THE LOOP

THE LOOP

JEREMY ROBERT JOHNSON

SAGA PRESS

LONDON SYDNEY **NEW YORK** TORONTO NEW DELHI

SAGA PRESS
AN IMPRINT OF SIMON & SCHUSTER, INC.

1230 AVENUE OF THE AMERICAS, NEW YORK, NEW YORK 10020

First Saga Press hardcover edition September 2020

SAGA PRESS and colophon are trademarks of Simon & Schuster, Inc.

For information about special discounts for bulk purchases, please contact Simon & Schuster Special Sales at 1-866-506-1949 or business@simonandschuster.com.

The Simon & Schuster Speakers Bureau can bring authors to your live event. For more information or to book an event, contact the Simon & Schuster Speakers Bureau at 1-866-248-3049 or visit our website at www.simonspeakers.com.

Interior design by Davina Mock-Maniscalco

Manufactured in the United States of America

10   9   8   7   6   5   4   3   2   1

Library of Congress Cataloging-in-Publication Data

Names: Johnson, Jeremy Robert, 1977– author.
Title: The loop / Jeremy Robert Johnson.
Description: First Saga Press hardcover edition. | London ; New York : Saga Press, 2020.
Identifiers: LCCN 2019038792 (print) | LCCN 2019038793 (ebook) |
ISBN 9781534454293 (hardcover) | ISBN 9781534454316 (ebook)
Subjects: GSAFD: Science fiction.
Classification: LCC PS3610.O35643 L66 2020 (print) | LCC PS3610.O35643 (ebook) |
DDC 813/.6—dc23
LC record available at https://lccn.loc.gov/2019038792
LC ebook record available at https://lccn.loc.gov/2019038793

ISBN 978-1-5344-5429-3
ISBN 978-1-5344-5431-6 (ebook)

To the ones who didn't make it through
And to the ones who acted with wisdom and kindness despite it all

No man is free who cannot control himself.
—Pythagoras of Samos

———

Paint "No Rules" on the water tower.
—Aesop Rock

Transcript Excerpt, *Nightwatchman* Podcast Episode 251, Uploaded 6/1/21, 03:47 a.m.:

Welcome to another broadcast for the thinkers, drinkers, freaks, geeks, smokers, jokers, fornicators, freedom fighters, and other fuckups who populate these early hours. As always, you're listening to the Nightwatchman, the only man brave enough to tell you the truth, the one media source you can depend on, throwing you the life preserver of legitimate facts in this ever-stormier sea of lies we call the big ol' US of A.

Now I know our listeners are chompin' at the bit for some follow-up on the Adam Colson case and what Brazil's sudden willingness to play ball and extradite a dual citizen means for the other war criminals currently sipping caipirinhas on the sandy beaches of Ipanema. And we'll get to that. I promise. But first there are a couple of particularly questionable items in the news that we want to shine a light on tonight with the return of a little feature we call the Yeah Right Roundup.

First, we've got the discovery of a new, even-more-insidious security-breaching "back door" on your phone, thanks to the undeletable MoonLite trashware app installed on most every device regardless of manufacturer. Now, I know regular listeners would never walk around with an off-the-shelf version of Stalin's Dream in their pocket, but maybe you're a newer listener who thinks these back doors aren't being exploited by the government and/or corporations in tandem. Maybe you think, *They'd never track me. They'd never listen to me.* And to that I say . . .

Yeah, right.

If you want a way to close these back doors, or find hardware that's built for clean, encrypted communications, stay tuned through the end of the show and we'll have some solid, NW-endorsed products to tell you about.

Next up we've got grimmer fare: a murder-suicide that seems 'bout as fishy as a deep-sea trawler. Open your ears for me and listen to this article from Turner Falls' local paper, the *Observer,* and tell me if any of this makes a lick of sense to you.

"Mother, Son Dead in Apparent Murder-Suicide

"Turner Falls, OR—Police are investigating a possible murder-suicide that left a young man and his mother dead.

"Officers found the pair just before eight a.m. Saturday in the 1700 block of Kensington Avenue.

"Police said they received a 911 call from a concerned neighbor who heard a struggle and checked in on the family only to discover the bodies of the deceased. First responders pronounced both the mother and son dead at the scene.

"'This is an incredibly difficult situation for everybody involved,' said Sergeant Bill Remar, Turner Falls PD.

"Police are investigating the case as a murder-suicide. Remar would not describe any injuries or possible cause of death, or release the names of the deceased citing the pending notification of next of kin and the ongoing nature of the investigation.

"The Turner Falls School District has confirmed the youngest victim attended Summit Ridge High School. The district released a statement saying it was heartbroken to learn of the passing of one of its students.

"The extended family of the deceased were contacted but gave no response.

"Update: The sheriff's office said Saturday that the victims are seventeen-year-old Brady Miller and forty-two-year-old Julie Miller, both of Turner Falls. They are survived by estranged father and husband Samuel Miller, a development lead for local medical supply manufacturer IMTECH. He is not considered a subject of interest in the investigation and could not be reached for comment.

"Update/exclusive: The *Observer* has obtained a statement from Constance Logue, the neighbor who discovered the deceased. Logue said, 'I heard yelling, and a car door slamming. Then the Millers' dog wouldn't stop barking, which isn't something we've ever had a problem with. We're friendly, so I walked over to check, and when I noticed the front door was cracked open I knocked to let them know I was coming in. I tripped over some luggage in the foyer and noticed that a vase full of flowers in the entryway had been knocked to the floor. Something about that, and the dog . . . I got goose bumps. You could feel something was wrong. Then I walked around the corner into their living room, and I found Brady and Julie. That poor boy . . . lying on the couch, a pillow still smashed over his face. And Julie was lying on the floor near him with an empty bottle of her heart pills on the coffee table. I thought about CPR, but I could tell by the way they looked that I couldn't help them. I ran back to my house and locked the door and called 911. While I was waiting for them I couldn't stop thinking that this didn't make any sense. Julie loved that boy. So did Sam. Even when they were splitting up, he was their little angel, you could tell. I can't picture either of them hurting a hair on his head, and I . . . They only ever wanted the best for him. It's senseless. It just breaks my heart.'"

So that's where it stands right now, listener. Obviously it's sad, and it's tragic, and at first glance maybe that's all it is. You can imagine a mom at wits' end, under some insurmountable pressure—maybe a husband who's about to take full custody—doing something like that. Because it happens. It does. People break.

But . . . BUT . . . longtime listeners know that we've had our eyes and ears on Turner Falls for a while now, ever since half the companies in Big Data simultaneously decided to build their largest-ever centers on the edges of the quaint little tourist-trap ski town. You can go all the way back to episode two thirty-five and give it a listen again for the full details . . . There was no specialized workforce, no environmental benefits . . . but all of a sudden the world's billionaires can't get enough of that high desert real estate. It. Doesn't. Track. AND the *Nightwatchman*'s crack research staff are taking a look at some other business, shall we say, *quirks,* in the area, and that *includes* this Samuel Miller's company, IMTECH. There's definitely something else going on, and we're peering as hard and deep as we can into that darkness to see the whole picture. So listen—you've got to be patient with us before we can report on *that*, because we like to rely on a little something the dying breed known as journalists used to call FACTS.

But, folks, even *without* all that, even if there were no other reason to give Turner Falls the old suspicious side eye, there are still enough things in this article to get your antennae up, aren't there?

We've got an estranged husband who is somehow NOT a person of interest in the kind of case where the husband is always the first person of interest. What does the Turner Falls PD know about this man that we don't? We've got a neighbor reporting signs of a struggle and the sound of a car door slamming, which could be a third party fleeing the scene. We've got luggage packed at the entry to the house. Now let me ask you, who packs up for a trip just before killing their child and themselves? On top of that we've got a forty-two-year-old woman overwhelming and suffocating a healthy seventeen-year-old male, who the neighbor describes as positioned on a couch like he was napping and not fighting for his life. And then we've got an overdose by heart medication, which, you know, we've researched, and that's not something people do. You go mixing nitrate drugs with something like Viagra, then sure, you could vasodilate yourself to death, but killing yourself with heart pills alone . . . wildly unlikely and uncommon. Now, we know that the murderers in murder-suicides have a tendency to leave the room where they've just killed, *especially* in family cases. The thinking is that the remorse pushes them away and drives their suicide. Most common place to find the murderer is the backyard, separate from what they've done. But here they find mom laid out *next* to her son . . .

You want to write it all off to madness, mental illness. Something. But when you've got this many questionable facts being reported, and a possible perpetrator who's been cleared with almost unnecessary expediency, you start to *wonder . . .* And I can tell you from years of shining the light that there's a pattern to this sort of senseless thing: you watch where these multinational corporations land and operate, and you watch for these kinds of deaths that simply *do not feel right,* and, pardon my French, but they go hand in fucking hand. You run out of pushpins mapping these things.

So when I look at this incident and the companies flooding into the area I start to wonder about Turner Falls: Is this just the case of a fractured mind committing an inexplicable tragedy? Or is it the beginning of something worse? Do I need to get my pushpins ready for whatever is next?

Folks, I know I'm sounding a little ghoulish here, but after a while you feel like you've seen too much. Learned too much. Honestly . . .

it does make you a little crazy, and you don't want to be right about the worst things, and it hurts when you are. So I want to believe this is an anomaly. I want to believe that these massive companies have the people's best interests in mind. Maybe they'll create a beautiful symbiotic relationship and jobs and money will rain down like mana and our corporate benefactors will usher in a new golden age of peace and prosperity.

It sounds nice, doesn't it, folks? But I can picture you out there, shaking your heads as you listen, and I know what you're thinking . . .

Yeah, right.

PART ONE

VECTOR/INSERTION

chapter one

A REPORTABLE INCIDENT

L ucy wrote "Fucking animals!" on a piece of notebook paper, and around those words she drew arrows pointing in every direction.

She wanted to rip the page from her binder and slide it to Bucket, but he was stuck two rows over, separated from her ever since Mr. Chambers caught them giggling at the absurd photoshopped pics on Bucket's phone.

Lucy *missed* sitting next to Bucket, and more with each passing week. He was the only other brown kid in class—hell, one of only four at the whole school—and it was calming when he was with her. She didn't feel so . . . examined. Bucket would never dare to touch her hair, or say he was "jealous of her tan," or worse yet, call her "exotic" and make her feel like a creature at the goddamn zoo.

But now he was across the room, face buried in his textbook, and she was alone, and she wished she'd never laughed at that picture of Wilford Brimley riding a manatee into an old-timey western sunset, yelling something about "diabeetus." If there was a dumber way to lose access to her best friend, she couldn't think of it.

Honestly, they could have been in worse trouble with the phone event. If Mr. Chambers had swiped deeper into Bucket's image files instead of turning the phone off and placing it on his desk, then he might have found the dozens of pictures where Bucket had pasted shots of himself into screencaps from lesbian porn: in some he gave an enthusiastic thumbs-up; in others he sipped on a cup of tea, pinkie out, or casually sat between two women who were about to, according to the film, "try kissing a little, just to see what it's like."

Bucket claimed his obsession with the videos came from his "model girlfriend back in Cali who totally went both ways," but Lucy had her doubts. Still, she wanted to understand Bucket's fascination. She even tried watching a clip from his favorite site—notjustroommates.com— but found the footage did little for her. She spent the day in a funk after that, hoping some switch would flip in her head and allow her to like girls. Seemed like that would be easier, somehow, especially once she went to college and left the uppity bitches at Spring Meadow High far, far behind.

But no—it was still Nate Carver's big hands and wide back and perfect smile she thought of when she rubbed against her pillow at night. Even worse, Nate was one of *them:* he lived on Brower Butte in a house so big it gave her vertigo if she looked up to its peak, and like most of the other rich kids in town his parents were both employed at St. Andrews—the hospital and IMTECH were the only two places in Turner Falls for making serious money, at least until the data centers opened. That hospital money meant Nate got a brand-new car for his sixteenth birthday. When he posted up on the basketball court, he wore custom shoes, which he bragged had to be insured before they could even ship. His brother was at Harvard, and Nate claimed he was headed there himself. Said his grandpa's name was on a plaque at the library. "I'm a slam dunk."

Lucy knew at least twenty kids smarter than Nate, but none came from money, and zero percent of them would ever feel comfortable describing themselves as "a slam dunk." So when Lucy thought about

Nate, she wished for two very different things at the same time: his beautiful body on top of hers, and his beautiful body utterly destroyed in a fiery accident involving his fancy new car and a telephone pole.

Lucy tried to focus on Mr. Chambers at the front of the room, but the dull hum of something about partial derivatives was interrupted when Ben Brumke unleashed a bone-rattler of a belch and the kids around him in the back corner moaned and raised their sleeves to their faces, anticipating the gut-rot stink of Ben's homemade protein shakes. Bucket, who often made the mistake of expressing his feelings aloud, said, "Brumke's eating roadkill again," and a few in the class laughed. But then Ben threw his pen at Bucket and said, "Shut your face, Sandy," and Mr. Chambers cleared his throat in a way that let everyone know they needed to calm down or face a lecture.

Half the kids at school called Bucket "Sandy," ever since they found out he came to the States from Pakistan, and all the kids knew what was *really* being said. Lucy got her share of nasty bullshit too—plenty of "Loogie" and "Go back to Mexico" and "taco bitch" and "donkey fucker," and after a while she didn't even care enough to tell them she was actually from Peru. She didn't feel like they deserved to know any true things about her, and she could imagine all the Paddington jokes at her expense. More than that, she didn't want them being able to research why she had been adopted by the Hendersons in the first place. Lucy Henderson had it bad enough—god only knew how they'd treat Lucia Alvarez, especially if they knew what her birth parents had done . . .

Lucy looked back at Bucket, the way he was holding in his anger. Their sophomore year had been so bad that they both ended up needing bite guards at night to save their teeth from grinding. Bucket's jaw was clenched now, his hands white-knuckled around the edges of his desk. Bucket made eye contact with her and Lucy did her best to send a message with her face.

This is temporary. One more year, and we both leave this podunk hillbilly bullshit town forever.

Turner Falls, Oregon, in the rearview mirror. Middle fingers up as we drive.

We leave these fucking animals behind.

Bucket took a breath. He released his death grip on the desktop.

Mr. Chambers sensed the tension and turned toward the class. "I know it can be tough to focus this close to the end of the school year, but we've got one more chapter to cover before the final on Thursday, and then we're done for the year. Can we keep the insults to a minimum, Mr. Brumke?"

"Sure."

"And Mr. Marwani?"

"Ben's the one who's belching right in—"

"*Mr. Marwani?*"

Bucket huffed. "Sure."

The class fell into a lull then. The too-brief excitement had drifted to nothing, and Mr. Chambers's monotone continued to recite the magic terms all the students would need to memorize before their next shot at the SAT's, and the school's meager, outdated cooling system did what it could to battle the desert heat, which transformed their big beige brick of a school into a low-key oven. For a moment the room drifted into a kind of soporific peace.

It was so surprisingly calm that it took a few minutes before anyone in the room even noticed the way that Chris Carmichael was twitching at his desk.

———

Jake Bernhardt sat right behind Chris, a few desks back from the front of the room.

Chris's family lived way out in Cascade Woods, a ramshackle assemblage of manufactured homes and trailers notorious for their meth lab explosions. You did your best to not take a wrong turn in Cascade Woods, lest you end up with some ganked-out tweeker shotgunning your ass with rock salt (or worse—rumors said there were bodies buried in the deep boonies).

Jake's family hailed from Brower Butte, and their property was so sprawling that they'd devoted a huge chunk of their backyard to an elaborate racetrack for Jake's remote control cars. At Jake's house, you did your best to jump from the roof outside Jake's window to precisely the right deep spot in the pool, lest you end up with a busted ankle like the one that cost Bradley England his senior football season.

So of course Jake always took an interest in Chris—he'd never scored such easy laughs before.

Chris doesn't shower for a week. Jake holds his nose, pretends to pass out. "Somebody forgot to take out the trash!"

Comic gold.

Chris wears the same shirt until a hole tears in the back. Jake flicks pennies into the hole and makes the field goal symbol with his arms.

Are you guys seeing this?

Chris's dad ends up in county jail on petty theft charges. A week later, Jake asks him if he has any big plans for Father's Day.

Classic!

Lucy never laughed, but she didn't always say something either. Jake's cruelty was a spotlight you didn't want swung your way—last time she told Jake to leave Chris alone, he ended up binder-checking her after class and sent her history notes flying across the hall. When she was on her hands and knees gathering her papers he said, "Clean it up, Loogie. Practice for my house."

What a crack-up!

High fives were had at her expense. Did Lucy notice Nate Carver laughing at her? She pretended she didn't.

Now Jake was back at it, holding up limp-wristed hands and mimicking the way Chris's body was shaking in his seat. His cronies chuckled. Jake bent his head to his desk and pretended to snort a line, then sat back up with exaggerated tremors. The laughter got louder.

Mr. Chambers rotated toward the class, and the laughs cut short. Lucy read Mr. Chambers's expression: *Please—I'm so close to being done with all of you. Be decent for once. Just finish this class so I can start my summer and I'll only have to see a handful of you at driver's ed training.*

Something in the back corner caught Chambers's eye. "Ms. Dufrene, can you turn off your phone or does it need to spend the rest of class on my desk?"

Patty Dufrene's thumbs were a blur, a concerned look on her face.

Chambers walked closer and spoke louder. "Ms. Dufrene, can I have your attention?"

No response.

Chambers walked over and placed an open palm directly between Patty's eyes and the phone. "Hand it over. You get it back at the bell."

Patty held her phone long enough to power it all the way down, then handed it to Mr. Chambers with an aggrieved whine. Her eyes followed the device to its resting spot on Mr. Chambers's desk.

Chambers scrawled more sample problems on the blackboard, his chalk tapping out a robotic rhythm. Loud and persistent as that sound was, Lucy was distracted by a new noise—Chris Carmichael's desk was squeaking. It reminded her of the time she drove to San Diego with the Hendersons to visit her "aunt" Molly. They'd checked in to a Super 8 at the halfway point down I-5 only to discover that their motel neighbors were having an epic screw session. Lucy remembered how embarrassed her adoptive guardians, Bill and Carol, had been, but mostly she remembered how steady and fast the springs were squeaking and how the woman's moans sounded more like something she was doing to pass the time until the man finally stopped thrusting.

Honestly, Lucy had thought the whole event was kind of funny, and the sound of Chris Carmichael's squeaking desk brought that all back.

She was about to laugh until she saw the way Chris's body was moving.

Something was wrong with him. Very, very wrong.

His narrow frame was slumped, pinning his weight against the metal support tube running from chair to desk. Lucy leaned forward and noticed a thin string of drool hanging from the corner of Chris's mouth. Sweat was beading on his forehead and soaking through his greasy black locks. His left leg was jerking back and forth at the knee while his foot pressed against the tile flooring so hard the sole was scuffing.

He's . . . fighting something. Like he's trying to force himself to stay at that desk.

Mr. Chambers finally caught on and turned to look at Chris.

"Mr. Carmichael, what's . . ."

And then Chris's neck bent back and he was staring at the ceiling and he yelled, "You promised you'd delete the picture, Ginny. Stop being such a bitch!"

Patty Dufrene stood bolt upright. "Shut your mouth, Chris. How do you . . ."

Chris kept yelling. "Why am I seeing this? Where am I? I don't want this!" and then he fell quiet, but the spasms in his body amplified, causing his desk to rock and lift and clatter against the floor. His head swiveled, eyes wide and panicked as if he were trying to see in the dark.

Have his eyes always been so blue?

Lucy swore that Chris had hazel eyes, but now they appeared blue and rheumy. Lucy wondered how that could be, but the thought was interrupted when his back and knees popped so loudly the sound echoed against the ceiling tiles. Lucy recoiled, imagining how that must feel inside Chris's body—his joints grinding and locking, unable to stop all that shaking.

Mr. Chambers was at Chris's side then. "We need to give him room until this passes. The key, is to, uh, to keep him from hurting himself. Megan, run down to the office and tell them to call 911." Then Chambers bent over Chris's thrumming body and rattling desk. "We need to get him as flat and stabilized as we can. Jake and Michael, you get his legs, and I'll lift under his shoulders." The teacher said, "Chris, can you hear me? I need to move you," and he laced his hands behind the boy's neck, and that's when Lucy realized she must have fallen asleep in class, because she swore that at that moment she heard something under Chris's hair *squeal* and then Mr. Chambers was backing away with a bloody hand, screaming, "What the fuck?"

And then Jake, forever dull and cruel and incapable of reading the goddamn room, tried to get in one more joke. He leaned toward the back of the class and said, "Chris is shaking harder than his mom's vibrator!"

But no one laughed. Even Jake's victory chuckle was cut short because within seconds Chris had erupted from his desk and was on top of Jake, had him trapped in his seat, and in a series of spasms Chris managed to raise one hand and plunge his right thumb directly into Jake's left eye.

Then in Lucy's nightmare she saw Mr. Chambers afraid to move forward but yelling, "Chris, get off him now or I'll have to report this," as if they were still in a situation where something like the rules of a high school might apply, and Jake began to bleed from the corner of his eye as he unleashed a slaughterhouse squeal and tried to bat Chris away with his arms, and then Chris's eyes rolled back in his head and a flat, even voice fell from his mouth saying, "Override protocol failed. Ops dispatched."

Mr. Chambers didn't seem to understand where the voice was coming from because he turned toward the door of the classroom, looking for the people who might be coming to restore order. After a few seconds ticked by, he must have realized that task fell to him, because he rushed over to his desk and pulled out a small black canister of pepper spray and said, "You have to stop that now, Chris! Stop or I'll spray you!"

If Chris heard, he paid it no mind. His thumb pressed farther into Jake's skull. Jake made noises that no one in that room would escape dreaming about.

Mr. Chambers stepped toward the boys and sprayed Chris's eyes and then aimed the stream directly into the mouth of the young man.

Mr. Chambers gained Chris's attention.

Chris untethered from Jake's coiled, screaming body and stood. Blood dripped from his thumb to the tile. The class sat paralyzed, coughing and gagging and trying to breathe fresh air through folded hoodies or sleeves. A crowd had gathered at the door to the classroom, some filming with their phones, some running when they saw Jake's body shaking its way into deep shock.

Chris straightened and looked at Mr. Chambers, then at his red, slick hand. "This *fixes it*. What I did. What you did to me. The signal . . ." His voice started to fade, airway tightening against the pepper spray assault. Chris shook his head from side to side and coughed. He blinked through hideously swollen eyelids. "It's not so bad, Mr. Chambers. They said I would be smarter, but they lied to me. They lied to my mom. But *you*—you really helped me. After all this time."

Then Chris bent forward, his movements finally smooth, and he picked up his precalculus book from the floor. He lifted the thick, sharp-cornered book up in the air with one bright red hand.

"This is the answer. You gave us the answer."

Then Chris Carmichael took two swift strides toward the front of the room and swung the textbook down into Mr. Chambers's face.

Mr. Chambers lost his legs and rag-dolled to the floor and then Chris was on top of him with the book raised high and he turned toward the class to speak.

"This makes it stop. This is real."

He brought the textbook down, using both arms this time. Something crunched.

"I could see it all before, too much, but now I'm *here*."

Another swing down. This time the arc of the book splattered the white tile ceiling with tiny red drops. Lucy could swear she saw something pulsing on the back of Chris's neck as his hair flopped forward.

"We are going to be okay, you guys."

Another swing. Mr. Chambers's hands fish-flopped on the floor, his wedding ring ticking against tile, his moaning buried beneath the sound of gargled blood.

"We are all going to be okay."

And then Lucy leaned forward in her desk because her vision had filled with tiny blinking stars, and she fought to stay conscious because there was a murderer in the room and she could barely breathe from the pepper spray and it was far too late for "Locks, lights, out of sight." She didn't know what the hell she was supposed to do. Part of her wanted to jump from her desk and restrain Chris or knock him off Mr. Chambers, but everything was moving too fast.

She heard men yelling in the hallway. Something rolled into the classroom next to Mr. Chambers's awfully quiet, immobile body, and Chris didn't even stop to acknowledge the purple smoke coming from the object because he was still swinging his book.

How can he hold on to the book with so much blood on his hands?

Lucy felt oddly guilty for thinking such a thing, but then her thoughts were wiped clear by the smell of the noxious purple smoke and the sudden, thunderous sound of close gunfire and then the sight of Chris's face slumping loose from his head and slapping against his chest.

The air was toxic with pepper spray and gunpowder and atomized blood.

Screams ran through the room at full surround.

Chris's body gave one last tremor and collapsed onto Mr. Chambers.

Then the school bell rang.

It was the final shock Lucy could bear. Some distant part of her mind thought, *School's out*, and she slid into static, then nothing.

chapter two

ESCAPE ATTEMPTS

Lucy's alarm sounded from the dresser across the room, waking her for another day of playing pretend.

"Yes, I'm fine today."

"No, I didn't have any nightmares."

"Yes, I care whether or not there are fresh blueberries at breakfast. The simple pleasures are important! Where are we without our day-to-day niceties?"

"No, I don't want another appointment with Dr. Nielsen. And there definitely aren't any details about that day that I'm concealing from her so she won't have me committed."

"Yes, I'm dealing with everything just fine."

"No, I didn't have a dream where I posted a picture of Chris Carmichael's exploding face to my account and then I pushed my phone down between my legs and rubbed up against the flood of buzzing notifications. Because that would mean that something is broken inside of me, right? And I'm doing great!"

"Yes, I think graduating is still important, and yes, it might be good to change schools. But didn't Nielsen say I needed to confront what happened on my own time? Thank you for being so patient with me. Thank you for reminding me every day that you've got my back! Yes, this is *our* challenge to face together."

"No, I haven't had any suicidal or self-destructive thoughts. Trust me, I'm going to be okay."

We are all going to be okay.

———

Lucy knew the Hendersons' every action came from a place of love. She knew how lucky she was to have Bill and Carol in her life, and how they were afraid she'd go back to being the near-catatonic little girl they'd adopted after the tragedy in Peru.

That being said, there were times after "the incident" when their love felt like a lead fucking apron on her chest and she couldn't breathe from all the goddamn heartfelt care and protection.

That afternoon she texted Bucket: Dying here. Bill and Carol treating me like a baby deer. Please come pick me up. Let's go to The Exchange.

———

The Marwanis did all right. They didn't pull St. Andrews or IMTECH money, but Bucket's dad had his own dermatology clinic, and his mom worked as a dental assistant, so they weren't hurting. They could have forked over enough cash to put Bucket in an older used sedan, but they wanted him to earn it, so he worked part-time at Culbertson's Grocery. As a result he always smelled like fresh-baked bread when he came to pick up Lucy.

She dropped into his front seat and inhaled deeply. "I love it!"

"It's bullshit, though. They don't even bake the bread on-site. They just pump in this smell to make you think they did."

"I don't care." Lucy sniffed closer and closer to Bucket, like a dog following a trail. "Smells so fucking good!"

"All right, all right. Cool your jets, weirdo."

"It's making me hungry, dude. Can we grab some big pretzels before we go to The Exchange?"

"I'll stop there, but I don't want anything."

"Your stomach still all jacked up?"

"Yeah. I mean, I eat, but I don't *feel* hungry. My nerves are kind of off now . . . you know?"

"I know. Can we not talk about it, though?"

Bucket gave a nod and boosted the volume on his stereo. Bass flooded up from the trunk and replaced Lucy's bad vibes. She couldn't make out most of the lyrics to the song, aside from some guy with an auto-tuned voice singing, "rub that yayo on your pussy/get that booty numb." The music hit the right dumb/dead spot in her mind, and she smiled a real smile for the first time that day.

"This is good."

"Yup. You want mall pretzels or you want to hit the corner market?"

Lucy thought about all the other kids who might be at the mall. Could be Chris Carmichael's friends. Could be Brady Miller's friends— Lucy barely knew anybody from Summit Ridge, but they'd had the prior week's hot tragedy, holding a candlelight vigil for the loss of their classmate. Supposedly he'd been killed by his own mom, which triggered feelings in Lucy that made her ignore the news about *that* crime in its entirety. Even if they didn't have to see people *directly* related to the awful things which had happened, other students would be there, and Lucy thought about how they'd pretend to be interested in her so they could drill down and ask about what had happened in Mr. Chambers's classroom.

I can't answer those questions. I don't want to. I'm not even sure what I really saw.

Dr. Nielsen spoke with her about the way adrenaline affects memory, and how slowly the truth might float to the surface and find its place, and how some of the things she may think she saw were only visions filling in the gap until her true memories were ready.

But there was something on the back of Chris's neck, right?

She hadn't yet saved up the courage to ask Bucket what he might have seen.

Her smile dimmed.

Enough of this. Enough thinking. And no mall.

"Corner market's fine. Can you turn up the music?"

"Sure. AC on or windows down?"

"AC, bitch, so I can keep smelling this crazy-good bread smell."

She sniffed at him again, closing her eyes, pulling exaggerated amounts of air. Then they both laughed and shared the smallest moment outside their haunted lives.

The Exchange was cool because nobody went there. Music stores had become halfway museums, the only clients being people so computer illiterate that they still used CDs, and a mix of hipsters, DJs, and old-timers who worshipped at the altars of vinyl.

Lucy liked the quiet mustiness of the place, and the feeling of slowly flipping through their vast rows of records.

Bucket liked it because one of the clerks was a twenty-five-year-old named Toni who was rumored to also be an exotic dancer over at the Boiler Room. She was covered in tattoos and had bright purple hair and big blue eyes, and one time she'd even asked Bucket his real name.

"There's no way you're actually called 'Bucket,'" she'd said. "Nobody is called 'Bucket.'"

"It's my name."

"Yeah, listen . . . I know it's not. I can feel it. I've got a few names myself. I'll tell you what. I'll tell you my names first, then you tell me yours, and we'll be good, right?"

Bucket squinted. Lucy had been impressed by how he'd stood his ground against Toni's charms.

Toni leaned forward across the counter. "The truth is, I have three names. There's Toni. It's what everybody calls me. And then there's the name my parents gave me, which is Antoinette—way too fucking fancy for me to use on an everyday basis."

It was Bucket's turn to lean forward. She'd suckered him in by dropping that f-bomb. She wasn't talking to him like he was a kid. He loved it.

"Then there's my third name, and I only use that in one place." Bucket's eyebrows raised. Lucy knew what he was thinking—*The rumors are true! Toni really is a dancer.* "So this doesn't go beyond here, but sometimes I go by the name Amity."

"Wait . . . Amity? Like in *Jaws*?"

"Well, that's not where I got it from, but sure. I like it because it sounds cool to the clients I work with, but I *really* like it because of what it means."

"Friendship?"

"Yeah. That's what my other job really is. My clients *think* it's one thing, and it *can* be that, but a lot of times they don't see what I'm really giving them. They need someone to say, *I'm here for you, and I'm open to you. You can trust me. I can listen to you. I will look at you because you matter. I'm your friend.* People are lonely, you know?"

Lucy looked over at Bucket's puppy-dog face and thought that this woman deserved to be called something fancy like Antoinette.

"So those are my names. Now it's your turn."

"Fine. It's not very interesting, really. It's Bakhit. Bakhit, that's all."

"Bakhit. I like that. Kind of, I don't know, exotic."

Lucy riled. *Exotic. Always fucking "exotic." It's a common name where he's from.*

Bucket smiled, putty in Toni's hands.

Toni asked, "So why Bucket, then?"

"Oh, I don't . . ."

"Come on! Nobody's been in this store for the last three hours.

The store cat's got fucking diabetes. He lies there *all* day." Toni pointed to a mound of tabby cat lumped in one of the store windows. "*Please.* Tell me something interesting."

"Okay. It's what my little brother Dalir called me, back when we lived in Pakistan. He couldn't get 'Bakhit' quite right. He'd follow me around saying, 'Bucket! Bucket!' and we'd all laugh."

"Oh my god—that's so cute."

"Yeah, but, uh . . ." Lucy saw something pass over Bucket's face— maybe the realization that she was listening, or that he was about to talk about a part of his past he kept closed away. "My little brother, he, uh, passed away. He got some kind of fever that made his brain shut down . . . and after that my parents were so sad for a long time. We barely spoke. And when they came out of that they decided that we had to move, to get away from . . . everything, I guess. So then we ended up in California, before we moved up to Oregon. And once we moved up here, I noticed they'd started calling me Bucket instead of Bakhit. At first it really bothered me, but after a while I kind of fig- ured it was part of . . . You know, it came from my brother. So I was cool with it."

"Whoa. Damn . . . I'm sorry."

"It is what it is, you know?" Bucket tried to lighten the mood. "Be- sides, this name is easier for me. Now I only have to spell out 'Mar- wani' when I'm on the phone. But everybody gets 'Bucket' right off the bat."

And with that, Lucy had learned more about Bucket than she'd been able to discover in two years of friendship. She figured the FBI should hire dancers to run their interrogations.

But Toni wasn't working at The Exchange today, and Lucy noticed Bucket's disappointment after he scanned the store. Diabetic cat? Check. Rows of dusty old albums? Check. The woman Bucket hoped he'd one day marry? Negative. Judah was working, and he was nice, and always smelled like beer and cigarettes, and it was fun to ask him

about the band patches all over his jean jacket, but still . . . no Toni/
Antoinette/Amity.

Plus, Lucy's corner-store pretzel tasted like it had been on the
rotating rack since the days of the pyramids, so it was a rough outing
so far.

*At least I'm away from the perpetually concerned faces. At least I'm
not answering all those carefully phrased questions meant to help me along
the path to healing.*

One thing about raising yourself as the child of two raging alcoholics was that you developed an allergy to being nurtured. Lucy liked
that about herself, but it really fucked with the Hendersons' parental
instincts.

Lucy ditched her shitty pretzel in the store trash, keeping one
small piece, which she offered to the store cat. The cat opened an eye,
batted the pretzel chunk with his paw, gave the offering one lick, and
then fell back into its diabetic stupor.

C'est la vie.

Album zone-out time—flipping through row after row of vinyl,
breathing calmly through her nose, giggling at the occasional album
cover, maybe even holding up the worst ones for Bucket to dig. Bucket
was fine hanging out—she caught him checking the front door for
Toni's arrival, though she never came.

Lucy wondered who Toni was with at that moment. And what did
her name mean to them?

She looked at Bucket again. He saw her looking, and pretended to
browse through a stand full of sleazy old comic books. But it wasn't
long before his eyes drifted to the door again.

People are lonely, you know?

After an hour, Lucy finally felt her shoulders drop for the first time
in too long. She let her fingers drift across some slip mats mounted to
the wall and felt them pull against her, and she felt a rare moment of
longing for the forests near where she was born, for the rough bark on

the trees and the way it abraded her skin and made her hands feel open and alive. She closed her eyes and tried to remember the smell of that place, the way it had felt like home before the authorities came to take her away and place her in the orphanage and put her name and picture in the adoption database.

It was no use. That place—the good in it—felt lost to her. *This* was her world now—sharp, brittle, sticky juniper trees and frigid desert nights where the air felt as empty and mean as the faces of the white boys who laughed at her and lusted after her at the same time. A place full of kids with no money and kids with all the money, and every once in a while, a kid with a goddamn bloody textbook raised above his head talking about signals in his brain.

Her shoulders were back up to her ears.

Goddamnit!

Time to go anyway. Bucket had work at Culbertson's the next morning. The Hendersons wanted Lucy to have a session with some grief counselor, even though she told them she was fine.

"I trust you, Lucy, but I'm having a hard time believing you're fine."

On top of having to deal with that overbearing grief bullshit, there was a rumor that the district was going to push for three more days of attendance, despite the tragedies at each school. Supposedly some of the more influential parents in the community demanded that the district *still* hold a graduation ceremony. If that was true, it meant that Lucy and Bucket actually had some homework to complete.

She tried to imagine sitting at the kitchen table and working on her differentials.

"This is the answer. You gave us the answer."

Then that crunching sound as Mr. Chambers's face collapsed.

Fuck the grades, she thought. *They can give me a pass.*

Bucket was up at the front counter, joking with Judah about buying a sticker for his car that read "Pipe Layers Union." He said, "I like it because it's subtle."

"Really? That strikes you as subtle?"

"Sure. I mean, if I got an honest bumper sticker, it would just say, '10-Inch Pussy Wrecker.' But this sticker lets the ladies know I can take care of business without being so direct."

Judah laughed. "You must be packing some serious heat."

"Well, I'm not going to talk too much about it. It's not really your business. But I can say that my girlfriend in California—"

"Oh, shit. Here we go," Lucy said.

"Pay her no mind. I was saying, I had a gorgeous girlfriend in California, before my parents moved us to this shitbrick city. No offense."

Judah held up his hands, palms out. "Hey, I'm not the mayor. And this town blows."

"So this girl, she was a model, so beautiful, but *so skinny*, you know what I'm saying?"

Judah nodded.

"And since I have what I have, it was tough for her. I'm going to be a gentleman about it, but I can tell you that I had to stick four fingers in her to loosen her up before she could take the D."

Judah laughed and shook his head. Lucy wondered why boys instantly lost fifty IQ points the moment they started talking about sex.

"So, anyway," Bucket said, "I better buy this sticker."

"You got it, buddy. On the house." Judah pulled the sticker from under the glass and passed it to Bucket. "I'll charge it to my employee account."

"Thanks, dude."

"No problem, kid. I could listen to you run bullshit all day."

Bucket beamed.

"Besides," Judah continued, "you two seem like good kids. Especially compared to what I put up with from some of those little Brower Butte bastards. Shoplifting shit, even though they have the money. Fucking with the cat. Little creeps. And you wouldn't believe the stuff they say to Toni."

Lucy instantly recalled the litany of names and gestures she and Bucket regularly endured—how easily those boys said things like "goat fucker" and "jumping bean"—and her eyes dropped to the floor. She looked over at Bucket and saw he was clenching his jaw.

Judah must have been watching them closely. "Yeah . . . you guys know, right? That shit never changes. Even when I was a kid. Different guys, same attitude. I lived over past Westerhaus, if that gives you some idea of how I was growing up, and I'd look at those kids and imagine having what they had, all those opportunities, no serious worries, and I was so jealous. And later, when I was selling a little weed, those guys wanted me around, so I'd hang with them. Their cars were cool, I guess. Sometimes I got laid rolling with them. But I was always nervous. Just something about them that felt . . . *off*."

"Like you're waiting for them to be mean?" asked Lucy. The few times she'd tried to be social with the Brower Butte kids, she'd felt like either an accessory—"My Ethnic Friend"—or a curiosity to be studied like a bug under the magnifying glass until they got bored and decided to start pulling off wings.

"Yeah. Sometimes it *did* turn mean. Like one night, I'm walking with a bunch of those guys, coming back from a party at Roake Falls, and Justin Norris sees a cat. Total stray, ribs sticking out. And Justin squats down and starts making little noises to the cat and holding out his hand like he's got food, and you know the other guys are making jokes right away. 'Justin thinks he can gets some pussy.' That kind of shit. So finally the cat kind of slinks over, hesitant, but he's hungry, and the moment he gets close enough, Justin grabs him by the back of his neck, picks him up, and then drop-kicks the thing as hard and far as he can."

"What?"

"Yeah. So I heard it yowl, and hit a tree, and behind me they're all, 'Holy fuck, Norris!' and, 'Oh my god!' and laughter. Mainly laughter. That was the worst part. Like this was the thing that finally lit them up and made them feel. But there was something underneath it, like they were scared too, I guess. Before that, they seemed so *bored*. I was always too busy working or worrying to be really bored . . . but these guys . . . I remember seeing Todd's freezer once, out in his garage, *packed* with fucking food, and he looked at it and moaned and said, 'I hate all this shit.' "

Lucy looked at Bucket, trying to figure out a subtle face that would say, *Dude's got issues.*

Bucket didn't look over at her. Instead he asked, "So what happened to the cat?"

"We could hear it howling out in the trees. And I remember Todd saying, 'You smashed that pussy, Norris!' and then for whatever reason we all started walking toward the sound. And when we found the cat, it was wrecked. Back leg bent the wrong way, bone sticking out. Blood coming from its mouth. So right away I grabbed the closest rock I could find and I bent down and finished it off. Fast and clean. One hit. I told myself I was saving the cat from more pain. That coyotes would have come. But the truth was that I could feel it, like in my bones, that those guys weren't done with the cat. That things were going to get worse."

Lucy pictured the way boys' faces would change when they were in a group together. It happened with girls sometimes too. Whatever was wrong in them, it was lined up like dominoes. Only took one falling over and the rest went bad.

Judah continued. "So . . . yeah. That was my last time rolling with that crew. I wondered what would have happened if I had told the police the next day, but my family always taught me that we don't talk to cops, and besides, Justin's dad was on rotary, and he owns, like, half the bullet factory. Plus, they would have flipped it on *me*. 'Judah freaked out and killed a cat.' All their voices against mine."

"Yeah."

"What's weird is I see Justin now, in town. He's over at St. Andrews, in *pediatrics*. Sometimes I see him out at the bars with his friends. Most of 'em got fat, had kids, that whole route, and they *still* look so bored. And it kind of creeps me out, because I look at them and I wonder what they're doing these days that makes them laugh the way I heard them laugh back then."

There was a long silence.

Lucy said, "Maybe they grew out of being like that." This had long been a secret hope of Lucy's, that time and age would make people better to one another.

Judah took a sip from his huge mug of black coffee and looked at Lucy. "Yeah. I hope so. But then I see their kids and they have that same look in their eyes. I don't know . . . My girlfriend says I'm classist as shit, but she grew up with decent money. But it's like their parents passed on a sickness in the genes. Or it's the money. I don't know . . . And *then* you have what happened over at Spring Meadow. That Carmichael kid was poorer than dirt, but obviously he was a psycho too. I'm friends with his uncle Scott, and he said it doesn't make any sense at all. That family's *definitely* got issues, but Scott said the kid didn't have a violent bone in his body. So what the hell? And the Miller kid . . . He always seemed nice when he came in, one of the good ones despite the money, the world lined up in front of him, and his own mom mercs him in his sleep? Jesus . . . What the hell is going on in this town? Sometimes it feels like things are fucked up in every direction, you know?"

A thick, wet-sounding ululating noise came from near the entrance of the store, pulling their attention away before Lucy or Bucket could say a word.

Judah looked at the clock on the wall and made an alarmed face as he was pulled from his soapbox into the now.

"Oh, shit—Blumpers!"

"Blumpers?" Lucy asked.

"Store cat. I'm late for his shot. Damn it." Judah bent behind the counter and rose with a small hypodermic needle in his hand. "He gets all crashy and weird without this. Falls off whatever he's lying on. The meds make his shit smell like that liquid smoke you use when you're making jerky, but I guess that's better than him dying. Sort of."

Blumpers mewled out another sad, strangled noise from his window seat, and the sound made Lucy think of that *other* cat, the one from Judah's story. She imagined how it must have felt in those last moments—hopeful, and confused, and soaring through the air, and crushed.

Then killed.

Rocks slamming down.

Textbooks slamming down.

Screams and purple smoke. Gunfire and blood.

Her anxiety rose. Her heart sped, skin hot across her chest and face.

What happened that day? What did I see?

Judah looked at her. "You all right?"

"Yeah . . . I'm fine."

But she wasn't, and she felt tears coming, and she guessed that if she started crying she might not be able to stop for a very long time, so she ran out of The Exchange and into the cool air of the early evening.

Once she made it to Bucket's car, she leaned forward and rested her arms against the roof and shook against a surge of fresh embarrassment.

Bucket followed, putting a gentle hand on her shoulder. "What's going on?"

Lucy turned and straightened, then sniffled and blinked back the tears, which wanted loose. "I don't even know anymore."

"Yeah."

"Like, do you ever feel like the last few weeks didn't even really happen? Like they *couldn't* have?"

Bucket leaned against the side of his car, and Lucy joined him. The sun was setting, and the air would grow cold soon. Lucy shivered as the first desert breeze rolled against her skin.

Judah was in the window to the store, bending over Blumpers to administer his meds. He looked out the window to Lucy and Bucket. His face read confused, but he offered a conciliatory wave before returning to his side job as a cat nurse.

Bucket spoke. "Sometimes, right when I wake up, I forget that any of it happened at all. Then I see my parents' faces, how worried they are, and it all comes back. You can't hide from it. Anywhere."

Lucy nodded and watched the sun lower in the sky, painting the clouds. They glowed pink, then shifted to dark purple.

Lucy smelled smoke again, and wondered what she had breathed in that classroom. And what was Chris saying about "ops" and "protocols?" Had she imagined that? How had those men with guns arrived so quickly? They hadn't even looked like cops . . .

Her breath shortened. Her head swam again.

"You think it'll always feel like this?" she asked.

Bucket thought for a moment. "It can't, right? My mom always says, 'The only constant in life is change.' When I was little that made me feel scared. But now . . . things have got to change, right? Because if it feels like this forever . . ."

"If it stays this way, we're going to have to see how far we can make it in your car." Lucy thought of when the Hendersons had arrived to take custody of her. Sometimes things did get better, for a while at least.

Am I better off here, though? Really? I just watched two people die.

Bucket slapped the roof of his car. "Run in this? It's on its last legs. Besides, what do we do for money?"

"Rob banks."

"Really?"

"Well . . . no. I can't stand wearing masks. But we could sell the shit we own. You save up your Culbertson's money. We hop hostels and live cheap. We go north to Portland. I heard they'll let you live in a tent there."

"You want to live in a tent?"

"Not really. But I don't think I can live here either. You heard Judah . . . It's not going to change."

"Uh, Judah's kind of a burnout. I mean, he's a nice guy, but he's stuck in high school, you know? And he's got a *Nightwatchman* bumper sticker on his truck. That's like all that conspiracy theory bull-shit. So maybe not a guy to run to for life advice."

"Fine. Fuck it, dude! If you're going to Negative Nelly all my shit, then you can take me home."

"Fine. Hop in." Bucket mope-walked around the front of his car and got out his keys.

Is this because I snapped at him? Or is he only bummed that Toni never showed?

"Wait."

"What?"

"Just wait . . . I'm sorry. It's not you. You know that. *Please.* I can't go home yet."

Bucket returned to her side. They both stared at the last of the sunset. The sky melted from purple-pink to dark blue as the outline of the mountains in the distance burned bright white

Lucy said, "This place is really pretty if you don't think about it."

Bucket laughed, then shivered. "How much longer you want to stay here?"

"Couple minutes. There's always one last color change after it drops behind the range."

"Fine. I want some tacos soon, though." Bucket pulled his phone from his pocket and started scrolling. "Fuck. Signal's still weird. Keeps popping me over to emergency-only bars."

"You gotta change services."

"I know. But Mom says if I want to switch, then I have to pay for it, so . . . It's not that, anyway. Kevin Gearhart told me his phone's been jacked too."

Lucy remembered seeing Bill walking around the yard that morning staring at his phone. What'd he say to Carol? "Desert wind's playing hell with the signal." Maybe Bucket was right. Lucy didn't really care—she'd been off her phone and social media since the incident. Dr. Nielsen said that was fine, and Lucy missed it less with each day.

Bucket was back near the store entrance, holding his phone aloft, his body contorted, his face lit by dim blue light. "Down to one bar. Damn. But I'm back on."

Lucy kicked at a piece of filthy ABC gum stuck to the sidewalk. She was ready to go. But Bucket was excited about something. He hopped in place for fear of losing his connection. "Holy shit. Yes. They did it! No more school for this year. They're just mailing diplomas to the seniors and calling off everything else. Looks like some parents are furious. They're organizing their own graduation event for the seniors out at the Ridgecrest golf course."

Lucy felt relief wash over her—they could give those seniors acid and fucking rocket launchers for all she cared. The important fact was that she wouldn't have to go back to Spring Meadow.

"And everybody's freaking out about summer being here. Sounds like there's a big party out at East Bear Caves tomorrow night. Brewer says he can drive us out if we want to come."

Lucy rolled her eyes. Danny Brewer was a loadie who covered his bad skin with a mop of dyed black hair and was constantly out of school on drug-related suspensions. He had a habit of offering things to Bucket, acting like he was a friend, but Lucy saw the way Brewer looked at her. She understood his angle.

He *was* actually kind of cute, somewhere under his blemishes and bad posture and greasy hair, but Lucy had a learned aversion to anybody who was constantly fucked up—she'd trust a wild animal first.

"That's a hard pass for me, Bucket. Have you seen all the dents in Brewer's truck?"

Bucket ignored her, transfixed by his phone. She saw a new, disturbed look on his face and felt fresh anxiety flutter across her skin. "What? What is it?"

"Jason Ward."

"What about him? His parents buy him another Jaguar?" Ward was a first-class collar-popping asshole who lived in an iron-gated compound so high on Brower Butte that it looked out over valleys on every side. He'd never said a word to Lucy, but he had a habit of spitting on Bucket's locker whenever he walked by, leaving fat green snot slugs during the winter cold season.

"No, it's nothing like that," Bucket said. "He's *missing*. Nobody has seen him for three days. Looks like his parents reported it yesterday."

What kind of parents wait that long to call the cops?

Lucy wondered if Jason's parents were like hers back in Peru—maybe they only noticed him when it was convenient.

"That's not the worst part. I don't want to lose the connection. You've got to come over here."

Lucy didn't know if she had space in her mind for any more "worst parts," but her curiosity got the better of her.

"Look," Bucket said. "Carrie Zielinski's comment."

There was Carrie's perfect face, a slight sideways tilt to her head highlighting her pricey cosmetics and long neck leading down to a cashmere sweater. The message next to her picture read:

saw him when I was working at Tastie's on Tuesday night
he was kind of pale and he kept rubbing a bandage on his neck
he bought a waffle cone with cookies and cream but wasn't eating it
and it started melting and when I told him he acted like he couldn't
hear me
he was looking straight ahead and he said something like they did
this to me and I said who and he said they don't care it won't stop
and his hands were shaking and then he dropped the ice cream and
ran out

sooooooo worried you guys oh my god

I am having a really hard time with this but my thoughts and prayers
are with his family

We love you Jason come home safe

Lucy shivered. She looked away from the phone to find she had missed the final falling colors of the sunset. It felt like all that was left of the desert was darkness and sharp winds.

"Fuck. Can we go home now?"

She and Bucket got in the car then, and neither said a word on the drive home because they knew they'd talk about Jason, and that would mean acknowledging the truth they could feel in their bones: Jason was not safe, and he needed more than thoughts and prayers, and when they got home they would have to work harder than ever to pretend that anything was okay.

chapter three

NIGHT RIDE

D inner the next night was Crock-Pot roast beef with carrots, pota-
toes, and a heaping helping of oppressive parental concern. The
Hendersons even had the dining room lamps dimmed like Lucy
had become some kind of albino newt which would shrivel and die in
direct light. The entire day had been polite knocks on her bedroom
door and quiet, calm voices and offers of favorite desserts, and the look
of faces drawn tight with worry. It felt like Bill and Carol held their
breath when she entered the room.

To be fair, she'd barely spoken to them since heading out with
Bucket the night before, and she'd spent the morning in bed, staring at
the wall. She wished she could keep faking it, partly for Bill and Carol's
sake, and partly so they'd leave her be—sometimes, she'd learned, you
need to shut the fuck down.

What did Dr. Nielsen call it? Avoidance?

That sounded fine by Lucy, and she was comfortable letting reality
drift away for a while like she'd done when the Hendersons first
brought her to the States. But she knew she didn't have long before
they started breaking down—a few months into her adoption, they'd

nearly divorced. She felt like they craved normalcy for her more than anything, a return to the routines that kept their family moving forward through time in a way they could all live with.

Well, fuck them. This is my life, and they haven't had to see what I saw. They'd be popping fucking Xanax and quitting their jobs by now.

Lucy observed that feeling, somewhere at the back of her mind.

And what did Nielsen call that? Reactivity, right?

When she finally, begrudgingly crawled out of bed to pee, she had walked by Bill's office, where he was watching the local news. He was normally pinned to cable news this time of day.

He saw her walking by and smiled. "Morning, Lulu."

"Morning. No CNN?"

"Nope. Cable's on the fritz now. Between this and the phones being down, I'm about ready to chew somebody's ear off. I always feel bad for the call center folks, but somebody needs to get us back online. Talked to the Danielsons yesterday and they said they're having the same problem, so . . ." Bill gave a *What can you do?* shrug.

"I'm sure they'll fix it soon."

"Hope so. *Local* news still looks like they're recording it in a coat closet. You'd think for a town with this much money, they'd be able to bring our station out of the '70s. Instead we get *this*." Bill held out a dismissive middle finger at the TV, and Lucy started to laugh until she saw the face on the screen.

Jason.

". . . with police reporting no new developments in the case of missing local boy Jason Ward. The Ward family and Turner Falls PD encourage anyone with information of value to contact the number below."

Bill looked over at Lucy, a question on his face, but he said nothing, since she was already turning away and bolting to the bathroom.

She'd flipped on the vent fan for noise cover, grabbed a thick towel from the rack by the tub, and sat down to pee. She folded the towel over twice and jammed her face into it and let out a scream as quietly as she could. It came out like a moan, or a growl, some animal sound she couldn't quite recognize, and that scared her worse. She tried to ignore the feeling that rolled up from her heart into her mind and made her want to tear the towel in her hands to shreds and smash the mirror and kick a hole in the door and keep rending the reality around her until all of it was subatomic and floating in a cloud around her anger. She imagined herself tilting her head back and opening her mouth to scream again, only this time her mouth kept opening and her jaw detached like a snake's and she kept splitting until she was cleaved in two and all that came out of her was white flame. She shook and waited for the bad energy to leave her mind, and wondered what happened to all the rage in her body when she trapped it inside like that. She smashed her face deeper into the towel and bit it and held her breath until she saw stars darting. The waves of anger fell to low tide, as they always did. She dried her eyes, then rinsed and got back to her bed and the comfort of doing nothing and thinking as little as possible.

She heard Bill and Carol later that day, their voices hushed but urgent out in the kitchen, Bill's voice getting much louder suddenly. "Well, what the hell am I *supposed* to do, Carol? Why don't you tell me, huh?"

They were breaking already.

So: dinner. Lucy walked out to the kitchen and watched their love for her soften both of their faces.

She said, "Pot roast, Carol? That smells *yummy*. Can we eat at the table tonight?"

"Of course, honey. I'll set it now."

A loud, wailing sound came from the street. Blue and red light flashed on the Hendersons' ceiling for a moment before zooming past. Lucy thought that was the first time she'd ever heard sirens in her neighborhood.

"Finally cracking down on speeders, I hope. I swear those speed bumps did nothing."

A second burst of light and sound as another police car came blasting down their residential street.

It *wasn't* normal, but Lucy was pretending to be all right, and she knew Bill and Carol weren't about to let some distraction ruin that.

Nobody said much of anything real while they ate, for fear of breaking the spell. Bill mentioned the weather, and how the wind dried his sinuses this time of year. Carol was excited that the western scrub jays were coming back to her garden this year. All three took turns complimenting the meal. Lucy tried to keep a light on in her eyes, and hoped she was smiling hard enough to be believed. Between every third or fourth bite, she swallowed back a burgeoning scream.

Don't break.

Look at them. They love you. They need you to be okay.

Lucy wanted to say the right things to them, the true things that would let them breathe, and she imagined herself saying, *I love you and I will always love you for saving me, even if I don't feel safe right now. But two boys and a teacher have died in the last two weeks and I saw something I can't explain and it's a nightmare I can't escape, and I'm terribly scared and I need you now.* And then she knew she would cry, in that way that left her shaking and far too open, and they would come to her and hold her and be grateful for the chance to love her back.

She felt the world swirling around her, how strange everything had become, and she realized that maybe telling them the truth was the only way to get back to any kind of safe place, and she braced herself in her chair and felt brave for a moment before another streak of red/blue light ran flashing across their dining room ceiling and the sound of sirens shot her through with panic and stole her courage to speak.

Still, she finished her meal, briefly joking with Bill about the cable outage and paying further compliment to Carol's cooking skills and carefully avoiding saying anything real.

Once the performance was complete, Lucy said, "Thank you," and excused herself from the table and walked as calmly as she could to the front door, hoping she might find more breathable air out on the front lawn.

It was a moonless night, and the stars swam in thick drifts across the sky. Lucy looked straight up and breathed deep and wished that something would take hold of her and pull her straight out into space.

She lived inside that dream for a moment until bright, unnatural light and a rumbling engine took over her senses. A horn blared twice, and her eyes adjusted to see an old, heavily dented red truck with duct tape covering a missing cab window. A mismatched gray canopy covered the truck bed and displayed years' worth of laminated trailhead passes and a peeling "Led Zeppelin" decal.

Fucking Brewer.

But it was Bucket who leaned out the passenger window. "Hey!"

"'Hey' back, dude."

"My phone's barely working, so I thought we'd drop by. We're going out to East Bear. You want to come?"

"Oh . . . no. It's not really a great . . ."

Brewer rolled down his window and leaned out. "Hey, Lucy. What up?"

"Nothing. Just finishing up dinner with my family."

"Oh. Are you, like, in the middle of it right now?" He seemed genuinely concerned he was interrupting. One of his eyes was hidden by his hair, but the other was looking right at her. His face was relaxed and friendly. Not concerned, or worried, or trying to *fix* her. "It's going to be awesome out at the caves tonight. You wouldn't believe how much of the Milky Way you can see out there when it's like this."

Did he catch me stargazing? And of course it's going to look awesome to him—he's probably high already.

Lucy looked at the boys, the excitement plain on their faces, and she imagined the rumble of Brewer's truck against her body, and the cool air that would rush in through the windows, and the long drive through the night.

She looked back at her house. It had never looked so small or heavy to her before. She felt the warm light from the windows on her skin like heat from an oven. She felt the Hendersons' *need* stretching out to her, wrapping around her chest.

She could barely lean in through the front door to let Bill and Carol know she was going out.

They told her they loved her. She rushed into the night before that truth could cause them any more pain.

Only after Lucy brushed aside the empty tallboy cans and found a belt that would actually latch was she able to settle into her seat in the extended cab and realize the consequences of her split-second decision.

I'm letting Brewer drive me somewhere.

Not just somewhere—to a party. In the woods.

Probably half the school attending. Everyone knowing I was in Mr. Chambers's room the day it happened.

Jason Ward missing.

The whole town's phones barely working—what if somebody falls into the fire? Josh Keener is out of juvie. What if he starts a fight and crushes somebody's throat again? Or worse? It could always be worse.

What if those cop cars I heard zoom by were already on their way out to the party?

There's no way this old beater of a truck has any kind of airbags.

Fuck.

By the time Lucy started to unbuckle and racked her panicked brain to conjure some excuse to exit, she'd found that the truck was already in motion. Right away, she felt a strange calm—she didn't know whether it was from leaving behind the pressure of her family home, or some vestige of the peace she'd felt as a little girl lying across the back seat of her parents' car with the sweet smell of the cherimoya groves drifting in through the window—and she decided that she would at least go along for the ride. She had a few books saved on her phone. If the party was too much to handle, she'd retreat to Brewer's rig and read until it was time to leave.

There was one thing she had to check on first. Lucy picked up an empty tallboy from the floor of the truck and tapped Brewer on the shoulder with the can.

"You drink these tonight? If you're drunk, then Bucket has to drive."

"Yeah, I drank all those tonight. Sat at the park with my music blasting and knocked 'em back. But then it was dusk and I saw a bat and I got scared."

"Seriously?"

"No. There were no bats."

"Dude, come on . . . You drank all these? You have to pull over."

Brewer laughed. "You need to stop. First, those are from a camping trip three weeks ago. Second, they're Bill Stanton's. I don't drink that fuckin' piss beer. Gives me bad headaches the next day. Third, I'm not sure Bucket can drive stick. And fourth, I'm not even drinking tonight."

"Oh."

"Yeah. You can cool your jets. I got these fuckin' rad mushrooms instead. Like all purple around the gills. Blue on the stems. They're crazy. But I can't drink with them or it stings my stomach something awful. Like, *Aaaaaah! Oooooh! My tummy!*" Brewer hunched forward and clung to his gut, then laughed. Despite being mildly terrified by Brewer's potential madness, Lucy laughed too.

Bucket leaned back in his seat and rotated his head toward Lucy. "I can drive stick, Lucy. I'll get us all home."

"No shit, bro?" asked Brewer. "Oh, that's great! I was only going to have a few stems and one cap, but now I can eat the whole fucking bag. That's awesome. You're my D and D, Buckminster."

"Designated *and* driver?"

"Oh, yeah. That's dumb. Whatever. Point is, I'm fucking stoked. Gonna see some galaxies tonight, dude." He held a fist out to Bucket. Bucket looked at the fist. Brewer said, "You don't bump this in the next five seconds, I'm going to slug you with it."

Bucket complied, and Brewer made an exaggerated series of explosive noises with his mouth. "That turned into a super-bomb, Buckwild. You can't let it build like that."

Lucy laughed again, and it felt like something lifting from her chest. She wasn't sure if Brewer was dumb or bugging out for kicks, but she liked the way he didn't seem to care about anything too much. He seemed free in a way she wished she could be.

Lucy noticed that Bucket was wearing the cologne his parents got him last Christmas. How much had he put on? The smell filled the cab of the truck, mixing with the odor of stale beer and that locker room musk she noticed whenever a couple of boys were in a closed space together. She had yet to decide if *that* was a good or bad smell, though sometimes it stirred something in her. She cracked the small tinted window to her right and leaned toward the cool desert air.

Then she caught Brewer looking at her in his rearview. She could see both of his eyes for once, with the wind blowing his hair out of his face. They held eye contact for longer than she thought appropriate, given that he was on the highway now and it felt like they were going way above the speed limit.

Brewer said, "Fresh air, huh? Is it Bucket's kitty-cat cologne or my nuts?"

"What?"

"I helped my cousin work on the pond at the Brubakers' farm, and I wore jeans like a dummy. Felt like I had swamp crotch all day, but when I got home I was so tired I napped instead of taking a shower. Honestly, I didn't think you'd come out, you know? Thought it'd only be me and Bucket and my mushies."

"So?"

"I don't know. I feel fine being filthy around dudes, but now that you're here I feel kind of weird. I mean, I can smell my junk from here. It ain't pretty."

"No. It's not that." She was going to say it was Bucket's cologne—the way it smelled a little like the spray they use to cover up the smell of pee at an old folks' home—but she stayed true to their friend code: they ribbed each other mercilessly when it was only the two of them, but never when there was a third person around. She wouldn't sell him out. "I like the fresh air, that's all."

"Oh, cool. Me too. Sometimes I even crack my bedroom window during the winter."

Lucy did the same, but she said nothing back. She noticed Bucket's shoulders hunching, and she imagined he was realizing he'd been used as a conduit and was quickly being third-wheeled. She decided to bring him back into the conversation.

"Hey, Bucket."

"Yeah?"

"You bring anything for the party?"

"Not really. I tried to call Tricia Howard so she could pick me up some beer, but my phone's shot. I rolled a joint using some crumbled-up schwag I stole from my parents' closet, but I don't have high hopes for it. The weed was really dry."

Brewer chimed in, using a cartoony voice. "How dry was it?"

Bucket had blown the fist bump. Lucy saw his face brighten at this new attempt to amuse Brewer. Bucket said, "As dry as Tina Plumber's second pussy."

The joke landed with Brewer, who snorted and shook his head. "Man, she is mighty confused, though."

Lucy wasn't fond of how boys talked about other girls in front of her—either they said demeaning shit as if she weren't there at all, or they recognized she was there and said *really* demeaning shit. Despite that, she was curious. Did Tina really have a second vagina? And if so, how reduced was her own social standing that she hadn't heard about it yet?

"What are you monkeys laughing about? Does Tina really have—"

"Oh no. It's gross, Lucy."

"Grosser than your swampy nuts?" She'd actually liked that he'd been so open about his body. She sensed that came from a place of confidence; he hadn't said it in the way that some boys would say disgusting things to her in an attempt to shock, or to let her know how little her opinion of them mattered.

Bucket chimed in, "Lucy's okay with gross. I showed her Guacamole Party on my phone once and she didn't even flinch."

Lucy hadn't flinched—she had yet to back down from an internet challenge—but she did cry for the girl in the video that night. Never told Bucket, though. He often told her he liked that she was "one of the guys," and she didn't want to let him down.

"Guacamole Party? Seriously?" said Brewer. "I don't even like to think about that one. In fact, I'm kind of pissed you reminded me of it. *So nasty.*"

"Wait," said Lucy, "is Tina's thing *that* bad?"

"Oh, not at all. Just that it might be . . . Listen, you know how people were saying that I smoked crack out of a light bulb at Ada Keizer's birthday party?"

"Yeah."

"But that was total Grade-A bullshit, and it got around so fast that two days later my cousin was asking me about it. So sometimes I feel like it's shitty to go spreading stories you aren't a hundred percent sure on."

They were much closer to the East Bear Caves. They'd gone past the range of the city's streetlights. Without any moon overhead, Brewer's headlights were the only thing illuminating the road as it rolled beneath them. Lucy thought about what Brewer had said. She'd heard a ton about him, and his cousin Rodney, and how their whole clan lived in a manufactured home compound out past Westerhaus. They were meth cooks, they were burglars, they were junkies, they bred dogs for fighting. Brewer smoked crack.

How much of *any* of that was true?

Lucy knew Brewer pulled good grades, when he bothered to show. She'd heard his name on the honor roll during morning announcements and didn't quite believe it until she heard it again the next quarter. She wondered what he was really like. She wondered what lies he'd heard about her. She said, "You don't have to talk about it, then."

"Well, now it's built up, though, isn't it? And besides, I heard it straight from Ben, and Tina's got that crazy in her eyes, so I think we can file this one under 'Maybe.'"

"Soooooooo?"

"You know how Tina is an Eastsider? Well, they were doing one of their megachurch events, like some boy-band concert. Lambs on Fire, I think, which is actually a totally metal name. Anyway, she goes to this concert, and at the end they have this come-to-Jesus kind of thing on the stage where you can make a 'Purity Pledge.' So she does that, gives her heart to Jesus, says she'll save her virginity for some schmuck who won't even know if she's good in bed until they're married."

"Oh no."

"Yeah. You see where this is going. Well, she was dating Ben Brumke at the time, and he's an Eastsider too, but only because his parents go. So he's there every Sunday, and Tina saw him there and figured he'd be a safe guy to date."

Lucy remembered the time Ben Brumke walked by her locker and said, "If you forgot your lunch, then I have something you can eat," and then started making nasty wet throat-gagging noises.

"Tina miscalculated."

"Yeah, you could say that. So Brumke keeps pushing and after a month Tina tells him that she can't give up her virginity, that's holy territory, but she'd been messaging some other Christian girls online and she had something else for him."

"The butt!" said Bucket, appearing to relish this part of the story in a way that gave Lucy pause—there were clearly thoughts Bucket had about women in general that he never shared with her.

"Yup. The butt. Which always seemed kind of crazy, to me at least. I always saw that as a bonus level. That's not the default game. Like, you have to beat all the bosses and collect all the stars or rings or whatever, definitely do a bunch of oral, and then maybe you get to the butt. But here goes Tina, throwing it out there like a level-one mid-boss. So of course Ben goes for it, starts thumping away. He said that she kept her hands clasped in front of her face the whole time, like she was praying, and toward the end he said she was crying. And then afterward they're lying there, and she's still crying a little bit and she looks at Ben with this weird face and she says, 'I can't believe you love me so much that you're willing to wait. But I swear you can have the rest of me once we're married.'"

"Nooooo." Lucy didn't know what she was more amazing—that Tina lived so far outside of our accepted reality, or that anyone would consider marrying an ape like Ben Brumke.

"Yeah. Makes me a little sad. You can kind of picture her eyes all misty, that room smelling like ass and big, sweaty Ben, and she's hearing wedding bells and thinking something special has happened. She invited him to come to dinner—*with her parents*—at the Beef N' Brew the next night. So of course Ben dumped her. Sent her a text that night saying that he'd thought she was a good Christian girl and that after what happened he didn't think he could see her again. Then she texted back saying she didn't understand and he sent back, like, a prayer-hands emoji and a message saying, 'I'll pray for you.'"

Bucket laughed. Lucy cuffed the back of his head.

"What?"

"You know what. Ben's an asshole."

"Yeah, but . . . the prayer hands. It's kind of funny."

Brewer said, "Ben sure thought it was funny. But you could also tell he was shook up over it. I mean, with a girl that confused or crazy or whatever, how far is it in her head from *This is the man I'm gonna marry* to *This is the man I'm gonna stab to death*?"

Lucy rolled her eyes on instinct. "That's bullshit, dude. Why is it that every time a girl has strong emotions, you guys say she's crazy?"

"How it feels, I guess. Besides, when a girl wants to marry you because you guys did some butt stuff, and that happened because she was afraid of the wrath of an imaginary sky dude, that's *actually* crazy. Like fucking bonkers."

Bucket said, "Yeah. That's coconuts." He leaned back toward Lucy. "No need to get all *crazy* about it."

"Har har, dude."

"Oh, shit!" Brewer said. "I just remembered the weirdest part about that story. So after Ben's done talking about Tina and the laughter cooled off, there's one of those lulls, you know, where the whole table is quiet all of a sudden and you can feel it, and then Jason Ward leaned across the table and looked Ben in the eyes and asked him, 'How much did she cry?' And at first I thought he was joking, but then I looked at his face and I realized he was very serious and very interested. Like, he *needed* to know how much Tina cried."

Lucy shivered. Something had always seemed a little off about Jason. The only time she'd ever seen him have any kind of facial expression was when Luke Olsen and Dale Rupp got in a fight. There was Jason, standing on the periphery, rocking on his feet and smiling.

"So we all got the heebie-jeebies from Jason's question, and I think Ben made some dumb joke to try to brush it all off, to make it about him and his anal conquest again. But guess who's going out three days later?"

"Jason and Tina?" Lucy had found that answers that caused a dull ache in the pit of her stomach were usually the right ones.

"Yup. Jason and Tina. And that always creeped me out. I saw them holding hands in the commons one day, and I remember when he let go there were white prints from his fingers on her skin. Her fingers were all screwy, and her hand looked crumpled, like a baby bird after it hits your window. And I remember feeling this hate for him then, this really pure sort of hate. So when I heard he was missing, I thought about that crushed hand and I thought about him wondering how much Tina cried and I felt like, *Good.* You know? Like, *Fuck him. And I hope they never find him.*"

It was the group in the truck's turn to hit a conversational lull. Brewer's *Fuck him* echoed in their heads for a moment, grating against the blasphemy of talking shit about a kid who might be endangered, or worse. Lucy couldn't decide whether Brewer was principled or vindictive, but then she thought of all the times someone like Jason had probably been curious about how much *she* might cry.

"Totally," she said. "Fuck him."

She caught Brewer's eyes in the rearview again. Squinting this time. Wondering about her?

Bucket said, "Hey—mile marker eighteen! We need to watch for the turnoff, right?"

Brewer switched on his brights, lighting the brush and lava rock on both shoulders. "Yup. Should be after this next curve, then past that juniper that got hit by lightning last year."

He comes here all the time.

Lucy saw the torched tree he was talking about, a ghost in the headlights, white and bark-free at its base, rent down the middle, its jagged, blackened branches reaching skyward.

Brewer said, "Here we go. Party time, y'all," and turned his truck onto the old dirt road to the caves. He navigated through the rocky crags and washed-out dips in the road as if from sense memory. Lucy saw drifts of dust in the headlights and felt flush with anxiety as she remembered they weren't the only people headed this way. Things had felt so good for a moment, so simple and real, with only her and Bucket and Brewer and the night breeze. She could have talked to them all night—there was something freeing about the way they spoke together. But now it was "party time"—she imagined that she'd soon be invisible to them both, erased by whatever other urges they'd come out here to chase.

She wanted to tell Brewer to turn around, to find a way to keep driving, but she also didn't want to seem weird.

Shit. I'm faking it again.

Lucy wondered where she might be at that exact moment if she hadn't spent so much time trying to be the right version of herself for those around her. But before she had the time to find any kind of answer, she found herself lurching forward as Brewer's truck came to a sudden sliding stop in soft dirt. Empty beer cans clattered over one another and fresh clouds of dust rolled away from the truck for a moment before Brewer killed the halogens and left them sitting in dark.

"Ain't nothing to it but to do it, y'all. Let's party this piss-poor fucking excuse for a school year into the ground."

Bucket drummed on the dash and let loose with a halfhearted "Whoop whoop!" It had been his ironic party go-to for months.

Lucy whispered, "Fuck," to herself, pulled the cab handle, and stepped into the cold desert night. She spotted a small fire in the distance that struggled against the wind and darkness of the moonless sky to mark the entrance to the East Bear Caves. Lucy zipped up her hoodie and shivered and felt her feet sinking into the churned-up, sandy trail leading to the party. The sounds of muffled bass and laughter and the rumble of other arriving engines sped her heart, but she kept walking forward, afraid of losing Bucket and Brewer and entering those caves all alone.

Looking straight ahead, she had forgotten all about the stars above.

chapter four

CAVING

They stood near the wide mouth of the cave, a few steps short of peering over the drop. "It gets pretty dark down there. Either of you bring headlamps?" asked Brewer.

"No," said Bucket.

"Would have been a cool thing to mention when you picked me up," said Lucy.

"Honestly, I was shocked you decided to come. Besides, I figured y'all had been out here before."

Lucy could count the parties she'd attended in the last year on one hand. She guessed Bucket had been to a few more, only because his incessant desire to get laid occasionally outweighed any other considerations.

"I have a light on my phone, though. That's about all it's good for right now anyway," offered Bucket.

"That'll help once you're down there, but a headlamp's way better when you're clambering over the rockfalls to get to the back. Plus, there's no extra moonlight to help tonight, which means it's going to get pitch-black a few feet back from the fire, unless they have a rager going. Probably only pallet wood and presto logs down there, though, since this wasn't planned and everybody's hucking down on a lark."

Three kids in North Face vests with bright white LED headlamps walked past Lucy, beer bottles clinking in their backpacks. They took turns climbing out of sight using the aluminum ladders that descended into the cave system. The top rung on one of the ladders was marked "Stairway to Heaven" in thick black Sharpie. The top of the other read "Property of Brundage Concrete" though part of the text was covered by a sticker that read "40 oz to Freedom." Both ladders wobbled with each kid's passage, shifting against the soft soil and sharp stone of the entrance, and Lucy wondered why neither was anchored to keep it from falling over backward.

Brewer patted his face with his hands. Lucy couldn't tell if he was trying to knock a solution to their new problem out of his brain, or if he was dealing with the frustration of being saddled with two amateur-hour party pals.

"Look," Brewer said, "Bucket can use his phone, once he's down there at least. And then . . ." Brewer riffled around in the front pockets of his hoodie and pulled something out in a closed hand. "You can have this." He gave a small black headlamp to Lucy. It smelled of sweat and his greasy hair, but Lucy was happy for anything that might keep her safe.

"Thanks."

"No worries. Besides, in about half an hour I'm going to have fucking full-spectrum super-vision anyway. Wolf pupils. Bat hearing. Purple-green wobblies everywhere. All that." Brewer reached into his other hoodie pocket, pulled out his Ziploc bag of mushrooms, and started mowing down the contents like they were potato chips. He grinned at Lucy and Bucket and spoke around his stuffed cheeks. "You eat 'em fast and you don't taste the shit as much!" He lifted the bag to his mouth and tapped out whatever fungal crumbles were left in the bag. Then he pulled another crinkling bag from his rear pants pocket.

"Wait. What's that? Are you eating more?" asked Bucket.

"Oh hell no, dude. An eighth is good for me, or I start seeing some shit that definitely doesn't exist. Saw a giant chicken once. Huge. Golden . . . It was beautiful. But then I got scared. *This* is only some Skittles so my breath doesn't smell like cow flop all night." He knocked back half the bag at once. Lucy heard the candies clacking against one another, smelled synthetic fruit on the wind as he chewed. There was something about the scent that made her feel carefree, and for a moment she was excited to be out at a party, and even more excited to be around someone new. She remembered a time when she was very young in Peru and a boy she didn't know sat down next to her and handed her a lollipop made from caramel and coconut, and how the day, like too many, had been horrible, but those moments where they'd both sat there eating candy had been perfect.

Oh god. I've officially snapped. I smell some fruit snacks, and now all is right with the world.

But Lucy decided that the feeling, however irrational, was one worth riding for as long as she could, so she slipped Brewer's headlamp over her hair, flipped on the switch, and said, "Okay. Let's party."

Brewer flinched, and she realized the lamp was shining right into his eyes. "God*damn*, girl. Watch where you're aiming. Trying to blind me by a big-ass hole in the earth?"

"Oh, sorry." She couldn't tell if he was really mad. She tilted the light on her forehead downward and looked up to see Brewer was smiling. Excited.

"Do that an hour from now and it'll be like shooting rainbows into my brain."

"Yeah, now that you mention it . . ." Bucket held out his hand with his palm up. Brewer passed him the keys to the truck.

"I'm trusting you, man. Don't go grinding my gears. And don't leave me out here, even if I tell you to leave me out here. Hell, *espe-*

cially if I tell you that. If I try to watch one more sunrise without blinking I'll be blind for sure. Greg saved me last time. He shook me and said, 'You can't stare at the sun. You're going to go blind.' Which, you know, totally true. So I'm forever grateful for that. But what if Greg isn't here to save me this time? Do you think he's here? I hope he is. Good dude."

Lucy and Bucket exchanged a look—*He's already starting to trip out.*

"Anyway, once more into the breach."

"What does that mean?"

"No idea. It's what my cousin says when we're about to do something crazy."

Then Brewer walked over to the drop-off, got down on his knees, and steadied the top of one of the ladders.

"Wouldn't take shit to anchor these with some tie-downs and rebar, but we have to pull these old guys in the morning. Used to be a nice staircase here, but the Forest Service removed it after some dip-shits spray painted a bunch of swastikas on the cave walls and left a dead dog down there."

"Seriously?"

"Yeah. They torched a bunch of hibernating bats too, which is super illegal. My aunt said she heard it was Satanists that did it, but I told her it was probably just regular assholes. Maybe the Jessup brothers. Maybe some kids from the Butte. Town's full of dicks. Close your eyes and throw a rock, right? Anyway, I'll hold her steady until you're down."

Lucy knew that Bucket would probably like a steady descent too, but he was already walking toward the other ladder and starting his climb down. They could both sense that Brewer was doing this for her specifically.

Bucket's ladder clattered against the stone, loose pebbles tumbling into the cave below. Brewer asked, "You got it, bud?"

"Yeah, dude."

Lucy recognized Bucket's flat tone—*He's getting bitchy. Is he nervous? Jealous? What am I going to have to deal with tonight?*

She really had no idea, but there was a cool boy with candy on his breath waiting for her, and that was enough to send her down the "Stairway to Heaven." She steadied her nerves as her legs hung over the drop, and after she found the first rung with her foot, she felt safe. Three rungs farther down and the horizon disappeared from view. She felt the cold and dark of the cave wrapping around her with each step. It was the same sensation she got from diving into the swimming hole out past the Pinewood campgrounds—the warmth was only at the surface, and everything below was beyond the reach of the sun.

Before she knew it, she'd descended thirty feet and was standing on the cave floor. She heard Bucket make landfall to her left. Brewer was already on the ladder above and rushing down.

Lucy aimed her headlamp up to try to help him, and saw a flurry of fast, flitting movement in the beam. Then she heard the high-pitched squeaking sounds and realized she'd never seen so many bats in her life. Maybe a hundred of them swirling up and out into the night, though these were so much smaller than the ones she'd seen darting around the dusky treetops as a child, and they were heading out much later than she thought natural. Something stirred under her skin.

Turn around.

But Bucket and Brewer were already plunging toward the light and sound at the heart of the cave. Lucy imagined the two ladders behind her emitting a keening metallic screech, like the tines of a tuning fork sending out a warning signal, calling out to her, pulling her back. But that felt crazy, and she was tired of feeling that way, so she ignored the bad vibes and joined her friends as they walked toward the bottom of an ancient hole in the world.

As far as lemons-to-lemonade scenarios go, maybe having your eye gouged out in a violent attack was worth it if it earned you a harem of sympathetic drunken cheerleaders. Lucy could see the jealousy on Bucket's face, watching as Jake Bernhardt sat by the party fire like a one-eyed king on his Coleman ice chest, Lisa K on his lap and Tiffany Pedersen rubbing his shoulders and three other members of the cheer squad listening intently to whatever he had to say. Their faces were all sympathy and sweetness. Jake was damaged, a survivor. And even after everything that happened, he had come out to celebrate with his friends. *So brave.*

"That eye patch is a pussy magnet, Lu. What'd that guy even do? Act like an asshole and then get beat? How is that—"

"What? Fair?" Lucy could barely hide her annoyance. She had almost fainted when she saw Jake, and even now seeing him reminded her of too much. She thought about Chris Carmichael and Mr. Chambers and how neither would be the hit of the party any time soon. She thought about purple smoke and collapsing faces and at last the gravity of her decision to come to the party had landed and sat like a stone on her chest. And here was Bucket, thinking he'd trade an eye for a series of sympathy lays.

The worst part, what she didn't even want to acknowledge, was that even if Bucket had been the one assaulted, he wouldn't be in the same situation. He'd be One-Eyed Sandy to them. An easy punch line. Another thing to make him an Other.

Lucy placed a hand on Bucket's back. He was right. "Fair" wasn't part of the equation. Bucket looked over at Lucy, and she nodded at him. They were back on the same track.

Meanwhile, Brewer had jumped their track, derailed by his mushrooms and the excitement of finally arriving at the party. Lucy felt a little embarrassed by the way his attention had her head swimming.

What was that? What did I think was happening there?

Shortly after they'd found the first big opening in the cave—a sandy circle surrounded by stone, with a small wood fire and a gathering of students at its center—Brewer had looked from his hand to the fire, then back to his hand, then shook his head as if coming to an important decision. Then he leaned in toward Bucket and Lucy, voice lowered to a conspiratorial whisper, and said, "One hundred fifty thousand years of animals falling through that skylight up there." He pointed up to a hole in the domed cave, which could barely be seen if you didn't notice the smoke escaping though its eye. "Bear, horse, elk walking around and then, *Whoops!* and they're down in the cave on broken legs, looking for a way out. That's why the Native Americans called this the Skeleton Cave before white guys rebranded it. Supposed to be cleaned up, but I can feel the bones, y'all. The bones are still here."

He looked to his hand, seeing some power there. "The vibrations are the same. This is a magnet."

And with that, he was gone.

Lucy looked around for him for a while, staying stationary by the fire but tracking for movement and watching as more and more kids from school came fumbling over the rocks with coolers and cardboard half racks of lite beer. None of them were Brewer.

"He'll come back around, Lucy."

"Who?"

"Brewer."

"Oh, I don't care."

"That's cute. Maybe your white knight can hold the ladder for you again on the way up. Watch out, though—you can tell he wants to bury his face in your ass."

"Shut *up*."

"You shut up. I'm just fucking around." He bumped her with his shoulder. "Besides, he has to come back. We have his truck keys."

"You really know how to drive stick?"

"Barely. But Brewer would think he's flying a fucking bone-hunting spaceship, so . . ."

"Yeah. It's the right call." Lucy looked around the cave and tried to ignore the looks of surprise and glares of resentment she caught when she accidentally made eye contact. This was not her crew. Nobody from band. Nobody from speech class. A ton of kids from the Butte. A few older guys she recognized from the skate park. Loads of girls from cheer squad and dance team, filling their phones with firelit duck-lipped selfies in preparation for the glorious day when everyone's service finally worked again. A dark shape was high up the rocks near the cave wall, already hunched over, vomiting. Short hair, so not Brewer. Probably some Butte kid who'd shotgunned his sixer right when he'd shown up. She imagined how he'd probably felt minutes ago, his belly swelling with beer, his friends yelling, "Whooo!" as he chugged. He composed himself then stumbled back to the party. He nudged a friend, who tossed him a fresh beer and yelled, "Rally, bro!" The boy muttered, "Yeah. Rally," in response, then lifted the new beer with a shaking hand and started the process anew.

No wonder the bats left.

"How long do you think we'll be here, Bucket?"

Bucket was looking across the fire. Ashley Jorgensen had arrived, which meant Bucket wasn't thinking anymore; instead he was dreaming about a world where Ashley was really attracted to him instead of playing him for help with math homework. Lucy knew Ashley only dated older guys, either snowboard bums or guys from the community college, but Bucket couldn't get over a text Ashley had sent. It read Thinking about U, and included a dimly lit shot of herself in a short gray tee and white sleep shorts. Lucy supposed it was a more romantic message than *Thinking about passing precalc without learning anything.* At least she'd sent him a jerk-off fantasy. Others had taken more from him, and been less kind.

Still, she knew that his brain disappeared whenever he saw Ashley, so she wasn't surprised he'd failed to hear her.

"Bucket?"

"What?"

"You wanna look for Brewer and head out, maybe, or . . ." She let the question drift off. Bucket was staring, laid low by fantasy. He was useless to her so long as the Idea of Ashley held sway. "Never mind, dude. And it's creepy when you stare like that. You've got to work on intermittent glancing or something."

"Sounds good." It wasn't much of a response, but the best she could hope for from a guy suffering dick-borne deafness. "I'm going to see if Tim Arnold has a couple of extra beers I can buy off him. You want one?"

She considered saying yes, but the situation already felt beyond her control. She couldn't imagine piling any other complications into the evening, and her tolerance was negligible. She pictured herself in one of the corners of the cave, throwing up while people by the fire laughed at her lightweight status. Maybe someone would even snap a pic and run it through a funny filter that gave her giant eyes and a dog nose, or turn her into a cautionary three-second slow-motion puke clip. LoogieLosesIt.gif.

"No. I'm good."

"Suit yourself, Lu. But I think we earned this. We earned *something*, at least, after the last couple of weeks. The world owes us. I'm going to have some fun tonight."

And with that, he was gone.

One boy hunting bones, the other hunting fun, and Lucy left to herself without a friendly face in sight. She watched the fire for a moment, zoning on the tiny wavering cities falling to ash at its base. Then, as she had learned to do as a child, she became a ghost and wandered among the living.

———

The Hendersons encouraged Lucy to embrace her heritage, whatever that meant. They wanted her to take enough Spanish classes to retain her grasp on the language, while she did her best to bury her accent and speak clear, overenunciated English. They connected her with a school advocate to help her with the cultural and linguistic transition, but Lucy stopped meeting with her once she realized how those visits made her feel alien, as if she were a different species needing special handling. The Hendersons even offered to travel to Peru with Lucy after her senior year, to help her reconnect to her "motherland" and revisit the places she managed to remember from her parents' near-vagrancy, like Pucallpa or the outskirts of Lima. She knew they meant well, but what they didn't understand is that the moment they adopted her she placed her past in a small box in her heart, and locked it, and said, *That time is done.*

Because Peru, to her, was not her culture, or a land to which she felt some intimate connection aside from a few pleasant sense memories. Rather, it was the awful and perpetually unsure world her parents had created for her there. Her Peru was knowing that nobody was waiting for you when you needed them. It was knowing that you found your own food in the morning because not even slapping your parents would rouse them, and by evening they'd be gone again, so dinner was on you too. It was a school system that grew tired of trying to save her from her home and let her fade away so they wouldn't have to face the shame of their failure. It was a place where nothing was solid, and often the only joy was found in drifting through the city as a hungry ghost.

She'd learned to be small and fast, so anyone who might try to stop her movement wouldn't see her for long. If someone stared, then she'd stare back and say, "I'm hungry," and that made her disappear again. Soon the only people who spotted her were those with bad intentions, and she'd learned to spot them too, and to flee.

She learned to listen, and found entertainment in the lives of others. She heard their stories floating from windows and felt she soon understood the city better than most. She fell asleep under cantata shrubs outside the nursery of a new baby named Sandro, stealing his lullabies for herself. She woke at dusk with tears in her eyes.

She learned which stores would look the other way if a ghost suddenly fled their store with a piece of fruit. She found the nooks and tuckaways in the city where the other ghosts would congregate and share what they had found. The memory of these riverside and concrete hiding spots was the only thing—aside from her favorite fruits—that she missed on occasion.

The truth was that Peru was gone, and the worst of it—that life of never-knowing, her parents' fighting, the accident, the orphanage—was something Lucy had turned into an abstraction. So when the Hendersons pushed her to "embrace her heritage," she felt they didn't understand—her heritage was a dangerous feeling in her heart that she did her best to reduce to a permanent ache, and she feared that if she embraced it she might burn to death, like her parents.

The only thing she allowed herself were a few memories—the feeling of the river current, the taste of fruit, the beauty of the highland orchids—and her ability to disappear into the world of ghosts.

———

It was harder to fade from view in the East Bear Caves. First, Lucy was wearing a headlamp. Second, the terrain felt alien and unstable beneath her feet. What had Brewer said as they climbed over rough rock on the way down to the party?

"These are all old lava tubes, even the caves on the north side of town. Don't know if you've ever fallen on lava rock, but I learned to ride my bike on this shit, and when I wrecked, it felt like I was rubbing a cheese grater on my knees. So plant each foot nice and steady and keep your hands ready to brace your fall because this stuff shifts all the time."

Lucy pulled up her hoodie and tucked her hair inside. She killed her headlamp and gave her eyes a moment to adjust. People's faces were moving shadows in the firelight. Within a few strides, she had found the darkness beyond the light of the fire.

She closed her eyes and tuned her ears to the noises of the cave:

explosions of laughter, drunken proclamations, competing stereos playing hip-hop and pop-country. The distant, repetitive slap of somebody getting fucked from behind, the sound louder as the couple's excitement overrode their desire for keeping their quickie on the low. The rattle of the aluminum ladders in the distance, new revelers pouring in. *Woooo* noises of growing frequency and volume, spreading like a sonic virus.

The party was heating up.

And what are you doing, creeper? Hiding again? Backing away? No wonder they treat you like you're weird. You're fucking weird. Go hang out by the fire. Talk to somebody. Laugh at some dumb jokes. Hit up Bucket for a beer, if he scored some. Come on!

But it was too late—Lucy had heard something else bouncing from the walls of the cave: the sound of another girl dropping her volume to dish in confidence. Lucy took it as both a challenge to her abilities as a ghost and an opportunity to learn some intriguing gossip. A game.

She crept closer. Three girls passing a glass pipe and butane lighter, shooting the shit. She had to get in range to hear what they were saying without the flickering light from their smoke session reaching her. When she felt she was close enough she squinted and aimed her ears, using her hoodie to press them forward. *I'm batgirl*, she thought. *Please, god, don't let them see me.*

". . . so anyway, I say to her, 'Life hack, bitch: don't have a fucking baby. He doesn't give a shit about you anyway. You think he can pay for a kid working night security at the furniture store? He can't even buy decent condoms.' And she's not a hundred percent sure she's pregnant. She says her body feels *different.* So the next morning she hits Fred's Pharmacy and took care of it, but then I talk to her a few days later and find out that maybe it didn't work, and maybe it wasn't even Ayden's baby. *If* there was a baby at all."

Who was that talking? Ginny Bucholtz? She had that weird vocal fry sound to her voice.

"No joke?"

"Seriously. And get this—she said it might be *Jason's*. She got a text from him a few days before he disappeared, and all it said was *Come over*, so she did, and then when she got there she said that he was shaky, and he was aggressive, like not even talking to her, and he grabbed her and turned her around, but you know she's always had a crush on him, so she was like, *I guess this is how this happens.* He was a shitty lay too, like he only stuck it in once and then barely moved it until he started shivering. And then when they were done, he just said, 'Get out.' So she did. But here's the crazy part. On the way back to her car, she saw Jennifer Schwartz pulling into the same cul-de-sac."

"What. The. Fuck?"

"Right?"

"Oh, and wait. There's more—she said the only time Jason really stopped shaking was when he was inside her."

"You think he's doing more than coke now?"

"Who knows?"

"All I know is Amy needs to start making some better life choices. At this rate she's lucky she hasn't had, like, a baby made out of herpes."

"Jesus, that's gross."

"Ha! Herpes baby. Herpes baby."

"What the fuck, though? Shut up! You're gonna make me throw up."

"Can't help it. Oh my god, this weed is crazy."

"You want to go back to the party?"

"I want some fucking Taco Bell."

"I want to eat a herpes baby."

"Ugh. You're the worst, bitch. I love you."

"Let's stay long enough to check out the other party."

Wait. What other party?

Lucy's curiosity drove her closer. On her second step, her heel slipped on a batch of crumbled, porous lava rock, sending stones skittering down toward the girls.

Fuck!

Lucy quickly curled into a ball and hoped her dark hoodie and pants and the girls' significantly stoned brains would conspire to conceal her.

"What was that?"

"Bats, maybe."

"Maybe. Tom said he's seen a coyote in here before. Either way, let's walk back over. Nate Carver should be here by now."

"Girl, no. He's an asshole."

"He broke up with Emily last week."

"Still an asshole."

"I'm not trying to marry him. You ever see him running in those short little track shorts? That's all I'm saying."

"Ginny wants Nate's herpes baby!"

"Jesus. Handle your shit, Trace. You're gooning out."

Trace? Lucy figured that was Tracy Scheimer. Why was it always the honor society kids who started acting out when they got high?

The girls and their stream of gossip and laughter moved away from Lucy and back toward the fire. Without someone to haunt, Lucy felt the truth for a moment—*We're here now because a boy is dead. And another was killed. And another is missing. And here I am, alone in the dark while everyone else celebrates.*

These were not observations she'd wanted, or a feeling she could bear. She roamed quietly in search of anything else.

She checked out the center of the party and spotted Bucket standing at the edge of the fire, slowly sipping a beer and nodding to the music coming from the closest stereo. She knew if she followed his eyes she'd be able to spot Ashley Jorgensen too.

C'mon, buddy. You've got to move past that.

Lucy wondered if Bucket only pined for unattainable women like Toni and Ashley because he knew he'd never have to form a close connection with them, or face being rejected. Then she wondered if all her sessions with Dr. Nielsen were turning her into an armchair psychiatrist. Then she wondered if maybe she shouldn't turn some of that insight inward and figure out why the fuck she was playing cave ninja. Or why she could barely manage to sit at a dinner table with the two kindest people she'd ever met. Or why she was having sex dreams back-to-back with dreams about her teacher's face caving in. Or why . . .

"Whatchadoin', Lucy?"

Lucy yelped and almost tumbled forward. How the hell had Brewer found her in the dark?

Wolf pupils. Bat hearing.

"You peeing? I can walk away for a sec."

"No. Jesus. I kind of have to pee now, though. You scared the hell out of me."

"Sorry, y'all. Wasn't sure you were even real till I got close. Thought you might be a small black bear, or a spirit or something. But when I got closer, I smelled that nice smell you've got. That and your shoes. I remembered your shoes."

"Uh . . . thanks."

"Look at that little tribe down there, all huddled around the fire. That's old, what they're doing."

Lucy figured that shit felt profound inside Brewer's addled mind, but she wasn't sure she wanted to play sounding board for his trip. The way he'd talked to her when he was sober had felt so playful and direct. She hoped for more of that. Plus, she didn't want him to ask her any questions that might reveal her transition into ghost mode. She aimed for diversion. "What have you been up to? You find any bones?"

"No. Kinda bummed. I guess the Forest Service and the volunteer groups really cleaned this joint out last time it got trashed. Only found used condoms and busted forty bottles, which, you know, double bummer. My best guess is that the bones I felt in my hand were buried. Maybe mastodon bones, way down there, from thousands of years ago. Strong signal."

"Probably."

"Hey, can I ask you kind of a personal question?"

"You can ask. Doesn't mean I'll answer."

"I like that! All right. Is it true that where you're from there's a pink dolphin that lives in the river and puts curses on people?"

How does he know I'm from Peru? Bucket . . .

What else does he know?

Lucy's skin flushed, but she answered quickly to keep from seeming flustered. "There are real pink dolphins. They call them botos. But they don't really do *curses*. Some people say they take on the spirits of the dead, and that's why they act so human. They're really playful. But other people think they're shape-shifters that seduce young women by the riverside."

"Wait! Seduce? Like how?"

"The boto turns into a handsome fisherman, and if a girl pledges her love, then they hook up. But if you catch them fucking, then the guy turns back into a pink dolphin. And if you *don't* catch them, then the girl gives birth to another boto."

"Whaaaaaaa? No!"

"Yeah. When I was a kid I sat by the river one day and waited for a fisherman to show up. I thought maybe I could have a boto baby and then we could live in the river together."

Why am I telling him this? Jesus . . .

"Yeah," he said. "When I was a kid I wanted a pet great white shark, but then I found out they die in captivity. I was sad for a whole year. No joke. Same as when I found out helium only floated as a gas. I had *plans* for that liquid helium! Floating castle-sized plans . . ."

"Kids are dumb."

"Super dumb."

"You think we're still dumb right now? But, like, less dumb?"

"Probably. You're definitely dumb. I'm borderline brain-dead. Like, why are we standing in a pitch-black cave right now, talking about magic dolphins?"

"I like it here, though." And it was true. Though it was sudden, Lucy realized she hadn't felt this good in ages. Brewer really was like the boy who gave her that lollipop—he gave her moments that were better in the middle of all the mess. It happened with Bucket too, but often that felt like survival—they were helping each other get through. This was . . . different.

"I like it here too. You're cool as hell, Lucy."

She hoped that the dark was complete enough to conceal her smile. She didn't want to seem like the kind of girl who flipped for a compliment.

What would a cool girl say?

"Yeah. I *am* cool as hell."

Too on the nose? Did I sell it?

"It's good you know that. Sometimes when I see you in the hall you seem like you're trying to hide. And that's a shame because you're easily one of the most . . . What's the word?"

If he says "exotic," I'll scream until this cave collapses.

Brewer continued, "I guess just . . . interesting. Seems like you have a lot going on. And I see the way that you talk with Bucket, how close you guys are, and I get kind of jealous. That seems like a really good friendship."

Lucy didn't respond. Was he playing her? Did she even care? What was this?

They stood in silence for a moment until Brewer tried to recalibrate. "Listen to me running my mouth like I'm thinking out loud. Fucking mushies, dude. Bugging out in the cave like this is some sensory deprivation chamber. I told you I'm du . . ."

But before he could finish his sentence, Lucy slid her hands onto the sides of his face and pulled herself up to him and kissed him as hard as she could. Then he brought his hands to her face, gentle in the darkness, and kissed her back. After a while, their lips softened and they slid away from each other and then each took a breath.

"Whoa."

"Yeah."

"That really happened, right?"

"What really happened? What are you talking about?"

"Oh . . . uh . . . *nothing*. Listen, I'm high as hell and—"

"No, I'm fucking with you. We totally kissed."

"Oh, thank goodness. 'Cause that was great. I'm glad it was real."

"Me too. But it's getting weird now, talking about it."

"Should we kiss again? To stop the weirdness?"

"Probably."

So they did, and Lucy found herself in another good place, a place where she wanted to stay for as long as she could, away from the fire and chaos at the center of the party, and this second kiss lasted until both their faces ached from it, and then Brewer pulled away and said, "I want to show you the cool part of the cave."

Brewer's hand wrapped around hers, and a wave of something she'd never felt before rolled through her entire body, and she smiled again and realized she was ready to go most anywhere with him.

———————————

After a few near tumbles over loose rock, Lucy remembered she was wearing a headlamp and—absent Brewer's blown-out pupils and familiarity with East Bear—she realized that she wouldn't be able to keep up with him without seeing where she was going. Ghost mode forgotten, she flipped the switch and squinted at the light beaming from her forehead.

They'd stayed to the dark instead of heading straight through the middle of the party, Lucy feeling like she and Brewer had formed this small and sacred space that only needed to contain the two of them together.

They'd held hands as they walked at first, but Brewer was right—you wanted your arms out for balance. He was leading her into rough terrain, a clamber over boulder-sized stones toward the upper back left section of the main cave.

Seeing Brewer in the light of her headlamp gave her pause at first—he was skinnier than the type she usually went for; his long, artificially colored hair barely concealed the fact that his head was too large for his body; and she now had confirmation that he had no problem ingesting a large amount of drugs.

But none of that mattered to her, not really, because when she thought about what he'd said to her, and the way they'd kissed, she felt a fresh rush of something pure and good through her heart and body, and she couldn't let go of that feeling.

"Almost there. See that spot where it flattens out up above?"

She saw the spot he was talking about, but beyond it was a small hole in the cave wall, maybe three feet by three feet at the largest. She didn't know if she could go in there.

She thought about the back of her parents' car after the accident, how she'd been pinned tight by the steel as the smell of gasoline spread . . .

Brewer looked back. Could he sense her panic? "It's a short belly crawl, that's all. All you have to do is lie flat and wiggle through like one of those army guy toys, and before you know it you're in a much cooler cave. And it looks like somebody's already got a fire lit over there, so you'll be able to see light at the end of the tube. You don't always get that."

Lucy looked at the narrow cave entrance and thought of the fire beyond, and memories rushed through her.

Smoke as gasoline ignited/the sound of screaming in the distance.

Purple smoke in the room/screaming a few feet away.

Both times: trapped.

I'm losing it.

I'm going to fuck this up.

He's going to know I'm damaged goods.

No.

"I'll go first. Okay, Lucy? So you can see it's short and it's safe."

In the distance, Lucy heard two girls yelling down by the fire in the first cave. Had a fight broken out? Some kind of drunken drama? Maybe Emily caught Ginny moving in on Nate Carver and decided to pull out a chunk of hair.

Ahead of her was Brewer, and he was kind, and he wanted to show her something. And she wanted to be brave and see it.

"You go ahead, and I'll follow. Do you need the headlamp?"

"No, I know the way. I came out here with my cousin once, and our flashlight died when we were all the way in the second cave. Took us four hours of climbing around to find the way out, but now I know these caves front to back. Also, I'm pretty sure there's a glowing map of the whole system built into the surface of my left eye like a heads-up display. So we've got this."

God. He's still tripping. Are you sure he's not going to crawl into some dead-end tunnel right now and take you with him?

More sounds from the party echoed off the cave walls. A sharp popping sound and another volley of yelling.

Were those fireworks? Did somebody throw a handful of .22 shells into the fire again? Was Bucket doing all right? Nursing his beer and waiting for Ashley to make her move?

Brewer reached out for Lucy to pull her up to the tunnel. Once she was next to him, they both squatted by the entrance. He leaned forward and placed a small kiss on her forehead. "Trust me. You're gonna love this!"

And with that he was gone. Lucy watched the stony mouth swallow him whole, took a deep breath, and dove in after.

chapter five

THE PASSAGE

She contemplated turning off her headlamp—actually seeing how small the tunnel became at its center made everything worse. Each short, borderline-panicked exhalation stirred the dust kicked up by Brewer's belly crawl.

Breathing in all this old dirt. Am I getting enough air?

She pushed her face against the sleeve of her hoodie and inhaled deeply, hoping the fabric might function as a filter. Instead she tasted more grime mixed with the taste of wood smoke and stale cigarettes.

This cave is filthy. We can't tell because of the night. If it were day, none of this would look or feel the same.

The sound of the parties on each side of the tunnel became a drone of compressed chatter/screams/laughter; all of it merged into a collective cacophony that matched the vibrating anxiety in Lucy's bones.

Brewer's voice came back to her, so small beneath the din, sounding nervous despite the fact that he had deepened his tone.

"Feels tighter through the middle than I remember. You really have to rotate your shoulder through to clear the section by the graffiti."

He wants to sound confident, but he isn't. Why? Who am I following? Back up. Tell him you're not into it.

But then she remembered how excited he'd been to show her the other cave, and she remembered his hands on her face, so strong and sure, and she wanted that again, more of *that*, and she wanted it enough to shuffle her body a foot deeper into the narrowing passageway.

Following a boy. No, not just a boy. Fucking Brewer, of all people. A few compliments, a few kisses, and . . .

"There we go. It opens up again in a couple more feet."

This time he did sound confident, and she noticed how far ahead of her he appeared, the way the tunnel stretched out in the thin light and swirling dust. She could barely see his shoes anymore. There was a wink of flickering flame against stone in the distance, and she guessed that was the fire from the second party.

"You coming, Lucy?"

He must have turned his head long enough to notice she wasn't moving. She felt embarrassed and thought about what lay behind her: Bucket and his dumb fantasies. An ever-worsening, ever-more-chaotic batch of kids drinking themselves into grunting animal states. Jake staring at cheerleader tits with his one dumb eye. Other strange eyes on her, judging her, seeing only the idea of her they'd catalogued under the cruelty of her nickname. "Ugh, Loogie's here." All of them acting like everything was great in the midst of everything wrong—smoke and sirens and shots fired, their peers dead or missing or worse—doing their best not to think about a single damn thing, chasing escape through doors leading nowhere.

The trap is behind me.

"Yeah, I'm coming."

Brewer sounded excited now. "I'm almost to the end. There's definitely another party over here. Sounds wild."

Lucy squinted, trying to block out the narrowing closeness of the tunnel walls even as she felt the heat of her body radiating back from the cold, gray stone. She saw the graffiti Brewer had mentioned—BILL Z BUB WAS HERE!—and wondered who would stop at such a shitty spot to write something that stupid. Had they inhaled too many spray paint fumes? What if they had died right there, lodged in the tunnel walls, lips blue, face speckled with red paint? What did their parents think when BILL Z BUB's body was finally found and pulled loose from the cave? What . . .

"Lucy, you there?"

"Yeah."

Don't overthink it. The only way out is through.

Her headlamp slipped on her forehead, the band shifting on a fresh slick of sweat. She pushed forward another foot, her head and right shoulder past the narrowest spot in the passage. She tasted her breath, felt the moisture of it on her face, and smelled a combination of camp smoke and roast beef and Skittles. She felt self-conscious for a moment, wondering how she had tasted to Brewer when he kissed her, but then she remembered he'd eaten manure-grown mushrooms, and she figured they had equally gnarly breath.

That kiss. Brewer.

He'd made it to the end of the tunnel and seemed unaware of how far back she was. "Oh, shit, Lucy, this is crazy. You gotta come see this."

Brewer made it through. He's bigger than me. Of course I can make it through.

She slid her other shoulder forward and felt the tunnel wall against her arm, the sudden and immense pressure of it. Her heart rate tripled. She tried to take a deep, calming breath but found she could not expand her chest.

Oh god. I won't fit. I won't fit. What did he say? I have to rotate?

She looked down the tunnel, toward Brewer. She saw only the shadow of his body against the flickering firelight beyond. She could barely hear him, and it sounded like he was saying something like

"NoNoNo . . ." though that couldn't be right. An echo, a trick. What did it matter what he was saying? She needed to move. Had to move.

She pushed with her legs but gained no ground. She felt her chest wedge farther into the narrowing. The pressure tightened with each breath.

She tried to yell for Brewer, but couldn't move her lungs enough to force out more than a whisper.

Instead his voice floated back to her, some unintelligible, weirdly panicked sound she could scarcely hear over her own heart thrumming in her ears.

What's wrong?

He's not looking at me. Why isn't he looking at me? I need him.

He doesn't know I'm stuck.

I'm stuck.

No.

Trapped.

She wondered if she could rotate farther and push her pinioned shoulder through, but then she realized she'd be on her back, faceup, still pinned under the enormity of the stone above her.

Faceup, like after the accident—watching the trees sway above, hearing the screams and the sound of men hammering away at the frame of her parents' car.

Faceup, like a body in the grave.

If she closed her eyes and opened them again, would she see BILL Z BUB on top of her, pressing down?

She felt something in her bones, an old feeling from the bad days in Peru, when basic survival had felt like the order of the day—*You have to move.*

So instead of inhaling, she exhaled and pushed all the air from her chest. She imagined herself shrinking, and dug her feet into the soil behind her, and she pushed and pushed until her shoulder felt like it would separate, and then there was motion and sudden relief as her body finally shifted forward and she managed to bring the arm closest to the ground away from her side and latched her hand like a claw into the soil ahead. That gave her more room to inhale, so she breathed deep and pushed again, and within seconds she had shimmied past the trap at the center of the tunnel.

Despite her newfound freedom, she felt the too-small stone gap closing behind her, a throat trying to gulp her down, and she waited to feel BILL Z BUB's bony hand on her ankle, pulling her backward . . .

Instead she found Brewer's calloused hand on her outstretched forearm, and the warmth of his skin on hers felt like life. A safe place, at last. *At last.* But then she realized that he was facing the wrong direction in the tunnel, and he had a tight grip on her arm and was whispering, his voice a childlike tremble, "Go back! We gotta fucking go back!"

Not a safe place. Something is wrong.

"You hear me? I think it's real, Lucy. We have to go back!"

"What's real? What are you talking about? Are you tripping out?"

"I don't think so. *Just go!* It can't be real, but . . . do you hear that?"

"This isn't funny, Brewer. What the fuck . . ."

And then she did hear it, and she wished for it to be a hallucination, that maybe kissing him had transferred his mania into her. But that was impossible, and she wasn't high. In fact, escaping the middle of the tunnel had placed her in her body with acute intensity, and so she was certain that she too heard the sound coming from the cave ahead: high-pitched keening screams, a tone she recognized from her parents' accident, the sound of trapped and injured humans crying out in agony, believing they were going to die.

And worse, amid all the wailing, she heard laughter.

Someone was terrified and dying/Someone was amused and joyful in equal measure.

Combined, it was the worst sound Lucy had ever heard.

Brewer pushed at her shoulders, bringing her mind away from the terrible noise. She saw a profound panic in his eyes.

He heard it too.

"I think they saw me, Lucy. The ones who already had those things on them. We have to go."

"Wait, what *things?*"

"I don't . . . It doesn't fucking matter. Christ! Start backing up."

Toward the trap. Toward BILL Z BUB. They'd end up wedged in together, fighting for air. Clawing at each other.

No.

"I can't."

"You gotta, Lucy! There are so many of 'em down there. There must be another entrance to that cave or something. C'mon!"

"I can't. I have to go forward."

"Bullshit. Start backing up or I'll start pushing you."

He's so afraid. Shitshitshit. Is this real?

"Okay, but I can't go too fast. I got trapped . . ."

"I think he saw me! Go!"

His voice—he's telling the truth.

Lucy pushed herself backward with her palms, the cuffs of her pants filling with dirt.

"Who saw you?"

"Jason."

"Jason Ward? He's alive?"

"Maybe. Just keep moving, okay? That's good . . . There was something coming out of his mouth, Lucy. Like wet black spiders. And there was something else, stuck to the roof of the cave. Something shiny. *It was moving.* I don't think the other kids could see it. It happened so fast."

Brewer shut his eyes, shook his head. When he reopened his eyes, Lucy noticed how wide and black his pupils were even in the direct beam of her headlamp.

No. Wait. This isn't happening. He's frying balls. And I'm almost backed into the narrows again.

"Keep going. They're coming. When Jason saw me, so did the rest. They all looked at me at once."

Brewer looked back down the tunnel, even as he kept shuffling forward. His head would be smashed into Lucy's soon.

"You hear that?"

Lucy did—there *was* a sound behind Brewer, closer than the awful noises and laughter. Stones falling. Another body, grunting as it entered a tight space.

"Oh, fuck fuck fuckfuckfuck, go, goddammit. They're right fucking . . ."

Then, as Lucy felt the passageway tighten around her again and just as she felt the weight of the cave walls pressing down and crushing the air from her chest, she saw something in the swirling dust, moving right behind Brewer. The sound of it rushed toward them, and then a pair of pale, trembling hands reached out and grabbed the first boy she'd ever kissed and pulled him screaming toward whatever he'd seen and tried to escape.

Lucy reached out for Brewer, to grab his wrists and hold on as tight as she could and pull him back toward her, but it was too late, and she hadn't listened, and she hadn't believed him soon enough, and within seconds his terrified cries merged with the chorus of violent animal sounds rolling up from the cave below.

She had only a moment to contemplate what had happened—to see the plumes of dust left by Brewer's body as he was torn away—before a voice reappeared, the one she felt in her bones and not the confused one that churned in her mind, and it said one thing:

RUN.

She exhaled hard and fast and pressed her chest to the ground as flat as she could and pushed away from whatever had taken Brewer.

As she retreated, she heard a sound over her own exertion. A boy's voice, flat aside from a strange tremble.

"Another one down there. I can see her."

Then grunting and the sound of hands slapping down swiftly over the rocky ground. Someone else in the tunnel with her now, obscured by the dust.

Lucy kept pushing back, away from the sound, wondering how long she'd have to go backward before she'd reach the cave opening, the truck, anywhere but the tunnel. She strained to stay low and fast, wishing her arms could move her faster, hating the fact that she couldn't see behind, terrified she might see more ahead. She caught a flash of BILL Z BUB's tag in her peripheral vision and knew that this time she had made it past the binding ring of rock at the center of the tunnel.

YES!

But still, she discovered, she was no longer moving. The sound of someone's labored breathing was far too close—*Is it coming from behind me? Did they come in the other entrance? Oh god.*—and it was only when she heard laughter that she realized she couldn't move because someone had grabbed a fistful of her hoodie and was pulling her toward them.

"Gotcha, bitch. I can use you. Put me back on."

She felt a second hand grab her hoodie, and this time a fistful of hair was rolled in with it and a searing pain shot through her scalp as she was pulled farther toward the center of the cave.

"Who are you?" asked a boy's voice.

The hands yanked her head upward and she was eye to eye with Ben Brumke. But he wasn't altogether Ben Brumke anymore—in the glare of her headlamp she saw his eyes were bright blue, the irises blurred at the edges. Shiny black fluid had pooled near his shoulder and stained his polo shirt. And his face . . . She had never seen a human face show so many emotions in such a short time, his excited grin moving quickly to a grimace to a frown to an involuntary spasm to a smile again, this time a rictus showing all his perfect white teeth.

"Fuckin' Loogie!"

Ben's eyes rolled back in his head for a split second and then focused on Lucy.

"He says we don't want you. He says I can feel better now."

Lucy remembered Chris Carmichael, those same blue eyes, his bloody textbook raised above his head—". . . *I'm here now. I feel better.*"—and she felt Ben's grip tighten on her hair and hoodie and she pictured how she was about to die, face crashing again and again into stone, and so she pushed her head up enough to shine her headlamp into the boy's eyes and then reached for his face with two hands outstretched like talons and dug in her fingers and clawed down toward the earth with all her strength.

New warmth on Lucy's hands, a guttural scream in her ears. She smelled Ben's breath, an aggressively nasty mixture of electric fire and rotting seaweed, and then his hands released enough that she could slide backward, leaving him holding only her hoodie.

She scrambled, not sure if he was following and reaching out for her again, wondering when something would stop her. But she felt the tunnel widening around her and picked up speed. In the distance, Ben stopped his howling, so she took the smallest moment to look back and see if he had cleared the center of the passage.

He appeared wedged in, unable to pursue her. His arms lay flat against the ground, and his blurry blue irises looked beyond her, unfocused on the world around them. Fresh blood ran in black rivulets down the trenches she'd dug into his face, and she realized she could feel the pressure of his stripped-back skin under her fingernails.

Despite his tortured appearance, Ben was smiling at her.

"Signal's bad down here, but I can see the picture. Green house. White trim. 1437. The Hendersons."

No.

How the fuck?

She was dead certain Ben had never been to her house. Most of the Brower Butte kids probably didn't even know her little suburb on the outskirts existed. So how did he know where she lived?

She saw Ben begin to shake, his whole body caught in some kind of seizure. He cried out, his voice no longer confident, the sound of a scared boy for one moment.

"Can't feel like this . . . Make it stop . . ."

He twitched again, then his face calmed.

"Program re . . . It's . . . it's . . . it's . . . it's *you*, Loogie. *Hey!* I see you. You're *meat*." Ben found his smile again, grunted and pushed loose from his rocky surroundings, then backed away from Lucy and disappeared.

Could he trap her? Would he be able to find the other side of the tunnel and crawl in behind her? Hadn't Brewer said there was another way around?

Brewer.

Fuck.

Lucy moved as quickly as she could to ensure that she broke free from the tunnel before Ben or anyone else could find her there. She felt as if she was crawling out of the throat of something that had tried to consume her whole.

As she backed out and saw the entrance to the passageway, she thought she had finally escaped some kind of nightmare, a reality too dreadful to exist, and she stood and drew her first full breath in what felt like forever. It should have been freeing, but instead her lungs filled with the shock of acrid smoke and she heard cries ring out from below and smelled something much too much like burning flesh. Then she looked up and saw the shadows of bedlam stretching out on the cave walls, and she realized that she had escaped nothing and her nightmare had become the world.

chapter six

IMPULSE & RESPONSE

Ginny Bucholtz was on fire, but the other girls kept kicking her anyway, their faces expressionless, hers buried somewhere in the sandy cave floor. She must have been shielding herself with her arms, because Lucy could see Ginny's interlaced hands had melted into the smoking black skin on the back of her skull, all of it bright red where it hadn't burned crisp, the girl's jacket aflame, her body moving only with the steady, thudding kicks on each side of her ribs.

Before Lucy recoiled and pushed flat against the cave wall behind her, she noticed a shape on one of the girls' necks—a small, shining circle, some kind of fluid oozing free from the shape. She imagined she saw something shift under the girl's skin, but didn't allow herself time to think about what it might be. What did it matter? Those girls had dragged Ginny though the fire and kicked the life from her; Lucy knew they'd do the same to her.

"*He says we don't want you.*"

"*You're meat.*"

Lucy tried to hold her breath, but her vision filled with static. She closed her eyes and waited to wake, to find herself pulled free from the swirling primordial reality of hiding, heart pounding, in a cave full of predators. She opened her eyes, and her senses felt cruelly honed—the smell of the burning girl so sweet and smoky that Lucy might have drooled had adrenaline not run her mouth dry, the sounds of grunting and breaking and a boy trying to shout through a crushed windpipe so loud and immediate she wondered if someone was dying a few feet away. And her vision was surely a betrayal, because all she saw before her was violation: bodies hunched over bodies, striking, biting and tearing, one girl straddled across another, her chin and neck awash in fresh blood, her eyes closed, her head swaying repetitively from left to right, and beyond her two boys holding another boy aloft by the backpack straps they'd turned into a makeshift noose, and beyond them more and more, a spiral of savagery spinning out from the heart of the party.

Lucy felt she was deep beneath the earth, surviving inside some absence that had never known the light of the sun, a place where the blood of others was the closest you could get to warmth. She wanted to be transported to some high place, some treetop that overlooked the mountain ranges, where the air was crisp and cool and didn't smell like Ginny Bucholtz's melted face.

Her want took her nowhere.

Her mind remembered that Ben Brumke was probably looking for her. If he knew where both sides of the tunnel ended . . .

She instinctively reached up to pull the hood of her sweatshirt over her head, to conceal as much of herself as possible, but all she felt was the back of her neck. Ben had stripped her hoodie and headlamp as she fled. Somehow she felt far more vulnerable with the skin of her arms and neck exposed.

What am I protecting myself from?

My classmates?

Other kids?

That can't . . .

Gunshots rang out, somewhere too close, *inside* the cave, shocking Lucy back into the unacceptable reality of her surroundings.

Don't wonder. Respond. Escape.

But what if those shots are coming from the men who came to our school? The men who killed Chris?

And though it wasn't the first time she suddenly imagined her fellow students being gunned down en masse, it was the first time the thought gave her such relief.

Maybe it is the SWAT team, or whatever that was? They stopped Chris! They knew about Chris, so they've got to know about this. Unless the cave is throwing them off. But I heard those helicopters, so . . . Maybe if I tuck in up here and lie low, they'll come through and save me.

Lucy squatted over crumbling cave stone and scanned left to right, waiting for an enfilade of purple smoke canisters and bullets to tear through the cave, praying for such a thing as if it were a cleansing white light. Instead she heard a voice, low and flat, echoing from the wall.

"There. By the other tunnel."

Two shapes below, backlit by fire, concealed in twisting plumes of corpse smoke. A boy and girl, both shaking. Lucy imagined their bright blue eyes locked in on her, something moving at the base of their necks.

The gunshots she'd heard were not coming from any savior. For all she knew, one of the kids below had a pistol and had already used it to kill.

But how can that . . .

She looked down and the trembling, smoke-shrouded shapes had disappeared from sight.

Not being able to see them stopped her questioning. She stayed low and close to the boulders she and Brewer had clambered up an hour before, sliding down the rocks, hating the exposed feeling of her back facing the party when someone could be approaching with a knife, with a gun, with a broken bottle, with a stone, with bare, trembling hands, with anything they might use to drain the life from her.

As she reached the base of the largest boulder, she realized there was a gap between the massive rock and the cave wall. She heard a pair of feet crunching toward her, and without giving it a thought she crouched and squeezed backward into the dark triangle of space behind her and took one deep breath.

Ghost mode. Be small. Be quiet.

Voices. Fuck. QUIET.

"I swear I saw someone."

"Better, better, better . . . I can't feel like this. Didn't want this."

The girl responded, her voice short and sharp and hungry. "Stop thinking about it, Carver. We need to do something."

Carver? Was Nate one of them now?

"There's a . . . fog. You see that? It hurts. Get me back on."

It was Nate. And he sounded weak, and scared, and Lucy's hate-crush was instantly undone and replaced by some weird sympathy. Whatever had happened to her classmates, not all of them were coping with the change.

"Yeah, yeah. Keep looking. We're heading up soon."

"I need it f . . . f . . . f . . . first."

"Find them first, then. Could be Lucy. We saw her up there."

"We?"

"Ben, I think . . . Can't see it all straight. This is . . . I need it too. He says we can feel like him, if we find more of them. Keep looking."

Lucy held in her breath, chest aching for air, heart vibrating her whole body.

Two sets of footsteps moved away from her hiding spot beneath the boulder, each going a different direction. She waited ten seconds more and released her breath as slowly and quietly as she ever had.

"We're heading up soon."

Up.

Into town.

No. The Hendersons. The Marwanis. The whole city.

None of them would see this coming.

I have to warn them.

Lucy started to back out of her hiding spot and was confronted by the sound of a body smacking against the rock wall ahead of her.

Nate and the girl had been looking for her, but they had found someone else.

Lucy took another breath, squeezed herself small, wishing she could turn to water and melt away into the ground.

"Hold his face against the rocks! Scrape him." Now Nate's voice had shifted from pained tremble to rising excitement.

"Scrape him."

Whatever sympathy Lucy had briefly held for Nate evaporated. He was just like the rest of them. Always had been.

"Yeah . . . Hold on . . . Help me rotate his face, goddamnit."

Lucy heard three people breathing hard, struggling. Then Nate yelped.

"He fucking bit me."

"Son of a bitch. I need this too. Now. I know what will make him scream. *Then* you scrape him."

Lucy heard someone grunting through clenched teeth, then a tortured yowl, then spitting. Two smacking sounds. A crunch. Then the sound of a face receding as it was dragged across rock.

"Told you he'd scream. Told you! Ears come off as easy as they say."

The sound of a boy crushed to earth, pulling sputtering wet breaths through a broken face.

"I can see you now."

Lucy squeezed back as hard as she could.

They spotted me.

"I can see you now too."

She realized Nate and the girl were talking to each other, almost casually, over the wreckage of the boy they'd found.

"But how long does this last? I can't be off again. There's too much information. Can't be off. I need this."

"Yeah. You feel *that*, though?"

"*Yeah.*"

"It could die, right? So we gotta hurry. Always . . . h . . . hurry! Hold on . . . You see that message?"

"Heard it. Saw it. Can't tell which. It's all, like, squished together."

"Ward wants us back at the main cave."

"We could find that girl, though. Lucy."

She shivered at the sound of her name and the flat way it rolled from Nate's mouth, marking her as an asset. An object to be exploited.

Prey.

"No. He's calling us. I think he has a plan. He knows how to make this feel good. We have to follow these impulses. Let's go."

Lucy heard the boy and girl running away from her but waited an extra moment before stepping out and crouching next to the wreckage they had left behind.

She couldn't ID the boy on the ground. His injuries stripped away most of what you'd use to recognize someone, but she could tell by the small sounds he made that he was alive. She remembered the voices she'd heard as she was rescued from her parents' accident, the way they'd offered comfort. She tried to do the same for the boy.

"You're going to be okay. I'm going to get out of here, and I'll send for help."

The boy moaned. Lucy looked closer and saw that his ear had been pulled loose and flapped against his cracked jaw, and she guessed her words were useless, so she put a gentle hand against his shoulder, figuring that might be the last human contact he knew. A kindness in all this. Then she stood, stepped over the boy, and crept slowly through the darkness toward the exit of the cave.

It looked like Bucket's fantasy had come true until you got close enough to see the way Ashley Jorgensen's body twitched over his and how she had her teeth clamped down on his upper lip and was pulling back to tear it free.

Then it looked less dreamy.

Bucket's high-pitched wailing gave Lucy another clue that this was not what he'd hoped for from tonight's party.

Lucy had made it so far without being seen, staying tight and high against the cave wall and moving in the direction of what she prayed was the exit. She even thought she'd seen the dim light of the moonless sky in the distance, but then she heard the moaning to her left, and it sounded enough like Bucket that she couldn't block the sound from her mind and keep moving.

At first it was confusing. She'd seen Bucket and Ashley tucked away in a corner of the cave, Bucket lying on his back, Ashley with her legs spread and lean torso stretched over his.

You're kidding me. Not only did they escape the slaughterhouse, but they're making out? Come on. I've got to warn them.

But then Lucy heard Ashley's voice, confused and agitated. "I thought it might work—*it usually works*—but there's no feeling."

Bucket started to protest, "Well, maybe if you—"

"No, we have to . . . I mean *I* have to do it the way he said." Ashley's head twitched rapidly. Her right shoulder hitched upward. If Bucket noticed, he didn't mention it for fear of breaking the spell. "I can make it stop. I have to do it his way."

"What . . ."

And that was when Ashley had leaned forward with her face inches from Bucket's, and Lucy had heard enough to know nothing sweet was happening.

She thought of the destroyed boy she'd left behind and knew she couldn't watch that happen again, so she knelt down and grabbed the closest stone she could find and charged toward the intertwined bodies just as Ashley bit into Bucket's lip and started to tear it away like a wolf stripping sinew.

Bucket cried out. Ashley pulled harder, lifting Bucket's head from the ground. Bucket lifted his arms to push Ashley away, but doing that must have increased Ashley's pull, because his cry rose to a shriek.

Under the cover of that noise, Lucy was able to cross the last few feet to her friend. Ashley caught the motion, released her bite, and turned toward Lucy.

There was never a plan. There was only Bucket, about to be killed, and Lucy, and her rock. And Lucy didn't have time to think about what might happen when she swung the rock toward Ashley, or the way Ashley's perfect little nose would collapse and spray blood on the three of them, or the way the descending weight of the rock and Lucy's momentum would drive the stone down Ashley's face into her teeth and crack her incisors straight back into her mouth, or how Lucy would trip over Bucket and fall on Ashley with her full weight and drive that stone even farther into the skull of that bright blue-eyed girl until she was all the way fucking dead.

That was never the plan. That was just what happened.

Then Bucket had his hand over his torn lip and was looking at Lucy, and Lucy was breathing hard and pushing up and away from the fact that she'd murdered Ashley Jorgensen, and neither of them understood why there was a high-pitched squealing sound coming from somewhere beneath the dead girl's neck.

"Lucy, what the fuck?"

"I don't know." The squealing under Ashley grew louder. "Get up. We have to get out of here."

"Okay. Hold on." Bucket reached down into his pants and adjusted himself, then shifted to stand up.

"Wait. You have a fucking boner?"

"Well . . . she was on me. It was hot."

"She was going to kill you."

"Yeah, well . . . It was great until then. She told me she wanted to pay me back for all the help with math, and it seemed like the party was getting too crazy, so we walked out here, and . . . fuck . . . you *really* smashed her."

"I know. I couldn't let her—"

"Kill me?"

"Yeah."

And then Bucket was just smart enough to put his arms around Lucy and hold her for a second. Lucy shook a little in his embrace and knew that if she were not terrified she may have wept. She ignored another feeling at the back of her mind—a deep, blinding anger that was growing from a spark to a flame.

They're trying to kill us.

I had to kill Ashley.

Why do I have to feel all of this?

Bucket let her go. "I'm sorry. This is fucked up. But thank you."

"It's all right. Whisper, though, okay? We have to be quiet." More aberrant noise from under Ashley—squealing replaced by the sound of something wet squelching inside the girl.

"*Christ.* What's wrong with her?"

"I don't know. But there are more like her, lots more, and they probably heard us. One of them said they were going to meet in the other cave, but who knows? If Ashley was over here, then there could be more. They could be coming to kill us. They already got Brewer, and Ginny, and . . . we just have to go. They're heading into town next."

"*Green house. White trim. 1437. The Hendersons.*"

Bill and Carol. They saved me when I needed them.

I'll save them.

Lucy and Bucket carried rocks with them and flinched at every sound on the path back to the exit. Then they heard sounds in the cavern behind them and hit the ladders running and climbed like they'd never imagined they could.

Had the meeting in the other cave ended? How many of those blue-eyed, twitching bastards were headed their direction? Headed toward the town? How could this be real?

Keep moving.

Even once they reached Brewer's truck and locked themselves inside, even once there was metal and glass between them and the night air thick with sirens and distant screams, they didn't feel safe. Even when the engine rumbled into life and Bucket managed to get the rig into fourth and build speed away from the death-filled cave, they knew that nothing had been escaped.

There was the world behind them, and the world ahead of them, and all of it wanted them dead.

Finally having that at the surface felt right to Lucy. The truth was that she'd always sensed the world's eyes on her, the way it objectified her and wanted to destroy her.

"You're meat."

She thought of the feeling of the rock in her hand, the way Ashley had collapsed under her. Something about that feeling gave her strength and sped her heart. It had its own momentum.

She looked at Bucket, the way he shook behind the wheel of a beautiful dead boy's truck. His erratic driving might kill them. He needed to focus.

"It's okay," she said.

"*'It's okay'?* It's the goddamn apocalypse, Lucy. You're fucking crazy cakes over there. You killed my fucking crush, and something that wasn't her was screaming inside her neck. Brewer's dead, and if you're telling the truth, then a bunch of other kids are dead too. And *what?* You want me to fucking calm down?"

"No." Lucy put a hand on Bucket's shoulder. "You don't have to calm down. That would be insane. I think we've been calm too long. That's what I'm trying to say. We're not going to be calm any longer. We're going to fight this. We're going to show these motherfuckers the truth."

"Oh, really? What's that?"

Lucy bent forward and picked up a heavy steel wrench from the floorboard of Brewer's truck. It felt stone heavy in her hands.

"We're not meat, Buck. Not anymore."

Next Venture Magazine Issue #112, 5/14/21:

DISRUPTORS IN FOCUS:

IMTECH TAKING "INTELLIGENCE" TO NEXT LEVEL

This issue, our "Disruptors" series takes us to the snowy slopes and summery splendor of tourist favorite Turner Falls, Oregon. Nestled among mountains, rivers, and world-class breweries, Turner Falls has long been known as a hub for outdoor adventure and homespun hospitality, so *Next Venture* was intrigued when recent news from the area actually centered on a small and specialized medical company called IMTECH (formerly known as Integrated Medical Technology, Inc.).

The company—best known for AcceptSkin©, a synthetic silicon tissue used to prevent the rejection of bioelectric implants in medical patients—recently captured minor media buzz after being granted a mind-boggling 2,835 patents for what it claims will be a single piece of technology. Add to that the fact that they've changed their corporate registration to the more compelling Immersive Media Technology, Inc., prior to announcing their SEC filing for Q4 public offering, and it's clear IMTECH is a company on the move. *Next Venture's* Jim Hargreaves sat down briefly with Media Relations Officer Preston Bernhardt for a provocative (if guarded) conversation about investment, intelligence, and "augmented existence."

Why the name change?

"Well, we feel our vision has expanded, as has our mission. And in keeping with that we wanted a name which better represented our focus going into the future. As Integrated Medical we changed the way the human body interacted with needed implants. We made the technology human, and saved lives, and we remain immensely proud of those accomplishments. Now, as Immersive Media, we will magnify that synergy in some very surprising new ways."

Can you expand on that?

"Not currently, though I can say that even with our extended focus we will continue to remain at the vanguard of biotech and bioelectronics. IMTECH is not done saving lives. But now we're also ready to enrich them in a brand-new manner."

Aside from the patent data and a few PR announcements, IMTECH has released so little information prior to its forthcoming public offering. Has it been difficult to demonstrate marketability or secure financing?

"Happily, I can say it's been quite the opposite! Our CEO [Katherine Prince—ed.] is obviously keeping information very tight, but she's a hugely confident woman, and those investors who have seen even a brief demonstration of what we're working on have taken us through three abundant rounds of financing. The expansion could not be going any better. With regards to the public offering, there's always this lament you hear about: *Oh, I wish I would have purchased*

Microsoft stock in '86 or Apple in '80, and honestly we feel that people will be saying that about IMTECH within this decade. People need to understand that this will be beyond a disruption. This will be a redefinition."

You mentioned financiers? Anyone we'd know?

"Ha! It's challenging not to talk about it, because there are always outside concerns about false promises and vaporware, and everyone says their idea is the next to change the world, so . . . listen . . . the recent influx of massive tech companies to the Central Oregon area isn't a coincidence, and they aren't only here for the world-class beer or skiing. Though that sure doesn't hurt! . . . Joking aside, we're engaged in some incredible partnerships, and the way those folks are working with us goes beyond investment and advocacy. Everyone we're partnering with is a true believer."

Well, you've certainly piqued our interest. Some market analysts, including Fiscal Post, *have claimed that IMTECH is radically overvalued. Yet* Bramberg Weekly *concurs with your view that IMTECH will be an "ultragrowth stock." So, two very different perspectives at this point in the rollout. Anything else you'd like to say to the* Next Venture *audience prior to IMTECH's road show?*

"Well, you've always got a few pessimists who skew negative so they can appear clairvoyant if something goes wrong. But that's the case with every prelaunch, isn't it? Once our underwriters present their professionally vetted valuations, I feel we can have *that* conversation in earnest. When the time is right, when we are certain that we've fully locked in and protected some *very* proprietary technologies, I'll be able to speak in greater detail. Which, you know, I'm aware of how hyperbolic this all sounds at this point, so I can't wait for our opportunity to show and prove. But at this stage,

I simply want everyone—and I mean *everyone*—to know that we've had some exciting developments that we believe will be industry game changers. As I said, our product line will no longer be only for those with medical needs—we're democratizing intelligence itself, in a brand-new way, and the appeal will be universal. Some might say essential, given our competitive marketplace. I'm quoting our last investor update here: 'We're going beyond augmented reality to augmented *existence* in a way that will change the way we interact with the cloud, with one another, with our health, and with the world.' I wish I could say more than that, but I promise all will be revealed when we kick off our road show at Collision Conference this summer."

Wait . . . augmented existence? Critics say IMTECH is using provocative buzzwords for what they predict will essentially be a health monitoring or biofeedback system.

"Well, those critics lack the kind of imagination and future-forward inspiration we have at IMTECH. I've already said more than I wanted to, so I'll leave it at that. But it will be a pleasure to watch those critics' response to our unveiling."

After a statement like that, I can assure you that I'll be in the front row, and I'm also certain that many of our readers will be eagerly awaiting IMTECH's forthcoming announcement and IPO. Best of luck on your launch and thank you for speaking with Next Venture!

"Always a pleasure, Jim."

PART TWO

DARK/DRIVES

chapter seven

LOCAL NEWS

The ambulance was on its side, emergency lights running, top side of the frame caved in where the massive Ford truck had slammed into it and rammed it over the soft shoulder and into the desert drop-off.

Bucket and Lucy had hung back in Brewer's truck, unsure of who'd been driving the huge, swerving Ford and positive it was better to not find out. Lucy told Bucket to kill the headlights, but with no moon and no streetlights Bucket said that was just a different kind of death sentence. They were about one hundred yards back when the Ford overtook the zooming ambulance and slammed into it at top speed.

They had not expected that the Ford would follow the ambulance over the shoulder, and it wasn't until they passed through the light-streaked wall of dust from the accident that they saw what was happening.

Three boys had hopped from the truck and were moving toward the smoking ambulance, one of them holding a hammer, another trembling so severely he could barely keep up. Lucy recognized the sticker on the back of the rig—an illustration of a rifle scope sighting in three wolves, the text reading "Smoke a Pack a Day!"—and wondered if Luke Olsen had been the one driving his truck or if he was back at East Bear bleeding out on the rocky ground.

Bucket stayed lead-footed on the pedal. Lucy looked back just in time to see the ambulance quaking.

The boys had made it inside.

"We have to follow these impulses."

Lucy imagined them smiling, hands suddenly steady. Feeling better already.

The lights were out at the Hendersons', aside from the flicker of the TV on their sheer window blinds.

"We run in, we warn them, and we call your parents from the landline. Maybe they'll know what we should do next. There could be an emergency meeting place, or maybe we call the cops and then bail out of town. But we have to be fast."

Lucy still had Brewer's wrench in her hands, and her voice sounded oddly confident, alien to even her own ears.

Brewer's truck lurched and died. Bucket had forgotten to shift out of fourth when he slid to a stop in front of Lucy's house.

"Smooth, huh?"

"Yeah. You did good, Bucket. Make sure you grab the keys."

Who is talking right now? Lucy questioned her sanity. First, she'd felt broken, reeling from seeing Chris and Mr. Chambers die. Unsure of everything. But now—*now*—she felt strong in a way she wasn't ready to abandon.

Well, Dr. Nielsen, I was having a lot of confidence and trust issues, and let's not forget the perpetual fear of abandonment, and as you know, the PTSD from the incident at Spring Meadow, but then I kissed a boy and a little bit after that I killed a girl with a rock and now I'm feeling fine. Should I assume this is the end of our sessions together?

Lucy was certain she'd gone mad. And once she'd survived the night and made it to a safe place with the Hendersons, she was certain she'd be headed for catatonia.

But for the moment she felt strong. She hopped out of Brewer's truck armed with a wrench and ready to swing on anyone who got in her way.

————————

Except: no one tried to stop her.

Though she wished they would have, once she made it inside.

Bill and Carol were in the living room, eyes transfixed by their sixty-inch flat screen. They sat low in their La-Z-Boys, heads tilted slightly. Both had crusted streams of blood running from their noses to the hollows of their necks. It didn't shine in the strange blue light from the screen, so whatever caused it must have happened earlier.

Bucket said, "You feel that, Lucy?" and pointed at the TV and the fluctuating static and snippets of sound emanating into the room.

She looked at the screen and instantly felt her bones turn to concrete. Her eyes floated back inside her head, ten feet, then twenty, the TV an abyss she floated above, the sensation in her body a reminder of the time Bucket had talked her into drinking a bottle of Tussin DM with him.

A voice came to her, but not through her ears. She felt the voice vibrating at the base of her skull and caught snippets of a man's urgent, slightly worried voice:

. . . message from the emergency broadcast system . . . potential leak in the storage of underground toxic waste at the now-defunct Handsome Valley Nuclear Power Plant. A low-level earthquake, barely detect . . . may have caused a fracture in the twenty-foot-thick concrete surround . . . Travelers . . . turned back for a thirty-mile radius around the Turner Falls area. Commu- nication difficulties created by high-intensity scanners being used to assess damage without actually unearthing . . . Handsome Valley site workers and federal and state officials are on-site and working diligently to assure safe

repair . . . vised to remain inside until further notice, and youth may be partic . . . effects including confusion, hallucination, paranoia, and . . .

Lucy felt the trickle of blood roll from her nose right before she felt Bucket's body slamming full speed into her ribs. Then they were both on the carpet and Lucy couldn't see straight, but she could smell the dust in the Hendersons' house and the faint odor of the pot roast Carol had cooked and then a wave of too-sweet cologne from Bucket, who lay on top of her.

She tried to say, "Jesus, Bucket, get off of me," but she was still hearing the transmission in her head and something wasn't connecting between her brain and her mouth and the best she could muster was, "Jeeb." Somehow he understood, pushing up and away.

"Sorry, Lu. I didn't know what else to do, and I thought of what the electric co-op people taught us to do when someone's being shocked, so I . . . Are you okay?"

Static stayed in her vision. The voice pushed at her mind. She closed her eyes and put her hands over her ears. The intra-brain broadcast faded. She was afraid to take her hands away from her ears, so she kept them there and yelled to Bucket.

"YES! I'BOKAY!"

"We have to turn off the TV."

Lucy couldn't agree more. She pointed with her head at the wrench she'd dropped on the ground. "DOANGETCLOSE! THOWIT!" Lucy felt fluid running from her face. More blood from her nose? Drool from her barely controlled mouth?

Did I have a fucking stroke?

Years of friendship and the occasional night of drinking forties must have taught Bucket how to understand Lucy in slur mode, because he reached over, grabbed the wrench, and popped above Bill's chair long enough to wing the tool into the heart of the brain-fogging broadcast. Thin shards of pricey nonreflective glass fell to the floor, followed by the brief but surprisingly loud sound of the television's wiring shorting out. The blue light and insidious sound echoed in Lucy's mind, but faded by the second. She stood and rushed to Carol.

"Carol. Wake up! It's Lucy." She shook Carol by the shoulders, afraid that slapping her might be too much for the woman's mind. "We shut it off. It'll go away in a second."

Carol's chest rose and fell, but beyond that there was no sign of life. She stared straight ahead, eyes fixed on the shattered television, which had held sway moments before.

Lucy moved to Bill, giving him a stern shake, then putting a hand on his face.

He didn't shave tonight.

He always shaves.

They were worried about me. Up late. Watching TV.

Waiting for me.

"I'm sorry, Bill." She put her other hand on the opposite side of his face. "I should have stayed after dinner. I'm sorry."

Looking at him she felt paralyzed in her own way by how pure the Hendersons' love for her had always been. She thought about all the moments where she'd wondered if she could return that love, and how she hated herself when she couldn't. Worse, they knew how she'd lived as a young child, so they understood why she was distant and loved her still, and always.

She felt she might cry. She imagined that old Lucy coming back. So confused. A wreck.

No. Do something.

She stood as tall as she could and swung an open palm across Bill's face. The slap landed. Fresh blood rolled from Bill's nose. He looked back toward Lucy.

He's seeing me.

Bill opened his mouth, letting loose a low moan. Then, slowly, he looked up.

"Can you see me, Bill?"

Bill's eyes fogged, but he spoke. "Tonight we come to you live with an emergency broadcast to alert you to a potential leak in the storage of underground toxic waste at the now-defunct Handsome Valley Nuclear Power Plant."

"No, Bill . . . no."

Lucy hung her head.

His voice carried the same unaccented inflections as the news broadcast. He continued his recitation. "Handsome Valley site workers and federal and state officials are on-site and working diligently to assure safe repair of the barrier. All citizens are advised to remain inside until further notice, and youth may be particularly vulnerable to the toxins believed to have been released. Be on watch for effects including confusion, hallucination, paranoia, and even unexpected or violent behavior."

"NO! *Bill!* Come on!"

And Carol began, to Lucy's right.

"A low-level earthquake, barely detectable at the surface level, may have caused a fracture in the twenty-foot-thick concrete surrounding the PUREX plant. Travelers are being turned back for a thirty-mile radius around the Turner Falls area. Communication difficulties . . ."

The broadcast was back in stereo, Bill and Carol running on dead-eyed loop, fresh blood darkening their teeth.

Part of Lucy that had always been waiting for this day, waiting for Bill and Carol to disappear as her parents had done. But another part of her had come to trust in them, over time, to let herself feel soft and safe in their arms, and that was the part of her that remembered that her life had become a living, breathing nightmare and all she could do was survive.

She turned her back on Bill and Carol and their incessant, repetitive lies on loop. She walked toward the destroyed television and reclaimed her wrench and thought to herself, *I am going to hurt whoever tries to stop me from escaping this dream. And it's going to feel good.*

chapter eight

PROTECTION PLAN

A fter the accident in Peru, Lucy never saw her parents again. She was informed they had died in the crash, and by the end of that night she'd been cleared by the emergency medical staff and unceremoniously bused to the orphanage, where she did her damnedest to ignore the taunts and threats of the other children by hiding under the thin blanket on her assigned bed.

With Bill and Carol, things were different. She felt abandoned again, but it wasn't their fault, not really, and she wanted to protect them from whatever plans those twitching animals who had emerged from the cave might have for the town. And who knew how many of them were out there? Lucy recalled the rushing cop cars she'd seen before dinner and realized whatever was happening to the town might have already been spreading before the party. She remembered the way something on Chris's neck had squealed when Mr. Chambers grabbed him, and how Jason Ward had a bandage on his neck before he disappeared. And what had Jason said to Carrie before he ran away?

"They don't care; it won't stop."

How long has this been going on?

Bucket walked back into the living room with the Hendersons' old-school portable phone in his hand.

"You got through to your parents?" Lucy asked.

Bucket shook his head. "Couldn't even get a dial tone. And listen, but only for a second." His voice was thick, on the verge of tears.

She held the receiver to her ear, and right away she recognized the odd warbling tone and the words emerging in her mind.

"Handsome Valley site workers and federal and state officials are on-site and working diligently to assure safe—"

Bucket ripped the phone from Lucy's hand, which she noticed had already begin to curl tightly around the beige plastic.

"No." She looked at Bucket, both of them wide-eyed with realization.

"Yup. It's on the TV. The phone lines. Probably all the local radio stations too. Only that message, over and over again, and that weird pulsing sound underneath."

"Fuck. How the hell do we . . ." Lucy went silent for a moment, thinking about all the houses surrounding them, and the way television light glowed in the living rooms of most on any given evening. Did it matter if you were watching cable when the broadcast began? Or was it infecting all forms of digital transmission? Did the town's cell phones finally light up all at once, carrying the broadcast? She pictured houses, bars, police stations, fire stations, 911 call centers, even the hospitals, all of them now coma wards filled with the bleeding blind, barely breathing and mumbling false warnings in tune with that awful thrumming frequency.

How can this be? It . . . can't. Or maybe the broadcast is telling the truth. There was a leak in Handsome Valley. East Bear is closer than the town. We all caught a megadose. Some of us lost our minds. But if that's true, what did I really do to Ashley? Did that even happen? What am I seeing now? Where am I? Strapped to a gurney, raving through radiation sickness?

Lucy lifted her right hand and moved it in front of her face. She breathed deep and took in the familiar smells of home—vanilla-scented candles, the evening's dinner, Carol's perfume. She stretched out her toes and felt a hole in one of her socks. She licked her lips, and they were chapped and a bit chewed. Her mind tumbled through a catalog of all the little things that made waking life less pleasant than dreams, and the truth was that she was here and hungry and thirsty and all of it felt oppressively, terrifyingly real.

Lucy started shaking. Bucket, seemingly unsure of what else to do, stepped toward her and gave her a hug. He said, "It's crazy, right?"

Lucy nodded and then gently broke away from him, fearing that being held any longer would throw her into a total meltdown.

"This is real, Bucket."

It was his turn to nod. "Yeah."

"How do we make it stop?"

"How the fuck do I know?" A panicked look spread across Bucket's face. "I think we need to run. Hop back in the truck and gun it for anywhere else."

"Oh, sure." Even if she was willing to leave Bill and Carol, Lucy imagined it wouldn't take long before she and Bucket were discovered by those twitching bastards. Run off the road like the ambulance, stomped in the wreckage. And if her murderous cohorts weren't in some way responsible for the paralytic transmission, then who was? And would *those* people let them leave town? They didn't even want anyone *moving*. Were they waiting at the outskirts with walls of speakers, waiting to drown leftover citizens under waves of weaponized sound?

But Bucket saved me from the broadcast. Maybe he's immune to it!

Lucy pointed at the shattered TV. "Wait, why didn't the broadcast pull you in when we first got here?"

"Well, I had a bad feeling about that when I saw that your parents didn't turn to look at us."

My parents. I never call them that, even after all they've done . . .

Bucket continued, "So I didn't look right at the screen, and I turned my busted ear toward the TV."

"What busted ear?"

Bucket tapped his right ear. "Got an infection when I was twelve. Eardrum burst twice, and my parents didn't want to risk any more infections after what happened with Dalir, so they had the doctor put in a little plastic tube. It never healed right after that. Sometimes it makes a whining noise after I sneeze, so I think there's still a hole in there."

"Whoa. Why didn't you ever tell me . . ."

"What? Brag about my gimpy ear? It's embarrassing. Sometimes when the volume is up loud in my car I can't even tell what you're talking about. That's why I always just nod and say, 'Yeah,' like I agree with you."

"Son of a bitch." Lucy smiled at him, even though it felt oddly dangerous.

I need to be the other Lucy now. That's the only version I can be, or I'll collapse, paralyzed like in Mr. Chambers's room.

"Well, your shitty ear saved me tonight. So thank you."

"No worries. I owed you, right? After Ashley?"

Ashley. The sound of stone collapsing her beautiful face. The strange noise that came from her neck.

The other boys, free of the cave, running toward the ambulance. Heading into town. And they knew where she lived.

They're coming.

No more overthinking. Protect Bill and Carol. Protect yourself.

Keep moving.

———

Lucy and Bucket had argued about the plan at first. He thought they might wait a little longer to see if the effects of the broadcast would wear off, thinking Bill and Carol would snap to and be able to help them. Lucy shook each of them again—this time more sternly than before—but when she looked at the dimness in their eyes she figured that even if they returned, they might not ever come all the way back to her. She pinched the top of Carol's hand, digging her fingernails into the skin. Not a flinch. No retraction. She moved to Bill and said, "I'm sorry." and then slapped him full force, hoping his eyes might clear once more. Nothing.

Fucking nothing.

Each effort made the pain of the forced separation even more apparent. She wasn't sure she could bear to try anything else. And she couldn't stand to see them mumbling that bullshit message anymore—each round of stimulus seemed to induce a new round of hypnotic chatter.

Bucket wanted to check his phone for ways to wake people, thinking ice water or bright lights might jolt Bill and Carol back to consciousness. Lucy sighed but relented, and was thankful when he discovered that his cell signal was finally one hundred percent dead. She was less thankful when he discovered there was a notification for a single voice mail from "Unknown Number." He and Lucy agreed it should be deleted immediately, but the phone would not allow Bucket to remove the file, so Lucy grabbed it from him, placed it on the floor, and bashed it three times with her wrench before he could even protest.

"Great! Just great! What if my signal came back and I could have contacted the police? Fuck, Lucy!"

Lucy pictured the swarms of psychotic youth descending on the city—the police weren't going to have anybody answering calls, and even if they did, the dispatch would be flooded. It didn't matter if they could be reached. She let her wrench thud to the floor and told Bucket the truth she could barely stand to force on him, though she had felt it since she was a child.

"I don't think there's anyone who can help us." She paused to watch his face, which shifted quickly from anger to grave concern. He was really listening to her—that was important if they were going to survive together. "And besides, that thing was . . . infected, or whatever. You know it."

"Yeah, I . . ." Bucket drifted off. Lucy saw he was covered in a sheen of new sweat. "I really loved that phone."

Lucy thought of the number of times she'd had to repeat herself because Bucket had been distracted by his phone. Worse, she thought of the despairing look he got on his face when someone inevitably popped into his feed to remind him of his place in the world.

For the second time that night, she was surprised by how rewarding it was to fucking smash something.

But Bill and Carol's sound coma wasn't something she could smash away. They were fragile like this, terribly vulnerable in a way that disturbed her too much to acknowledge, and she knew that their best bet was the one she'd relied on as a small child.

"We have to hide them, Bucket. I need your help."

———

Bill had put on a lot of weight over the last holiday season—he had a tendency to get nostalgic and mopey and buried his pain in bloating booze and belt-busting peanut butter fudge—so Lucy and Bucket moved him second.

Both Bill and Carol had gone silent, their robotic bullshit about the radiation leak finally tapering off as Lucy and Bucket settled them into bed.

Once they were both sequestered, Lucy grabbed an extra down comforter from the hall, and she and Bucket pulled it over their bodies and tucked it under their arms. Then they left two full glasses of water on Bill and Carol's nightstands and quietly exited the master bedroom.

Lucy ran to the hallway bathroom and returned with a key. She locked Bill and Carol's door and slid the key into her pocket.

Bucket whispered, "What's up with the lock?"

Lucy made a circle with her forefinger and thumb, then repeatedly inserted the index finger from her other hand. Bucket feigned disgust, and she left it at that. The lock was actually extra security to protect their valuables when they traveled, but she thought it was funnier to make Bucket imagine Bill and Carol having sex. And she didn't tell him how proud she'd felt on the day when they showed her the little ceramic cat sculpture in the hall bathroom, and how you could twist off its head to get the hidden key. She'd felt then that they trusted her. She hoped she was keeping that trust now.

I'm abandoning them. I should have at least been brave at dinner. I should have told them I loved them.

But then I would have stayed with them tonight. Joined them on the couch with some popcorn. Joined them after that, bleeding, in a coma, waiting to be harvested by the things from the cave.

No.

They know I love them.

Let me believe that.

She put one hand and her forehead against the bedroom door and squeezed her eyes as tight as she could and whispered, "Please. Protect them," to anything good that might be listening.

Then she gave Bucket a nod. The Hendersons were secured. It was time to check on the Marwanis and hope they'd escaped the corrupted transmission that had poisoned the airwaves over Turner Falls.

Light flooded the living room as Lucy and Bucket descended the stairs. Lucy felt a rumble in her feet, and her eyes adjusted enough to see the bright lights washing over the room came from a large pair of halogen headlamps and fog lights on the front of someone's truck.

Fuck. It's too late.

"Bucket, grab a knife from the kitchen. They're here."

Lucy found her wrench by Carol's La-Z-Boy and braced herself.

Can I do this again? Can I kill someone?

"Bucket, hurry up!"

Had he fled out the back door? She wouldn't have blamed him. It was the reasonable response. But she knew—from what Brewer had described, from the look she'd seen in Ben Brumke's eyes as he tried to crush her skull—that reason had left them.

Another abandonment.

What was left?

A door slammed in the street. Someone sick was on their way to kill her and her family.

For *fun*. To "feel better."

She tightened her grip on the wrench, ready to swing it with both hands and put the weight of her body behind the blow.

I'm not meat.

Fists at the door, pounding. Bucket reappeared at her side with a serrated carving knife, which, while large, was kind of a shitty choice. The blade was thin, and she could imagine it breaking off after one good stab. It shook in Bucket's hand.

He was not ready for this.

A voice from the other side. "Lucy, goddamnit, I know y'all are in there. I can see my fucking truck. You gotta open up!"

Brewer!

But how? Was it a trick? If these blue-eyed sons of bitches could find her address in their thoughts, what else could they do? Were they mimicking Brewer? What was this? One more cruelty before they charged in and killed everyone she cared about?

"Open up. I don't think we lost 'em for long, and Jake's hurt real bad. Please."

Lucy ran to the front window, craning her neck to see who was standing at the door, waiting for them to spot her and come crashing through the glass.

Jake Bernhardt's truck was idling in her yard, halfway onto the lawn, tires full of churned-up turf. The dome light was on, and she saw Jake leaning against the passenger-side window, holding a bloody T-shirt to his head.

But wouldn't Jake be with *them*? Every kid she'd seen or heard hunting their classmates in that cave had been part of that scene. Brower Butte kids. Popular kids. A few jocks. The ones who already fucked up her life on a regular basis. And what had Ben said to her?

"He says we don't want you."

Jason Ward, or whatever Ward was now, calling the shots inside their heads. Telling them who they could use.

There was some sick goddamn hierarchy, even here, at the end of the world.

She yelled out the window. "Fuck off. You're with them. You come in here, I swear you fucking die."

Bucket offered a halfhearted "Yeah!" in support, but his voice carried more fear than aggression. She hoped he'd be worth a damn if she needed him.

The boy on the front step responded. "See, I knew y'all were in there. And listen, Lucy, I *know* you believe me by now. Maybe you didn't when we were in the tunnel, but I can tell by your voice that you know I was telling the truth. I still am . . . just . . ."

Something distracted both of them. A new pair of headlights turning onto Lucy's street.

"Oh, fuck. They found us."

"How do I know that's not more of your crew? How do I know you're really Brewer? Maybe they got to you."

She pictured Brewer looking at her with new, bright blue eyes. Where did he stand in their little hierarchy? Would they keep Brewer and reject her?

"Open the door, please! You'll see."

"No."

The approaching truck was halfway up Lucy's block.

"Listen, listen, *listen*, damn it . . . all right, what's . . ." Brewer's voice drifted off, then returned brighter. "Lucy, when you were a kid you wanted to fuck a dolphin."

And Lucy knew that while what he'd yelled was both somewhat inaccurate and totally inappropriate, it was also something only Brewer would know, or be willing to yell.

Or is he manipulating me? Maybe whatever got into the Brower Butte kids is in Brewer, and it knows what he knows. How do I . . .

The eyes!

More pounding at the door.

"Get on your tiptoes, Brewer!"

He did as he was told. Lucy rushed over and looked out through the small half circle of decorative glass at the top of the door, but she could only see Brewer's mop of hair from that angle, some of it matted, some of it shining wet.

Blood. He's hurt too. Of course he is. They dragged him away. How is he even here?

"Pull back your hair. Let me see your eyes."

Brewer swept back his bangs and cringed. A fresh trickle of blood rolled over his left temple. He raised his brow, showing her more of his face than she'd ever seen.

His eyes were muddy brown by porchlight, and some part of Lucy that she could barely register was delighted.

It's really Brewer. He came back to me.

Then he was yelling her name again, but this time a new panic had entered his voice. Lucy reached out to open the door to him, and the front of her house exploded inward.

The picture window that framed her idyllic street view became thousands of flying glass shards as a huge gray Bronco with an absurd lift kit came smashing into her living room like it intended to drive right on through.

Lucy dropped back from the door, shaken by the impact, wondering how there could be a truck inside her goddamn house, and what part of it was leaking gas, and how long she might have before the whole rig ignited and turned 1437 Juniper Street into a kamikaze blast zone.

The Bronco must have been from the pre-airbag era, because whoever was sitting shotgun had been thrown halfway through the windshield. Her torn torso flopped and vibrated on the hood as smoke billowed from the engine beneath. Lucy spotted a dark bulge on the girl's neck—*she's one of them*—right before the girl turned her head with a nauseating pop.

The girl smiled through a fresh gout of black blood from where the crash had peeled back her scalp. Her eyes drifted for a second, then snapped to attention on Lucy's face. "It's *you!*" Her smile disappeared and her eyes rolled back and she murmured, "Found found found found . . ." but Lucy's attention was pulled away by Brewer's screams from the porch and the sound of the driver's-side door of the mangled truck creaking open.

"Lucy, are you in there? Can you hear me?"

Lucy didn't respond because she was already on her way over to the truck, and she'd found her wrench, and she was alive in this new world in a way that she recognized as simultaneously very wrong and very right at the same time. So as Bucket recovered from the truck's impact and rushed to let Brewer in, Lucy was ready to accept the fact that there was a flaming goddamn truck in the Hendersons' living room, and that she was ready to deal with the problem.

Brewer was through the front door then, saying something like, "What are you doing? You gotta get away . . ." but Lucy had already grabbed the side mirror and pulled herself up onto the chrome running board and she had the truck door thrown wide within seconds and the driver, who had been holding on to the handle, was flung to the floor.

Lucy recognized Bradley England's face, though the overly blue eyes threw her for a second. Then she saw Carol's favorite wineglass on the floor next to Bradley's head, and remembered that Bradley had just rammed a truck into her house with the intent of killing everyone inside, and so it was easy to ignore Brewer yelling, "No!" and it was easy to ignore the disturbing way that pain and pleasure flickered across Bradley's stunned face as he reached for a shard of glass on the carpet, and it was easiest of all to jump from the running board with her wrench in both hands and bring it swinging down with the full force of her body weight.

For the second time in one night, Lucy felt the vibration of a crunching human skull echo through her arms. This time she knew it was coming.

This time she was able to enjoy it.

Bradley's hand was still reaching for the shard, and her first swing hadn't made nearly the hole she'd expected, only a dent in his forehead, so she made sure the next swing came down by his eye, and with that the orbit crunched and gave way. Bradley's hands fell limp. He must have sensed it was the end, because he too began to say, "Found," over and over again, and Lucy didn't know how these things—

Humans, Lucy. They're humans.

—might be communicating, but she knew she didn't want to be found, so swings three and four ruined Bradley's smile, and he couldn't say a word through his shattered jaw, though his face clicked and sputtered and his one good eye stared straight at Lucy.

What does he see?

What do they see?

And she knew she was screaming then, and it felt good to let loose inside the house, where she'd always kept any extremity in check. It felt *so* good.

I am not the Hendersons' daughter. I am not Bucket's friend, or Brewer's

girl, or Dr. Nielsen's patient, or a goddamned orphan. I'm not Loogie or all
the jokes at my expense. I'm not a product for your use.

I'm only me. I'm right now. I'm here.

Maybe I've lost my mind, but this feels right.

I wish I'd lost my mind a long time ago.

She looked straight into Bradley England's face, a devastated mess of
jutting bone and flesh only recognizable as human because of the blazing
blue iris that glared upward, looking through her as if she were nothing.

"You want to send your friends a message, huh?"

She hocked back as hard as she could and spit in his one good eye.

"Show them this, Brad."

She raised the wrench, screamed again, then swung down and
struck the boy blind.

———————

Lucy stayed inside that moment for as long as it felt like a victory, but
then Bradley's body began to shake underneath her and his throat was
pulsing, and something about that made her stand and recoil.

She saw Bucket near the base of the stairs, hunched and vomiting
on the floor.

She saw Brewer looking at her, and his face brought a fresh ache to
her heart.

He's afraid. Of me.

And seeing his face like that made her feel something other than
anger, and she knew that what she'd done would never be undone, and
that maybe she should be afraid of herself too. But then she heard the
girl pinned to the hood of the Bronco slowly choking on her blood as
she muttered, "Found," and some machinery inside the truck ruptured
with a cracking sound she felt in her spine, and she remembered the
beauty of staying in motion.

She approached Brewer, who looked like he was ready to bolt. His
eyes met hers.

"Well, fuck, Lucy. That was . . ." He fell silent.

She couldn't read the look that came into his eyes next. Judgment? Confusion? Reverence? Maybe all of them.

Two thoughts rose simultaneously.

What have I done?

And: *What does it matter?*

I saved our lives.

The Hendersons were still upstairs. She wondered if all the noise below had set loose another round of mumbled warnings from them. She wondered if they'd ever come back.

Both she and Brewer rotated at the sound of a gunshot a few blocks away, the sound expanding through the suburban night.

More of *them*. Or someone fighting back, discovering that being home behind a locked door meant nothing if the wrong people were on the other side. Or someone deciding to escape the world at shotgun speed. Regardless, it was the sound of someone dying, and it wasn't time to join them.

"Bucket, there's a fire extinguisher in the garage, and another in the kitchen. Grab the kitchen one and help me spray the truck."

Bucket righted himself and moved quickly from the room, apparently grateful to have something to do other than witness the inexplicable trauma that had become their new reality.

"And you." She turned to Brewer. "You're going to get us out of here before more of them are drawn to this house. We're going to grab the Marwanis, I hope, and anybody from your crew who hasn't had their brain wiped clean by that goddamn broadcast, and then we're going to do what we should have done a long, long time ago and get the hell out of this bullshit town."

chapter nine

RUN DOWN

They decided to take Brewer's rig because Jake's truck was almost out of gas and a concerning amount of blood from Jake's and Brewer's head injuries had pooled along the crevices of the tan leather interior. It was messy enough that leaving it behind might make anyone in pursuit think they'd already been killed. Also, Brewer insisted. "Jake's truck looks nice, but that engine is soft as pudding. Little V-6, faux-wheel drive. No guts. I've got four-wheel, and that suspension can handle shit off-road."

Bucket protested. "We don't need to rally right now, dude."

"Goddamnit, I know that, Buck. But I saw a couple big-ass JLTVs headed out toward the US-26 access with mounted gunners and every-thing. Not sure we'll be able to get out of here on the regular streets."

Bucket and Lucy exchanged a worried glance. The broadcast rolling through town, now fucking soldiers headed to the outskirts . . . What was being contained? Was there really a leak at Handsome Valley?

No matter the truth, they had to escape.

Lucy was halfway to Brewer's rig when she heard a slurred voice coming from Jake's truck.

"Howdafuckeryoualive, though? Truck hitchoo." Jake made a collision sound before his good eye rolled back and his head thumped against the partially rolled-down window, leaving a fresh slick of blood.

For a flash, Lucy saw Jake as a liability, damaged cargo that would hold them back. She remembered his past unkindness and was ready to leave him. But then she pictured what would happen when *they* found him.

"Scrape him."

She pictured Jake violated, torn limb from limb by the pack of feral animals that used to be his friends.

Then she imagined the look on Bucket's and Brewer's faces if she said, *Leave him.* They were already afraid of her, and what she'd done. If she lost them, who was left? So she accepted the risk and resentment which came with Jake's bad ballast and took the initiative.

"Bucket, help me move Jake. Brewer, get your truck started."

Bucket threw Brewer his keys and ran to her. They moved quietly and quickly to Jake's truck and grabbed the boy, trying to ignore the shallowness of his breath and the way his body rag-dolled and lay too heavy across their arms. Lucy had Jake's legs and Bucket lifted under his shoulders, and together they ignored the fact that each of them had, at some point in the last year, quietly wished for the same cruel boy to disappear.

Lucy looked at Jake's body now, how vulnerable it seemed, and she watched his one visible eyelid twitching—whether from dreaming or dying, she could not know—and she imagined him peacefully at rest in his bed, his mother looking over him, and she blinked back an oncoming wave of confused tears and continued moving the boy.

"Aw, shit." Bucket grimaced and turned his head to the side. Something about the way they were moving Jake had caused a gout of blood to surge from the deep wound in his scalp, spraying Buck's shirt and neck. Lucy glanced down and saw that she too had taken on a new coat while removing Jake from the truck. Fresh blood smeared over the darkening stains of the evening. Lucy looked down at all that red and thought, *That's never coming out.*

Lucy couldn't look in the rearview for two reasons. First, she couldn't stand to see her family home drifting away behind her, smoke rolling from a barely contained vehicle fire in the living room while the Hendersons lay coercively comatose in the upstairs bedroom. Second, she was afraid to see her own eyes, knowing that would make her real again. Fragile. Afraid. Abandoned. Or worse—she'd see the new Lucy reflected, eyes wild, droplets of blood drying on her face, and know that's who she really was.

Each option unacceptable. Acknowledging what she might be losing could crush her, and thinking about what she'd done—about how right it had felt to destroy, and how good it had felt to finally have a way to exert control—might paralyze her. But death was surely headed her way, and life, whatever that meant now, could only happen somewhere far from here.

The present became everything, and action overrode thought, and that was how it had to be.

She rode shotgun. Brewer drove. They nestled Jake into the side of the extended cab with the duct-tape window replacement and angled his body to keep his head from lolling forward. That seemed to slow his bleeding. Bucket sat behind Lucy and gave Brewer the Marwanis' address. He said it overcarefully and clearly, and Lucy sensed he was speaking like that to keep from crying because he suspected they would find the same sad scene they'd uncovered at the Hendersons'. And if the Marwanis were just another batch of bad noise replicators, then who could they turn to? Did Brewer have parents?

She looked over at Brewer and saw his white-knuckled grip on the steering wheel and the tight worry knit across his brow, and he looked so small, and young, and scared, and she had to look away for fear that the way he felt would infect her too.

A deep ache rolled from Lucy's right shoulder down to her hand, which felt huge and heavy and throbbed with her pulse. She looked down and realized she'd kept a death grip on the handle of her wrench.

We're going to get through this. You have to stay strong.

She felt the heat coming from the truck's defrost vents warm her skin, and she realized she hadn't grabbed a jacket or sweater from her room. Didn't grab the first aid kit from the Hendersons' bathroom either. Should she have searched their closet for a gun? She couldn't imagine Bill owning one, but she also realized that if he did have a firearm, he'd probably kept it secret from her for her own safety.

They want me to live. They believed that they could give me that. They believed they could protect me.

And now I'm fucking this up. I'm not thinking enough. I'm not doing the right things. I killed two kids. But they would have killed me. And they weren't them anymore. Those eyes. That dead ocean smell. Christ, what happened to them? What's happening to me? How long can I survive like this? What am I—

"How the hell did you get out of the caves?"

Lucy was grateful that Bucket spoke up. His question to Brewer halted the spiral of thoughts that were unraveling what little resolve she held.

"I, uh . . . I don't want to talk about it. I need to drive."

But Bucket was right. Brewer had been in the lair with them. He had seen Jason and some other weird shit. If he was in that snake pit and survived, then he might know something that could help all of them.

Lucy pushed. "Please, Brewer." She placed her left hand on his leg and watched his face loosen at her touch. Based on the way he'd looked at her in the house, during the attack, she'd half expected him to flinch. Instead he sighed at the contact—none of them were breathing enough—and then he nodded a few times as if to say, *I can do this.*

"They pulled me back. It was Ben and Luke, I think, but it was hard to see anything because right after they pulled me out of the tunnel I felt kicks coming from every direction. I tried to curl up and protect my head. That's what Rodney always told me to do if I got jumped. But even with my hands on my head, something got past me and they split my scalp with a rock or I got kicked with a work boot or whatever and I was passing out and I remember thinking, *Let them kill me before one of those things that came out of Jason's mouth gets to me.* And it was weird . . . Maybe it was the shrooms or the blow to the head, but I felt this sense of peace outside of the pain. Like the pain was this batch of red, radiating signals trapped in my body, that I had to feel it *because* of my body, but soon I wouldn't be that anymore. Soon I'd be the same as the rocks and the smoke in the cave, just there." Brewer's voice caught in his throat. He cleared the tremble and continued. "So I was on the ground dying, I thought, and I heard other people dying in that cave and I felt so . . . like, sad for them, but not for me, and something hard and heavy crunched into my shoulder, and then I heard more noise and thudding sounds, but they were *next* to my body instead of in my body, and I opened my eyes to see Jake on top of Luke."

"What?"

"Yeah. I don't know what got into him, or why he helped me, but he was beating Luke on some honey badger shit. Totally vicious. Like he didn't care if he killed him or not. And normally my instinct is to break that shit up. Makes me sick to my stomach. But in this case I was so glad I wasn't being hit anymore, and I didn't know where Ben had gone, but he wasn't attacking me either, so I stood and watched for a second, until I remembered what I saw at the bottom of the cave, and I realized one of those spider things might be coming for me. Then I turned around to back away from the whole mess, and that's when Dale Rupp rushed up the rocks. I could barely understand how he was walking, he was twitching so much, but he got close enough I could see he was smiling, and he had a little raptor flip knife in his hands and he grabbed Jake by the hair and started slashing away at his scalp. And I realized I had backed away into the dark and I think I could have run, but then I heard Jake's voice. He was screaming, and it was so high-pitched it was almost like when a baby cries, and I couldn't take that sound, so I did the first thing I could think of and I ran behind Dale and grabbed him by his ankles. Like a snake, you know, to stay away from the sharp stuff at the other end. I pulled back as hard as I could, lifting him up in the air like we were playing wheelbarrow, and Dale let go of Jake and fell face-first to the ground. Then he was making this gurgling noise and I saw he had an arm trapped underneath him and my guess is he fell on his knife. But that's not my fault, right? I mean he shouldn't have had a knife out in the first place. He shouldn't have attacked us."

Lucy sat silent, believing Brewer already knew the answer. And if she acknowledged his feelings of guilt, she feared that might unlock those feelings wherever she had hidden them in herself.

Dr. Nielsen had told her that compartmentalizing was toxic. She told her she had to merge all those feelings together to be her honest self.

Dr. Nielsen got her truth from books. Dr. Nielsen had never felt the truth of the world in the ways Lucy had been forced to experience.

Dr. Nielsen could fuck right off. Lucy made another compartment in the depths of her mind and locked away the voice of the woman who had to be paid to provide care and advice.

Brewer continued. "So Jake was still pretty with it then, from the adrenaline or maybe he hadn't bled too much yet, and I gave him the nod to follow me so we could get up and out of there. We stayed in the dark and made it to the east wall. There's a little section there where some rock jocks illegally installed a bunch of climbing bolts in the lava rock, and there was enough light from the fire to catch the glint of 'em. I looked back at Jake to make sure he saw how we were going to get out. And then I looked back down to the party one more time and I saw maybe two or three dozen of those fuckers standing in a circle at the bottom. Most of 'em were bloody, and I knew most of that blood wasn't theirs, and they were all shaking and staring at one another, but not one of them was saying a word."

"Ward wants us back at the main cave."

That meeting saved our lives, thought Lucy. *That was the only way we were able to escape the swarm.* Despite that truth, she found the idea of all those empty blue eyes gazing at one another left a cold pit in her belly.

They have a plan.

Brewer stayed quiet a second longer, his lips pursed. Lucy thought he looked like he was hesitant to say whatever happened next. Then he sighed again and said, "So y'all are for sure going to think I lost my mind, or I was tripping or whatever, but I swear this is the truth. All right? And I swear all those kids stopped twitching and then they all looked straight up at the same time, and there was something big and black and shiny attached to the roof of the cave and it was moving around too, like a mama dog's belly rights before she litters, and some kind of squealing sound was coming from it. And when we saw that it was like we caught a cattle prod up our asses and hit that wall like fucking spider monkeys. Jake was probably a gallon low on blood by then, but he beat me to the top of the climb, and through the fissure up to the desert, and he didn't pass out until we made it to his truck."

Lucy took her eyes away from scanning for pursuers and looked over at Brewer, who was shivering a bit even though by now the truck was officially hot with mildewed air from the vents. She weighed everything she'd heard against her experience of the night, and it took her all of two seconds to make a decision.

"I believe you, Brewer. I believe all of it."

"So what the fuck do we do, then?"

"Same as before. We stay alive. We grab our people and get out of here."

"Should we call the cops? Or maybe there's something on the news. I could turn on the radio and—"

"No!" yelled Bucket. Lucy had to restrain herself to keep from smacking Brewer's outstretched hand with her wrench.

Brewer flinched. "Okay. Jesus. No radio. What the fuck, man? There's got to be someone who can help us in a situation like this."

Lucy reached over and detached the face of Brewer's audio deck and threw it out the window, aghast that she hadn't already thought of that and had left them at risk of hearing the broadcast. She imagined all of them bleeding from their noses, mouthing synchronized lies about the PUREX plant as the unmanned truck careened off the road and ran full speed into a juniper tree.

"There *should* be someone who could help us, but something else happened in town since after we left for the party. There's a broadcast . . ."

And then it was Lucy's turn to sound completely fucking crazy. In their broken world, even the truth felt like wave upon wave of lies, so reality crumbled and drifted further from the world they inhabited, and their shared nightmare coalesced as they drove the streets of Turner Falls in search of anything that might return them to the world they once knew.

———

The entrance to Bucket's suburban subdivision was flanked on both sides—an ornate decorative rock sign reading PINEBROOK VILLAGE on the left, and a three-tiered cascading water feature on the right. It wasn't until Brewer's headlights were pointed directly at the fake waterfall that they spotted the neighborhood's private security officer floating faceup, belly sliced and spread, spilling loops of intestine, which shone yellow-pink in the aqueous shimmer beneath the fall's spotlights.

The truck lurched to a sudden stop.

"Oh, fuck." Bucket leaned forward, squinting. "That's Darryl. They got fucking Darryl."

Lucy and Bucket had always laughed at the way Darryl patrolled Pinebrook steely-eyed and deadly serious, when everyone knew all he was really armed with was a phone for calling the real cops. Sometimes, for kicks, Bucket and Lucy would drive slowly behind Darryl's security car for as long as they could until he'd stop and step out to usher them by with a frustrated nod. *"All right, kiddos, I get it. Now let me get back to the serious business of watching porn on my phone and talking down Mrs. Habersham after a squirrel runs across her roof."*

And now, for once, there had been an actual threat which Darryl had needed to stop, and he had tried, at least, and been split wide open to bloat in the unnaturally blue chemical-saturated waters of the neighborhood he'd failed.

Lucy looked beyond the Pinebrook sign, up the main street that fed into Bucket's subdivision.

"There! Brewer, kill the lights."

Three blocks in, a sedan spewing thick exhaust, brake lights bright red. Even from a distance, Lucy could see the car was shuddering on its wheels.

They're in there. Waiting. Trembling.

Is it a trap? Did they see us?

The brake lights turned off.

"Shit! Go, Brewer. Slow. Leave the lights off."

"You think they saw us?"

"Do you want to find out? Just go."

The truck curved back toward the streets. Lucy kept her eyes on the sedan, which hadn't yet moved. Bucket whispered, "We can go around. We can head out Knott about a half mile and cut back in on Kubelko. There's another entrance."

"What makes you think that'll be any different?"

"It's barely visible. No sidewalks. Unpaved. I don't think they'd expect us to go that way."

"Bucket, they knew right where I lived. They'll know where you live. They could definitely be waiting for us to come for your parents."

"Lucy, we have to try. If you guys won't come with me, I'll try on my own. There's a chance my parents weren't watching TV when the broadcast hit, okay? If we stop on Kubelko, we can hop fences from there to get to my backyard. I can't just leave my family. What if the kids in that car get tired of waiting for us?"

They both knew the answer. Even if they'd been lucky enough to dodge the broadcast, the Marwanis would be easy prey. They were gentle and unsuspecting and loving people.

Which, in this new world, meant that they were fucked.

Lucy looked back at Bucket, anger in his face, tears welling in his eyes. She looked at Jake, so pale, drawing the shallowest of breaths. She wondered what was happening back at the Hendersons', and why she hadn't thought to load them into the back of Brewer's truck (as if she'd had time to think). And then she realized that by the time the sun rose over their city, it was possible Bucket might be the closest thing to real family she had left in the world.

"Okay. We'll take the back way. Brewer, you know where Knott is?"

"Landfill road, right?"

"Yeah."

Brewer smiled.

"What?" Lucy asked.

"Nothing. Just a dumb memory. Rodney used to have a flatbed trailer, and we'd help clean out old people's houses after they'd passed on."

"So?"

"So sometimes we'd see how far we could chuck all that old, shitty furniture into the landfill pits. Stuff would totally explode when it hit bottom. We'd leave those houses, everybody all strung out from mourning, and then we'd go to the dump and have the best fucking time throwing everything away. Winging that stuff until our backs ached, watching birds scatter. Seeing big old leaded mirrors shatter into a thousand pieces."

"That is dumb."

"Yeah." Brewer shifted into fourth, pushing up their speed even though they couldn't see much road between the intermittent street-lights. "It was great, though. Got paid. Got a workout. And we laughed like crazy."

Lucy watched Brewer's face soften with his laughter and wished memories gave her the same comfort. She was watching him, forgetting to scan the roads, feeling again that there was something sweet and wild in him, which she wanted to stay close to for as long as she could. She didn't smile—that would have felt like madness—but she imagined a future with him where she could.

Had she not allowed herself that moment of fantasy, she might have seen the headlights round the corner behind them. They might have been able to escape.

She felt the shock of the impact through her bones before the sound of the gunshot reached her ears. Then came the sound of tempered glass crumbling, and she looked back to see the rear window of the canopy had disappeared. The actual rear window on the cab was cracked but had not given way.

If that canopy weren't there, I'd have Bucket's brains all over me.

Brewer swerved and started to slow.

"What are you doing?" Lucy yelled.

"It's a blowout. If the hole's not too big, I can . . ."

A second shot echoed through the air, but it went wide and cratered a road sign reading TRANSFER STATION/LANDFILL 3 MI.

Lucy watched how quickly Brewer's mind reassessed their situation.

Exploding sign/lights in their rearview.

Not a blowout.

Hunted.

They spotted us the same time we spotted Darryl in the waterfall.

He flipped on his headlights and slammed the pedal. There was a whirring sound for a moment as the RPMs flew out of control and then the engine caught up and Lucy was slammed against her seat. She smelled scorching metal and melting rubber through the vents and wondered how long Brewer's truck would hold out.

The car, low and fast, gained on them despite Brewer's best efforts to gun his engine. A third blast rang out, and Lucy saw their rear right lights had been destroyed by the shot.

The tires. They're going for our tires.

They're not shooting at us. They want us for themselves.

Lucy wondered if it was mutually assured destruction to turn the truck around and charge at them head-on. Probably. But she felt that desire in her bones. The moment each new threat arrived, there was a rush of blood through her body, and her muscles felt strong and tight again, and she wanted nothing so much as to crush whatever had tried to harm her. She felt it like fate, magnetic, pulling her toward conflict.

This has always been inside of me, but I never let it out.

I was a ghost instead. For too long.

She looked back at Bucket, ducked down and wide-eyed in the extended cab, and she saw in his face that he understood—there would be no rescue missions. Perhaps the best they could do was draw the sedan farther away from his parents' house. His nobility had been cut short by a shotgun blast, and nothing could be done to help anyone if

they were run off the road and torn to pieces like the men in the ambulance.

But where to go?

Already on the outskirts where Bucket's family lived, their exces-
sive speed sent them hurtling past the Turner Falls city limits in less
than a minute.

LEAVING TURNER FALLS. THANKS FOR VISITING
THE CITY OF MOUNTAIN VIEWS!

Another blast. Lucy heard metal shearing, saw sparks as a chunk of
the tailgate broke free and skidded across the asphalt. Then she looked
forward and saw an unnatural glow in the distance. Too bright, like the
massive light rigs that sent crispy dead moths twirling down at the
baseball stadium.

*"I saw a couple big-ass JLTVs headed out toward the US-26 access
with mounted gunners and everything."*

The lights had to be military. Lucy wondered if they had blocked
every arterial out of town. If they knew what was loose in Turner Falls,
would they have a "shoot on sight" policy? She thought of their crew—
one fucked-up loadie, a brain-damaged rich kid with one eye, and two
brown kids who happened to be coated in the blood of some of Turner
Falls' most-appreciated young folks—and she couldn't picture a scenario where they'd want to approach nervous, trigger-happy men with
guns.

As far as "rock and a hard place" scenarios go, it was a fucking
doozer. She looked down at her wrench in her hand, weighed the options, and made the call.

"Flip it, Brewer."

"What? We're building speed. Look back! I think we can ditch 'em.
Maybe they're running low on ammo."

"Look way out there. See all that light. That direction's all desert.
Should be dark. So that's got to be the military guys you saw, right?"

"Yeah, but . . ."

"Or cops. It could definitely be a police roadblock."

"Shit."

And Lucy learned a lesson: if you ever want a loadie to go one way, point the other way and say, "Cops."

Brewer flipped it, fishtailing in gravel as he spun through the soft shoulder, but bringing the truck back to true as the front wheels gripped the asphalt. In the back, the inertia flung Jake onto Bucket, who yelled in surprise as he caught a fresh spray of warm blood from Jake's Grand Canyon scalp wound.

That's good, though, right?

Lucy had watched enough episodes of *FBI Files* with Bill to know blood only spurts when someone's heart is still beating. Despite Jake being shit on the inside, he was young, and very fit. He could survive. And he'd saved Brewer, so for her friend's sake she hoped they could find a way to keep him alive.

Bucket pushed Jake off him, and Jake lolled for a moment, muttered something which sounded like, "Truck stinks," then collapsed the other direction, the slightly less bloody side of his head coming to rest against the gooey adhesive interior of Brewer's carefully constructed duct-tape window.

And then Jake stuck.

Bucket's mouth dropped open. He looked at Lucy, and she looked back, sharing his amazement, and one of them might even have laughed if Brewer didn't yell out, "They're coming up!"

The distance between the truck and car was closing too fast. If they pulled off a shot in proximity, they might really blow out one of Brewer's tires and send their desired cargo to a spinning stop.

Lucy scanned the road and the land beside it. The shoulder was gradual, and only a foot above the desert floor. No trees, only brush, tumbleweeds, and the glinting eyes of a rabbit or snake.

So, just as they were approaching the car, as she saw a boy with a too-wide smile emerge from the back window of the sedan with a shotgun shouldered, she grabbed the steering wheel and yanked to the right.

Lucy had heard the term "rally" before, but she had never randomly rallied someone's vehicle from the passenger side, so she wasn't prepared for the tiny second of antigravity she felt as the truck soared over the shoulder, or the body-wide thud she felt as the vehicle slammed to the desert floor.

The boy in the car didn't have time to recalibrate his aim, and he took his shot at the place where the truck should reasonably have been. Meanwhile, the truck was spewing soft dirt, the bottom scraping and thumping against huge chunks of lava rock, which Lucy hadn't seen when she decided to steer for a second. Then she felt the left side of the truck lift off the ground and Brewer's hand was on her arm and pushing her hand off the wheel and he could have been yelling, "Goddamnit," but there was so much noise from under the truck that Lucy couldn't be sure. She was certain that when she slammed against the passenger-side door and looked left she saw more sky and less road than you'd normally want to, and she could feel they were going to tip and roll, and by some minor miracle Jake Bernhardt's head was still stuck to the duct-tape window, and she thought that would be a funny thing to see before she died.

But: Brewer corrected the wheel and accelerated at exactly the right time, and then the left wheels were once again earthbound and tearing away at the silty soil beneath them.

Another shot echoed through the desert, but—thanks to all the dust sent skyward in the near-wreck—it missed its mark. Within seconds, Brewer returned them to the road, and this time he had the accelerator pushed down as far and hard as he could manage, like he had the world's most venomous snake pinned under his sneaker.

Lucy saw the headlights of the sedan come round behind them, but her near-deadly desert diversion had gained them serious ground.

"LUCY!"

"What?"

"LUCY! WHAT. THE. FUCK?" Brewer pounded his flat right hand against the steering wheel with each word.

"I saved us."

"I KNOW! JESUS! BUT YOU NEARLY KILLED US!"

Brewer rolled his shoulders and took two long deep breaths.

"I'm sorry, Lucy. It's only . . . This is insane. I don't know where to put that feeling without yelling."

Lucy nodded. She one hundred percent understood.

"You're alive. Yell all you want."

"Yeah, yeah. Whatever you say, psycho." There was an edge to his voice, which Lucy figured was part adrenaline and part exhaustion, but she could tell he wasn't trying to be mean. He was just a wreck. They all were.

Lucy watched the headlights behind them, drifting up and down with the rolling street, staying close enough to keep eyes on them but no longer trying to rush them.

She ran scenarios:

They're waiting for us to run out of gas. Then they attack.

Or, however these things are communicating, they've signaled ahead. Their friends are waiting.

Or they've calmed down. Chasing us, firing guns—that was enough to stop them from writhing. To get them "back on." But that won't last forever, and the hunt will continue.

Or whatever Brewer saw hanging from the roof of the cave has found its way to the surface, and we're heading right back toward it and the boys in the car behind are smiling and whispering, "Found found found found," while they escort us back to their breeding grounds.

No matter what, she thought, *we're fucked.*

But there was some magic she felt in responding to their madness with her own. If they had to exist inside some everlasting death dream, at least she'd found a way to feel alive.

She'd never been so trapped.

She'd never felt so free.

Brewer said, "So we're heading back into Turner Falls?"

"Sure. Why not?"

"You think we should go to one of the neighborhood emergency meeting spots?"

"We could drive by," she said. Then she thought, *Let's see if any of those uptight parents who claimed they "don't even own a television" were telling the truth. Let's see who's left that isn't a mumbling coma patient, or a twitching murder junky, or a soldier enforcing containment protocols under bullshit pretenses. Let's see if we can find someone, anyone, who can tell us why the fuck our city fell through some black hole into an alternate universe that's even more magically fucked up than the one we already lived in.*

Then she realized something: if they knew her address down to the house number, if they could see that info inside their heads, then they'd definitely also be able to pull up all the neighborhood emergency site info. Hell, Jason Ward and his crew may have gone to those first. She pictured all of those nicely dressed Brower Butte kids, blue-black oil dribbling from their necks and pooling at their clavicles and lower backs as they spasmed and jerked. Did they close their eyes and see a grid of the city with a smattering of bright red dots? Did they hear Jason Ward in their heads, or did the squirming black mass above them send its own special messages?

Go to these places. You will find the elderly and parents who don't know where their children are. You will find the very young. They will be tired and confused and worried.

None of them will be ready for you.

None of them will stop you.

They are yours to harvest.

They are yours to use.

No, she thought. *No emergency sites.*

She pictured playgrounds littered with human husks, bodies rendered obscene by the newly cruel hands of boys and girls who had once played on the nearby jungle gym.

Even with all she'd witnessed, Lucy found she couldn't bear the thought of seeing that in real life. She smelled the burning gas and melting metal of her parents' accident at the thought of it.

Block that out. Not an option.

"Actually, Brewer, fuck the emergency meeting sites. They won't be safe by now. Never mind." She sighed. "There's nowhere good to go." She looked back at the headlights in the distance, and Jake "If You Can't Duck It, Fuck It" Bernhardt, and she looked at Bucket, who had seemed to realize that the Marwani rescue mission was officially out of the cards—his eyes were glazed and he stared, mouth open, out the windshield.

"What do you think, Buck?"

"I don't care." His dead voice. She hadn't heard his tone that flat since the day Luke Olsen secretly hocked a snotball into his soda.

"Some cans come with a special surprise, Sandy!"

All that laughter. Every sneering face a reminder that you didn't belong.

But this was worse. He might have lost his parents. Lucy knew that feeling—numb, no hunger, bones feeling like balsa wood, then suddenly you remembered what you'd lost and were crushed flat.

"Hey . . . They could be all right. Maybe they were playing chess or mancala, and they went right to bed after that, and they don't even know any of this is happening. And if those guys were only in your hood so they could find us, we've dragged them away now, right?"

Silence. The back seat was bummer city.

"What about you, Brewer? What do you think we should do?"

"I don't know. I mean, Rodney and I always had this plan, like, we'd joke about what we'd do if there was zombie outbreak or martial law or a, um . . . like, a race war or whatever. Not that I'd want a race war or anything . . ." He glanced nervously at Lucy. "But we were only talking about different scenarios that *could* happen . . ."

"Ugh. Shut up, dummy. What was the plan?"

"Yeah. That's all foolish. Ignore that. Main point, I guess, is that if any kind of shit went down, we agreed we'd meet at the Double D Truck Stop."

"The Down and Dirty?" Bucket asked, a little life returning to his voice, proud at knowing the nickname of one of Turner Falls' most notorious businesses, an oddly structured combination diner/truck stop/dive bar that operated in defiant violation of most truck lines' "bottle to throttle" visitation policies. "What are you going to do? Get hammered?"

"No. I mean, sure, you could. They got hella-cheap White Russians, free beer backs, two-dollar well drinks, and . . . but no. That wouldn't be the point anyway, unless you were in a full 'bombs dropping, end of the world' kind of scenario, then sure, drink up. But no. There are better reasons to go to the Double D. None of the rumors about that place are really rumors. You *can* get speed there, for sure, and that could help you stay alert. And there are a couple guys who run guns through there. I watched Sean Landers buy a sawed-off there, no serial number, and he sat in the booth with the dealer and they shot the shit over one of those big, greasy omelets. And a bunch of the late-night crew are there for the vets' discount, and loads of those 'Nam and Korea guys have concealed carries on 'em."

Bucket, who Lucy knew had a soft spot for vicarious sleaze, had actually perked up in his seat. "So you and Rodney wanted to meet there because they have guns, drugs, booze, and soldiers."

"Sure. And coffee. And the omelets are greasy, but they're also pretty fucking delicious."

Lucy liked the way Brewer sold the idea, and she liked the way that Bucket dropped his dead voice at the thought of the place, and she felt exhaustion and collapse creeping in from the wings to take her down. Maybe this would be a chance for them to hole up and get some rest.

Besides all that, she secretly believed that no matter what they did, there was only more death ahead of them. They might as well take a shot at scoring some pancakes.

"All right," she said. "Screw it, then. Let's go to the Double D."

chapter ten

CRUISING THE RUINS

L ucy could tell that sleep deprivation and delirium had finally over-
whelmed her, because everything was getting worse yet she was
smiling, even holding in laughter lest her friends in the truck know
she'd finally snapped. Despite the immediate mortal peril of their crew
being pursued by *two* vehicles intent on running them down, and despite the deeply worrisome chugging/grinding noises coming from beneath Brewer's truck as they raced over a paved pathway through the
town's oldest cemetery, she'd taken to repurposing famous sayings to
fit their current situation:

Life is what happens when you're busy making plans. But in this
case "life" is "being hunted down by an even larger pack of enraged
classmates" and "making plans" is "rolling into town right along the
main thoroughfare on your way to some dirtbag pit stop you near-
arbitrarily selected as a place to hide out while the apocalypse blows
over and discovering that a jacked-up Ford full of homicidal assholes
was waiting and watching for you from the parking lot of Hendrix-
son's Grocery."

Or

Wish in one hand and spit in the other, and see which one fills up first. Or: wish in that first hand, that's fine, but maybe use your other hand to hold tight to a blood-encrusted wrench and feel your palm sweating around the heft of the weapon and secretly fantasize about the moment your truck finally runs out of gas and how you'll get a chance to feel the crack of the metal against the skull of another one of those blue-eyed Brower Butte bastards. But don't think too hard about the excitement that stirs in your heart or the way your fantasy makes heat spread up from below your belly because really we're trying to focus on hands right now.

Or

Sometimes you eat the bear, and sometimes the bear is a metaphor for something less reasonable like a batch of vibrating, Dead Sea–smelling, potentially telepathic murder-junkie kids with a vendetta against anything moving, and that kind of bear really shouldn't exist, which means the laws that were supposed to hold the universe together were faulty, which further meant that the decorum and respect of the old world meant shit-all and it was okay that Brewer had made the last-second call to jump a curb and crash through a single, paltry security chain so they could cut across the town cemetery and lose their pursuers because they had to do something, and sure the vehicles in pursuit had raced past because they hadn't seen a road where Brewer had but she was certain they wouldn't give up the hunt . . .

"LUCY! Which direction will cut through to Elk Creek Road?"

Brewer sounded angry. Lucy realized she was gently rocking in her seat.

What am I doing? What's happening? Shit!

We're going to die.

She tried to blink away the membrane she felt clouding her mind and focus, because that was her job, somehow: to stay alive long enough to . . . what?

"LUCY!"

The truck barreled down a pathway barely wide enough for a hearse and she wondered if they were breaking the all-time cemetery speed record—would there be a trophy?—but she did see the red-and-white mortuary building off to her right, which meant heading that direction should take them back to a city street and away from the depths of the cemetery grounds.

"Go right!"

And he did, but later than he should have, so he barely avoided crashing into a white marble mausoleum, and right after that one of his rear wheels dipped into the open blackness of a freshly dug grave and sent a new surge of creaking and snapping sounds through the frame of the truck. Lucy paid that no mind as her thoughts had tumbled back beneath a disorienting veil of shock and trauma and her lids felt heavy and she was wondering who was the first person to say, "Come visit my dead body at this fancy little house I bought. Bring the kids. Snacks are on you." And she liked to imagine it was invented by some guy with the name Dale Mausoleum and she felt what he'd created was no stranger than any of the rest of it, that was certain, because when she looked out on the field of tucked-away corpses and stone monuments it felt so distant and abstract that she might as well have been racing in a lunar rover above alien glyphs and even the grass was unnatural here, to the point where she thought they might have painted it because in the headlights the green looked like it was really more of a dark blue

Or

Purple

Or

Blue

Or

Purple

Or

Oh god I can't do this anymore we're going to die and they'll pull us

from the truck and put their quaking hands on us and laugh while they rip us to shreds and we'll bleed down into the soil until the bones beneath us are stained red again.

And though her eyes were open, vision left her. For a split second between passing out and her face hitting the dash, she was blissfully free of consciousness.

She returned in static, confused, a dull throb in the bridge of her nose growing more distinct as thought crept back in to her oxygen-starved brain.

No mercy here.

Mercy mercy me.

Merci beaucoup.

Beaucoup bucks.

Buckminster Fuller.

Fuller House.

House M.D.

Empty House.

Wait, was that last one a thing? Lucy decided it was. Close enough. Nailed it! But someone was angry. The world was vibrating beneath her. A boy was yelling.

". . . damn it, Lucy, did you pass out? We've gotta . . . you can't . . ."

No, the boy wasn't angry. He was *scared*.

The window next to her slid down. The shock of fresh, cool air racing over her skin reminded her where she was.

"They found us again. Look!"

Two sets of headlights, growing closer. The sedan from the desert and the truck from the grocery store had caught up to them. The car dropped back, and the oversized Ford accelerated fast enough to make its headlights lift.

Lucy felt pressure on her ribs, then a sudden and sharp pain as Brewer grabbed and twisted and pulled down at any skin he could manage to pinch.

"OW! What the fuck?"

"I need you here. I don't know what else to do. Keep breathing, all right? I've heard you can pinch that bundle of veins and nerves or whatever under your tongue to stay awake."

She looked back at the predators behind them, knowing they were willing to bide their time, knowing they were waiting for her to collapse. And she had.

It's happening. Too soon. This is how people die—they just run out. They wear down. Battery at zero, and you stop, and that's the end.

She tried to remember what Bill had always told her when she was wandering around the house in zombie mode after a night of no sleep. Something he liked to quote from all his Jason Bourne books. He'd say, "Why don't you take a nap, kiddo? I'll wake you up in thirty minutes. Remember, 'Sleep is a weapon.'"

Sleep is a weapon.

But how will I ever sleep again?

She thought about how deep a sleep she'd finally be allowed once her light was fully snuffed.

I want that.

But then she looked at Brewer white-knuckling his dying truck through the cemetery, and she turned and saw Buck staring straight ahead with dull eyes, iron grip on the cab's *oh, shit* handle, mouth open, doing his best "*Saving Private Ryan* soldier resigned to die" face, and then she saw Jake, motionless and too white and tucked against his duct-tape nest, and she wondered if he was alive, and further, if he *was* still kicking, how they were going to separate him from all that adhesive without accidentally peeling loose his slashed-through scalp. So the back seat was still bummer city, and the front seat was harried survival without end, and she wondered where she fit in all that. And she wondered why looking at all their faces filled her with a new energy. Why had the will to live drained from her, but the will to protect these poor, terrified boys was flooding into her mind and aching body?

They're all I've got now.

She hoped that the Hendersons were tucked away safe, but she'd spent every moment since they'd come to drive her from the orphanage secretly believing that they too, would be taken from her. And once they were gone, *that* fear could leave her.

You didn't have to worry about the dead.

But these boys, right here and now, were what she had left. Her connection to the world. And if there was something in her—this terrible rage she'd harbored for who knew how long—and if that thing might protect them all, then she had to . . .

"Wake up, Lucy!"

She'd been swaying again. Drifting away.

No.

She pinched under her tongue as Brewer had suggested, her fingers squeezing against the thin, slick ropes of connective tissue. There was a jolt, but not enough.

When do I feel most awake? Most alive?

When I'm moving.

When I'm fighting.

Lucy dropped her wrench to the floor of the truck and balled her fists and pounded them into the dash in front of her. Her blood quickened, the pain lighting up her fists and arms and aching chest. The molded plastic dash cracked. She yelled, the pitch high and unrestrained.

Brewer flinched.

"Jesus, Lu! Are you shot? What . . ."

"We have to do something. They can chase us forever. They're *fucking with us,* and this truck is dying."

"What should I—"

"We can lose the car, maybe the truck. Go through the graves."

"What?"

"Go through the fucking graves!"

And Brewer must have trusted her instincts, because he wrenched the wheel hard to the left and headed straight into a field of jutting stones.

Lucy felt a couple of dull thumps against the undercarriage, then yelled, "Shit!" when she realized they were about to collide with a four-foot-tall concrete statue of a praying angel. She imagined the statue bisecting the truck, but instead it tumbled under with a spine-rattling thud. Immediately the truck slowed. She pictured one of the angel's wings latched onto an axle, the other plowing the cemetery soil beneath them, anchoring them to waiting death.

We can't stop here. We don't have the numbers. We've got to lose them or find some other regular human beings.

"Gun it again, Brewer!"

Brewer slammed the accelerator down. The truck revved like mad, and the sudden surge dislodged the angel. The statue was ejected from the rear of the truck, tumbling end over end toward their pursuers, both of whom managed to swerve handily around the buzz-sawing stone divinity.

Lucy huffed.

Thanks, god. You totally had a chance to prove you existed, and you went and fucked that up.

Worse, Lucy spotted new movement—a boy in a mask climbing from the passenger-side window of the truck behind them.

No, not a mask. There were four dark red vertical stripes running parallel down the boy's face. Even from a distance, Lucy could recognize her handiwork, the long, savage gullies she'd dug into the boy's face.

Ben Brumke.

He's found me.

"You're meat."

For a moment she wished that during that moment in the tunnel she'd had the forethought to go for Ben's eyes. Fingers dug in, pulling back, the warmth of his scream on her face.

If I ever get the chance again . . .

Another thud beneath her as their mobile desecration parade tore its tornado path through the cemetery. Ben was holding tight to the dusty truck, one arm in the cab, body leaning out, one arm pulling him toward the cargo bed.

A flash from the headlights on the sedan behind the truck allowed Lucy to see the outline of a giant bull's-eye decal on the window, a silhouette of a wolf in its sights. The text on the design was backward, but she recognized it. "Smoke a Pack a Day." Luke Olsen's truck—the one she and Bucket had seen drive an ambulance from the road like injured prey.

Shit. Brumke's going for Olsen's secret stash.

Hunting was a cultural centerpiece of Turner Falls life—students at Spring Meadow could even take unpenalized weeks off at the beginning of bow and rifle seasons, a holdover put in place by their forefathers back when far more people filled their fridges with elk and venison as a means of subsistence—but guns were long since banned from school grounds. Still, the Spring Meadow policy was more lenient than most schools': first offense got you a warning, second earned a three-day suspension and mandatory gun safety class, and the third strike left you expelled.

Luke Olsen was a frequent enough offender that he was nearly expelled last October, after a parking lot patrol reported rifles in his rig for a third go-round. When he reappeared on campus, he was all smiles. "Dad has a Rotary friend who's tight with the principal. Besides, he says the whole thing is 'nanny state bullshit.' I wasn't even in trouble, dude. He was, like, *proud* of me."

But it also became clear that his dad might have used his last favor with the school district, because one week later Luke showed up for school with a locking, custom-molded gun rack built into his truck bed.

"Truth is, now I can fit twice as many guns, and they can't even tell whether or not I've got 'em with me."

Thanks, Mr. Olsen!

So now Ben Brumke was on his way to an unknown arsenal, ready to put the final nail in the rolling coffin that was Brewer's badly battered and nearly fuel-free truck. Lucy imagined that whatever was functioning inside Luke's and Ben's Cro-Magnon minds found the situation both familiar and exciting. School was out and Turner Falls' newest hunting season was in full bloom.

She pictured herself strung up by her feet, body split from pelvis to ribs, her guts gathering flies on the concrete floor of Luke's garage.

What would I feel, before I became meat? How long would I feel the knife slicing through my skin? Would I feel their hands inside me as they tore away?

Her heart fluttered then returned to its panicked thumping. She felt, at last, all the way awake. The bad energy she'd felt as she screamed quietly in the bathroom the day before—a time that felt worlds away—was what drove her into the future. She remembered the white flame she'd imagined when she pictured herself torn right in two, and she knew *that* was the feeling that had allowed her to survive.

She imagined that flame spreading, filling her with light.

There.

Now keep going.

She spoke to Brewer. "That's Luke's truck. Ben's going for the hidden rack. More guns. We have to go faster."

"Truck ain't exactly in 'go faster' kind of condition right now."

"It has to be. Cut back to the pathway. Get to a road."

Lucy looked back. Brumke had dropped out of sight, likely opening the concealed case.

Bucket woke from his daze behind Lucy. "Oh, fuck."

"What?"

"Jake kicked me. He's awake."

Lucy turned to see Jake flapping his right hand in the air, his remaining eye scanning the truck, his patch being pulled loose by the duct tape that gripped one side of his head. She tried not to be curious about what was under the patch, but she wondered what Chris Carmichael's claws had left behind in the boy's skull.

"Uh. Uhhhh." His raised hand steadied. His eye locked on Lucy, then looked up at his hand.

"Hand!" Jake sounded frustrated, though his speech was the clearest she'd heard it since he'd arrived spilling blood from the cavern in his head.

"High five?" Lucy asked.

Jake growled, childlike, impatient.

"Answer!"

And then Lucy realized he wanted to speak, but needed to be called on first, and she imagined what he must be seeing through his concussed mind, and wondered which teacher she might resemble, and she remembered that they had all been students once, before the trembling beasts came tumbling from the mouth of the cave.

She pointed to his hand. "Yes, Jake?"

His hand dropped. The slightest smile spread across half his face, though the rest remained slack. But Lucy knew that grin, and had seen it before any number of Jake's cruelties. She braced herself for the awfulness that was bound to come from his mouth.

Jake spoke, as slowly and clearly as he could. "We, we . . . we . . . went shooting around out China Hat Road. *Everybody* except Brumke bagged . . . confirmed kills. He can't shoot for shit. Couldn't eeeeee . . ." Jake stalled out, eye rolling back, the tenuous connections keeping him conscious and speaking flickering out for a moment. "Couldn't even clip anything with *snake shot*. One foot spread on that. We all got squirrels, some quail. Brumke got shit. Went home moping with his little dick in his hand. Teeny-tiny little Brumke dick. Aaaaaaahhh . . ."

Jake tried to laugh at his own insults, but whatever weak signal was broadcasting from inside his damaged mind had given out again. His head lolled along the wall of duct-tape adhesive, further ensconcing the left side of his face, pinning him like a mouse struggling against a glue trap.

Lucy tried to appreciate the snippet of good news Jake had provided without thinking too deeply about the way he'd clearly linked a boy's capability for murder to his dick size.

This is the way these guys thought before *they were infected by whatever was in that cave.*

The deep rattle of Brewer's dying truck suddenly lessened, and Lucy saw they'd made it back to the paved pathway, and beyond the trees outlining the periphery of the cemetery she saw a regular streetlamp. That meant they'd almost made it back to a city street. But what had they gained? Their diversion had succeeded only in devastating the bottom of their ride and waking Lucy from her body's attempt to collapse.

But when she looked in her side mirror, *they* were behind, still hunting, and she realized she could see Brumke leaning over the top of the truck cab behind them. A tiny flash of light came from in front of the boy, and then she couldn't see a thing because the mirror she'd been using had ceased to exist, and it wasn't until the sound of the blast reached her ears that she realized Brumke's first shot had come inches from shattering its way through either her or Bucket in the same way.

What happened to "He can't shoot for shit"?

Maybe he's not shooting like Brumke because he isn't only *Brumke anymore. Whatever is in his head, whatever told him my address and told him he'd feel better if he killed me, it's making him* more *than he was before.*

Another shot and Brewer's side mirror was shards.

They're blinding us. They'll hobble us next. Nice and slow. Toying with us. We showed them we're dangerous, so now they're trying to soften us up for the easy kill. Getting their kicks.

Those shots didn't hit the cab because they want to put their hands on us.

"*I can't be off again. Can't be off. I need this.*"

Lucy imagined Ben Brumke's hands, suddenly stable on the rifle, calmed by the chase. She imagined how much better he would feel if he could put those hands on her.

"They're going for the tires next, Brewer."

Brewer nodded and tightened his grip on the wheel as they slid by the black wrought iron fence that separated the cemetery pathway from Elk Creek Road. Two quick jolts as the truck jumped the curb and slammed down on the thoroughfare. Brewer pushed the pedal hard enough that his leg straightened and his body rose in his seat, and they finally picked up speed.

Lucy looked back despite the eerie feeling that she'd turn to see another muzzle flash and then nothing at all, ever again. She could see Brumke, rifle up and leaning over the cab. She could see the sedan, limping along behind Luke Olsen's rig, one of its tires flattened and sending off smoke as it tried to keep pace.

"Yes! The car's dying!"

And that was how it really felt to Lucy—the car was an animal; it wanted to kill and eat them, but by some luck the creature had been injured and might in turn die. She saw the shapes of what once were children in that car, now slaves to their spasms and worst urges, and she hoped that the car would burst into flames and they would burn alive in the belly of the beast they'd enslaved and brought into the hunt.

A streetlamp twenty yards out exploded, and both Brewer and Lucy flinched at the sound of another shot from the rifle.

"Why the fuck doesn't he shoot *us*?" Brewer asked.

"I don't know. Having fun? Like this gets them off or fixes whatever is wrong with them, for a second. So maybe they're edging right now, and once they get ahold of us, once they kill us, it's all over. That nut's busted, and they have to find more people."

"Maybe they think we know where there are more people?"

"Could be. I mean, they're fucking crazy, so who knows? Can we still make it to the Double D?"

Brewer shook his head. "They ran down our gas. And listen . . ."

Something under the truck was clanking hard, metal on metal keeping pace with high RPMs.

"What's our next-best option?"

"Downtown, maybe?" Lucy had an idea, but pegged it as a massively hard sell given Brewer's loadie instincts. "We could pull into the police station parking lot."

"We come charging through inside whatever's left of this truck and they'll think we're infected or whatever. They'll shoot us."

"Yeah . . . maybe. But at least they'll shoot those shitbirds behind us too."

And Lucy knew Brewer must finally be as bludgeoned as her, because she could feel them both nodding and thinking, *Fuck it. If we die, we die. But at least we'll take those murderous cocksuckers down with us. And then it's over.*

So Brewer cut left at the next roundabout, the one with the huge bronze bear that Lucy used to be quite fond of back when she lived in a world where someone could stop and give a damn about something like a sculpture. For another two blocks, the world rolled by, familiar streets she'd known now rendered alien in zoetrope headlight flickers, every angle and shadow new menace, every possibility feeling like inevitable death, and Lucy wondered if her jaw would ever unclench or if her teeth would be ground to dust. She figured people were born with a certain amount of mileage their hearts and minds could withstand, and she was running hers down at top speed.

If seeing "the incident" at school gave me PTSD, what is all this *doing? What happens if the trauma never goes "post"? And even if this ends, what will be left of the world? What will be left of me?*

Lucy blinked against the notoriously bright streetlamps that indicated they were entering the downtown shopping district. They were ostensibly installed as antitheft discouragement at the urgings of the Turner Falls Business Commission, though; an alternate theory said they were put in place to disorient drunk drivers, as they consistently neglected to turn on their headlights as a result of the artificial wall of sun streaming down. Either idea seemed plausible to Lucy, though both transgressions felt quaint in light of what the city was up against this evening.

Your big bright lights can't stop what's coming.

She looked back to see the sedan had finally gone from limping to full collapse. Four kids—Male? Female? Did it matter?—rushed from the vehicle, running to catch up, vaulting into the bed of Luke Olsen's truck, which sped back into pursuit before the last new passenger was even aboard. The kid didn't get a solid grip and went tumbling from the truck bed, head striking the curb at an angle that Lucy, even from a distance, could tell was deathly wrong. The kid was immobilized, but Lucy could imagine the screeching noise that was surely coming from its neck.

The sky behind the truck was shifting, a light purple tint that made the mountains glow. A new day was on its way, and Lucy's eyes floated from the sunrise to the truck and back to the light and wondered if the sun might help to end the nightmare, or if it would only make everything more real.

Good morning, Turner Falls! Murder squads, military blockades, and mind-pulverizing audio transmissions got you feeling like you woke up on the wrong side of bed? Head downtown to try one of our newest offerings: suicide by cop!

But maybe we don't have to die . . .

"Bucket, what are you wearing under your jacket? Same old shirt?"

He wore a tight-fitting white T-shirt with a breast pocket almost every time they went to a party. Ashley Jorgenson—god rest her face-biting, rock-demolished soul—once told Bucket it looked good on him. Even asked him if he'd been lifting. So of course he wore it to *every* party after that.

"Yeah. My good-luck shirt. Why?"

"I think we can surrender. Let the cops know we come in peace."

Bucket pulled the zipper down on his hoodie. "Fuck." A section near the top was bloodstained—His own/Ashley's/Jake's? All of the above?—but the rest was pristine white.

We can wrap the bloody part around the top of my wrench. Conceal it.

"You think we can roll up and show 'em a T-shirt and they won't feel froggy enough to shoot?" Brewer asked.

"One hundred percent maybe. They see us waving a white flag, then look back and see a batch of shaky assholes aiming a rifle, maybe they can figure it all out."

"The Turner Falls PD?"

Brewer's limited faith came with good reason—the Turner Falls Police Department was so bad at investigation that in the early '90s they actually made a list of small towns with the greatest number of unsolved homicides, prompting a Jay Leno monologue joke where he said, "So, if you need to murder somebody, maybe head on over to Turner Falls, Oregon" (further prompting the studio audience to laugh in a way Lucy was sure would be appreciated by the families of Turner Falls' still-unavenged murder victims).

"I know. Maybe they figure it out. Maybe they don't. If you're sitting on a better idea, you can fucking . . ."

A stop sign a few yards ahead of their truck folded in half, pocked by silver craters. The sound of the gunshot came from closer than before, causing everybody but Jake to flinch and look back.

Luke's overloaded truck was closing the distance.

Can they sense we're planning something?

Brewer said, "All right. Let's try it."

"It's my favorite shirt, you guys."

"Buck, I'll fuckin' buy you a new one. Besides, that stain ain't comin' out. Trust me."

Lucy liked the way Brewer understood what it was like to deal with bloodstained clothing.

Jesus. When did I turn into a fucking cave girl? First real kiss and my first time committing multiple murders happened the same night. There's no way that's not hardwiring something shitty into my brain right about now. I'm not sure who I was ever supposed to be, but I can't be . . . this.

Lucy imagined some future where the Hendersons awakened to discover their adopted daughter—who they had saved and cared for in every way they knew how—was listed among the other teens responsible for a citywide murder spree, and she saw her body shrouded after their police confrontation, riddled with too many defensive rounds to allow for an open coffin, and she realized she would leave the Hendersons with nothing but empty hearts and a series of unanswerable "whys." Or worse, they'd answer those "whys" by damning themselves, and it would destroy them.

I have to live. For these boys. For the Hendersons.

She was about to wonder why she hadn't placed herself on her own list of reasons to stay alive, but the thought was too frightening. She pushed it away.

"Give me the shirt, Bucket. You look hotter in your red polo anyway."

"I do?"

Was he blushing?

Bucket Marwani, king of situation-inappropriate biological responses.

"Shit, dude . . . You always look good to me." She'd never said anything like that before, but it was true, and he had to know that their mutual low-key crush was part of what sustained their friendship. And they were probably going to die soon anyway, so she figured she might as well put it out there. "Now give me your fucking shirt."

She turned all the way around and reached her hands into the back seat to hold Bucket's jacket while he stripped off the white tee, looking beyond him and wondering if the kids in the truck would soon catch on to their plan and deliver a fatal shot through Brewer's head and hope the rest of his cargo lived long enough to kill. With that thought, she felt flush with anger again, and she hated *them* for making her feel that way, but her fury only amplified.

All of this is a trap. They rigged the game. How do I stop playing . . .

And then Bucket had one arm out of his shirt, and Lucy saw his eyes widen, and suddenly he was yelling, and Brewer said, "Holy fuck!" and slammed on the brakes. Lucy faced forward and saw that they had finally made it downtown, where all the businesses were closed and a few were engulfed in flames. Even stranger, the streets weren't as empty as they'd hoped, because just to the left of their truck was a man in khakis and a dress shirt screaming and waving at them, and dead center in their headlights was a girl who had staggered her way to midstreet, her head wrapped in tinfoil, her fingers furiously probing an angry red-and-black shape on the back of her neck, and she turned to look at the oncoming truck with terrified bright blue eyes, and then Brewer cranked the wheel hard left and was lucky enough to steer between the man and the hunched-over girl, but was also unlucky enough to slam the front of his rig directly into one of the hyperactive streetlamps, which lit the area like noonday sun.

Lucy felt their momentum transform, the seat belt a python around her chest, something moving too fast between her and Brewer and slamming into the windshield as her own head sledgehammered the dented dash. Then ticking and hissing and gasoline and melted rubber, and she was a little girl again and Mom and Dad weren't making a sound and she was trapped, always trapped, always in that moment, a girl who never had control.

But that couldn't be true because there was no bus this time and no one yelling in Spanish, and to her right, in the flickering of the dying streetlamp, she saw a jacked-up Ford attempt to navigate the sudden wreckage by pulling right too far and too fast and the center of gravity would not hold and the monstrous predator-ridden beast that had pursued them ejected its subhuman cargo in a rain of bodies as it rolled.

There would have been joy in that moment—seeing her hunters vanquished, the rifle split in two, the modded truck crunching inward, bodies slamming into asphalt and brick walls, bones shattering and skin peeling back and painting everything in red and strangest blue—but Lucy wasn't sure there was any glory left in all this destruction, because her friends were far too silent and all she could hear was tempered glass rattling down and in the distance a girl was screaming, "Why didn't they kill me? *Why can't I fucking die?*" and that was the last thing she heard before the streetlight above ceased its flickering and slipped with Lucy into darkness.

Transcript, *Nightwatchman* Podcast Episode 258, Uploaded 6/8/21, 02:14 a.m.:

Welcome to another broadcast for the thinkers, drinkers, freaks, geeks, smokers, jokers, fornicators, freedom fighters, and other fuckups who populate these early hours. As always, you're listening to the Nightwatchman, the only man brave enough to tell you the truth, the one media source you can depend on, throwing you the life preserver of legitimate facts in this ever-stormier sea of lies we call the big ol' US of A.

We gotta start tonight's show by talking about the latest hot spot for what has got to be a coordinated dis-info program. I'm speaking, of course, about the idyllic tourist trap of Turner Falls, Oregon. Now, if you go back to episode two fifty-one, you'll recall Turner Falls was the site of the Miller family murder-suicide, which was sadly just the beginning of this town's recent troubles. And if you were listening to episode two fifty-seven, you know all about the incident with the disappearing school shooting. If you've forgotten about *that* or you need more info, please head on over to our special member site and peel that onion and input your user-specific Nightwatch code and see what I'm talking about. Might be we've got nothing at all, and I say that for the fake friends and fed fuckwits out there, because we know you're listening.

Or it might be we've got a handful of the screen caps, which have all but disappeared from the web, showing there was both a student-on-teacher assault, possibly even a homicide, and then some kind of unidentified but heavily armed response force that either ended that student's life or took him into custody. We don't know, we really don't know the scope of what went on there at Spring Meadow High, but I'll tell you what we DO know:

1. There were over fifty-eight video files of the event, shot from different angles, some actively witnessing and some only in proximity to the event, and those videos all surfaced across social media within minutes of the occurrence. And then, minutes later . . . NOTHING. Vanished, aside from a few photos saved by intrepid members of the Nightwatch, because we know a thing or two about how the truth can simply disappear.

2. Not only did we catch the rapid erasure of those files, but any and all attempts at phone follow-up were met by the sudden failure of ALL cell providers who service the Turner Falls area. Are they blocked on their end? Are we blocked on our end? Are they letting a few family calls through to prevent panic and outside interest? I couldn't tell you. And there's no explanation forthcoming—nothing about satellite blockage or sunspots or windstorms. NOTHING. Now, I have to tell you, when we've seen that kind of prolonged silence in the past, when they don't even try to offer some feasible propaganda . . . that gets my hackles up even worse. You add in the fact that some people are reporting that emails and PMs regarding the Spring Meadow incident have ALSO mysteriously disappeared, and it becomes clear that we're looking at something beyond a cover-up. What-

ever this is, it's got arms and legs, folks, and even if we can't see all the connections yet . . . well, you can feel them at work, can't you?

So, since we remain devoted to the undiluted truth, and since we could tell that standard methods of communication weren't going to illuminate shit, we've done what they USED to do in real journalism and sent an ace. Longtime friends of the show know we have our sources among those discontent with the restraints placed on their ethics and veracity by the corporate conglomerate info pimps who call themselves the modern media, and one of those brave knights has already been dispatched to the Turner Falls area. So certainly stay tuned for that.

In the meantime, our crack team of researchers and even some of you over at the forum have been doing the deep dive for dirt on the Turner Falls area and the probable causes for this unconscionable media blackout, and I've gotta tell you . . . something *stinks.* I'm not just talking about those skunky, overhopped IPAs they keep pumping out of the region either, though, as you'll hear, they could be part of the problem. No, I'm talking about the kinds of things we find when we FOLLOW THE FUCKING MONEY. I'm talking about the scorpions and rattlers you reveal when you flip a few rocks out there in the high desert.

Some listeners are going to say, "What are you talking about, NW? The wife and I visited Turner Falls last year. We hit the slopes, did the brewery tour, then ended the evening having champagne in our hot tub while the sun set over the mountains, and it was lovely." And to those listeners I would say the following:

Did you know there are two different proposals in place to route massive irrigation lines into the Turner Falls area? We're talking years of work, hundreds of millions in taxpayer funds. They want one line coming out of the Columbia, another coming over from the Snake. Hundreds of miles of line pulling water from two rivers to a town that's already got its own river running right through the damn middle. Now, if you told me it was solely to replenish eastern Oregon agriculture—and there is mention of that in the proposal—I'd give it more credence. But they want these lines running all the way into Turner Falls. And for what? Golf courses? Breweries? I don't buy it. They have their runoff, their river, and fresh water coming straight off the Metolius too. So does it have to do with the possible privatization of the assets linked to both rivers? The new administration would LOVE to shift all that hydropower out of fed control and into the greasy grubbing hands of their corporate buddies. Or is it possible that the proposal is linked to the proposed multimillion-dollar prepper community that happened to launch at the same time all those massive data centers got approved for their regional tax breaks? Is it insane, folks, is it really that crazy to think that the ultra-rich people who are buying up all that beautiful land might also want to ensure they have a steady-flowing supply of fresh water in and around their enclave? Imagine you have access to all the information and the brightest minds money can buy. Imagine you can see what's coming—the uprisings, the mass displacements, and especially, ESPECIALLY, the water wars. You can see it because you had a hand in engineering it. Now imagine you found exactly the right territory to ride out the next revolution, with a power grid that flows as easy and cheap as the mighty rivers and a wall of mountains between you and a rising ocean. Is it crazy to think you might want to consolidate your sources of power—all those data centers—and your electric power and your state-of-the-art survival housing, and most important, your food and water all in one damn region? So, yeah, anybody who isn't paying attention to fresh water as a finite asset, anybody who isn't watching where that water's being routed and secured, anybody who doesn't think the ghouls at the top would be willing to hoard those assets when the going gets tough . . . well, I don't like to disparage, but that person would be a damn fool.

So get this, folks . . . I wish those pipeline proposals were all we'd found. I WISH. But when you make a career out of flipping rocks and shedding light, you see a lot of the darkness. And it's tough, because the mind starts to boggle. You want to shine a light; you have to . . . It's an American duty, hell, a HUMAN duty, but sometimes you see these demons at work and you want to turn away. But we won't do that. I promise you. So I gotta tell you, there's more.

Did you ever hear about a little Turner Falls company that goes by the name of IMTECH? If you were paying extra-close attention back around episode two fifty-one, the name might seem familiar, and we'll get to that. But it's not a name that rings out for the general population, and I have a funny feeling they've mostly liked it that way up until now. So IMTECH . . . They started out small, specializing in synthetic, silicon-based skin. By all accounts they did well with their area of expertise, and their skin helped a lot of folks, including burn victims and people who had heart attacks or epilepsy. Their product did a lot for our vets in this era of the cowardly IED. And I applaud all that. But lately it appears they've changed focus. We've got sources indicating that financials released to investors reflect the company's assets at twenty times what they were in the prior year, including a new research and development facility on the outskirts of Turner Falls. Now, canny listeners will pick up on that phrase "research and development" and have some idea of where I'm heading with this. Would you be surprised to hear that two of IMTECH's executives, the fellas who launched the company back when it was called Integrated Medical Technology, Inc., got their seed money from Tremmel Logistics? Again, not a name that rings out, but an important one, because Tremmel Logistics designed the computer chips that guided the Patriot missiles we used in our quaint little Desert Storm, which further means that Tremmel Logistics had their paws deep in the DARPA pocketbook.

So now we've got ourselves a small medical company that's suddenly not very small at all, run by missile-making eggheads with DARPA connections. And according to their own press release, they're working on something that stands to 'revolutionize the way we interact with our world.' These folks, this once-tiny company nestled in a tourist trap, filed more patents than Google last year. You know what kind of capital that takes? More than you're going to get hawking fake skin to burn victims, that is certain. But more concerning, dear listeners, far more concerning, if you ask me, are the FDA "device approval" filings our sources have unearthed. Because normally, folks, normally, if you want to sell an implant, something that the consumer will permanently place inside their body, you have to jump through some hoops. I'm talking institutional reviews and test monitoring and premarket monitoring and early feasibility studies and animal testing and periodic reviews and device clearances and risk assessments, and all of THAT has to happen before you can even talk to a human being about paying them to be a test subject. Which normally I might call government overreach, but when you're making an object that might be installed inside the body of a loved one, well . . . this might be a case where the rigor is warranted.

However, my friends, I have to tell you that our research does not show IMTECH meeting any of those rigors. Rather, the records we've obtained show the FDA rolling over like a family dog that wants you to pet its sweet little belly. Within one month—ONE MONTH, folks—of IMTECH's initial application we see a note reading "Unanticipated adverse device effect concerns sufficiently mitigated via extra-agency verifications. Requirements of 21 CFR 812 met, Investigational Device Exemption (IDE) *granted.*" As an easy point of comparison here, let's talk about the nicotine patch. That thing only sits on the surface of your skin and contains a chemical that had already been heavily researched. And guess how long it took for the FDA to approve that? Thirty-nine months. How about the pacemaker? Eighty-three months. Even now, slightly improved pacemakers can take years to reach the market. But you're telling me that this little company out of Turner Falls makes a device that not only goes inside the body, but contains more groundbreaking technology than the Google overlords managed to conjure up last year, and THAT gets an exemption?

You can't hear it through the microphone, folks, but I just got goose bumps. Because there it is: the same people who taught missiles how to sneak down a chimney like Santa Claus—the same people who live in a region rapidly filling with gargantuan data centers from some of our most powerful and pernicious corporations—might be using DARPA money and influence to fast-track some kind of bioelectronics device into the bodies of American citizens. In fact, the good people at IM-TECH say we may see this product demonstrated as early as this summer, lucky us, and by Christmas you can even buy their stock. Rest assured, we will have a member of the *Nightwatchman* crew on hand for the debut of this new technology. And you can also rest assured that if this product is in any way another effort to place chips in the bodies of free human beings, we will be calling for an immediate global boycott of their stock and other offerings. I've said it before, and I hope there will be a day in the future where I don't have to say it anymore—I don't think they want to chip us with the Mark of the Beast, I think they want to chip us to mark us as beasts.

Now, you're wondering something . . . I mentioned the Miller case earlier, that tragic—and tragically questionable—murder-suicide that seems nearly quaint in light of what we're now discovering about the area. You happen to remember who the father in that case, Mr. Samuel Miller, happened to work for? I bet you can guess. But would you guess that new revelations in that crime, and maybe even pressure from our devoted NW listeners, have led to him finally being sought as a person of interest in the case? Which certainly makes sense. But now—and thanks for playing along at home—guess who cannot be located by the police? That's right! Samuel Miller, development lead and high muckety-muck at IMTECH, has disappeared. Relatives we spoke to say they haven't heard from him. IMTECH stonewalled our communications. And there's no indication the police force has any idea where he's gone. On top of that, our requests for something as simple as a cause of death for either Julie or Brady Miller have been met with sternly worded emails about Oregon's disclosure laws, and claims that we've presented neither "legitimate" nor "substantial" interest in that information. Which tells you how much they value THE TRUTH as a justification. But get this . . . They've also denied that information to the Miller's next of kin. So all I see here are walls going up. All I see are bureaucrats and corporations protecting themselves from the light we're trying to shine.

Holy hell, folks. Holy hell . . . Like I said, I hate when I'm right about something like this, but it is now an undeniable fact that something is terribly amiss in Turner Falls. So obviously we'll be keeping you posted as this situation develops. We're waiting on remote contact from our ace in the area, and there may even be unscheduled new podcasts as we discover more. Because obviously, OBVIOUSLY, the events in Turner Falls, Oregon, are being obfuscated by some kind of pernicious cover-up. And I know, because the internet is full of ding-dongs, that within the hour there will be memes with pictures of me screaming, "THEY'RE STEALING WATER AND MAKING GAY ROBOT MERBABIES" or some kind of nonsense, because the folks who know what's happening in Turner Falls don't want you to hear my voice. THEY don't ever want us to know the TRUTH. These are the people who forgot to put the word "Destruction" in between "Patriot" and "Act." These are the people who want you to forget running behind DDT trucks, and Tuskegee, and MK, and nuclear ashes falling over Tularosa. At least the army saw fit to claim the Los Alamos detonation was only an "ammunition explosion." In Turner Falls, right now, no one is claiming anything at all. They don't want us to talk about it. They don't want us to know about it.

But we will, folks. We will. Because the night is long, our watch is eternal, and our eyes are sharpened by the light of the truth. And if that's the kind of truth and the kind of reporting you need in your life, and with my hand over my heart I believe it is, then be certain to like and subscribe, and even better, become a contributing member of the *Nightwatchman* crew and get early access to the merchandise that allows us to keep this tiny candle lit out here in the deep dark.

And as always, dear listener, stay tuned and stay free.

PART THREE

CLASS/WARFARE

chapter eleven

TRAPPED VOICES

L ucy figured she'd murdered her way right out of heaven, but wherever she'd ended up after she died in the truck crash seemed pretty nice. She hadn't realized how cold she'd been all night, but now her body, wherever it was, felt warm. She couldn't tell where her arms began or ended, but she sensed they were pressing against something soft. There were other sensations—flat, hard concrete beneath her, a throbbing across her forehead and eyes—but they floated in and out enough to be disregarded. One eyelid felt like it had been cut open and stuffed with hot cotton, but the other was only tender. She tried to open it, but a beam from someone's nearby flashlight shot in and transformed the throb in her forehead into a fist hammering down, so she decided she didn't need to see.

Nobody was screaming. Nobody was threatening her. Nobody was hunting her.

Maybe it *was* heaven.

Being dead was so easy.

Voices came in waves. They didn't speak Spanish, so Lucy knew she hadn't been reunited with her parents or her ancestors, but she

recognized all of them, or thought she did. Though they were sometimes too loud or fearful in a way she thought might pull her from this
good place, they were also concerned and caring and she allowed them
to enter the space her mind occupied as it floated in and out of the
silent, divine nothingness she hoped she'd one day be allowed to join.

———————

"So is that all you have here?" An older man's voice, worried. New to
Lucy.

"Yeah. It's enough to satisfy OSHA requirements. It's not like we
have a lot of on-the-job injuries." A younger man's voice, slightly an-
noyed.

Judah? From The Exchange?

"I have a mini first aid kit in my car, but that's over at the Boiler
Room, and there's *no way* I'm going back out there." A woman's voice.

*Toni/Antoinette. But something has happened. I've never heard her so
shaken up.*

"M'okay, I'mokayanyway." Slurred speech from a boy.

Maybe Jake? He was still alive?

"Actually, this *is* the best he's been all night. I thought he was
dying earlier, but now it looks like the duct tape accidentally fixed him
up. What are the fuckin' odds, man? But I guess it was invented for injuries anyway, right? Or was that super glue?"

Brewer.

"It was super glue."

"Yeah, you're right. But maybe duct tape should be used more for
this kind of thing too. I mean, that chunk that ripped loose from my
truck window's holding his scalp together real nice. You gotta fix that
eye patch, though, Jake . . . It's rough to look at . . . Careful . . . Jesus,
you're being too sloppy with your mitts . . . Here, I'll help ya . . .
and . . . *there.*"

"Thanks."

"Anytime, bud."

———————

The older man's voice again. "There's swelling we need to worry about with each of them, and I think the Indian kid might have an internal bleed."

Is he talking about Bucket?

"You keep saying that shit like suddenly this place is going to turn into a hospital. What we have is what we have, all right? I'm here almost every day, and I know for certain there's no hidden operating room or stash of medical supplies. Just stacks and stacks of CDs that nobody is ever going to buy, some novelty crap, and a few black light posters. So if we can't help these kids with some gauze and a couple of ice packs, then we need to get them out of here. And if you have an awesome idea about how we can pull that off without attracting a gang of those fucking psychopaths, then I'm in. Otherwise you have to stop asking."

"I'm sorry. You're right. I only . . . I want to help."

"If you want to help, maybe don't go treating a used music store like it's the triage center at the ER. Or better yet, don't go chasing weird little girls with tinfoil hats into traffic, or causing multiple wrecks, or talking to me like I'm some subordinate of yours."

Judah's pissed. But he always seems a little pissed.

Is that girl here too?

Why can't I hear her? Why can't I hear Bucket?

———————

"It's not right."

Toni was whispering, standing above Lucy.

She doesn't think I can hear her. Am I dead? Maybe I am dead. *Am I stuck in this body?*

Lucy tried to open her eyes again, and instantly regretted the pain that washed over her. She attempted to soothe herself.

Be still. Stay calm. You're at The Exchange. I think the boys that were chasing you died in the wreck, and you're still here. And if more of them are coming for you, then you have to rest right now.

Judah whispered back to Toni. "You saw her eyes, though. She's one of them. Even if she's not trying to attack us right now, she could. She has to stay tied up."

"What if she dies? Right here, in this building, while we have her fucking tied up. Are you ready for that? What if Steve gave her too much of Blumpers's insulin?"

"He said it was a small dose. Just enough to keep her woozy and disoriented. And it's cat medicine, right? She's way bigger than a cat."

"Yeah, that's what we'll tell a judge, Judah. *We helped a strange man tie up that little girl and inject her with insulin because she had fucking blue eyes and we were afraid she'd murder us and she was bigger than a cat.* That should work out great."

"Think about what they did to Trevor in the parking lot. You ever see two kids do that to a grown man? To a *bouncer*? His leg was goddamn *backward*, Toni, and they were laughing. This isn't a 'rule of law' situation anymore. Whatever's got into these kids, they're fucking crazy now. And that girl is sick like them."

"But Steve says she's different."

"Sure. And who exactly is Steve? That might not even be his name. And what was he doing, following this girl around?"

"He seems like he knows a lot of medical stuff, at least."

"Really? Like I couldn't tell you to put ice on swelling and wrap injuries in gauze."

"Listen, I don't know him any better than you. It's true. He could be some Grade-A fucking super creeper for all I know. But when those trucks wrecked, he was the first one to rush in and start pulling those kids loose, and they all seem to be alive for now, so that's something."

"Okay. I get that. But I'm not giving him any more of the cat's insulin. I'm not going to watch him kill that girl in front of us."

"Me either, all right? I promise."

And Lucy heard the rustling of clothing as Judah and Toni embraced, and she heard each of them try to take deep breaths and fail.

———————

"So it was mostly kids from the Butte who got infected?"

"I think so."

Judah and Brewer. They're close to me. Exhausted. Delirious.

Brewer continued. "There was a second party in the back cave. Nobody I knew was invited. Jason Ward was back there, and those . . . *things* I told you about came out of him and swarmed the other kids. So fast. Then they lost their minds. Started twitching. Killing people. They've been hunting us all night."

"So now those guys have gone from selfish little assholes to super-charged murderous assholes? That's *great*."

"I don't know. They weren't *all* assholes. Some of them were only along for the ride. And some of 'em were decent if you got 'em alone. They were, like, assholes by contamination. Definitely some bad eggs in that crew, though."

"Sometimes I used to think it was because they had everything handed to them, right? They got whatever they asked for. No stress or worries, so they did all that fucked-up shit because it was their way to finally feel something. Then they get hooked on that, and there are no consequences, not really, and it becomes a habit. That's how it felt when I was at Spring Meadow, at least."

"Still bothers you, huh?"

"Yeah. Which I know is fucking lame—like here I am, in my hometown, still mad at the rich kids and jocks and general psychopaths, and all the awful shit they got away with—but I can't help it. When you're a kid, that's when you feel everything so much. Everything counts. Everything is as intense as it will ever be. Now, with this adult bullshit, it's all so repetitive that a year disappears in a blink. It's like I only half feel any day that I live, even the great ones. It sucks . . . It's not just sour grapes from my high school days, though. The divide runs between the adults too. Remember that big coke bust back in 2008? Kenny Parsons and Brian Heald got busted doing the same shit, but look at which one of them is still in jail. Once they seized his assets, Brian was back to having nothing, but Kenny had his parents' money to lean on. They bought his way right out of jail time. Couple weeks ago I was looking at the paper and saw Kenny won some 'Developer of the Year' award from the chamber of commerce. So even after high school, man, they live in a different world from us. Same city, but a different world."

"Not anymore, though."

"What do you mean? The situation is the same as ever. The rich kids are just faster and better at what they've always done."

"What's that?"

"Using us. Throwing us away. And you know whatever's gotten into them was made by some huge-ass corporation, and when the dust settles the executives will all get golden parachutes and float on over to the next empty spot waiting for some asshole to fill it, and all we'll be is a footnote. A casualty statistic."

"Shoot, man. Maybe. That's usually how it goes, right? But I don't know about this situation. This *whole city* is on fire, man. I don't think these guys are checking bank balances before they start murdering people. Could be the old rules, rich, poor, none of it means much anymore. These kids are like rabid dogs. You can feel bad for 'em because they're sick, but there aren't a lot of choices when you cross their path: you gotta run and hope you're fast enough, or kill 'em as quick as you can."

"Yeah. It's fucked up, but I used to *dream* of a day like this. Pitchforks and guillotines. The people's uprising. 'Eat the rich' and all that. This scenario should give us carte blanche for that."

"But now?"

"I don't know anymore. It was only a fantasy. It's like you get sick from the anger and the helplessness of living in this fucked-up system, and you feel like destruction might be the only way to shut it all down."

"Sure."

"But when I try to picture a utopia, where we, like, all rise above, and we're kind and we grow as a species, I can't see it. So either I'm too dumb to have that kind of vision, or I'm just smart enough to know that humans could never pull it off. It's *way* easier to imagine dystopia, and war, and all the bullshit we've been living in. But now that's here, it's right outside our door, and I hate it, and it's weird, but I feel like it's kind of my fault. Like I should have hoped for more. Done more."

"That ain't fair, dude. That's some delusional superhero shit. But I get what you're saying. It's hard not to feel that way. I used to wake up around three in the morning with this crazy anxiety, feeling that way, like all the world's problems are mine to fix. I told my grandma about it, back when she was still trying to raise me and Rodney, and she told me I was a fool. She said, 'Every morning when you wake up, I want you to make two promises to yourself. One, you'll do your best to stay healthy and keep living. Two, you'll be as good as you can to others and yourself.' And that's it."

"You think if everybody did that we'd have a utopia?"

"Fuck if I know, dude. I know it helped me, for whatever that's worth. But then you get into a situation like this one, and doing any of that shit feels pretty much impossible. So what I'm hoping for now is to find some way that me, and Lucy, and all of us can find someplace away from all these assholes where we can at least try to be good again."

"That's a nice idea."

"Yeah. It's all I got."

"There's no employee lounge? Some little kitchenette in the back?"

"Nope."

"How do you eat lunch during a shift?"

"We're downtown. I walk somewhere and grab a bite."

"What if you're alone on your shift?"

"I nuke stuff with the little microwave under the counter, then burn a stick of the nag champa we use to cover up the smell of Blumpers's diabetes shits."

"Any tinfoil under there?"

"No, dude. I just told you, we only have the microwave. You think I'm throwing tinfoil in there?"

Judah sounded on edge, but also restrained in a way she hadn't heard from him before.

"What about a mini fridge for leftovers or drinks? Maybe there's some old food wrapped in foil?"

"Nope. I am a proud first-round finisher of burritos, and Toni brings homemade stuff inside a little plastic freezer bag."

"Okay . . . *fuck*." The older man—*Steve?*—forced a breath out through his nose, clearly frustrated. "How's your cell signal here?"

"It's shit. I mostly have to browse on the work computer and get landline calls. These old brick building are pretty, but they definitely don't help my signal."

"That's good, then. We've got that going for us. Any idea if there's a metal frame under the masonry? Have you seen any exposed metal beams?"

"No. I mean, I have no idea. Why?"

"If there was some way . . . a generator in a nearby building, or maybe if we could kill the breaker and tap the main electric line and run it to the metal, we could turn this whole place into some kind of Faraday cage . . . but even then we couldn't do any kind of frequency control to match the satellite—"

"Wait. You want to send a countersignal? Didn't Iran do something like that when they didn't want people seeing the news about the revolution?"

"Yeah, they did. But how the hell do you know about that?"

"Dude, I work at a record store. All I have is time. I mostly read and take care of Blumpers, so . . ."

"Salt. What about salt? You have any by the microwave?"

"Now you're talking, dude. No canister of Morton's, but we have a big-ass bowl of take-out condiments, and there are a bunch of salt packets in there."

"Good." Lucy startled as the man clapped his hands. "That's *something*. You pour those out, and I'll sort the salt."

"All right, man."

"And we'll need some kind of plastic or metal basin. Best if it's metal. Please tell me you have something like that."

"Maybe in storage."

"What about water? Is the bathroom sink all you use for that?"

"No. We've got a spigot in the receiving bay that we use to fill the mop bucket."

"Even better. We need that mop bucket filled with fresh, clean water, and we need to saturate it with as much salt as we possibly can."

"I'm on it. But you mind telling me what we're doing? I'm not about to waterboard that little girl . . ."

"No. No! Of course not. Listen . . . there's a device inside that girl's neck, in Marisol's neck, and it's malfunctioning very, *very* badly, and despite that she's been able to control what's happening to her in a way that most of the test . . . most *people* have not been able to. And if we're going to try to stop what's happening, we need to find out what makes her different and then *maybe* we can help the others who have been affected. But that device in her neck wants to communicate with a satellite with an incredibly strong, very specific signal, and if they get back on a full uplink . . ."

"Those things will find us."

"They'll find us. They'll know what we're trying to do. And they will tear us, and her, to pieces."

Lucy heard Judah crossing the store toward the receiving bay, moving with new urgency.

"Istrue? Yer a . . . dancer over at Boiler?" Jake's speech was improving.

"It's true. I am a dancer," said Toni. "Or I was. Your friends burned that place to the ground tonight. Killed my friend too. I think they would have killed me. Some girl wearing a Coach backpack jumped on me the same time your pals started kicking my bouncer to death."

"Not my pals."

Lucy heard the hurt in his voice.

Is he seriously mad that his Brower Butte buddies hadn't brought him into their fucked-up fold? Is this his first time feeling rejected?

"Really. You guys aren't friends anymore?"

"Theybeenweird since, uh . . . since the incident. Said I screamed too much when I got attacked. Said I was a little bitch."

"Have any of them had their eyes gouged out?"

"No."

"So how do they know how you're supposed to act?"

"I know. They said I shouldabeen able to beat Chris back. Brumke said it wasn't like Chris had any muscles because all he ate was government cheese. But theydin'tfeel how strong he was. How crazy."

Jake sat in the silence of his memory for a moment, then said, "Can I ask you 'nother question?"

The tone in his voice changed. He's embarrassed. He feels weak. He's going to try to push that away.

Toni said, "Sure," and Jake said, "Is it true you suck parking lot dick for money?"

Toni made a clicking sound with her tongue—a tiny noise that

Lucy managed to hear as both disappointment and *This motherfucker*—
then asked, "Do I look like your mother?"

"No."

"Are you sure? Because you seem to have mistaken me for a whore."

Lucy heard the hard *clack-clack* of Toni walking away and then she
heard Jake's voice, quiet and sad.

"Shit . . . I'm sorry."

Toni turned. "Really? Sorry because I walked away? Or sorry because you said some stupid, disrespectful shit?"

"Both, I guess."

"You guess?"

"Don't call my mom a whore, though. That's how my dad talks."

"Yeah?"

"Mmm-hmm."

"Well . . . that sucks, kid. I'm sorry for that. But you don't have to
be like your dad, all right?"

"Okay . . . okay."

And then Lucy heard Jake sniffle back snot, and she thought he
might be crying. To her further surprise, she felt Brewer's breath warm
on the side of her face and heard him say, "What do you know? Maybe
all that head trauma did Jake some good," and she realized that he'd
been sitting on the floor beside her for who knew how long.

———————

The thought of Brewer beside her had lulled her into the smallest sleep,
and she tried to stay inside that peaceful place, but then she felt his
hands on her shoulders and he was saying, "You gotta wake up, Lucy.
Wake up," in a way that sent a bolt of electricity through her entire body.

Something's wrong.

They found us.

She sat up too fast and the pressure in her head thudded from front to back and threatened to spill her over, but she wouldn't allow it, and her hands searched the cold concrete floor for her wrench because they had to go, they had to fight, they had to . . .

Brewer's arms wrapped around her, and she tried to push back at first, but then she managed to open her right eye just a slit and the look on his face didn't say *panic*.

It said something worse.

"It's Bucket, Lu. They think he's goin'."

Brewer lifted Toni's shawl from Lucy's chest and then wrapped his left arm through and under Lucy's and helped her to stand.

She knew what Brewer meant, knew it right away, but she told herself she wouldn't believe it until she saw Bucket. They took a series of gentle steps through the store, passed Jake, who had converted his crusty hoodie into a pillow and fallen asleep on the floor, then passed the corner of the jazz and bluegrass vinyl bins, and finally she saw the crumpled shape on the beige love seat by the listening station, and she knew they were right.

Brewer said, "He was the worst off, so we gave him the couch. Steve thinks he's got a rupture inside, from the wreck."

"The wreck. We were distracted. I wanted his shirt. That was *my* plan. He should have been holding on to that handle. Maybe . . ."

"No. That's bullshit. We were being chased. *They* did this, Lucy."

She looked at how small Bucket seemed. They'd folded his thin arms over his chest, and it reminded her of the time a baby bird ran into the big bay window at Bill and Carol's house and they buried it in a shoe box in the backyard.

The man that had to be Steve stood frowning near the head of the couch, his dress shirt now rumpled and half-untucked and smeared with blood from rescuing them from Brewer's truck.

"We don't have the facilities . . . I'm sorry. His blood pressure is dropping fast. He's already in hypovolemic shock, but he might be able to hear you. I thought you'd want a chance . . ."

"Yeah." She shook her head yes as her voice caught in her throat. "I do."

Lucy walked to the edge of the couch and gently lowered herself onto her knees.

They had used paper towels to wipe away most of the blood that had covered him after the wreck, but even without that, it was clear his face had been torn in five directions at once when he hit the windshield. Lucy wanted to kiss his forehead, but she was afraid that his face was one touch away from sliding off his skull, and so instead she lifted her right hand and placed it on his left and tried not to gasp at how cold he already felt.

How is this happening?

It's not. Still dreaming.

But it feels real.

Is real.

Goddamnit.

No.

She looked at him and leaned in toward his ear to help him hear, and she only managed to say, "Hey." before the tears came. And she thought that two days ago she might have felt embarrassed—all these people watching her, the sound of her crying so ugly and deeply personal to her—but when she looked at Bucket, and how certain it was that his life was ending, she no longer cared. Let them watch—this moment was hers and Bucket's and no one else's.

"I hope you can still hear me, Buck, because I need you to know that I love you, all right? I really do. I feel like I'm so, so grateful and lucky to have met you. I mean, you know that. You know all that. You made me feel like I wasn't so alone. Even when you were being a dick, it was like . . . oh god . . . we saw each other. We understood each other. And now, I don't know. This is fucked up. It sucks, it just fucking sucks, because we were supposed to leave this place together, right? And now *you* get to leave, *you* get to fucking bail, and I'm fucking stuck here all alone. And I don't know if I can do this without you. I didn't think I would have to. But I hope you hear me, Bucket. I hope you do. Because I love you, and I want you to know that you were a good person while you were here, okay? You were good."

And then she felt quite suddenly as if there was nothing more to be said, and she sat there with her hand on his and cried and felt her tears hot on her split and swollen face. Then she sensed a delicate hand on the center of her back, and she heard Toni say, "Can you help me? I want to help him go," and somehow Lucy understood, and so she worked quietly with Toni to lift his tortured head and narrow shoulders, and then Toni slid into the couch and laid Bucket's head across her lap. Lucy placed her hand back on Bucket's and Toni placed one hand on his barely rising chest and began to whisper, "It's okay, Bakhit. It's okay. Shhh. Shhh. Shhh. It's okay," and they stayed that way until the boy's chest failed to rise at all.

chapter twelve

MARISOL & STEVE

Lucy believed it was a good death, as far as those final moments were concerned, and even in her grief she found herself surprised that Bucket, the king of inappropriate bodily responses, had not recognized Toni's voice and touch and left them all with a stunning display of angel lust.

She nearly laughed at the thought until she realized his internal bleeding had probably killed his ability to erect that final gravestone. Instead she felt embarrassed, and a new wave of grief rolled through her.

My best friend is gone.

He found a way out of the nightmare. But he left me here, and I'm thinking about hard-ons next to his dead body.

Really healthy mind you got in here, Lucy.

She looked back at Bucket's face, so small and awfully pale.

It doesn't matter what I think. He thought filthy, depraved shit all the time and told me most of it. Imagine the stuff he wouldn't *tell me.*

And he was awesome. So it doesn't matter. We're all fucked up.

With that decided, she realized that she no longer felt any desire to be near the stillness of Bucket's body, so she stood and shook the tingles from the legs she'd trapped beneath her.

She looked at Toni. "Thank you."

Toni nodded.

"You want up?"

"Yeah, I think so."

They lifted Bucket once more, and Toni extricated herself and shook and shivered.

Toni said, "You feel him move through you when he went?"

"No."

"My mom was a nurse, and she told me that sometimes you feel them slide through you. Like their last energy or whatever it was that made them truly alive flows into you for a moment, then out, then they're gone. For what it's worth, I didn't feel it either, but . . ."

Lucy swayed for a second, and from beneath her she felt the surety and finality of Bucket's death reaching up to pull her down to the floor, deeper into her grief than she was willing to go, so she stepped forward and grabbed on to Toni and wrapped her arms around her and pressed the slightly less pummeled side of her face tight against the woman's chest and felt the beating of her heart.

One-two. One-two. One-two. One-two. The beating came into her, strong and steady, and there was joy in the sound of life continuing, the persistent motion of the heart and the feeling of it reverberating against her skin. She knew that she wanted to stay in that place for longer than Toni or the world would allow, so she held tight.

Then, as she had suspected, the world decided that Lucy could not stay inside that beautiful feeling, because there was a louder noise in the distance—thumping and muffled screams from what was probably the receiving bay—and then Judah emerged from behind the door with a panicked look on his face and yelled to them, "She's awake!"

The room smelled of cardboard shipping boxes and sweat and something worse beneath those which made Lucy think of seaweed rotting
on the shoreline, swarming with sand fleas. The girl sat, restrained by a
mixture of bungee cords and plastic stretch wrap, in a cheap wooden
chair which creaked with her incessant movement. A rickety metal
storage rack had been placed above her, its lower shelves removed,
its top shelf holding what Lucy assumed was the saltwater-filled mop
bucket. The girl's black hair emerged wild and curly from the edges of
the foil wrapped around the top of her head, and her face stayed in motion, the same series of vacillating tics Lucy had seen on Ben Brumke
when he pursued her in the tunnel.

"Can't feel like this . . . Make it stop . . ."

Steve slid past Judah and Toni and pulled a small flashlight from
his pocket and hunched close to the girl and said, "Marisol, I need you
to look straight at me if you can."

Marisol's head shook violently, but Lucy saw her jaw clench and
the vibrations waned and she managed to slow her body to a low
tremor and look into Steve's flashlight. And while one eye still radiated
an unnatural smear of bright blue, which seemed to have seeped
beyond the iris, Marisol's other eye, though bloodshot, was a plain
brown.

"What does that mean?" asked Judah. "Is she getting better?"

"Quiet, please." Steve sounded both excited and irritated. "I need
to speak with her."

Lucy felt Brewer come into the room, close over her right shoulder.

"Where were you?" whispered Lucy.

"I, uh . . . I used that shawl to cover Bucket. Seemed right."

Lucy wondered for a moment where and how this boy found the
decency and kindness that he radiated, and she felt a little less alone.
But then she pictured Bucket, so small and motionless beneath the
shawl, and she shivered.

Steve placed a hand on Marisol's knee and said, "I'm sorry we did all this to you. We couldn't risk it if you lost control. Or if *they* could see through you. Can you hear them right now?"

Lucy thought that the girl was about her age, maybe a year younger, but her voice emerged like a ninety-year-old's, thin and cracked and wavering with her uncontrolled movements. "I'm off, but I feel it calling. It itches, inside my skull. It wants back in. I need it, to stop this feeling. Please. Can I . . . can I let it in?"

"I wish you could, Marisol. I know this hurts. But if you connect to them, they'll pull you back into their loop. You'll want to hurt us. They'll come to help you hurt us, and we can't have that. If that happens, I can't help you."

"Please? Please. *Please*. It hurts."

"No." He paused for a moment, then said, "Do you remember what you did to Dr. Spencer?"

"Yes." Her face was pained for a second, then dull, then angry, then Marisol squeezed her eyes shut. "I'm sorry. I'm so sorry. I couldn't help it. I don't want to do anything like that ever again. I'm *trying*."

"I know. I know. *It wasn't your fault*. You have to know that. I'm not blaming you, all right? But that kind of thing can't happen again."

"Can you at least press on the spot, then?"

Lucy remembered the first time she'd seen Marisol, seconds before the crash, hunched and dazed and probing the back of her swollen neck with slick, shiny fingers. For a moment she blamed the girl for Bucket's death, but then she looked at her again and realized what Brewer told Judah was right: that was as fair as blaming a rabid dog.

"I'm not sure we should do that anymore, Marisol."

He keeps using her name. Humanizing her. Reminding her who she is.

Steve continued. "I think if you keep pressing, you might kill it. Then we won't be able to remove it, and if your body thinks the device is an infection then it'll attack itself and your brain will swell and—"

"That's fine. I can die. You can let me die. I deserve it for what I did."

"No. You don't deserve it. None of you deserve what's happened to you. This is our fault. Me, Marisol—it's my fault. And the other doctors. The engineers. The programmers. Everybody. We all should have known. But they're dead now, and I'm not sure what to do. I only know that if I don't fix this, it'll all get worse. So I need you to help me stop what's happening, okay?"

Lucy had never heard an adult sound so guilty and so desperate at the same time. Now she understood the urgency of his movements around the store, and the way his shoulders slumped beneath an unseen weight, and why he had saved them from the truck, and why he was trying to save them all.

He can't live with what he's done.

But does he know this can't be undone?

She hadn't felt such simultaneous worry for and anger at an adult since her birth parents died.

Marisol asked, "Can you take it out of me? I feel so sick. Something is moving inside me."

"I think it might be retracting. We gave you some insulin to stop you from communicating with them, and it made you very sick for a while. There's a chance—if it thinks you're dying—that it's going to look for a new body. I don't have a mirror to show you, but one of your eyes is better now."

"My right one. There's no blue or red anymore. No images."

"That's good. That's great!"

"But I can't see the bad scene anymore either."

"The bad scene?"

"What happened." Then, quietly, "*Dr. Spencer.* I shouldn't tell you, but I found a way to close my eyes and see that again. And I hate it, but it made the feeling stop for a little while. But now I'm so tired from whatever you shot into me. And there's something else. A new feeling, not only in my neck anymore. I feel it down low, swelling. So tired." Her trembling worsened as whatever control she'd exerted over her shaking faltered.

Steve put his hands to his face and slowly drew them down while he took a deep breath.

He doesn't know what's happening.

He's not in control.

None of us are in control.

Judah moved toward the girl, walking behind her and making certain the water bucket was centered over her head. He looked to Steve. "You sure this is blocking the signal? How do we know she isn't sending them our location right now?"

"If she were connected, her tremors would smooth. There's something happening in the transmission that's releasing enough dopamine to keep them moving. To keep them from being crippled by the twitching. And I think her other eye would turn blue again."

"You think? And how do we know those kids from the wreck haven't told them where we are? I swear I saw one of them crawling into the alley."

"We don't know. We have to hope that the trauma of the accident was sufficient to damage either their neurological capabilities or the Oracle device itself."

"Device, huh?" Lucy felt Judah's tone rising. Panic? Fury? She couldn't tell. Judah pointed at the back of Marisol's neck. "Oracle? Is that what you're calling this fucking tumor or whatever that's leaking oil down her neck?"

"It's not oil. I think it's hemocyanin. And I have no idea why it's leaking that, or why it's flooding her irises. That wasn't supposed to happen. There were synthetic barriers we'd proposed. Expensive, but they—"

Marisol's eyes grew large. She interrupted, pleading to Judah. "Mister, please press on that thing for me. You gotta make these feelings stop for a second. Press it a couple times, quick."

Steve stepped forward to stop Judah, although Lucy could tell Judah found whatever he was looking at too repellent to touch. Steve said, "The exhaust port hardens . . . It develops a sort of beak over time. If you touch it, it could bite you. And we're not sure what happens if that secretion gets—"

"Don't listen to him," said Marisol. "Just rub around the edges. Squish down on it a little bit, until it squeals. It pushes out the blue. Help me feel good. *Make this stop.* Please . . . It's moving in me. It's growing."

But Judah was already backing away.

"You can make it stop." Marisol shook harder in her chair, the legs lifting as she rocked it from side to side. "Make it stop." Her shoulders crashed into the already-stressed support rods of the storage shelving around her, causing one to snap inward. Judah reached out to stop the falling rack, but it was top-heavy, and the saltwater bin tipped. The gushing gallons exploded across the floor. Marisol rocked harder, threatening to topple her own chair, screaming, "MAKE IT STOP!"

And then it was Toni who came rushing forward, pushing back Steve so she could reach the girl and drive another hypodermic needle filled with insulin into Marisol's leg. Steve yelled, "No!" but Toni had already pressed the plunger. Then, just as quickly, Toni pulled the needle, threw it at the wall, then turned and slapped Steve across the face so hard he staggered back against the roll-up door of the receiving bay.

Steve hit the wall and was dazed when Toni lunged at him. It was clear she intended to choke the man. Judah pulled her back. She struggled to break free, but Judah held strong, so instead she spit at Steve and yelled, "What the fuck did you do to her?" and Steve slid down the wall and curled into himself and was quiet for a moment before he found the courage to answer.

———————

"They kept us separated, so none of us could see the whole scope of the project until we'd reached testing. Even at that point, I think they were telling us different things. Whatever they believed would keep us motivated, working through the all-day crunch.

"I felt lucky to have the job—there's a certain point where your specialization narrows where you can work, and there aren't a ton of positions open in integrated neuromorphic engineering. And since IMTECH worked outside of the research university system, they offered even better benefits. There was a sense of security in not always wondering if grants would come through. They paid to move us out and even helped us find a house. Paid off my med school loans. It all happened so quickly. I was already in their lab system two weeks before my family landed in Turner Falls. And when I realized who else I was working with, I understood that this was truly the cutting edge.

"Which, you know, I can read your faces, and I know you don't fucking care about any of that, but I want you to understand how fast, and smart, and aggressive they were. And I bought their lies, even when I had questions. I asked them why we had to build the visual interface, and they joked that all technological revolutions ride to success on the backs of porn and video games, but then they reminded me of the scope of the project. The media aspect was a minor acquiescence to ensure commercial viability. But in the big picture, we had a chance to save humanity from pain, depression, addiction . . . *every-thing*. We were going to give people a broad-spectrum tool for truly controlling their lives, and minds, and bodies. Oracle was going to cure society's ills. I was a true believer. We all were.

"There were moments when I should have stepped back. I can see that now. First, when I started spotting military on-site. That should have told me something. They came in civilian garb, but I

could tell from the way they moved and spoke. And security protocols kept bumping up, and I suddenly had a lot less access to other
development teams. Then there was the day they brought on
Dr. Spencer. I'd read about her work on the plastic-eating algae out
at Woods Hole. Admired that, and her. But then I told my supervisor
that we'd want an ethicist on board, maybe even an oversight com-
mittee, if we were going to shift from synthetics to biotech. And you
can guess what he did."

"He laughed?" Judah asked.

"Not quite. He pulled me aside and said, 'Did I ever tell you, Steve,
that my mother has Parkinson's? And I have to ask you, how ethical do
you think it is to tell her, or the millions of other people who we can
help, that she has to continue on this slow downward slide because
someone got nervous about making real progress and had to call in a
bunch of glorified philosophy professors who'd sit there and pretend
to understand what's happening at the vanguard of blue biotech?' And
I started to say something else, and he could tell I didn't buy that line
and instead he gave me the brush. He said, 'You know what? You
could be right. Can't hurt to dot all our *I*s here. I tell you what—how
about I bring it up at the next conference call? I want to be sure you're
happy here, after all. You do like this job, don't you, Steve?'

"Then I thought about how my kid liked her new school, and how
well she was doing at snowboarding, and I thought about my wife, and
how much she loved our new house and her yoga studio, and I said,
'Well, it can't hurt to mention it, but I understand if it isn't an immediate need.' And he said, 'There are a lot of balls in the air here, but
your concerns are definitely worth thinking about.' And that was the
last I ever said about ethics, and my paychecks kept coming in.

Steve sat silent for a moment, and Lucy sensed this was the first
time he'd said any of this out loud. She couldn't tell if it was lifting a
weight from his chest, or crushing him further. She also couldn't quite
tell which of those options she'd prefer.

"So we kept working, and Dr. Spencer was *brilliant.* I had some understanding of biomimetics, but her ability to conceptualize ways we could use nature's most successful mechanisms on such a tiny scale was astonishing. I mean, some of it was far out, even beyond what we were actualizing. She thought we were maybe fifty years away from being able to turn humans into what she called the 'universal animal,' that between 3-D-printed cartilage and epidermal electronics and nanotechnology we might be able to allow humans to emulate the best qualities of other creatures in nature. Sometimes I even felt like I was slowing her down. She made my head swim, and the novelty rate of our discoveries came hard and fast. It felt like a crusade. And I just . . . I stopped thinking about anything other than making Oracle the miracle we believed it could be.

"She was the one who recognized the malleability of octopus tissue. It was my job to find a way to culture the modified samples she provided in a way that it could mesh with our silicon skin and the latticed microcircuitry that would facilitate the biofeedback and stimuli outputs. And it was then, during that part of the project, that I should have quit. But knowing what I know now, I don't think they would have let me. I would have had a heart attack, or a car accident, or . . . I don't think there was any quitting IMTECH, even knowing only my little compartmentalized piece of the project.

"It's not like I didn't do my research, but all the same things that concerned me about the octopus tissue—the cellular autonomy and regrowth, the RNA editing capabilities, the way the protocadherins mediated connections to the neural cells—were also what made it so *perfect* to work with. And the insane senescence of those cells meant that we didn't need to worry about device decay or carcinogenic effects. So we kept working and handed in our results. Then, far faster than we expected, there were rumors of a prototype. But we had no idea they were going to do . . . *this.*"

Steve stood and stepped toward Marisol. Toni moved to cut him off, stopping Steve in his tracks. He said, "Do you know how much insulin you gave her?"

Toni said, "No."

"Well, neither do I. I only want to check her vitals. She's barely breathing. It's possible that dose will send her into shock, and she'll die."

"I had to do something. That *thing* you put inside her is torturing her."

Steve looked up at the ceiling, then flatly said, "Yeah. It is. But she's also the only subject we know of who managed to override the adverse effects of the Oracle in any way. And I know this won't matter to you, but I never would have put the device in her, and I want to find a way to take it out. But that's no good to her if she goes into a coma and dies, so please . . ."

Toni stepped aside, and Steve labored over Marisol for a moment, then made a curious face. "Her heart rate and pressure are both higher than they should be."

"That's good, right? That means she's going to live?"

"I don't know. That was only a U-40 syringe, but a second dose could be lethal. Something's off."

"You're fucking right, something's off. But that's your fault. You guys were the ones who thought it would be okay to pop a fucking octopus computer into somebody's neck."

"I didn't know, I swear. I thought we had years of testing ahead of us. We *should* have. We would have seen these same neurological responses in mice, or monkeys."

Judah spoke up. "They didn't even do any animal testing?"

"I heard there was an exemption, but I didn't know about that until they'd already done installations on the first three subjects."

Lucy said, "Jason Ward. Chris Carmichael. Who was the third?"

Judah ventured a guess. "Brady Miller?"

"Yeah. I'm not sure on that third, though, because he died before displaying any signs of adverse effects."

"*Adverse effects?* What the fuck, man?"

"I'm sorry—industry jargon is tough to shake. All that clinical language was part of how reality stayed distorted around us, I think. But Judah's right . . . It didn't make sense, what happened to him and Julie, and Sam disappeared from IMTECH just after that, so it felt like something was wrong. I don't know. Brady's dad, Sam, was one of the driving engines behind Oracle. He talked about getting a tattoo of a scroll with every patent number he'd had a hand in, and it didn't feel like he was joking. He looked at Katherine, our CEO, like she was some living prophet. Some of my coworkers thought he was in love with her, and that's why his marriage was falling apart. But I still don't understand how he could have offered Brady up for an early trial of the Oracle, or if he even did. It's possible Sam wanted it for Brady, and his wife didn't."

"I listen to this *Nightwatchman* show," said Judah, "and when they were talking about the case, they kept pointing out the packed bags in the entryway and how the neighbor heard a car door slam."

"So?" asked Toni, her voice making it clear what she thought of Judah's podcast choices.

"So what if that was the dad? What if he wanted his kid to have the Oracle, and the mom refused, and she was going to bail with the kid, and then things went bad? You think your friend Sam could have done that to his family?"

"I don't know. He wasn't really my friend. Could be IMTECH—or whoever was deeper behind the Oracle project—did that to prevent discovery. Could be Julie really committed those crimes, to protect her and her son. I don't really know anything anymore. Things that felt certain a month ago seem like complete lies today. You could feel it happening at the company, gradually, this sense of things shaking apart, but we just . . . ignored it. We needed our mission to be true, or else what had we been doing with our lives? And I kept deceiving myself, saying things were okay, and that the path to true progress had to feel chaotic, but for the last couple months before this happened, there was a kind of *mania* spreading through the halls. We'd entered deep, deep crunch time on the project, based on a rumor that a group working out of the University of Tokyo was developing a similar device. And they had all the big names on staff—Kondo and Tikoshi and Kitazawa—and supposedly they already had PMDA approval. If they launched before us—and they *were* scheduled to make an announcement at BIOcon—then it would have gutted our launch, and right before the company stock was set to go public. So IMTECH decided to rush to market. Somebody pulled the right strings. They told us to keep working. Keep refining. But at some point they decided the prototype was functional enough to test. That was a few weeks ago, and most of us had no idea what they'd done. Then I heard the news about what happened with the Millers and at Spring Meadow, about how the subject—"

"Chris," Brewer said. "His name was Chris."

"I'm sorry. You're right. About how *Chris* had been exhibiting some kind of tremors before the conflict occurred, and I knew they'd fucking done it. Because that was one of our main focal points—if you can control dopamine regulation, if you can track those fluctuations and teach the brain to stabilize itself, you have the golden key. But if you throw something untested in there, you start messing around and starve or overexcite the neurons in the ventral tegmental area toward the middle here"—he pointed near Marisol's ear—"then you create the exact opposite of what we intended. Too much dopamine in your system and the impulsive and destructive behavior goes through the roof. Too low and the body goes into a kind of twitchy agony. And however they engineered this, whether it's the way it's interacting with the network signaling, or something unexpected coming from the biological side . . . it's putting these kids through hell. They're looping through cycles and releases faster than the brain should be able."

"But why did it take so much longer for Jason Ward to become sick? Why didn't he lose it at school the same day as Chris?"

"No idea. Maybe their installs weren't simultaneous. Only other thing I can think of is a rumor that was going around IMTECH. Jason's dad, Gordon, was our CFO, so I was shocked when I heard his son had been one of the subjects. Then I remembered what Kristi in accounting had told me. She said Gordon used to joke about his kid being a psychopath. He would say, 'Chip off the old block, I guess. Should help him in the corporate sector.'"

Lucy and Brewer shared a glance.

"How much did she cry?"

His dad wasn't joking. He knew.

He thought the Oracle could fix Jason.

Steve must have caught Lucy and Brewer's surprise. "So it's true, huh? Because that would have slowed down the mania created by the device, if he had lower levels of gray matter in his insula, or if he was already accustomed to using cruelty to control or stimulate his levels. I guess Gordon was even more of a true believer than the rest of us."

"But wait . . . How did they get Chris to volunteer?" asked Brewer.

Judah said, "I think I know. *Jesus.* His uncle Scott told me that Chris's mom was about to be evicted from her trailer, but all of a sudden she stopped mentioning it. And she drove home from the funeral in a brand-new minivan. She said it was from insurance money, but he doesn't even think she's got a policy for herself. So . . ."

"Fuck." Brewer hung his head.

Lucy couldn't stand the idea. She said, "Maybe she thought the device could help him in some way. Or give him an advantage, or . . ."

"That was one of the main selling points," said Steve. "The belief was that the connectivity of the Oracle meant that anybody who had the install would be able to access our collective intelligence as easily as their own memories."

Lucy thought of something she'd read in the *Observer* when Brady Miller and his mom were found dead. What did their neighbor say?

"They only ever wanted the best for him."

She could imagine the doctors, leaning forward with a release for Chris's mother to sign. *We can give your son advantages that most of us have never dreamed of. Plus, anyone who helps us with this phase of clinical trials will also receive a substantial stipend.* Everyone in that room smart and smiling. True believers all. Opportunity and money on the table. A better future for the one you loved most, there for the taking.

And hadn't Chris seemed smarter that morning? Hadn't he been answering the teacher's questions? Lucy wanted to believe that.

"So it's possible," Steve said. "Maybe she thought she was helping him."

"I don't know," said Brewer. "I hung out with Chris when I was younger. He used to boost ramen and eat the noodles raw in the park because his mom already spent her paycheck on cigarettes. Didn't seem like Mom of the Year material."

Lucy remembered a time last year when Chris had stolen a brand-new shirt from Bucket's cubby during art class, and how Bucket knew but didn't say anything aside from telling Lucy, *"It sucks. But he needs it more than me."*

With that memory, she felt Bucket's absence pulling her down again, because he was gone and their reality only grew worse with each revelation.

What are we dying for, Buck? A stock offering?

She felt fury rising in her, and she knew that if it was unleashed, her first instinct would be to kill the man who'd helped to design the long-suffering world she'd been thrust into. But Steve seemed so sorry, and he knew more than the rest of them about how they might make it all stop, so instead of lashing out, she breathed deep and grabbed Brewer's hand and crushed it until his knuckles ground together and went white. And he must have understood, because he did not pull away. Once the immediate urge to attack had drained, she said, "Okay, so IMTECH made every greedy, fucking stupid asshole decision they possibly could. I get that. But what do we do *now*? Is there some way we can get to the IMTECH buildings and shut down the signal? Would that stop them or deactivate the devices?"

"No. First, because I don't think it's a local signal these kids are receiving. We were told the device needed to work with a gigahertz frequency instead of megahertz, so we're dealing with satellite communication. They might have on-ground relays or signal amplifiers around here, but even if we take one of them out, it wouldn't stop anything. And second, IMTECH is scorched earth. Whoever is really running the Oracle operation must have realized they had an outbreak on their hands, because yesterday evening they sent in a squad of hazmat-suited goons with some kind of sonic weapons, and they started executing staff. Full cleanup. Never heard a single shot fired, only these weird, low rumbles."

Lucy looked around and confirmed Jake was still out in the store. At some point, he'd woken and crawled his way into a chair, where he sat and swayed, mumbling something to himself. Didn't his dad work for IMTECH? Hell, half the rich families in town had one parent or the other working for them. Jake seemed fragile right now, and Lucy wasn't sure he was ready to hear his dad had probably been slaughtered in a military cover-up. Poor guy had already had a really big day.

Steve continued, "Luckily, I'd been organizing samples in a sub-zero storage freezer when they came through our wing. I heard those rumbles and something felt instantly wrong. When I peeked out from storage, I saw two of the goons rounding the hall corner, and behind them I saw my supervisor sprawled in the hall, blood coming from his ears and nose. I stayed low and made it to my office, thinking I could call my wife and kid from the landline and tell them to leave the house and go to a hotel for a day or two without telling me where. But of course the line was dead. So then I ran to warn Dr. Spencer, and when I entered her office, Marisol was on top of her.

I have no idea how she got there, but right away I could see that she had . . . uh . . . she had chewed out Dr. Spencer's throat. Dr. Spencer was trying to fight her off, and Marisol was holding her hands down and trying to bite deeper. And I guess she did, because when I finally managed to grab a chair and knock Marisol loose, she had her mouth full, and she tore away more of Dr. Spencer's throat, and that . . . that was it for her.

"I turned to hit Marisol with the chair again. At that point, I didn't even know why she had attacked Dr. Spencer. It was just . . . chaos."

Lucy nodded and remembered what had happened to Ashley Jorgensen. You either attacked, or you ran.

Steve continued, "But when I went to hit Marisol with the chair, she didn't duck or try to hide, or attack me. She only stood there in the corner, staring ahead, twitching. And I noticed her eyes were wrong. She had the dead expression of a dopamine crash for another moment, then suddenly she was crying and trying to back farther into the corner. She said, 'I didn't mean to. I didn't mean to. There was a voice. It said I'd feel better. It said we'd all feel better if we did this.'"

Jason was in all of their heads, preaching murder as salvation. And once he was proven right the first time, they knew they needed to get back into the light again, and again, and again.

"I'd never heard of or seen Marisol before, but right away I knew they'd decided to keep testing, and I knew they'd put what I'd helped design inside of her, so Dr. Spencer's death was on my hands too. I asked Marisol if she thought she could stop herself if that urge struck her again, and she said she didn't know, and then we heard a rumble and a thump in the hallway, so we hid behind Dr. Spencer's desk until another of the suited-up killers had passed. Then we ran for it and managed to make it out a shipping door unnoticed. We made our way through a little patch of preserved wetlands behind the lab, then cut back into town, and then Marisol started muttering and making claws, and her tremors became far worse, so I pulled her into Payton's Drugstore on Greenford and wrapped her head in foil and used some Clorox wipes to clean the blood from her face. It seemed like she was stabilizing. Maybe the fear and stress helped her regulate, or maybe the signal had become weaker. It was awful to see her poking the device, but that seemed to help too. I asked her if she was fighting bad urges, and she said she was, so maybe she's figured out a way to control what's happening in her head. But willpower can only stand so long against biochemistry. That's ingrained in us, to ensure we survive. I don't really know how she kept from killing me, and I'm not sure that I didn't deserve that death . . ."

Steve drifted off, exhausted. Maybe wishing he'd let Marisol kill him.

"You can probably figure the rest. We left the store and worked our way toward downtown, thinking there'd be strength in numbers if we could find some kind of congregation or emergency meeting spot. From there I hoped I might find someone to help me secure the girl until we could figure out what the hell was going on. But there was no one, not until we saw your truck headed our way. I swear, I didn't realize what Marisol was going to try until I saw her bolt into the street. And now we're here, and she might be dying, and if I was being totally honest I would tell you I don't know how to help any of us and all I really want to do at this point is get back to my wife and kid and make sure they're safe."

"But even if they're safe now, how long will that last if this keeps spreading? You have to think. There has to be a way," said Lucy.

"It's all guesswork at this point. Maybe the satellite that's connected to all these kids isn't in synchronized orbit. If that's the case, then this could pass soon. Or if this really is a military containment situation, there have to be emergency protocols in place to stop it. If they've realized that the device can spread, that it's multiplying, then they'll have to contain it like a disease. They'll have to take action."

Lucy thought about all that Steve didn't even know:

First, there was the malicious Handsome Valley broadcast that had laid the town dormant. It was like the nuclear bomb version of the weapons he'd seen the cleanup squad using in the IMTECH slaughter. She wasn't sure she had the heart to tell him that even if operatives hadn't been sent to his house, his wife and kid were probably fucked up regardless, babbling propaganda and bleeding in the dull glow of their television.

Next up was the undulating, shiny black mass that Brewer saw hanging from the roof of East Bear Cave, and the way that he had described black spiders spilling from Jason Ward's mouth before they found themselves at home inside the necks and minds of Turner Falls' best and brightest young folks.

Last but not least, there was the sizable, gun-heavy military presence blockading the roads out of town, shining sun-bright lights on anything that tried to leave this little high desert paradise.

All of which led Lucy to believe that no cavalry could be expected. They weren't treating this like an accident. They had quarantined a whole town and made no effort to charge in and wipe out the infection they had knowingly unleashed. And if they weren't treating this like an accident, that's because it was something else. But what? An experiment? These weren't scientists. They had to be military—controlling the environment, observing from a distance. Watching the fallout. Waiting to see the totality of the damage.

Maybe it wasn't an experiment.

Maybe it's a fucking weapons test.

And I'm not sure they plan on any of us making it out of here alive. Once it's all over, they can sell the Handsome Valley story, amplify it from a leak to an explosion to explain away all the death—a national tragedy that we must never allow to happen again. Maybe a nonweaponized version of that message is already being broadcast. Maybe, to the rest of the world, we're already dead.

The bastards.

Lucy was still mulling over how she might be able to tell this sad, shattered man and the other kind and unwilling test subjects in the room how much worse things really were when Marisol sprang back to life with a message of her own.

chapter thirteen

HECTOCOTYLUS

H ungry. So hungry."

Marisol's voice was lower than before in a way that felt wrong to Lucy.

It's changing in her neck.

Judah said, "I've got a candy bar up front, unless her blood sugar's already too fucked up. Should I . . ."

Marisol moaned low and rolled her head. A seam in her foil hat began to separate.

Judah said, "We've got to tighten that up, right? And shouldn't we put some around that device?"

"No. The Oracle has a latching arm that slides into the base of the skull and then unfurls over the surface of the brain, and all the receiving circuitry is in there," said Steve. His tone was casual, Lucy thought, like a man who was describing a convenient way to patch drywall rather than the manner in which his untested biotech chimera was violating Marisol's mind.

"So hungry." Another moan. Her eyes rolled back, and when they returned to the room, they were distant, clouded.

Worse, both were bright blue.

She opened her mouth wide and a gurgle rolled up from her throat, along with a smell that reminded Lucy of the time she walked by the Sushi Train dumpster on a ninety-degree day.

A third moan. Marisol clenched and unclenched her hands. "You need to get me *some food*. I'm burning up. I can feel it growing."

"What's growing, Marisol?" asked Steve.

"Something in me. Something in here."

"In this room?"

Marisol looked directly at Steve, her upper lip curling with revulsion.

"No, you *cocksucker*. In *here*." She opened her eyes wide to show him—*they're in my mind*. "It's red. I can see Dr. Spencer. I can taste her. It's making me hungrier."

"Are they communicating with you again? Is it Jason?"

"There's a trickle, but I can't get back on. And there's no more Jason. Something hollowed him, and it's bigger now, in all of us. We can . . . *I* can feel it over my left shoulder. It's growling. It's in here with us, but it wants out. *So hungry*."

"I want to help you, but I don't think we have anything you should eat."

"It hurts, though. *Everything* hurts. They're doing this on purpose. You have to make it stop. I need a hospital. How close are we to the hospital? I need a real doctor. My belly feels . . . wrong. I don't even know where we are. I'm scared. Please."

She's trying to manipulate us. She wants to tell them where we are. Can't they track her signal by now? Or is that foil all that keeps them from seeing a flashing red dot that says "Murder Them Here"?

"I can help you, but I need to ask you a question. Can you see what they see?"

"Not yet. The signal is stronger now, but something is blocking me. It's worse this way."

"Why are they blocking you?"

"I don't . . . aaaah . . . my belly. We don't know. I don't know. It's an absence. It hurts here. You made me this way. You have to fix it." Marisol smiled. "You can fix it, Steve. Put your neck in my mouth. Let me taste you, like Dr. Spencer. You look so sad. I can fix you if you come closer."

"No. Marisol, you have to fight it. I don't know what you were doing before, but it was working. You have to do that again. This isn't you. It's the device."

Lucy saw new malice in the girl's eyes, the way the blue was growing brighter.

Can they see us through her right now? She could be lying. We need to cover her eyes.

Lucy looked around the bay for a loose swatch of fabric or piece of clothing they could use to blind the girl, and was surprised when she looked back to Marisol and saw the girl had already closed her own eyes and was rocking her head back and forth.

"There *are* messages in here. They barely reach me, but I can see them better like this. They are not smeared across the light anymore. They say . . . they say the change is coming, and they want you to know that it is too late for me to fight. I'm growing. Soon there will be no more Marisol. And very soon we will find *you*, Steve, like we found your wife. Like we found your daughter." Marisol's head lolled back, but the smile did not leave her face until something caused her to hunch forward and resume moaning.

Steve backed away, breathing fast.

Marisol lifted her head, calmed again. "You made me sick, but they will heal me. They will bring me back in. They're playing a vision for me, Steve, to ease my pain. There's a dark gray bedspread, and your wife is on top. She's wearing a silver necklace with a tiny charm on it. A shooting star with a diamond at its center. Oh, it's *beautiful*."

"No."

"They have been at your wife with knives, Steve, and opened her up like a flower in bloom. But something's wrong. Even after they split her ribs, they still could not fit your daughter back inside of her. She's too big now, and she's crying, and the noise is awful, but they will stop that soon. They will—"

Toni yelled, "Enough!" and ran behind Marisol and pressed her thumb, hard, again and again, into the grotesquerie pulsing in the back of the girl's neck. Marisol's eyes rolled back, and she moaned, but this time the sound was one of deep pleasure rather than pain, and Lucy tried not to think of the lesbian porno she'd watched with Bucket and failed and knew that another part of her mind had been forever corrupted and bent inside the power that had taken control of her world.

Then Toni yelped and jumped backward, watching in shock as a drop of blood welled on her thumb and then rolled down to her elbow, a red streak on white skin.

Marisol looked around the room. The features of her face softened. "You made it stop. Oh god, that's better." Her voice was lighter again. Only a girl. She swiveled her head, trying to look for Toni. "Are you hurt? I'm so sorry. I'm so sorry. Why is this fucking happening to me? Please don't let them back in. I can't control anything once they're in my head. They're getting so much stronger."

Lucy was nodding, her eyes concerned, seeing that the girl was in there somewhere. She wanted to give some kind of comfort to whatever was left of Marisol in that sick, infected body. "If we keep pressing your neck, do you think that will help?"

"I think so. And don't stop, all right? I'm so sick. Why am I *so sick*?" The girl began to cry. She looked over at Steve, who was back against the bay door and staring miles out at nothing. "Do you think it's true? What they showed me? Maybe it's not true, Steve."

He didn't look at her, and spoke in a flat tone. "It's true. They knew about the necklace. I bought that for my wife the day I found out I got the job at IMTECH."

Lucy almost opened her mouth to tell Steve how sorry she was, but then she saw the look on the man's face and realized he had fallen into a place where her words could not reach him. She returned her attention to Marisol.

"Do they know where we are now?"

"I can't tell. The connection was weird. Worse than before. *Meaner.* And I don't know where we are, anyway. I'm not even *from* here. I was with my friend Jaelyn at a mall in the 'Couv waiting to see this guy we met online. He was going to pay each of us two thousand bucks to be in a music video, but he never showed, and then I woke up in some lab, and now . . ." Marisol's face scrunched up. New tears came. "I only want to go home. I'm so sick. The director at my group home is going to freak if I'm not back soon. They'll kick me out, I know it. Can you help me?"

Lucy told her the truth. "I don't know. But I'm sorry this has happened to you."

"You're sorry? *Sorry.*" Marisol's voice dropped into a lower register again, thick in her throat.

Lucy said, "Toni, can you press on the device again?"

Toni held out her bleeding thumb. "Yeah . . . *no.* Something is stinging in the bite. Fuck that. Let's blindfold and gag her."

Marisol spoke again. "Please, somebody. They're coming back. It's burning, inside. It's moving . . ."

Brewer stepped behind the girl. "I'll do it."

"Keep your finger to the side, yeah? Don't let it bite you."

Brewer extended his arm, his hand unsteady, moving in slowly, as if he was waiting for the nodule on the back of Marisol's neck to erupt and strike him like a snake. Right before he was about to touch it, he shied away.

"It's . . . beating. Like, it's thumping with her pulse. That blue shit is oozing from the center. I . . . I mean, what is this? I can't touch it, not like this. There's got to be something in that cleanup kit y'all had out when you were tending to us."

Brewer left the room. Marisol said, "Will one of you motherfuckers please press it now? I can feel them coming back. It's like they're breathing inside my head. Pushing at my guts. I *can't* feel this anymore."

Brewer came back, pulling on a second purple latex glove, a small puff of powder airborne at the snap.

"Only doing this long enough to keep them from coming back. And don't go moaning this time. That shit ain't right." Brewer reached closer with his gloved right hand. "Are you doing that, Marisol? You making it push out at me like that?"

"No. I swear . . . Press it, please, they . . ." Marisol rolled her head from left to right, her eyes bulging.

"It's coming out like it wants me to touch it."

Steve, from the same room, but also from the new world where his family was being tortured and murdered, said, "She trained it. It wants the stimulus. That's all that really matters to it—feeding, fighting, fucking. Dopamine, serotonin, oxytocin. It lives for the chemical reward, like us. Maybe to propagate. That's it. Touch the fucking thing. It doesn't matter."

So Brewer did as the man said, his face a knot of revulsion, his finger lightly stroking the outer right rim where the pulsing tissue of the Oracle met Marisol's torn and seeping neck.

Marisol's eyes rolled back. The moaning began again, a pure biological response unrestrained by any sense of thought that might have held it back, and Lucy wondered if she would ever feel as good—as free of herself—as Marisol appeared to in that moment, but the thought was cut short by a second sound, a high-pitched squeal that grew in volume so rapidly that everyone in the room lifted their hands to their ears and moved away from the bound girl at their center.

"What is that?" yelled Judah.

"Exhaust port," said Steve. "But it shouldn't be that loud. Or that constant. Something is broken."

Something is broken.

Really, Steve? You think? Wouldn't it be easier at this point, Steve, to look around the room and list the last few things that aren't *catastrophically broken?*

Lucy wondered where Steve was in his mind, and if it was a place she'd already been to in the course of her evening, or someplace even worse. She wanted it to be the latter, because Steve had had a hand in creating this world and because it meant that she wasn't trapped in the depths.

She looked at Steve, the way his mouth hung open, his ashen face, and for the smallest moment she'd found a new metric by which she could feel like she was doing all right.

Then the moment passed, because Marisol began bucking in her chair, kicking at the concrete floor. Her neck became ropes of exertion, her face a rictus. Her teeth were grinding together, and Lucy imagined she could hear them cracking even over the incessant squeal of the object in the girl's neck. The girl screamed through her clenched teeth until the sound transformed, the low rumble of something inside of her rolling upward. She kicked at the ground again and managed to topple her chair, and only then, as Brewer and Toni jumped to the side and Marisol fell back and slammed her head to the ground with a nauseating cracking sound, did the venting and screaming all come to a sudden stop.

The remnants of the thin metallic hat had flown from Marisol's head.

Marisol's eye's snapped open, swimming blue, the irises no longer even visible.

Her jaw unclenched, and she let loose a cough from deep in her chest, spraying her face with droplets of dark blood and something that shimmered blue-black and rolled faster from her skin.

Lucy and Brewer and Judah and Toni and Steve all watched, but none moved forward.

Lucy remembered the first time she'd heard Marisol's voice.

"Why can't I fucking die?"

She hoped the girl had finally gotten her wish.

Then Marisol reopened her eyes and spoke.

"User interface error four-point-six-two. Initiate salvage sequence."

Lucy said, "Steve, what the fuck does that mean?"

"I don't know. I wasn't in programming. It may not mean anything. So much was untested."

Marisol's head rotated swiftly toward Lucy, eyes wide, smile a blood-streaked abomination, her voice robotic and malicious at the same time.

"Means used up. Means new me coming. Means old me erased. Means more of us on way. So many more. Means we see you now. Means we see through you now. Means you're next . . ."

Then something surged inside the girl's chest and her jaw opened wide and she coughed once before a stream of blue-black oil gushed from her mouth and began spreading across the floor. With that, Marisol's face softened again, and Lucy realized that the Oracle had allowed the girl's consciousness back into her mind so she could experience whatever was about to happen to her dying body, and something about the immense cruelty of that delivered Lucy to the bright and fiery core of herself, and she realized that she had to kill Marisol. No matter how she did it, the act would be a mercy.

Lucy brushed aside a "What are you doing?" from Brewer and frantically searched the corners of the room as a terrified scream from Marisol gained volume.

I can't touch her. I have to find something I can kill her with.

My wrench—out in the wreckage.

There's got to be a hammer. Or a screwdriver. Or a . . .

There!

Then Lucy was back from the corner of the room, and had stepped over the puddle of shining ichor the girl had vomited forth. She was about to kneel down with the E-Z Glide utility knife she'd found so she could slit Marisol's throat and end her suffering, and that was when the girl exploded.

The first rupture came from her abdomen, below and to the right of her belly button. The skin, already pulled tight by her bindings, pushed upward, some force beneath rising without concern for what held it back. Lucy imagined someone beneath the girl, slowly pushing a spear through Marisol from below. The tip of the rising protrusion grew bright white, then tore audibly as the skin slid to the side, allowing the shape to emerge from the girl, shining in a mixture of fluids that smelled intensely of both decay and new life.

Lucy's momentum toward the girl halted when she saw the shape rising toward her and she instinctively kicked away from the body on the floor. She heard Marisol's screams grow unbidden, and she knew that her attempted mercy had come too late.

More of the shape unfurled from Marisol, whipping in the air. Beneath the slick of its birth fluids, it was fleshy in color, though Lucy swore that she saw a ripple of blacks and purples shimmer across its surface like passing clouds. The end of the thing looked sharp, almost bone-like, and appeared to be ridged by tiny teeth, but its size and shape fluctuated in a way that reminded Lucy of her own tongue. The thing uncoiled to the length of Lucy's arm, and farther down its length she saw suction cups contracting and expanding like suckling mouths.

Lucy glanced to Steve for some understanding. Some answer. Some way to make it all stop. Even in this new reality, where an aberration had literally torn its way into their world, she could see he was still thinking of his wife and child.

Judah was backing away. Toni shook her head and had her hand over her mouth.

She's breaking.

And Brewer? Lucy realized he had a hand around her right arm, near her elbow, pulling her back.

He thinks I might attack with my knife. Even with that thing waving in the air.

He thinks I'm crazy/he doesn't want me to get hurt.

Then, his voice from behind her.

"Holy fuck, we gotta burn this." He addressed Toni and Judah. "Y'all got anything? Gas or rubbing alcohol? Thinner? Hair spray?"

"Nos" from The Exchange staff, their eyes pinned to the emergent species weaving cobra-like from its nest in the girl's abdomen, the head of the whipping appendage expanding and contracting as if it was tasting the room, taking them all in.

A yell, distant but urgent. Jake's voice, alarmingly clear, as if the fog in his mind had been cleared by adrenaline. "Fucking company, you guys!"

Jake was right—Lucy saw the ceiling and walls of The Exchange turn bright with light. Two trucks out there. Who knew how many infected? The front door was locked, but the whole store was a fucking fishbowl—glass windows around three-quarters of the exterior.

There would be no holding them back once they shattered through.

What do we have going for us? A box cutter?

Lucy pushed her thumb forward and extended the razor blade an extra half inch. It lacked the heft and extension she got from the wrench. It felt small and sad in her hands, and she could imagine it turned against her in the swarm.

This is it. It's fucking over for us.

Bucket gone. Turner Falls in ruins. Hendersons brain damaged, maybe for life. Maybe even dead by now.

Can I do it?

She saw in her mind how fast and sudden it would have to be. She'd turn and slit Brewer's throat in one slice, then raise the box cutter just as quickly and slit her own. She'd drop the blade and try to hold the boy and let her eyes tell him, *I'm sorry. We're done. This is mercy.*

Maybe they could have one last good, quiet moment, and the nightmare would finally be over.

She tightened her grip on the blade.

A thud came from the glass front of The Exchange.

From below, Lucy heard a girl's voice, so small, so afraid.

"Kill me."

Lucy felt Marisol's eyes on hers, and wondered at the pain in them. What had Marisol's life been before this? How did she end up in a group home? Who had she lost? What had she lost? What had she done to survive? Why was she allowed to hurt so much? And what could anyone do to deserve this kind of end?

Nothing.

No one deserves this.

Make it stop.

Lucy lunged, but Brewer grabbed her other arm and tightened his grip, pulling her back against him to lock her in.

The uncoiled thing reared back for a moment, as if it had sensed the threat. Then it curled down and extended itself from Marisol's gut up to her head, where the tip quivered and twitched for a moment before tightening into a conical shape and pushing itself into Marisol's right ear.

The girl's scream tore into Lucy, an accusation—*You could have stopped this*—that echoed and distorted and grew louder as the thing grew rigid and flashed through a cycle of blues and greens and golds as it pulsed and hunched and drove itself farther into Marisol's skull.

The length of the thing began to vibrate and build up, a mass of bunched, wrinkling tissue by Marisol's ear. It churned at its base as more of it was born, drawing fresh blood and black fluid from the wound in Marisol's abdomen.

How much of that is still inside her?

Lucy struggled against Brewer's grasp, unable to stand the sound of the girl's suffering, wondering how fast she could saw through that thing before it pulled free from Marisol and found its way into her ear. But then Lucy saw the thing tremble again, and Marisol's head started smacking involuntarily against the concrete and fresh blood poured from her scalp, and then the thing in Marisol's ear gave one more rapid shake and flexed inward and penetrated her head so deeply that the side of Marisol's face split in four places and her jaw snapped loose and the screaming was finally over. The girl's body was suddenly still, save the movement of the slick, shimmering thing, which was even now coiling deeper and deeper into the warmth of Marisol's shattered skull.

Behind Lucy, she heard the sound of breaking glass. Laughter in the distance. Jake yelling from his chair, "They're through!"

Why hasn't Jake run to us?

Marisol's stillness was short-lived. Her torso hitched and shook. New sound gurgled up from her chest and over her torn, too-wide lips.

Lucy remembered the time she'd helped Bill remove a basketball-sized paper wasp nest from one of the trees in front of their house, and how they'd sprayed it with poison and snipped the branch it hung from, and how it lit up with angry life the moment it dropped into the black trash bag Lucy and Carol had been holding below. She'd never forget that feeling, the way the bag buzzed and raged and how the creatures inside wanted nothing more than to escape and attack her and unleash their endless hostility.

Then she thought of what Brewer had said about Jason at the caves.

"There was something coming out of his mouth, Lucy. Like wet black spiders."

Lucy thought to yell, "Step back!" but Brewer was already pulling her away, and the others must have sensed that something more was coming, because all of them had pushed against their respective walls and were looking from the entrance, where young men with bright blue eyes were crawling over tacky foil window displays, to the ground, where a young woman had become much less, something completely used.

She was Marisol, thought Lucy. *Now she's meat.*

Then the girl ruptured for the second time, her unmoored jaw flapping in a grotesque mimicry of speech as the blue-black things rushed over her lips.

Part of Lucy's mind thought, *Not spiders. Not octopuses. No eyes. Fast*, while an overriding and basic part of her mind simply knew they should be escaping. She nearly toppled both herself and Brewer, and so he let go and they instinctively moved in the direction of the store.

Except: that's where *they* were, the malignant mass of boys and girls who had breached the windows of The Exchange—shaking, laughing, brushing off glass, hands heavy with machetes and baseball bats.

They were circling Jake, who was swaying in his chair. They paid no attention to the crew in the delivery bay, as if they knew that had become a birthing zone for the thing they served.

Behind Lucy, Toni screamed. Judah yelled, "Get them off me."

Lucy thought, for a moment, that she'd been given another chance to save someone. That she could dive into the fray surrounding Jake and start slashing and that if she was very lucky she might save his life.

Then Jake looked back at Lucy and Brewer, and there was something in his face she hadn't seen before. He mouthed the word, *Run.*

No!

But it was too late.

Jake gave a resigned sigh, turned back to his prowling classmates with one middle finger raised, his other hand limp at his side, and said, "Buncha shaky little fuck boys anyway. You guys can eat my fucking ass."

They fell on him like wolves.

Lucy looked long enough to see Nate Carver—or at least the boy who used to be Nate Carver, who she had fantasized would one day take her virginity—grab a fistful of the duct tape clinging to Jake's torn scalp. Nate bent to look in Jake's remaining eye, then pulled downward with his fist as fast as he could, peeling Jake's scalp and the left side of his face and a strip of his neck away with an audible ripping sound.

Whatever they did to him next, the resulting scream never even escaped his throat.

Then Lucy and Brewer were running back toward the delivery area, and Steve was already rolling up the bay door, though it seemed to be stuck a third of the way open and Toni and Judah were batting at themselves and trying to squeeze out through the thin crack. Lucy saw something on the floor near the bay, and when it mewled in agony she realized that Blumpers the store cat must have come on instinct to investigate the skittering noises in the back space and found himself swarmed by the creatures pouring out of Marisol. Were they puncturing into him now, searching for a way to penetrate his panicked mind with their latching arms?

If I can reach down and slash once, maybe he'll bleed out before they can change him. Maybe he'll suffer less.

Brewer pulled on her free hand. "Lucy, come on!"

No one would be saved. Not today.

Steve finally managed to unhitch whatever had been stopping the bay door's upward roll. He threw the steel handles upward, and light flooded the wreckage of The Exchange, blinding Lucy for a moment.

Carol Henderson had always encouraged Lucy to "keep a positive spirit." She told her life would be full of challenges, even for those who had already suffered so many, and that humans had proven capable of enduring despite all this. And when Lucy had a really hard night, Carol would always say the same thing.

"No matter what happened, tomorrow is a new day. Each morning is another chance to make things right."

Lucy blinked away her sun blindness and stepped over what remained of Marisol, whose eyes had now been pushed loose from their orbits by the monstrous appendage that had grown from her own belly.

Behind Lucy, the soundscape was threat and laughter and the sound of another boy being broken to pieces by those he'd called friends. Behind Lucy, finally relieved of this hellish existence, was the frail body of one of the only people on Earth who she'd ever been sure truly loved her.

Ahead of Lucy were a handful of kind souls, deluding themselves that there was somewhere they could run to escape the constricting coils of cruelty to which they'd been damned. She wanted to stop them and tell them, *Each morning is another chance to make things right*, and then they could stand there and laugh and laugh in the new morning sun until doom descended upon them in one of its many guises.

Although there was *something* about the feeling of the sun on her skin, and Brewer's hand on hers as he pulled her into the alley behind The Exchange. No matter what they had taken from Lucy, from the city of Turner Falls, maybe from the world, she was alive.

Another day. Still here, despite these motherfuckers.

Still not meat.

She tightened her grip on the utility knife in her hand until she felt its sharpness as an extension of herself. And though she didn't allow herself Carol's sweet delusion that anything could be made right, she did allow her feet to carry her forward into the bright new day.

chapter fourteen

MAN ON THE STREET

S *teve is our injured baby gazelle.*

Whether it was his age, or the events of the day draining his will to live, or a genuine desire to suffer the wrath of what he'd helped to create—maybe even a fun combination of all of the above—Steve was lagging hard. Brewer and Lucy had bolted from the alley and onto Dalton Street first, followed closely by Judah, then Toni, who had kicked off her heels and was probably dying for the cool Converse she must have left at the Boiler Room.

But Steve—he might as well have been out for a casual stroll.

Did one of those spider/octopus things get into him? Is that what's slowing him down? How long before he starts twitching and running after us?

Lucy didn't know if she was willing to go back and help him. Why would she put herself at risk for that man? But he seemed to know a ton about the "device" that was infecting Turner Falls' kids, and he did manage to keep Marisol disconnected from the grid for all that time. He had tried to save that girl. Had really wanted to. And then she thought of all he'd lost, and what they'd done to his wife. His poor daughter. She could imagine their terror.

We have to help him.

This time she knew well enough to start running the other direction before Brewer could stop her.

He'll save me over someone else, every time. Veer wide.

"Lucy, no."

Damn it. He saw me.

And then Brewer was in chase, and Judah and Toni made confused faces but did not stop their full-tilt sprint up Dalton Street, and Lucy realized how mad she must look, running back in the direction of the boys who had probably finished mainlining every last ounce of Jake's suffering into their bodies and would be looking for their next high.

What do I even do when I get to Steve? He's not fucking Yoda. I can't just throw him in a backpack and go bolting the other direction.

She looked beyond Steve and saw that she had to reach him soon or it would be the death of them both. Three blood-spattered kids, two boys and a girl, came running around the front side of The Exchange and were headed straight for them, moving faster than usual, their gaits smoothed over by the way they'd used Jake. One carried a machete, the blade now darkened, while the other two appeared to have done their wet work with bare hands.

Steve looked back and saw the hunt had found him, and some basic switch in his mind must have flipped to "flight," because he finally picked up the pace.

Still too slow, though. What if he's our only chance to survive or even escape this?

Lucy imagined the machete slicing Steve's back, opening up flesh and fat and muscle and exposing his ribs and spine to the morning sun. She wondered if the kids would take turns swinging after Steve had been felled. Would they prolong his suffering, avoiding a fatal blow?

Stay away from his neck. He's got four good limbs. You pull on his hand while I swing.

The kids closed the distance faster than Lucy could. The boy raised his machete.

Too late. Always too late.

At least, that's what Lucy thought before she saw the beat-up 1985 Cadillac Eldorado round the corner onto Dalton, banking so hard two of the wheels smoked as they spun against the wheel wells.

More of them? One of us?

The hideous, trembling children in pursuit must have assumed the latter because they didn't look back, even when the driver gunned it and the engine rumbled so loudly Lucy felt it in her guts.

There was a wrongness to what was about to happen—Lucy knew that. The exact same event happening only two days prior would have been an emotionally devastating tragedy for the entire town. Three of Turner Falls' best and brightest, mowed down by a hulking Caddy with an out-of-state custom license plate reading "VER1TAS."

But on this particularly broken morning, the exact same occurrence was not tragedy but triumph. And at that exact moment in time there was a feeling in Lucy's heart, and though she chose not to name or acknowledge it, it was surely joy ascendant.

The boy on the right was pulled under the car first, his left shoe snagged by the front wheel, his body dragged and compressed beneath the burning undercarriage. The second boy bounced from the hood and was sent airborne before he hit the brick wall of Anderson's Optics and nearly bisected himself at the waist with his own machete. The girl was slightly ahead and looked back in time to see the car and try to leap safely to the side. She was too late—the grille caught her legs, and the impact sent her swirling across the asphalt, spinning so quickly the street stripped away her face like a belt sander.

Just as quickly, the Caddy veered up onto the sidewalk to avoid hitting Steve, plowing through a plastic box of local newsweeklies before it squealed to a stop.

Judah and Toni had finally turned toward the commotion and

were running in the direction of the car. Brewer caught up to Lucy, his eyes wide, his head nodding yes again and again, though Lucy didn't think he even knew it was happening.

Lucy was first to the Cadillac, although she flinched and stepped back when the driver's-side window started rolling down.

One of their tricks? Another cruelty? Are they feeding on each other now?

There was a man behind the wheel with a tightly shaved head and what appeared to be a bleeding bite mark on his left cheek. Lucy looked him in the eyes.

Not that terrible blue.

One of us.

The man spoke directly to Lucy. "You fucking crazy too?"

And though she was most certainly crazy, she knew what he meant, and so she answered the question with an honest "No."

"All right, then. Hop in." He leaned across and unlocked the passenger-side door. Lucy ran around the front and kicked the remnant of a news vending box out of the path of the car. Brewer caught up with her and opened the car door first, sliding into the front seat. Lucy hopped in after him.

A truck engine roared to life in the distance.

The rest of the crew from The Exchange.

Lucy yelled, "Hurry up!" Within moments Judah, Toni, and Steve had piled into the back.

Brewer held up an oversized silver pistol he'd found on the seat of the car.

The man behind the wheel said, "You mind holding that for me, buddy?"

"Sure."

"Keep your finger outside the trigger guard. Not quite sure how I'm still alive at this point, but it'd be a real shitter if you killed me on accident. Everybody in?"

Nods or "Yeahs" from all.

"Let's scoot, then. And once we're clear of this shit, maybe one of you can tell me why some kid with his legs on backward just tried to bite my goddamn face off."

With that the driver shifted gears and plowed back into the city street, dragging the remains of a fresh kill, dark blood trailing behind.

"I should have known. I *really* should have known. I mean, I saw some of the military guys laughing as they let me through the barricade, but I figured that was on account of my working for the *Nightwatchman* show. Not everybody gets what we do."

The man reached down by his hip and slid out what appeared to be a self-laminated piece of computer-printed ID. He passed it to Brewer and Lucy. It featured a faded picture of the man in happier, less face-bitten days, along with the words "PRESS PASS, Emmett Grayson—The Nightwatchman. Irrevocable Authority of the Press Hereby Invoked as Granted by the First Amendment of these United States of America." Lucy handed the pass back to Judah behind her.

"Now I almost wish I would have taken that CNN internship. I mean, the corporate agendas would have driven me crazy, but at least then those brutes at the barricade would know somebody would be following up and checking in on me. But with the *Nightwatchman*, I think they figured I'm just another loon. 'Sure, let him through. He won't make it out. He won't be missed.' Jesus."

Lucy shifted in her seat. Two bottles—an empty Maker's Mark and the last dregs of some Cuervo—clinked against each other. A half-roasted joint rested in the upright prongs of the ashtray jutting from the dash. Sober or not, he'd rescued them and evaded their pursuers for the moment.

"So they let me through, and there I am, thinking my name is finally preceding me, thinking I might be about to get a serious scoop, and I realize, *Holy shit, I'm driving through the desert at night. It's time.*

It's time to go full gonzo. So I pull over, and the night is beautiful, but, *man*, it is cold, and so I had a little to drink and decided to sharpen up with a few lines and a gummer, and there you go. It's the dream, right? But then I finally make it into the city, and right away I wished I were playing it straight. I mean, I'm not trying to cover some desert rally, or go flopping around Las Vegas like a libertine, so maybe it was poor timing on my part. Nobody's dropping acid while they report in Syria, you know? And something feels so *wrong* once you hit this town. My shitty old radio fried out the second I turned it on, and I couldn't get a phone signal worth shit to call home base and find out if there was any new info out of the area. And worse, there's *nobody* moving around, like even the tumbleweeds left town, and I tried to tell myself, 'Well, it's a sleepy little tourist burg.' but then I passed this school, Mountain Crest or something like that, and there's a light coming from the gymnasium. When I drove closer, I saw there was a body holding the door open, so of course I parked and jumped out to see if I could help, and also, honestly, I wanted to verify that the whole town hadn't been evacuated. But then I got closer and this smell came from the gym. Worst thing I ever smelled my entire life, and I grew up by a mushroom farm and worked at a dairy for three years."

Lucy had a sense of what Emmett was about to tell them. She had worried about it before, but swept it from her mind. Mountain Crest was one of the Community Emergency Hubs. Folks were supposed to meet by the open-air basketball courts, away from structures in case the emergency was an earthquake, but she could picture all the tired families who'd somehow managed to dodge the initial Handsome Valley transmission gathering there by default after their lines of communication broke down, paradoxically pulled from their homes by the endless parade of sirens in the city streets. They'd be confused, still wearing pajamas. Little ones crying, alarmed by all the loud noises, sensing their parents' fear. Those same parents wondering why they'd heard screams in the street/why their phones weren't working/why the cops wouldn't even stop in the street when you waved them down. Was that an explosion in the distance? Why was there so much smoke in the air? Was it really coming from downtown? Maybe someone from the school opened the gym so those gathered could warm up and congregate until someone who knew what the hell was going on showed up to guide them. Someone must have the answers, right? Someone must know what we're supposed to do when reality breaks down.

Instead of answers, the children had come, familiar at first, greeted by smiles until their twitching bodies and bright blue eyes told the adults something was terribly wrong. But by then, it would have been too late.

Lucy said, "It was a slaughterhouse."

Emmett said, "Yeah. I think so. There were cars parked around the school. Toppled strollers in the playground. But I didn't see *anyone*. And once that smell hit, I was almost too scared to get any closer. Thought I was going to retch. But my duty to the truth comes first, right? It has to, or what am I doing?"

No one answered. Lucy wondered if the ideas of "duty" and "truth" felt as abstract to everyone else as they did to her. They seemed fancy, ornate, positioned somewhere high up on a tower, absurdities compared to the reality of her known world. She wondered at how fast the idea of values could disappear from your mind when your classmates started scraping open people's faces against cave walls.

"I'm guessing it was a blessing in disguise now," said Emmett, "but I never got to see what happened in that gym. I was about ten feet out from the light in the entrance when the body holding open the door started to crawl toward me. It looked like they'd been attacked. They were bleeding from a puncture wound in the back of their neck. I yelled to them to stop moving. Said I was coming to help. When I finally got to them, I saw it was a man, and his hands were covered in blood. I crouched, and he lifted his head, and that's when I realized things were even worse off than I'd thought."

"Weird blue eyes?" Lucy asked.

"No. I wish, almost. *No eyes.*" Emmett paused a moment. "I mean, he had them, but they'd been pulled out of the sockets, and then, uh . . . they'd been crushed. There was something clear seeping from them onto the man's face. I was shocked. I popped up and swiveled, in case whoever had done that to the guy was coming for me next, but then I didn't see motion coming from anywhere, and I realized I should try to help him. I told him to lie still, that I'd find a way to get an ambulance out to help him, but then he rolled onto his back and started talking, and that was the worst part. I'm not sure I can remember everything right, so . . . listen to this."

Emmett swiped away an image of the *Nightwatchman* podcast logo on his phone, then pulled up an audio recording. Lucy heard an older man's voice, harried, rambling like a madman:

"It's too late for me. Help Emma. Please. Is she still here? The demons have her. They sprang from her mouth. They tried to enter my spirit, and I felt them taking my eyes from within. But I called on the Lord, and He guided me. He showed me the way to return to His light. It was a small sacrifice, nothing compared to what He's given. But the Devil showed me his world first, before I could pluck my eyes. I saw *too much*. You must know! . . . Warn the others. There are mothers, like Lilith, growing beneath us, protecting their dark children in caverns. More of the creatures are growing. They will rise soon. There was a vision, inside my head, *inside my spirit*. Two girls. They looked like friends of my Emma, maybe Amy and Jennifer, but that couldn't be. Something was terribly wrong with them. They were swollen, naked, and trembling. Bloated and holding their bellies—another of the Devil's mockeries, that they held themselves like the Virgin Mother. They were scared and screaming. Their skin tore and softened and sloughed away in places, and beneath that was something shiny and sticky and it bubbled over their muscles and the black sacs that had become their wombs. They lay on the ground of the Devil's realm, though their faces said they wanted nothing more than to leave, and they cried, 'Why, god?' and found no answers and then they moved by the Devil's hand and their bodies began to slide up the very walls, oozing like slugs until they hung heavy from the roof of their rocky hell. Then they slid together at the top and their bodies seemed to merge and their bellies peeled farther back and left something heavy and shining and black hanging from the roof. And still, they screamed, until the Devil peeled the skin from their chests as if they were flaps and they slid over their faces and grew dark and I could see nothing more than the shape of what they'd birthed above me, shimmering. The Devil wanted me to see all that. To know what was coming. To give myself over to his powers. But I felt god in my hands, and I was strong, and now I am saved. But what of my Emma? What of my sweet Marjorie? I called for them both, but for a long time there were only cries and moans, and then nothing. Can you find them, please? Surely it is His divine guidance that brought you to me. Can you help me save them? Can you tell them that the Devil needs their eyes to hold their souls? Please. *Please.*"

The recording reached its end. Everyone stared ahead for a moment, feeling the rumble of the Eldorado beneath them as Emmett navigated side streets and incessantly checked his rearview for signs of pursuit. Lucy and Brewer shared a glance—even if Emma's father delivered the confirmation like a mentally ill street preacher, Brewer *had* seen eggs on the roof of East Bear.

Emmett continued. "What do you even say to that? How do you respond? I wanted to believe he'd lost his mind, but he was so sincere. I grabbed him one of those metallic space blankets from my emergency kit in the trunk, and I laid it over him, and I told him I'd do as he asked. I said, 'I'll find Emma. I'll tell her about the eyes.' Guy didn't have long, I could tell. Even without his trauma, there was some kind of bruising and swelling inside his throat. Blood crusted around some hole in the back of his neck. Pale as a ghost. I figured it was the least I could do."

He paused again, but it seemed to Lucy it was only so he could take another breath and resume talking. She wondered at his ability to keep speaking without any input from the folks around him until she remembered what he'd said about "a few lines and a gummer." She imagined a headline: "COKEHEAD JOURNALIST HAS BIG NIGHT, WON'T SHUT UP ABOUT IT." But then she realized she only resented him because everything he'd just told her and the sad, scared voice on his recording threatened to destroy the tiny remnants of hope that flickered through her heart and kept her moving.

Those poor girls. What did Jason Ward do to them?

Emmett said, "Then I got back in my car, wishing I'd brought an old-school paper map instead of depending on this piece of shit for everything." He gestured to his phone in its holder on the dash. "Because I realized that—scoop or not—it might be time to get the hell out of town. I thought maybe I could find an old logging road, get by the military blockades. If I'm being honest, I was looking for a real map right before I found you guys. I went into that Oregon Only shop downtown, but all I found were chocolate-covered hazelnuts and smoked salmon and novelty mugs, and when I turned to leave the store, I got pulled to the fucking ground and some shaky teenager with a scraped-up face and his legs twisted the wrong way 'round was climbing up my body. Even all messed up like that, he was so fast, and strong, and before I could fend him off he had pulled himself up to my torso. I was dazed from my head slamming into the tile, and then I smelled burnt calamari and I saw a mouthful of half-shattered teeth coming at my eye and I moved and started to push back, but he managed to do this shit . . ." Emmett pointed to the swollen, circular bite mark on his cheek. "I barely got the guy off me, and that's when I decided, *Screw a map*, and realized I was going to wing it out of here on a hope and a prayer before I got pulled any deeper into whatever is happening to this goddamn town. Because, honestly—and I'm far from a religious guy—it kind of feels like somebody opened up the gates of hell and we'd all be better off if somebody just dropped a goddamn nuke and wiped Turner Falls off the fucking map."

"Nuke's already been dropped, in a way," said Steve. "I'm not sure if it was an accident, or if this was the plan all along, but it's clear now that they've seized the opportunity. They're studying the aftermath. You, me, everybody in this town—we're at ground zero. We're already statistics."

Lucy was surprised to hear Steve speak—having thought him forever lost to his grief and shock—but she was less surprised by his resigned tone.

Steve's figured it out too. The more they hurt you, the more they strip away what you love, the easier it is to understand what's happening, without all that messy hope or projected morality getting in the way. Then you can tell the truth.

"Only question now," said Steve, "is how long have we got before they have to start their cleanup? Even if they're pushing the Handsome Valley narrative, they can't risk that running for too many news cycles in a row. What if someone manages to communicate past their perimeter? How long until a concerned relative calls their senator demanding answers? And most important, if someone really is sitting in a control room, watching the feed from all these Oracle devices, how long will it be before they realize they've lost control?"

"*Wait* . . . Something is supposed to be under control here?" asked Emmett.

"There were rumors about features built into the Oracle—the thing that's infecting people—that were supposed to be advantageous for the people upstream. Theoretically, there would be ways to activate remote shutdowns, maybe reduce or even stop criminal behavior. Ways to drive commerce too. I think they developed it all under the banner of consumer logistics."

Judah said, "That's a pretty fucked-up euphemism for 'mind control.' "

"Sure. That's not the angle they used to sell us on the idea, though. They pitched it as innocuous. Beneficial, even. There was going to be a lockdown feature."

"Why?"

"To stop violence before it even happened."

"Yeah, well . . . *nailed it*," said Judah. "And how the hell would that work, anyway?"

"There were patterns we could identify and report. There was going to be a way we could send a visual override if we thought something dire was about to happen. Say the system IDs a kid with flattened serotonin levels who's trying to buy an AR-15. We could report that, stop it before it starts. Or we thought maybe we could even send a visual inhibitor."

"I heard one of them say their vision had gone all red."

"Yeah, it was going to be something like that. But all of that was beta work—only the *frameworks* for those are in the software we built."

"What about that thing that burst out of Marisol and drilled a hole in the side of her fucking head? Was that in the beta work too?" asked Brewer.

"Wait, *what*?" asked Emmett.

"Don't ask," said Lucy. She thought of the sound Marisol's head made when it shattered and let the tentacle worm its way into her mind.

"That's what I'm saying," said Steve. "None of this was supposed to happen. The animal side of the device is activating and manipulating the programming, bypassing its safeguards. There were cellular inhibitors engineered into the device. All of these side effects and mutations—the hemocyanin in the eyes, the hyperaggression and severe looping dopamine fluctuations and tremors—they show a level of contamination that we never saw in the limited lab testing we were able to do. But the really worrying aspect is the multiparous reproduction . . . I think that thing you saw coming out of Marisol was called a hectocotylus, and I think it grew from one of her ovaries. Could have been carrying eggs, or spermatophores, or nothing. I don't know. Maybe it was a dead-end mutation."

"But why the hell would it want into her head?"

"Instinct. The mating arm—the hectocotylus—is normally inserted into the female octopus via one of her siphons, and reaches all the way back to a specialized gland in her mantle."

"That's like her head?"

"Yeah. So that thing that came out of Marisol located the closest facsimile it could find and penetrated. When it could sense that method of reproduction was failing, that's when those smaller versions of the Oracle came crawling out of her, which I can't even explain aside from guessing that cells from the Oracle immediately begin to create some kind of specialized organ inside the human body once the device is installed."

Lucy could feel the way Steve took comfort in his knowledge. Even though what he described was monstrous, she sensed his mind clinging to—almost worshipping—the information inherent to his specialized world.

There's safety, for him, in science.

What makes me feel safe?

She wanted to imagine Brewer, his arms around her. Instead she felt a swinging wrench in her hands, the vibration of steel striking bone. She pushed the thought down.

"Now," said Steve, "what's even *more* concerning is what Emmett told us, because if the man he found was telling any kind of truth, the Oracle has found a third method of reproduction."

Amy. Jennifer.

"There are mothers, like Lilith, growing beneath us . . ."

"He was a shitty lay too, like he only stuck it in once and then barely moved it until he started shivering."

"Jason Ward," said Lucy. "I think he grew his own hecto . . . his own octopus dick or whatever. He did that to them, before he disappeared."

"If you've heard that they had sex, then it's possible. If the Oracle was already in him at that time, his dopamine deficiencies would have destroyed his ability to have intercourse or receive sexual gratification. That's probably the only thing that has kept the infected from, well . . ."

"Raping us?" asked Toni.

"In short, yeah." Steve sounded almost cheerful at the realization. "Sex is one of the main dopamine drivers, but with the Oracle causing so many ups and downs they're forced to find other ways of regulating their neurochemicals."

"Like killing us with their bare hands, or turning us into egg farms?" asked Judah. "That's fucking great, Steve. I guess we really got lucky, huh?"

Lucy felt Judah's anger, palpable and rising. But she also understood why Steve felt his inappropriately placed happiness—if his hypothesis was correct, then at least his wife and daughter weren't raped before they were murdered.

Is that where we're at? Finding joy in the prospect of slightly diminished atrocities?

"That's not what I'm saying, Judah. There's no luck in any of this . . . I'm simply saying that if the Oracle was already in Jason, the rapid fluctuations would have shut down his nitric oxide reactions, and his ability to have an erection. Which means that any reports of human sex after that are likely in error, and what really occurred was parasitic implantation."

Lucy imagined Jason Ward, shivering in his parents' bathroom, neck seething with the device they'd installed in him. He can't understand what's happening to him, or why, and then he looks into his underwear and sees something coiled there, growing from one of his testicles, sending chemical signals to his brain: *It's time to mate.* Then, instead of running to the hospital, or calling out to anyone else for help, *he called those girls.*

Christ.

Chris Carmichael lost his mind. Marisol tried to fight it, at least. But Jason . . . He was the perfect host, always willing to do the worst to fulfill his urges.

"Although," said Steve, "I don't understand how those essentially alien spermatophores would be able to interact with the eggs of a human female. Maybe the mating arm carried eggs too, and only needed a womb. Or maybe it was the way we sheathed them and engineered them to avoid rejection . . . It's like I built them a Trojan horse," said Steve. "But that's why I never wanted to work with octopus cells in the first place—their change and adaptation capabilities remain radically beyond our understanding."

"Wait! *You're* with IMTECH?" asked Emmett.

"I was. But they're gone now. Whatever this project *really* was, whoever was driving it, it's clearly only one thing as of today."

"What's that?"

"A bioweapon. But I don't think the people watching this understand what they're dealing with. When you're talking about bombs, you can think in terms of the radius and kilotons of force and half-life. Even with other bioweapons, there's a period of efficacy and then a rapid drop-off. But this . . . whatever the Oracle is becoming, it's adapting and spreading faster than they'll be able to understand from some satcom feed. And if they don't realize that soon, if they don't write off the whole venture and kill the satellite signal and actually nuke this place and spray the blast crater with toxins that'll neutralize cell growth for a thousand years, then—"

Steve didn't finish his sentence because he didn't have to. Lucy felt the implications of what he was saying roll through the car as undeniable truth: the Oracle would be the end of the human experiment, a ravenous, rapidly spreading cancer rendering what remained of humanity unrecognizable. Or maybe the Oracle wouldn't stop at human hosts. It would keep changing, adapting to each new challenge, and then the surface and seas of the Earth would become a perpetually shifting, rupturing animal, linked by a synthetic mind, malicious without purpose aside from consumption and growth . . .

Bad meat.

Lucy looked around the car. All the faces—aside from Emmett, who hadn't seen what they'd seen, and was *maybe* just high enough to have dodged letting their new reality set into his bones—were desolate. Lucy looked to each of them, and imagined their pain and what they had lost, and felt the good in them, which had allowed them to survive until that moment, and she thought about the Hendersons, and the space in their hearts they had opened up to her, fully knowing she may never find the strength to enter, and she thought about Brewer, and the way he made her feel, even now when her mind recoiled from feeling much of anything at all.

Then she thought of Bucket, and how they had made islands of each other, each one a safe place for the other to weather the petty day-to-day violence of growing up in Turner Falls, and she felt that there had to be so many other people like him, out there in the world—trying to get by, trying to be kind—unaware of what was about to be unleashed upon them.

She knew then that her heart was broken and would never mend. But she also felt how small a thing that was compared to the suffering that awaited the world if someone didn't do something to stop what was coming, so she found the courage to break the heavy silence inside the '85 Eldorado and say the truth they all needed to hear.

"There's no escaping this. Not for us. We have to accept that. And then we have to find a way to make the shitbirds who are watching us destroy this entire fucking town."

chapter fifteen

HITCHHIKER

Of course, any time you propose suicidally triggering a nuclear assault, there's bound to be some dissent. As Lucy suspected, Emmett hadn't been trapped in Turner Falls long enough to understand the gravity of their situation.

"Listen, that's all very noble, but I have a long-standing preference for not being vaporized by an atomic bomb. So how about we find a gap in their perimeter, make a run for it, and find some way to communicate the situation with the military once we're not in the middle of the bull's-eye?"

Judah said, "You're assuming there's a gap, which is kind of funny. I listen to *Nightwatchman* sometimes, and you guys are always talking about urban warfare drones. Surveillance drones. This is high desert territory. Open plains, minimal tree cover. Even if we managed to take this big metal boat off-road, what are the odds their perimeter isn't buffered by drone coverage? And Steve said they're using sonic weapons."

Lucy pictured Bill and Carol, mumbling in their living room, staring at nothing. She confirmed Steve's assertion. "They've already used them on most of the town."

"Exactly. So maybe we go gunning across the high plains, we even find a way out to the south where we're not trapped in by river canyons . . . and then what? We go stealth in this hooptie? It's impossible. They'll spot us, we hear some kind of weird boom, and that's it. A Caddy full of heart attack victims plowing through the sagebrush."

"Dude—'ghost ride the whip,' " said Brewer.

Judah laughed. "Yeah. Except it won't be as cool when we eventually drift into a juniper tree and then they come out in hazmat suits and cart our bodies off for testing."

"*That's* what I'm afraid of. It's why we can't risk escape," said Steve. "Everyone in this car has had some kind of contact with the infected. How do we know that *we're* safe? How do we know for certain that some new vestige of the Oracle implant isn't growing inside each of us right now? And how will they keep this from spreading before they even begin to understand what they're dealing with? *No.* We can't risk it. Would any of you want to be the Typhoid Mary who brought this to the outside world?"

Lucy could feel Steve's anger. She recognized it in herself.

He wants revenge. And he wants to die. He wants all of this undone.

But he's also right. It's like Emma's dad said—these are demons. We can't understand them. All we can do is destroy them.

Emmett still wasn't buying it. "This is all a trap. There's got to be some way out, if we can think hard enough. We're only *reacting* right now. They're doing what they always do—controlling us with fear, keeping us from using reason, making violence the dominant paradigm. They're choosing for us. It's what they do. It's how they stay in power."

Steve said, "You're not hearing me, Poli-Sci 101. You're still thinking about humans. And sure, we're mostly animals, and the worst of us rise to power and oppress the rest. That *is* why they're doing this to us now, searching for new methods of control, believing they'll find safety and stimulus in power, protecting what they think of as a 'proprietary technology.' All of that requires that they do what you're talking about:

destroying our empathy and reducing our faith in reason. Those guys on the border laughed when they let you through because you're not even *human* to them. You're a unit of something else. They rename you 'test subject' or 'enemy,' or they assign you a race or a nation or a class—and then they don't have to think about *you* anymore. It's a weakness, an evolutionary leftover, and it damns us, but listen . . . *That's old news.* If we're *lucky*, then all of that's a fight for another day. What we're talking about here is a lot less civilized, okay? I'm talking about absolute and violent physiological control. No hope. No options. Not even the illusion of free will, or the possibility of change. I'm talking about every human being on Earth used and discarded. Or worse, the Oracle figures out how to force us to propagate. They maximize us for consumption. *They farm us.* And there's malice here that I don't understand. I think they would allow our minds to remain intact. They'd want us self-aware, so we could feel what they were doing to us. They'd feed on that."

"And very soon we will find you, Steve, like we found your wife. Like we found your daughter."

Steve was right. There was something beyond physical need thriving inside whatever poisonous collective mind these Oracle things were sharing.

Lucy remembered Marisol, moaning in her chair as the Oracle used every inch of her to grow more of itself.

"It's in here with us, but it wants out. So hungry."

Per his MO, Steve again left everyone around him in a state of silent terror and contemplation.

He must be great at parties!

Lucy looked at the gun in Brewer's lap. She wondered how many bullets it held. The weapon was oddly repellent. She imagined herself pulling the trigger and wondered if the gun would dull the sensation of killing someone. She guessed the physical distance would create an emotional distance from the act, and that idea felt dangerous to her.

Dangerous?

Or unappealing?

You don't want to feel that distance, do you?

You want that high again. You want that sense of control.

This was always in you. And if you survive, if you make your way to Brewer's 'someplace . . . where we can at least try to be good again,' then he'll see you for what you are.

An animal. A user. A murderer.

Just like them.

Is that why you're ready to die? So you never have to face that moment?

Brewer broke the silence, and Lucy was grateful, at first, that he had halted her spiraling shame party.

"So you're saying this Oracle device or whatever gets loose, keeps mutating, and spreads everywhere, then it figures out how to harvest us like some *Matrix* batteries or whatever, except instead of sleeping in sci-fi pods and playing virtual reality all day we'd get turned into involuntary breeding stock and egg sacs and murder toys and they'd stay wired into us so they could get kicks from our suffering until something finally brought an end to life on Earth?"

"That's my hypothesis. It could be worse."

"Worse? How the hell does that get worse? I thought you said the face-fucking tentacle thing was a one-time mutation. Are we adding that back into the equation, or—"

"No. It's the 'end to life on Earth' part. Some researchers, given all the anomalies we've learned about the octopus—the senescence, the odd DNA sequencing, the RNA editing capabilities—think that we might be dealing with a species that evolved from a creature of unearthly origin."

"Fucking *aliens*, dude?"

"We don't know. But think about everything you've seen in the last two days, and how little of it makes any sense to us. What if we took an alien intelligence, altered it in ways that allowed it to manipulate and parasitize us, and then as a bonus we gave it access not only to the minds of the infected, but to our collective wisdom as a species? The programming inside the Oracle is interacting with a far more complex version of the internet than any civilian would be allowed access to. I don't know if the organism is able to communicate in a clear way yet, but it's definitely evolved in the short time since the testing launched, and will continue to do so."

"So eventually it knows all the dumb shit we think we know. So what?"

"Well, we managed to *create* the Oracle with everything we knew. Who knows what *it* will be able to figure out? We can't assume it is any less intelligent than us. And if it truly is an alien species, and one that had to have, at some point, figured out intergalactic travel, what's to stop it from attempting that again?"

"Oh . . . god."

"Yeah. So even the blessing of our solar system collapsing, or being swallowed up by a red giant, both of which are almost incomprehensibly far into the future, wouldn't save us from our subjugation to this thing. I'm talking about all of humanity, our consciousness and physical manifestation and being, interwoven with and forever tortured by the Oracle throughout the depths of the universe."

Emmett lost it. "Are you all fucking *high*? I'm the only one who knows where my coke is, right? Because you guys are trying to make it sound like some busted mutant iPhone is about to unleash hell on Earth, and I've got to tell you I've heard less crazy out of the pants-shitting meth-heads who call in to *Nightwatchman*. You guys have got to calm the fuck down or I'm going to—"

But no one in the car ever got to find out what Emmett was going to do. Any threat he could have issued was cut short when Toni reached up from her seat behind the journalist and then used both hands to pull a screwdriver back toward herself with such great force that it entered his mouth, punctured the meat of his throat, and exited the back of his neck in one swift motion.

She gave a second pull toward herself, part of her hands entering Emmett's mouth, driving the tool farther through the resistance it met near his vertebrae.

The point of the Phillips-head screwdriver slid through the space between Emmett's seat and headrest, but stopped a few inches short of Toni's clouded bright blue eyes.

Emmett screamed around the intruding device, and Toni seized that as an opportunity to grab his cheeks and pull back, exposing his newly bloody teeth as they clacked involuntarily against the plastic handle of the tool she'd run through his face.

His hands flapped against the steering wheel. His legs went stiff, jamming the accelerator to the floor.

"Brewer," yelled Lucy. "Lift his leg. Grab the wheel!"

Brewer's hands were occupied, the gun in his lap ignored. Lucy grabbed the weapon, surprised by how heavy it felt in her hands. She swiveled in the seat with her finger on the trigger.

Lucy noticed the tip of Toni's thumb, blackening and puckered blue where the Oracle in Marisol's neck had attacked her. Toni continued to pull up on the flesh of Emmett's face, trying to edge her damaged thumb toward one of his eyes.

"Something is stinging in the bite."

No.

But Judah was already leaning away from her and covering his ears. He knew what was coming, and so did Lucy.

Toni looked over at the barrel of the gun and smiled.

I'm sorry, Toni.

Lucy pulled the trigger.

It was not a clean shot. Lucy's aim was thrown off because she hadn't expected the kick, and the barrel shifted lower than she'd wanted. A perfectly round hole appeared in Toni's cheek before Lucy heard the blast, which set her ears ringing. She did not see the hole that appeared as the bullet exited, though she did see a fragment of skull flop over Toni's ear, tethered by a ribbon of scalp. A gush of blood spilled from Toni's mouth and then her head dropped forward. A tiny puff of smoke rose from the hole in the back of her head. Toni moaned once, coughed up another gout of blood, and stopped moving.

It was clear that Emmett remained alive, but his spine had been damaged. His hands had fallen to his lap and twitched there without purpose. Even over the instant tinnitus of the gunshot, Lucy heard his breath hitching against the wound in his throat.

Brewer finally managed to get a foot on the brake pedal, though he'd had no way or time to shift to a lower gear. The Eldorado skidded to a stop, then lurched and stalled.

For a moment, aside from Emmett's involuntary spasms, the people in the car were still.

Then Toni—who was sadly and certifiably in the throes of death—began to move. A small tremble in her head and shoulders, but enough to let Lucy and Judah know that there was life in her, and *that* life, sensing its host had perished, was ready to abandon its home.

Though it was obscured by the blood from Toni's head wound, something pulsed above her shoulder blades.

Judah said, "Oh, Jesus, let me out, Steve. She's infected. It's coming out of her neck."

"That can't be. It couldn't have grown inside her so quickly. Not from a bite."

Judah wasn't going to wait to find out. He reached over Steve and popped the door handle himself, letting in a gust of fresh air, which stood in sharp contrast with the smells of gun smoke and burnt flesh.

Toni's shaking became more severe. A single pinpoint drop of blood emerged above the mass in her neck. When it spilled to the side, a high-pitched whine emerged from the hole—the exhaust vent/beak announcing the arrival of a brand-new Oracle.

At that, both Judah and Steve burst out of the car. Brewer pushed against Lucy.

"C'mon. We gotta get out of here."

Lucy had other ideas. She didn't think Toni's last moments should be spent giving birth to an abomination. She said, "Forgive me, Antoinette," then pressed the barrel of the gun directly against the center of the squirming, squealing mass in Toni's neck, and fired again.

This time she knew to brace the gun. The shot was straight and true, and the thing in Toni's neck had been sent to the oblivion it deserved.

Blood pooled in the wound for a moment. When it ceased to bubble over, Lucy knew that Toni's heart had pumped its last. She would have wept, had she any tears remaining.

Steve was pacing on the sidewalk in front of Sammy's Deli, signs for Video Lottery and the "$2 Happy Hour Taquito Basket" flashing behind him.

"I mean, at this point how do we know the Oracle hasn't gone airborne? What else can this thing do? That gestation period was miraculous. Were there salivary papilla growing in the beak, injecting new cells? Or eggs? No, it must have converted *her* cells rather than growing its own. But how does it do that without creating an immune response? How is it shutting down our defenses? I don't think we can kill this thing. Maybe it's already too late. It's too late, right? TOO FUCKING LATE."

Steve crumpled against a lamppost.

Judah said, "Hey, you need to be quiet, man. There are more of them out there. They hear you, they'll come running."

"You don't *understand* . . . They may not even need to hear us. They could be watching us right now via their satellite uplink. I don't think it's working perfectly, but they could be receiving surveillance footage, an overlay wired into their visual cortex. Or maybe they've got the GPS data coming from Emmett's phone. Or who knows? The Oracle that grew in Toni might have already connected to their . . . *hive*. I think they know where we are. I think they're fucking with us. Playing with us. Even their anticipation could be triggering dopamine, feeding into their cycle. They're *savoring* us."

"Yeah, well, at least we know Emmett was right. We do sound like crazy people . . . But maybe you're right too, and they know where we are now. But if you're wrong, let's not give them any advantages."

"They have *all* the advantages. We're already dead. And I *did this*. For a company. For a fucking PAYCHECK."

Judah tried to help the man. "No. You couldn't have known. They didn't tell you everything. You thought it would help people, right? There's no way . . ."

"I killed them. Oh, Christ. I fucking killed them." Steve buried his face in his hands and began to cry.

Lucy approached, still holding the gun.

Judah was doing his best. "No. That thing inside Toni caused her death. And we don't know that Emmett—"

Lucy interrupted. "He's talking about his family." She looked at Steve on the ground. She contemplated the gun in her hand, and its potential for mercy.

I could finish this for all of us, right now.

She looked back at Brewer, who was leaning into the Caddy and trying to comfort Emmett.

"Let him cry, Judah. I need your help with something."

———————

"Do you think we can get that screwdriver out?"

Emmett's eyes had glazed, but he blinked when he realized Judah and Lucy were talking about him.

"No idea. Steve's the one with the medical expertise—"

"Steve's a fucking wreck. He's losing his damn mind right now, and I'm asking *you*."

Brewer was inside the car, holding Emmett's hand. "He's cold as hell, y'all. I don't know if taking out the screwdriver's gonna fix this."

"He could be right. What if we hit a vein when we pull it out?"

Lucy stood up straight and whispered to Judah as low as she could while trying to be heard over the ringing from the gunshots. "What the hell do we do? I don't know what the plan is, but I know we could really use this car."

"Maybe we could bandage him up and he could lay across the back seat. The four of us could squeeze into the front. Because even if we made him comfortable, I don't think we could leave him behind. Who knows what those infected twitcher things would do to him?"

Lucy imagined one of them sitting on Emmett's chest, slowly pulling the screwdriver out and then forcing it back through his neck at new angles.

"No, we can't leave him behind. But if we're going to put him in the back, we need to clean *that* up." Lucy nodded toward Toni's war-torn corpse.

"Oh, shit . . . I . . . I don't think I can . . ."

"You cared about her, right?"

"Yeah . . . a lot."

"Then you need to help us do this last thing for her."

———————

Sammy's Deli hadn't opened that morning, but its windows broke just fine, and within minutes Judah, Brewer, and Lucy had gathered a bag of premade deli sandwiches, a pallet of bottled waters, and a box of bar towels they could use to staunch Emmett's bleeding and to clean the back seat.

Judah wrapped Toni's head in a towel, gingerly replacing the section of her skull which had blown loose. He laid another towel across the entry wound in the back of her neck, per Lucy's suggestion.

"I don't think we should ever assume that whatever's infected her is all the way dead. There could be more growing inside her right now. Think about Marisol."

They did their best to be respectful as they moved Toni's corpse, but Lucy despised the revulsion that ran through her body and left her eager to drop the woman like a bag of trash.

They ruined her. They made every inch of her a weapon.

Lucy and Judah both shivered with relief once they'd deposited Toni's body, laying it sideways across the large red semicircle booth at the back of the deli.

"Was she religious?" asked Lucy.

"Raised Episcopal, I think, but now she only goes . . . she only went on holidays to keep her mom happy."

"Should we do the sign of the cross?"

"That's for when you're dying. She's dead now. She won't care."

"For her mom, I mean."

Tears welled in Judah's eyes. "Okay . . . yeah."

Both of them made the closest facsimile of the sign they could. Lucy said, "Rest in peace," then walked away, praying the monsters embedded in Toni's flesh were truly done with her.

———————

They opened all the car's doors in hopes that the smell of death might be lessened, then used bunched-up handfuls of bar towels to swipe as much pooled blood from the back seat as possible. Lucy and Judah tossed the saturated red rags into the street.

Littering. We've finally descended into a postapocalyptic society.

Lucy held back a smile because she was certain it would look like madness. She stepped out of the car to gather herself before she horrified the others.

If Bucket were here, I could have shared that joke with him.

She looked around at Steve, crumpled and silent, and Brewer trying to comfort Emmett as the man grew ever more pale, and Judah cleaning the last of his friend from the back seat.

No. No jokes.

Bucket and I grew that together. We had a place where we could put our worst thoughts.

That's gone now.

But maybe it doesn't have to be.

Lucy imagined a room in her mind. The ground was earthen and covered with ferns. Bucket had a weird affinity for the plants—said he liked the look of them and the tiny bumps under their leaves. The walls of the room were papered with all the notes she and Bucket had passed back and forth in class, the tiny tethers they'd used to feel less adrift. The room was lit by four large flat-screen TVs playing lesbian porn and hip-hop videos on loop.

Bucket was there, in the middle of the room, smiling, free from the massive injuries that had crushed his mind and stolen him from her life.

This is your place, Bucket. You can stay here.

Please stay here.

"Lucy!"

Brewer yelled from inside the car, tearing Lucy from her idyll.

"Something's happening."

Both Brewer and Judah had backed away from Emmett, who was shuddering in the driver's seat. His eyes had rolled back in his head, and his teeth were clenched around the handle of the screwdriver.

Lucy called over to Steve, who didn't acknowledge her in the slightest.

"Fuck. Did she infect him?" asked Judah, as he backed out of the car.

"I don't think so. His eyes are fine. Nothing's gonna grow in his neck. It's all torn up," Brewer said.

Still, Lucy didn't trust . . . well, anything anymore. "Get out of there, Brewer."

He popped out of the seat and ran around to the driver's side, watching the man with Lucy and Judah. Emmett's shivering worsened.

He's going to rupture. They're coming. A flood of them, and this time there'll be no Blumpers to distract them from swarming us and drilling into our necks . . .

Emmett's eyes rolled back into place. They were clear and scared. He looked toward Lucy and the others, but the screwdriver jutting from the back of his neck hit the right post of the headrest and he screamed in agony. His eyes rolled again, then refocused on the people staring at him from the street.

"Hep ee. Hers. Herso uch. Hep ee. Ay I sop."

Help me. Hurts. Hurts so much. Help me. Make it stop.

"It could be a trick," said Lucy.

Emmett pleaded with his eyes. A new surge of pain rolled through him and he yelled.

"HEP EE. HEP EE. EES GAH."

HELP ME. HELP ME. PLEASE, GOD.

Judah moved forward. Lucy tried to hold him back.

He turned to her and held out his hand. "Give it to me!"

"He could be infected."

"Maybe. Either way, there's only one way we know how to help him."

Lucy looked at Emmett, the depth of his injury, the whiteness of his face bright next to the blood cascading down his shirt.

Brewer said, "*Lucy.*"

She didn't want it to be true—Emmett had saved them and tried to help, and this was how the world rewarded him—but she also saw he was beyond any rescue outside the finality of what Judah was offering.

She handed over the gun.

She wasn't sure why she tried to watch what happened next. She told herself it was so she could help if Emmett really did turn out to be infected, but she didn't move any closer as Brewer and Judah grunted and lifted Emmett from the seat and carried him screaming to the sidewalk. They set him down and leaned his back against a dark blue post office box with his head tilted to the side. Judah held the gun by its barrel and offered it to Emmett, but the man's shaking worsened and he barely managed to gesture back in Judah's direction.

You.

You do it.

Emmett looked toward Lucy, his eyes wild and scared and human.

Not infected.

Then he closed his eyes, waiting for deliverance. Hoping, as Lucy had so many times in the last day, that the pain might stop.

Judah raised the gun. He stepped closer to ensure his aim would be true on the first shot.

He's been here before.

Lucy closed her eyes and imagined Judah with a stone in his raised hands, standing over the cat that Justin Norris had punted through the trees for no reason at all.

"Fast and clean. One hit."

The stone descended.

The gun fired.

Lucy opened her eyes on a world with one less kind soul, and wondered if such mercy would ever be afforded to her.

She turned back toward the rising sun and the bloodstained Eldorado, thoughts of a good death driving her toward whatever hell waited in the distance.

We have to end this, Buck, all of this, *before they win and this becomes forever.*

Bucket looked up at her, from his room in her mind, and smiled.

chapter sixteen

COMPOUND

I t was only when they popped the trunk of the Cadillac that they discovered how serious Emmett had been about going "gonzo." His suitcase boasted mostly weather-appropriate clothes, but a vintage TarGard cigarette holder and yellow-tinted specs were nestled in the middle, along with a dog-eared copy of *Hell's Angels*. It was the brief-case, however, and its panoply of tiny plastic liquor bottles, pills of all shapes and sizes, and barely dented bags of cocaine and mushrooms, that revealed the depth of Emmett's hero worship. Lucy saw Brewer's eyes light up at the discovery, but she could tell that he realized just as quickly that now was not so much the time for "gonzo" as it was the time for "hyperaware predator-prey evasion mode."

Besides, Lucy was much more interested in the two file folders tucked behind the drugs. The first had reams of info on IMTECH, mainly pertaining to patents and FDA filings. Nothing she hadn't al-ready learned through Steve, though the sterile language being used regarding the Oracle—personal integrated electronic device, synthetic guidance relays, two way media interface, et al.—caused bile to rise in her throat.

No one spoke the truth of it—"untested, highly experimental half-octopus mind-control implants" wasn't the kind of verbiage that garnered stamps of approval. But the employees had created their own reality where they were going to save us all, and they bent the language and the forms and the money kept moving, and now these documents read like the shittiest, most deceptive obituary the human race would ever get.

The second folder was a mystery to her. More permits and bureaucratic forms, but beneath that a batch of topographic maps and water table measurements and pipeline installation schedules. A single Post-it note attached to the front of the folder read, "Who needs this much water?"

Another question she couldn't answer. Another chance to sense how fucked up the world was becoming without any accompanying idea of how to stop all of it from getting worse.

She threw both folders back into the open trunk and put her hands on the bumper. Her head swam. Her vision went static for a moment, and when she returned there were tears in her eyes.

How am I supposed to fight this?

She felt the sun on her back, imagined that heat as weight bearing down on her.

This isn't fair. I'm only a kid. A fucking kid.

Holy shit. We're all going to die.

Everyone.

She started rocking uncontrollably.

How am I supposed to stop this?

She felt like grabbing the briefcase and gun and disappearing to the woods with Brewer.

We'll just get fucking high and ignore all of this and survive for as long as we can. And when they come for us, we'll do what we have to do, and it'll all be over.

She felt Brewer's hands on her back. "Lucy?"

She turned and squeezed him as hard as she could. She buried her face in his chest and hoped the sound of his heart would be louder than the panicked heartbeat she could feel inside her head. "I can't, Brewer. I can't do this anymore. I thought I was strong, but—"

"It's okay." His right hand rubbed her back, and part of her wanted to stay in that space and feel good for one fucking second, but then something about the way he'd tried to placate her so simply, the deep lie hidden in his kindness, caused her to burn inside.

It's okay?

The old Lucy, the one who clung to survival at all costs, had been ignited, and she cursed Brewer for accidentally setting off what she knew she couldn't contain. She imagined her spine glowing white until it was blinding and inescapable.

"It's okay? It's *okay?*" Lucy pushed away from Brewer and straightened herself. "We're *dying*. They're hunting us. For *fun*! We don't know how to stop them or even what they are, and there's nothing about this that will ever, ever be even remotely close to fucking okay!"

"Lucy, that wasn't what I meant. I just . . ."

But she was already walking away from him, her mind set to action, the only way she knew to calm the rage tearing at her insides.

She ran to the front of the car and grabbed her utility knife from the passenger floor, sliding the blade into her back pocket. Then she walked over and squatted in front of Steve, his face soaked with tears, and grabbed fistfuls of his shirt on each side of his collar.

"Get up, you motherfucker. You had your time. You don't get to cry your fucking goddamn crocodile tears anymore, all right? You're going to get up and fucking help us because *I can't goddamn do this anymore*, but I can't let them make the whole world like this fucking shitbrick town, so *you* stand up right now, and you do right by all the people you did wrong and you use that fucking big nerd brain of yours to figure out a way to fix what you started. *Then* you can lie down and die. But not right now. Not today. *Today you help.* Today you make this right, or I swear to god I'll fucking kill you myself."

For a moment Lucy could feel Brewer and Judah's eyes on her, and she remembered the way Bucket and Brewer had looked at her when she killed the boy in her living room, and then she felt like a witness too, standing behind herself, observing this other Lucy and realizing that she was telling the truth and that they might all watch her draw her blade and slice open Steve's neck from ear to ear.

This second Lucy stood silent witness behind the first, feeling broken and small and exhausted. Then Steve finally focused his eyes and lifted himself from his mourning and rose to his feet. He met Lucy's eyes and nodded.

"You're right. And I'm sorry."

"Fuck your 'sorry.'"

"Yeah."

"Just fight."

"I will."

Then the second version of Lucy merged with the first, and she was whole again, and she couldn't tell if she was more scared or furious, and she wasn't sure if she should hug the sad old man in front of her or slap his face, so she did neither and returned to the road.

No one was willing to sit in the back seat, for fear that the stains of Toni's murder might carry some kind of blood-borne pathogenic offspring of the Oracle. Emmett's mess had also proven difficult to clean in its entirety, so they draped the driver's seat in towels and called it good. Brewer drove since the Caddy was a stick, and Lucy sat next to him, packed in with Judah and then Steve to her right. They kept to quiet residential side streets while Steve pored over the documents from Emmett's briefcase.

Finally, Steve ceased nodding and mumbling to himself and said, "We have to open their eyes, and then we have to force their hand. I think there's a way we can do that, but first I need to know if any of you can get your hands on an explosive device."

"Yeah, that's funny, Steve," said Judah. "Let's drop by my house and we can grab some C4 and detonators."

"I'm not joking. Not at all. And it doesn't have to be C4. Anything strong enough to blow open commercial-grade PVC piping will do."

"Well, if *that's* all we need . . ." said Judah.

"I know where we can get something," said Brewer.

"We can't risk going to the Down and Dirty," said Lucy. "Look what happened last time we tried that. And now it's daylight. The town is crawling . . ."

"It's not in the city. My cousin Rodney's place. His storage shed."

"What kind of device are we talking about?" asked Steve.

"Pipe bomb. Big one."

"What the fuck?" said Judah. "He get that from the Jessups?"

"No, he doesn't run with them anymore. They got too far into that Nazi shit."

"Why the hell does he have a pipe bomb, then?"

"It's dumb . . . Sometimes we like to go out to the desert and blow shit up."

Lucy remembered his story about throwing furniture into the landfill, watching it explode. Seems like Brewer had a deep affinity for watching things be destroyed.

Is that why he likes me? Could he see that destructiveness in me, even when I couldn't see it myself? What did he say about me? "Seems like you have a lot going on." He didn't know the half.

Lucy found she was smiling.

Maybe he likes the worst in me. Maybe I should too.

"Rodney and I were waiting for his summer bonus, then we were gonna use some of it to buy a junker car, some shitty little hatchback,

254 JEREMY ROBERT JOHNSON

and drive it out near Burns and blow it up. Throw a party afterward. Bonfire in the wreckage."

"Jesus." Judah laughed.

"Well, it's something we liked since we were kids . . . but I don't think we're gonna get that chance. So that thing is sitting there, unless Rodney managed to bail from his place and he took it with him."

"What's inside the bomb?" asked Steve.

"Mainly BBs. Handful of screws. You think that'd do what we need?"

"I do."

"But why are we blowing up some pipe?"

"There are maps in Emmett's files that show there's a preliminary stretch of this pipeline expansion already in place, open and running aboveground. The pipeline is maybe half a mile north of the East Bear Caves."

"So?"

"If what you saw, and if what the man who blinded himself outside the school thought he saw, if that's all true, then I think the Oracle has been filling the East Bear Caves with eggs. You saw a black shiny mass clinging to the ceiling, right?"

"Yeah."

"So what if that man's vision was correct, and that's really all that remains of two girls who were impregnated by the first test subject to receive the Oracle? What if they've figured out a way to replicate by the thousands, on a scale far beyond what we've seen in the regular human hosts? If that's the case, if we can show the people watching this test how dangerous this organism has become, then maybe that triggers their protection protocols, and they wipe it off the face of the planet."

"Sure," said Lucy. "But how do we know they haven't already seen that through Jason's feed? Maybe, because they're the kind of fucking assholes who feel fine killing civilians for research, they don't care. Maybe they're only curious."

"That's why we need the explosive. If we rupture the pipeline, the topography slants toward the river. The water table there is high. The lava caves exist like they do because they were once perfect conduits for anything flowing through the area. If the water rushes through the caves, which I believe it would, then it'll carry the Oracle eggs with it to the groundwater and all the little tributaries feeding into the Deschutes River. After that, there's no stopping the Oracle from infecting the rest of the world. They'll know that."

"And these protection protocols—that's them dropping a bomb on us, right?"

"I hope. And maybe more than one bomb. They'll know it has to be a massive strike. Total destruction. Even the cave systems collapsed. But they've got the Handsome Valley leak for cover. Full media containment, so far. They seal off the area afterward, ban flyovers. They wouldn't even need to use the gold codes. The president would be granted full deniability. Hell, maybe they even get to test a new kind of bomb."

"But we're not really going to blow up the irrigation line, right?"

"Shouldn't have to. We only need one of their drones or one of the infected to see us setting the thing up for detonation, and they should launch their cleanup preemptively."

"But how will they know what we're doing? Or where to find us?"

"We're going to walk right up and tell them."

Then Lucy listened to the rest of Steve's plan, and though it seemed like madness Lucy found herself believing in every word of it because of what she saw in the man's eyes: more than anything he wanted revenge against the Oracle and all the people, including himself, who were responsible for the death of his wife and child. Beyond that was his sadness, and his desire that his life might finally end.

As far as architects for kamikaze death runs went, Steve had all the right stuff.

The plan was agreed to, and Brewer steered the Eldorado onto Westerhaus, toward the place he'd once called home.

———————

Lucy could tell Brewer grew nervous as they got closer to his property. His hands fidgeted on the wheel. He sighed and took long breaths.

"What is it?" she asked.

"I shouldn't say. It's dumb. Like a leftover thing from before all this other shit went down."

"Dumb's fine. It doesn't matter anymore."

"Yeah, right? I, uh . . . I've never brought anybody by my place, so I never had to say this before, but . . . my family doesn't have much."

It's burned into him. This sense of being poor, of being less because of it. This fucking town.

"I'm the only one who even made it this far into high school. My whole family, we're pretty much full-on white trash. Some of 'em sell drugs. Or *sold* 'em. Who knows? I don't know if any of them are alive anymore, which is crazy. But I know those rumors are true. And my aunt treats her dogs like shit, but she doesn't *fight* 'em. Those rumors are bullshit. I've got a cousin in juvie for rape. Another one was in jail for selling meth, but he OD'd on heroin when he was inside. And then my whole family got five-star shithoused at his funeral like none of them got the message. Just hopeless. And Rodney's pretty racist, if I'm telling the whole truth. So—"

"Stop."

"I just don't want you to think I'm something I'm not. I don't want you to be, like . . ."

"Disappointed?"

"Yeah."

I can't watch him freak out like this. It's the end-times, right? Might as well go full disclosure.

"Danny Brewer, you are the least disappointing person I've ever met, okay? In fact, if I had a chance to know you long enough, I'd probably fall in love with you. Maybe that's already happened. I can't process anything like that anymore. But know that, all right? I think you're fucking awesome. And I don't give a *shit* about your family, or mine. My birth parents were the worst alcoholics I ever met, and they barely managed to keep me alive, and they almost never kept me safe. And then one day they took me out for a drive and my dad passed out at the wheel and drove us right into a fucking school bus. Then, before the Hendersons saved me, I was in an orphanage where the older girls beat me and locked me in a storage closet for fun. After that, even though the Hendersons did so much for me, I never figured out a way to let them all the way into my heart, and now they're probably dead too, and I'll never get the chance to let them know what they meant to me."

"Fuck. I'm—"

"Don't be sorry. Just . . . don't be. Because our families were our families, all right, and they're part of us, but they're also not *us*. We are who we are, together, *right now*. And that's all there is to it, all right?"

"Okay . . . yeah. Yeah, that's good. All that being said, though, there's one other thing."

"What the fuck?"

"Not a biggie, but I don't want you to get weirded out if you notice, all right? Because there's hella porno in my room. Like, *racks* of it."

"DVDs?"

"Yeah. And magazines."

"Really?"

"Sometimes the internet goes down."

Lucy laughed then, and she missed Bucket, and she also wanted to cry because she could feel how much of being young and stupid had been stripped away from her, and how weird and glorious it all could have been. But in the end there wasn't much time to feel any of that, because Brewer turned onto a rocky dirt road, and they were approaching his family's muddy manufactured home compound and when they got close enough they saw that two of the buildings ahead of them had been burned to the ground. All that remained of the first were a few fixtures and the charred stubs of cinder-block supports. There was more left of the second, but what was left behind was far worse.

———————

Judah had Emmett's gun, so he ran up to the buildings first, then hollered back.

"I don't see anybody. I think they're long gone. But, uh . . . I don't think you want to come over here."

Brewer pulled the keys and handed them to Steve, who had returned to his grief coma. Then he hopped out of the car, his face ashen. He swallowed hard. Lucy got out after him.

"Whatever you see, you never forget," said Lucy.

"If our plan works, then how long do I have to remember, anyway?" asked Brewer. He walked toward the husks of his family's housing. "I need to know."

She wanted to hold him back, and wondered if he noticed the acrid smells floating from the wreckage.

He has to know they're dead. Isn't that enough?

She realized he wasn't going to stop, and ran to catch up.

Brewer took one bound to the top of the poured concrete steps, looked through the space where there used to be a doorway, and stopped in his tracks.

Lucy looked over his shoulder and found it tough to know—among all that bone and melted fat and flesh—who had died, and how. A small body sat in the remnants of a La-Z-Boy, the charred corpse supine, its jawbone hanging loose, its arms laid to its side, a third, larger arm erupting from its mouth. On the floor were the remains of two adults, their legs bound with steel wire. They might have been men, based on what was left of the hair. The torsos of two dogs lay between them, their ribs interwoven in a way that must have happened before they were set afire. But all of their limbs—man and dog—were in disarray. One man was missing an arm, and Lucy guessed that was the one that had been planted in the skull of the body in the chair. The others' arms were missing, and had been replaced with the dogs' heads, their burnt faces retracted into permanent snarls. The left body had its torso opened up, the organs pulled free and slopped to the side. The right body had its chest caved in, a partially melted mono-grammed bowling ball resting in between its shattered ribs.

The letters on the ball read "RPB."

Rodney Brewer.

Fuck.

"My aunt would have been watching her stories in that chair. She told me she had days of soap operas saved up," said Brewer. He turned to Lucy. "You said the message was coming out of the TVs right? So maybe she was in that coma before, uh . . . before they got to her. But Rodney and Eric . . . You think they felt all that? You think they made them watch?"

Lucy wasn't sure there was time built into their schedule for Brewer to lose his mind, so she lied.

"No. They were strong guys. I bet they killed them first, then did all this to send us a message."

"You think they did this *because* of us?"

Shit.

"No." More lies.

Make this better.

There is no "better."

Lucy suddenly understood the simplicity of Brewer telling her, *It's okay.* Sometimes you were only trying to keep the other person sane, and there was no true consoling to be done.

She said, "Have you seen anyone moving in the city, aside from Emmett? I think they came for everyone who was still breathing. I think they washed over Turner Falls like a wave."

"They knew where I lived, though. What if I'd never sold drugs to any of them?"

"They'd have known where you lived anyway. They have *all* the information, remember? This isn't your fault." She tried to turn his gaze away from the carnage, toward her. He wouldn't budge. Lucy wasn't sure he was breathing, and wondered if she could catch him if he lost consciousness.

She took a step closer, and at first she thought the cracking sound she heard was a floorboard giving way beneath her. But the next sound, Judah crying out in pain, told her otherwise.

She rotated toward the scream and saw Judah staggering to one side, pawing feebly at the axe blade that had been buried in the back of his head. Their gun tumbled from his waistband and hit the ground with a dull thud. A girl of maybe eleven stood behind him, smiling in purple pajamas, the spasms in her face smoothing as she watched Judah tumble to the dust.

The Community Emergency Hub. They infected more of the town.

What did Emma's dad say? "The demons have her. They sprang from her mouth."

How many of them are there now?

"Brewer!"

He finally turned, his eyes moving from one shock to the next, but he was no longer paralyzed by what he saw. Whatever anger Lucy'd found in herself seemed to have infected Brewer. He leapt from the ruins of his house and ran to Judah's body, placing one foot on his friend's back and prying the axe free from his skull. It made a squeaking sound as it was unmoored from the sheared bone, and Lucy saw a brief glimpse of Judah's exposed brain before the gash filled in with new blood.

To Brewer's right, the little girl and Steve were both scrambling for the fallen gun. Brewer approached with the axe. Lucy anticipated another cracking sound but never got to see what happened.

One moment she was standing, the next something had a vise grip on her ankles and was pulling her feet from beneath her. Her head smacked to the blackened floorboards, then swam.

A voice from above her.

"Loogie. You came. We knew you'd come."

Who the fuck?

"Rolling with that fu . . . fu . . . fuckin' crackhead, Brewster, huh? Did him a favor, burning this shit down. You should have seen Rodney. Crying like a bitch, that bowling ball thumping in his chest while his heart was still beating. I think I can . . . yeah . . . I can see it again. Getting better . . . at . . . this."

Ben Brumke. But the nail marks she'd torn into his face were healing fast—too fast. And he was standing above her. When Emmett had seen him, his legs were on backward. How . . .

His eyes were even bluer and more clouded than usual as he revisited his memories of slaying Brewer's family. Then, as quickly as they had fogged, the opacity drifted away and his eyes were sharp and cruel again.

"We've been hoping for another chance to play with you."

He swung a hammer down within an inch of her face, splintering the floorboard next to her.

"You see that? They're making me *stronger.* I thought I was done, after the wreck."

He swung the hammer down a second time, by the other side of her head.

"But we *grew.* They made the connections work again. They made me feel so good. And all I have to do is shit like this." He pointed to the corpse-strewn floor. "Honestly, I wish I always would have done this shit. Feels better every time, like Jason said it would. And now he's gone, and there's something bigger growing in *here.*" Brumke tapped his head with his hammer. "The more we feed it, the less time we spend in the empty space. The better it makes us feel."

Behind Lucy's field of vision, the little girl was screaming. Gunfire rang out.

Was she attacking someone? Being attacked?

Brumke looked up, apparently curious to see the source of the wailing.

Any chance to see another death.

Lucy seized on the moment's distraction, and what happened next was a blur. Lucy swung her left leg as hard as she could, sweeping sideways through both of Ben's shins, and whatever tissue the Oracle had rewoven through his spine and legs must not have been that strong, because she heard something inside him snap before his body even slammed to the floor. Then she was on top of him, and his arm was swinging back, hammer in hand, but she saw her own right hand descending faster, a shard of splintered wood flooring in her fist, and when she drove it into his left eye he lost the will to attack her any further and the hammer clattered to the floor.

Not that Lucy noticed his collapse—she'd become the *other* Lucy again, a fire burning in her chest, and only knew that whoever or whatever was beneath her would never get a chance to attack her again. She made certain of that by driving her left thumb into his other eye and then pulling to the side until she felt something give. It was only then that she returned to herself and heard the pitiful voice coming from beneath her tensed body.

"Where am I? Oh god, where am I? Mom. MOM! IT HURTS!"

It's Ben in there now.

Not the Oracle. Only a boy.

But how?

Does it matter?

"PLEASE. HELP ME."

Lucy honored his request, and helped him the only way she knew how.

The hammer felt good in her hands, and she raised it as high as she was capable, hoping she could cause brain death with the first swing.

There was a cracking sound, which echoed in the desert air. The hammer struck deep. Ben Brumke stropped screaming, but his hands spasmed at his sides. Lucy cursed herself for not succeeding the first time, and swung again.

This time she knew she'd succeeded because of the awful high-pitched whistling that emerged from the boy's throat.

The Oracle needed a new user.

Lucy felt revulsion roll through her and drove the hammer down into the squealing mass that twitched in Brumke's neck, striking until his skin split and the inside of his neck pulped and flattened and finally the sound of the growth inside of him squelched to a stop.

Then she stood and turned to see Brewer, the boy she thought she might love. He was barely standing, leaning his weight against a bloody axe and breathing hard. Sweat trickled down his face. The remains of the parasitized little girl lay before him, a gunshot wound in her abdomen, her head separated from her body and rolling toward the rocky driveway like a drifting tumbleweed.

Lucy waved to him with her free hand, unsure of the world, her sanity, everything. Then she said the first thing that came to her mind.

"It's okay."

She started laughing, unsure she'd ever be able to stop.

The axe made easy work of the padlock on the storage shed. Lucy was glad when they found the bomb, though it was smaller and simpler than she'd imagined.

According to Brewer, Rodney had rigged the pipe bomb with a long delay ignition fuse, partly because he wasn't that technically adept, and partly because he'd liked the idea of lighting the thing like an old-school stick of dynamite. However, Steve had said that for his plan to work, the bomb would have to have the appearance of being rigged to a handheld electric detonator, and after a few minutes in the shed Brewer rigged up what he hoped would be a reasonable facsimile.

Then they'd wrapped the pipe bomb in a bundle of Emmett's clothing and carefully secured it in his luggage in the trunk.

Knowing the bomb was in the car with them made Lucy inherently nervous, but less so than if she wasn't already planning on dying that afternoon.

They left Judah facedown in the dirt, finally too exhausted for the ornament of funereal proceedings. She figured each of them knew he'd been a good guy, and each of them knew how very dead and carefree he'd become.

Brewer and Lucy loaded into the car first. He shook Steve into awareness, grabbed the keys, and started the engine. Lucy's delirium had finally subsided, and she felt emptied out. She leaned her head against Brewer's shoulder.

Steve opened his mouth as if to ask them what had happened, looked at them for a moment longer as he registered Judah's absence, then said, "Fuck. We have to get going." He hopped out of the car and after a few moments of searching through the trunk, returned and closed the passenger-side door.

He held out a two-foot-by-two-foot piece of poster board. The side facing them read "GO SARAH! ONE MILE AT A TIME & BEER AT THE FINISH!" The other side, luckily, was blank.

Steve said, "Daylight's wasting. Let's head east."

He uncapped a fat-tipped Sharpie pen and began to write on the blank side of the poster board. They drove away from the Brewer compound with high hopes that everything they'd done and seen there might soon be turned to dust.

chapter seventeen

CELL DIVISION

S teve's handwriting wasn't aces, and he'd crammed a lot of info into the sign. Beyond that, half of it read like code. Lucy realized she'd simply have to trust that what he'd written would be enough to convince them to do the unthinkable.

We want them to destroy a prominent American city with a nuke. And we're depending on a grief-stricken scientist with a little piece of poster board and two teenagers with a pipe bomb to do the job.

We're fucking doomed.

Lucy read Steve's sign one more time:

RISK LEVEL 5
M.-ORG. EVOLVING BEYOND CAT. 4
NO CONT. PROTOCOLS ADEQUATE
NO TREATMENT POSSIBLE
MULTIPHASIC/MULTIPAROUS
WATERBORNE SPREAD INITIATING @ 1400 HRS
43° 57.016 N/121° 10.638 W
TACTICAL/TOTAL ERADICATION ONLY OPTION!

She handed the sign back to Steve.

"You think it's enough?"

"It has to be, right?"

"And what's this here? All the numbers."

"According to Emmett's documents, that's the latitude and longitude of where you're going to blow the pipe. Or where you're going to plant the bomb at least. I marked it on the map I gave to Brewer. He said he knows the area. And however they surveil you, you need to be certain they see the detonator in your hand. That's all that'll keep them from killing you and sending in the bomb robots to extract the device. So you need to be close together, with your hands entwined on the detonator."

"And what about you?"

"What about *me*? I don't know. They'll kill me. I don't think they'll risk trying to quarantine me, though it's a best-case scenario if I can lay out the entire situation for them in person."

"Oh, you think they'll invite you in for tea?"

"Right." Steve found it in himself to laugh. "No, they'll probably kill me from a distance. I just have to make sure they see this message first. Maybe they incapacitate me, and you guys do what you need to do, and I live long enough to see the blast."

"You'd want that?"

"I want to know that the Oracle had been entirely destroyed. If there's an eternity waiting, that's the only thing that might save me from damnation and let me join my family."

"Wait . . . you believe in that stuff?"

"Didn't before. Hardcore atheist. But what I've seen the last two days . . . If there is a hell, that's what we've unleashed. So maybe there's something else out there too."

"Yeah . . . maybe."

Lucy didn't buy his line of reasoning, but she felt what he was saying—he wanted to be saved from himself.

Join the crowd, pal.

Brewer turned onto the highway headed east. A few new residential developments dotted the landscape, but soon they disappeared, and all that was left was the black road and the green-beige desert and the distant snowcapped mountains, and—somewhere between them and the rest of the world—the men and women who were perfectly fine with watching them die.

———————

They drove until they could see the blockade—layers of concrete barricades and military vehicles, vans and communications towers, and behind them what looked like a gargantuan wall of speakers crowned by bright, shining silver balls.

"What the hell is that?" asked Brewer.

"No idea. Never seen anything like it before," said Steve. "You hear that humming sound?"

Lucy heard it. She looked down at her arms—all the fine little hairs were standing on end.

It's where the broadcast is coming from. It's how they paralyzed the whole town. Or it's what they're using to block our cell signals. Or it's designed to shut down the Oracle uplink if any of the infected make it this far.

It's massive. *How long has the equipment been out here, or stationed close by?*

How long have they been planning this?

"You know where you need to go?" asked Steve.

Brewer nodded. "It's only about a mile and a half the other way, then a little side road, and we'll be there."

The Eldorado was already pointed the other direction, doors open, engine running. Steve's highlighted topographic map showing the location of the pipeline sat on the front seat, weighted down by Emmett's half-emptied gun. The pipe bomb had been moved up to the back seat. Brewer had one of Emmett's lighters in his pocket in case they had cause to light the bomb's real fuse, which was now clipped perilously short. Lucy had the hammer in her left hand and the utility knife in her back pocket.

The last time she'd come out this way with the Hendersons, they'd picnicked near a popular climbing area, and Bill had shown her how to extract nectar from the bulbs of honeysuckle flowers. She'd had fun until she accidentally picked a flower with a bee nestled beneath the petals, and she received a vicious sting on the border of her lower lip. Then Bill made her an ice compress with a paper towel and some cubes from the cooler, and he made a few dad jokes about how Lucy should "bee more careful," and things were good again.

A different world. A different existence.

Before we went to war.

I'll never know a feeling like that again. But maybe we can keep that world from disappearing altogether.

Steve looked at his watch.

Lucy imagined the digital readout: "TIME TO DIE."

If Steve was afraid, he didn't show it. He picked up his sign, made sure the right side was facing forward.

Brewer put a hand on the man's back. "Good luck."

"Thanks," said Steve. "You too. And remember, if your watch says two and they haven't taken any measures, you have to light the real fuse. You have to force their hand. Are you sure you can do that?"

Brewer looked at the distant blockade. Lucy wondered if he was thinking about his family, and how what little he had was savaged and burned to the ground. Or was he imagining a future where he was the person responsible for unleashing that terror on the rest of the world? What if the military didn't believe them? What if Brewer brought down the flood and no one stopped those contaminated waters from rising and infecting the planet, city by city?

Fucking hell. We should be getting milkshakes and sitting in the park right now.

Steve should be with his family, sharing popcorn on the couch, watching some dumb superhero movie.

Lucy closed her eyes tightly and wished for one moment that the madness of their lives would be burned away, like a fever spiking and fading. But then she opened her eyes and Steve said, "This is it," and began walking toward the blockade.

"Steve, stop." He paused. Lucy ran to him.

"I want you to know that I'm thankful that you got back up, all right? Thank you for fighting."

Steve smiled. "You were going to kill me."

"Yeah . . . but you probably wanted that, anyway." Steve hung his head. "That would have been easy for you. *This* . . . isn't. And I think your family, wherever they are now . . . I think they would have been proud of you."

Steve looked up at the sky, then blinked a few times and looked back to Lucy. "Okay, kid. I have to go. There's no more time."

He was right. She couldn't even guess how long ago they'd passed the point of no return. All they had now was the plan. Steve raised his sign above his head and continued down the road.

Lucy walked the other way, back to Brewer and the car. She wasn't sure that what she'd told Steve about his family was the truth, but even if it *was* a lie, it was the right thing to give him before he walked toward his death.

———

They watched through the rear windshield of the car. Brewer already had the Eldorado shifted into first, one foot on the brake, the other hovering over the accelerator. Steve had wanted them to drive off immediately, before any pursuit might be attempted, but Brewer and Lucy *needed* to know that Steve's message had been received. Otherwise, what was the point? What if they sped off and found themselves sitting by the pipeline, cradling an explosive device, and no one even knew they were there? Or worse, what if more of those twitchy, murderous assholes crawled up from the cave system beneath them and attacked before anyone back at the blockade had a chance to verify that all of the threats, human and inhuman, were real?

Emmett hadn't left them any binoculars in his stash. Lucy tried to use the zoom feature on Steve's camera to watch his approach, but the image shook so drastically with each of her thunderous heartbeats that she kept losing sight of him.

Brewer turned away. "I can't watch. We need to *go*."

"One more minute. *Please.* I need to know."

Steve grew smaller with distance, shrinking away from them. Lucy squinted to block the noontime sun from her eyes.

Brewer's right. We need to go. Can this hooptie outrun anything they'd send for us?

Wait. Where did Steve go?

She scanned the horizon, then realized she'd lost him for a moment because he wasn't in motion.

"He stopped."

"Are they talking to him over loudspeakers?" Brewer rolled down his window to listen. "Are they sending someone out to talk to him?"

Lucy saw motion. A small drone, hovering ten or twenty feet above where Steve stood. She couldn't see much of it—a thin black frame, some kind of white container attached to its undercarriage.

"Not someone. Something. A drone."

"Fuck yes. They'll see the sign. They'll know!"

Steve appeared to think the same. She could see him adjusting the position of the sign, tilting it toward the hovering machine. His body and hands shook—was he yelling at them?

Whatever Steve was doing, it seemed to trigger an immediate response. Something on the underside of the drone sparked.

A flash? Surveillance shots of Steve and our sign?

But then Lucy saw a shimmer in the air beneath the drone, and a thin, black shape extending from its center, persistent bright light shining at the end of the mechanical proboscis.

Not a flash.

"Oh god," said Lucy.

The drone dropped to Steve's height.

He had turned to run, still holding the sign, when the spark of light became a jet of flame, engulfing him in one bright burst, his body swiftly saturated in whatever propellant came streaming from the flamethrower mounted to the drone's underbelly.

Lucy yelled to Brewer. "GO!"

The Eldorado lunged forward, almost throwing Lucy over her seat and into the contaminated rear of the vehicle. She braced herself and watched as Steve took two steps, then three, then collapsed atop their sign, all of it burning bright white and spewing thick curls of jet black smoke into the sky.

Did they see the sign?

They had to see it, right?

She pictured the drone jockey in his control station, seeing motion, the man coming closer to their perimeter.

What if all he saw was a threat, another of the infected attempting to break free of the company-controlled testing zone? What if his job was simply to torch everything that moved?

Did they see the sign?

She looked away from the flaming carnage. Steve had done all he could. He had tried, and now he was gone.

But did his message get through?

FUCK.

She looked at Brewer, his hands like a death grip on the wheel of the car, skin flushed red, eyes wild. His face so young, and terrified.

We're all that's left.

Do they know what they have to do?

Behind Lucy, Steve and the message were smoldering, a black blot of ash on the desert floor.

Ahead of her lay only uncertainty. One final hope remained, repeating on loop, vibrating in her bones.

Please let them understand,
And make them kill us all.
Save us.
Please.
Save us from what we've done.
Burn us from the Earth.
Amen.

After a minute of checking the skies and the road behind them, Lucy realized that she'd almost been hoping for pursuit. Something that would show they'd received Steve's message. Something that would show they gave a damn.

Chase us to the caves. I'll show you where two girls oozed up to the ceiling and ruptured into a thousand baby Oracles.

Nope. No JLTVs roaring up the highway. She leaned her head out the window. No drones overhead, no helicopters sighting them in. If it weren't for the rush of air through the windows and the thrumming of the Caddy's engine, the silence would be absolute.

"You think they saw it? Before they burned him?"

She imagined a group of military brass and scientists and businessmen watching a bank of monitors, their faces emotionless. Viewing results. Running the numbers.

Contemplating future opportunities.

She imagined the trigger-happy drone pilot, bored near comatose, activating the weapon on his toy the moment he saw motion, thinking a moment later, *What a minute. What was on that sign?*

A single mistake that would cost them the world.

Lucy recognized the deep panic in Brewer's voice, his rapid breathing and pallid skin.

He's losing it.

Which is totally the right response.

We shouldn't have to bear this weight. But it's ours, and there's no one else to carry it.

So—another lie, the sound of it allowing their death march to continue: "I think they saw it, and they believed him. That's why they weren't taking any risks. That's why they killed him right away."

"They're gonna start their cleanup?" His voice lifted.

He needs these lies, the hope.

So do I.

"I think so. So let's make sure we get to the pipeline before one of those drones catches up and we get crispy crittered in the front of this old-ass car."

She imagined a wall of flame rolling in through one of their open windows, felt the heat on her skin, pictured how they'd be burning, trying to scream through melting skin as the Eldorado careened over the shoulder and drifted into the desert with smoke rolling away behind it.

He must have imagined it too. They both reached out and rolled up their windows.

They passed a small green metal sign reading 19. A charred tree was in the distance, its stark whites and blacks in high contrast with the living green around it.

The juniper that was hit by lightning.

Brewer told me about that in another world, before we went down into the caves. Before I came out a murderer and spent my summer vacation watching everyone die.

They reached the turnoff for East Bear Caves, Brewer driving so fast that the rear of the car fishtailed a moment before straightening out.

Lucy remembered what Brewer had said to her and Bucket the

first time they turned down the old dirt road. She decided they needed to mark the occasion once more, and said it again in the best Brewer voice she could.

"Here we go. *Party time, y'all.*"

The sound of it broke her heart a little this time around, but then Brewer said, "Holy shit, Lucy," and they both laughed, and it was good to have something that was theirs, if only for a moment.

The pipeline was bigger than they expected, standing nearly as tall as Brewer. The black plastic PVC looked thick and hard, and gave off a noxious chemical smell that increased as they approached. It was held in place by a series of concrete supports and bolted rings, and it looked to Lucy to be sturdy and indestructible and basically the end of the fucking road as far as their little plan was concerned.

"You think Rodney's little bomb is going to put a dent in this?"

"I think so, yeah. If we can tuck it underneath, right by one of those supports . . . Won't be much room for the bomb to release its energy. Firecracker in your palm gives you a little burn, but you close your fingers around it and it blows them off, right?"

Lucy was amused but not surprised to discover that enough people had been fucking stupid enough that the effects of closing your hand around a lit firecracker would be a commonly known thing. She hadn't heard that before, but she trusted Brewer.

"Right. So where do we put it? He didn't give us a lot of line on the detonator."

"Well, this side is facing the caves, so . . ." Brewer walked along a length of the pipe, peering underneath the bottom. "There's a gap here. We can wedge the bomb in, layer some duct tape from the trunk over it to be sure it stays in place. Then we spool out the line to the detonator, wrap our hands around it, and wait for the cavalry to show up and confirm we're crazy enough to turn this whole place into a floodplain." Brewer looked down at his watch. "What time you got?"

She thought: *Time to realize this plan is madness, the last sad ravings of a man who wanted to believe he could redeem his unredeemable acts. Time for you and me to hit the Caddy and drive as deep into the desert as they'll allow us, so we can do all of Emmett's drugs and fuck our brains out until we overdose or they send out goddamned flying robots to set us on fire. Time to give up this hero bullshit and grab whatever time we have left to just be Brewer and Lucy before it's all over.*

She remembered: Steve's predictions—Earth's living creatures as one festering mass of Oracle-infected flesh, subservient and suffering for eternity.

She said: "One forty-eight. I'll grab the bomb."

Lucy didn't know that despair was something which could fall over you in layers, or that the weight of it increased exponentially with every minute after an expected apocalypse failed to show.

Their hands were clasped together on Brewer's jerry-built imitation detonator, and both of them could see the time on his watch.

2:03 p.m.

Not dead yet.

Oracle still spreading.

They didn't see Steve's message. Or they didn't believe it.

Or they don't care.

At least, Lucy thought, *I'm with Brewer.* He'd sat with his back against one of the supports for the pipeline. She'd sat between his legs and leaned against him, feeling the rapid rise and fall of his chest, the heat of his skin through their shirts. She wanted to press closer to him, to feel nothing between them, but they had to remain ready. She needed to see something, *anything*, watching them. Someone had to acknowledge that they were there. Someone had to do the right thing to stop them from bringing down the flood.

Are they calling our bluff?

Maybe Brewer's watch is fast.

Gray clouds rolled in over the desert—Lucy was always amazed at how quickly the clouds moved when you were out in the flatlands. The sun was dimmed, and a breeze rolled across the ground, whipping through the two-foot gap beneath the pipeline, drawing shivers out of Lucy and Brewer. He held her tighter. Warmth bloomed in her chest, the feeling another comforting lie.

Like Steve said—Oxytocin, right? More stimulus and response. I'm a slave to it as much as those twitchers.

But she allowed the feeling, and tried to ignore the anger that swelled in her when she realized how much more of this she deserved.

Be quiet, Lucy.

She closed her eyes, wanting her world reduced to only what radiated from inside of her.

Just feel this.

She pushed farther back against Brewer, her head rising above his chest, her temple resting against his cheek.

Then he spoke, and she felt his the heat of his breath on her skin before her mind acknowledged what he'd said.

"Someone is coming. Look!"

Her tiny reverie, broken.

Panic returned.

It wasn't military approaching.

It was one of *them.*

A girl, running, hundreds of yards out. Struggling against her own tremors, racing toward Lucy and Brewer, looking over her shoulder.

She's afraid. What the hell?

Brewer's right hand remained with Lucy's on the detonator. He reached over with his left and picked up Emmett's pistol.

Only two bullets left.

Lucy hoped Brewer wouldn't have to fire the gun. If she had to choose between being burned alive by a drone or eating a bullet . . .

The girl drew closer. No weapon in her hands. Dark torn jeans. Light gray hoodie stained with blood.

Her own? Others'?

Brewer eased his finger onto the trigger. Lucy thought of the utility knife in her pocket.

Fuck holding on to Steve's fake apparatus. We have to fight.

Brewer's body tensed behind her. They could hear the girl's ragged breath.

Then a new sound. The girl was yelling . . .

Lucy tuned in on the sound, and it became clear.

"No! NO NO NO NO NO!"

A trick? A trap?

But then, fifteen feet from Lucy and Brewer, the girl collapsed to the ground, sliding on her arms and knees, stirring up a cloud of dust.

"No. Please . . ."

The girl vomited a thin stream of bile, which told Lucy it was not her first time puking that day.

Then the girl looked up at them, a string of clear drool hanging from her mouth, one eye clouded over blue, the other hazel and deeply bloodshot.

"Don't shoot. *Please.*"

"Ada?" said Brewer.

Ada Keizer? A party pal of Brewer's?

She'd dropped out a year back, but Lucy heard her name now and then. She was supposed to be more of a loadie than Brewer.

As if to answer Lucy's guess, the girl reached into the pouch pocket of her hoodie and extracted a plastic baggie. White powder inside, along with a small copper key. Ada tried to steady her hand, brought the baggie as close to her face as she could, scooped the last dregs of powder from the bag using the key, stuck the payload into her nostril, and snorted long and hard.

The hand that moved away from her face has ceased its trembling. She dropped the baggie and key to the desert floor and Lucy watched as the bright blue storm clouding her right iris shrank away until her eyes were mostly hazel.

"That's the end of it. Oh, fuck, that's *it*. I can only . . . stay gakked up for so long. At first it broke the signal, but . . . I can already feel them. It's barely working anymore."

"Ada?" Brewer's voice was small, confused and concerned.

Another friend lost.

The veins in Ada's neck strained. "Oh, fuck. It's so *angry*."

"But how are you . . ."

"I was at the party in the back cave when it went bad. I thought Angie Patterson had dosed me again. Tried to settle into it. *Worst trip ever,* I thought. Tried to wait it out. Then Jason Ward started puking spiders. Then I fell. Passed out, or thought I did. Woke and I ran. But the trip wouldn't end, and I felt awful. Tried to wander the desert. Thought the daylight might help, but it only got worse. So much pain. The tremors. My head . . . They show me visions. The *worst* things. These are things they've *done*. Thought the coke might straighten me out. It did for a second, but they got stronger and stronger. Then you were in a vision, setting people free. And that's all I want. So no more questions, right? Just promise."

"What?"

"That you'll kill me too. Please. I need that. *You can't let them have me.* I saw you, in here." Ada pointed at her head. "Saw you at your place, through Brumke. Saw you coming out here, through the drone. The coordinates on the sign. That's why I had to come—I can tell you what they're doing. But you have to *promise*."

With the last sentence, she looked straight at Lucy.

She's seen what I've done. She knows I'll kill her.

But Brewer spoke up first. It was *his* friend.

"I promise. I won't let them have you."

Lucy could tell he meant it.

He's broken now too. They've bent him into this. They're reshaping all of us.

"All right, so *listen*. I bumped before I ran your way, but we can't tell what they can see anymore. It's spreading so deep. We feel it reaching into us. Taking over. So maybe they saw. Maybe they're coming right now."

"Who?"

"The ones from the cave. The ones who are preparing. They're moving the eggs down." Ada's body shook. One of her arms nearly collapsed beneath her. "We don't have to wait for the rains anymore." Her voice had deepened.

She's losing her hold.

Ada shivered and clenched her jaw, determined to have her say.

"They *want* you to blow the pipeline. But you *can't*. It only helps them, and the thing growing in our heads. It's figured out how to intercept. Edit. Block. The satellite is *theirs* now. It's part of what's growing in us. The people on the other side don't know what we've become. What we're doing. They *never* will. The satellite matched the drone signal, controlled it. Fed us everything, left them nothing. Not the old man. Not the sign. Nothing. They're *blind* over there. Confused."

Lucy watched ripples of blue spreading around Ada's irises. Her voice lowered again. "No one will help you. All you can do is run. Take the bomb. Find a way out. If you don't, we'll find you." Ada smiled, her head twitching uncontrollably. "We'll unleash the river ourselves."

Ada lifted her right arm, struggling against her palsy, and slammed a balled fist into the back of her neck. Her voice returned to normal. She pleaded. "Don't let it back in, okay? It's coming. I can feel them. They're coming. Please." She crawled closer. Lucy felt Brewer's body tense behind her. Ada's face froze, an awful space between a smile and agony, drawn tight as a mass of scar tissue. Her voice became a cry. "You *promised*. Don't let them in. I gotta die outside of them. *Please just fucking kill . . .*"

Brewer lifted the gun and pulled the trigger. Ada's face collapsed, the bullet's momentum folding her upper teeth into her brain, all of it slamming into the rear of her skull and toppling her backward.

Lucy imagined all that bone and torn brain compressing and swelling around the tendrils of the Oracle where it had woven itself into Ada's mind. She knew what would happen next—the Oracle, struggling against the dead wreckage of its host, squealing and squirming its way free.

Born again.

She thought of Marisol, and Ada, and even Chris, and how they'd fought the influence of the device, even when they were trapped within its realm, struggling against control.

She thought of the feeling of violence in her bones, and the uncontrollable destructive momentum of the new Lucy who'd been born inside the Oracle's nightmare version of her home.

She thought of a new world, where no one would ever feel what she'd felt in Brewer's arms, the human animal stripped of whatever kindness it might experience, cultivated only for its ability to suffer the whims of something cruel beyond comprehension.

Lucy made her decision.

She could see the surprise in Brewer's eyes when she turned and kissed him, forcefully, her hands on his face again, the echo of their first moment in the caves rolling through her. She knew that feeling would never last, never long enough, so she pushed back and stood, leaving him with the gun in one hand and the detonator in the other.

"Lucy?"

"The message has to go through. They have to know what's coming. I'm going to fight it, like Marisol. I'm going to find a way through."

Brewer started to stand, detonator in one hand.

"No," said Lucy. "You have to stay there. Don't ruin this. We have to force their hand, *now*, or there's nothing good, not ever again. I'll show them the message. I'll show them you, and the bomb."

"If you can't? What if you disappear in there? What if you come after me, or try to trigger the explosion?"

"Then you save us both." She pointed to his gun.

One bullet left. He'd have to risk capture and infection.

No more good choices.

"Fuck, Lucy."

"Ada wasn't only Ada. They're on their way."

She pictured the quivering, snarling children of Turner Falls crawling through the caves, their hands slick from handling the eggs of their new god. Even now they'd be climbing up the ladders. She imagined them falling on her and Brewer, blue eyes and blind rage, the cancer in their necks thrumming with expectation.

They'll break our bones, jam us in by the pipe bomb just to see what happens to the meat when the screws and BBs and shrapnel tear through what's left of us.

No.

No time left.

Find a way through.

She made her way to Ada's corpse, rolled her onto her face. The utility knife made short work of the soft, suppurating tissue around the Oracle.

She dug in with her hands and grasped the meat of the creature and pulled, and for one moment she felt how deep the thing—much larger than the ones she'd seen erupt from Marisol—had sunk its arms into Ada's neck and skull. Then, as if sensing its extraction, or perhaps the warmth of her skin and the still-moving blood beneath, the arms of the creature retracted from Ada with a squelch and rotated back, latching into the thin skin of Lucy's hand. She saw it then, and realized it was surely a mutant descendant of whatever prototype they'd put in Jason, because the thing in her hand was so repellent even the best marketing team would die trying to sell it. This was no *device*—the Oracle was a living tumor, a warped nodule of blue-black cell death with eight squirming arms, each of them bearing what appeared to be tiny black bone saws at their tips. An obsidian beak squealed at its center, and circuitry shimmered beneath the viscid mucosal jelly that coated the thing. There were clear, tiny cysts deeper inside, in which something even smaller—Eyes? Eggs? Larvae?—swirled and swam, speeding at Lucy's touch.

She wanted to throw the Oracle to the ground and smash it under her heel until nothing of it remained, every last cell split and oozing and unrecognizable.

No.

Don't think about it.

You can't. Your mind won't bear it.

Just do what you have to do.

So she did, and it was motion without thought or reason—the Oracle raised to the back of her neck—and she felt her hand freed from its grasp. There was a moment of no sensation at all, and she wondered if the thing was dying from the effects of the gunshot that cratered Ada's face, or from her rapid extraction technique.

Then she realized that less than a second had passed, and it had been wishful thinking to believe the creature dead, because it was, in fact, very alive, and the lightness she'd felt was the Oracle leaping from her hand to her neck.

It landed and latched.

Sensation returned—her neck on fire. She heard skin tearing, felt a drilling sensation, which she feared would split her head from her body, then something was inside of her, spreading beneath her skin, reaching up along her spine, unfolding over her mind, insisting it had been there all along.

The sky was red for a moment, then black, then back to gray and blue.

Lucy fell to her knees, her head swimming with the smell of burning gasoline, cherry blossoms in bloom, the mold deep inside a pile of decaying fall leaves

And

Dust and vomit and juniper pollen

And

Brewer's family and dogs, burnt and sickly sweet, and she saw the outline of their violated corpses again, not as a memory but as a layer of her vision, as real as the trees and mountains in the distance.

At the bottom of her sight, a stream of data rolled by, programming language she couldn't understand. Vestiges of IMTECH's programming efforts—so clearly subsumed within the Oracle—appeared as a third layer. The remnants of a menu interface, corrupted icons lighting up as her eyesight floated over them. It dizzied her, but she blinked and it disappeared. She blinked again and saw flames climbing white drapery, and she felt as if she were watching a camera pan back, but then she heard laughter and it sounded like Luke Olsen and as he stepped farther and farther backward she realized that she was seeing what he had seen when he burned down someone's home, and the very worst part of all is that something about his vision made her feel good and excited, and when she looked down her hand was steadied among the flames and she could feel a smile spreading across her face.

"Lucy, did you connect to them? Did it work?"

A voice, distant.

Worried.

Weak.

Another voice, closer, inside her head:

You were always one of us. We understand you. How you feel.

You can feel that way again.

The boy is behind you.

He trusts you. He has something we want. Your knife is sharp.

The absence is coming.

Lucy ignored the voice, its promises and threats and the way her body had begun to tremble again.

You're not listening. We will show you.

Electricity in her mind, vision a thicker red.

Her parents, burning in front of her. She'd breathed in their smoke, tasted them as they died.

No!

Then the closet at the orphanage. She never knew when the light would return. She was shrinking away. A mildewed mop in the corner. Girls laughing on the other side of the door. She had to pee and couldn't help it anymore, and when they set her free they saw what she'd done and they rubbed her face in it and called her "*perro*" and then she was deeper in memory, smaller, and so alone, and when you were all alone you weren't safe and you had to run from a certain kind of man and woman, you could see it in their eyes, something dead but hungry at the same time, and you tried to tell your parents but they heard nothing that wasn't the voice in them calling for the next bottle and then you were in the closet again, and then you were trying to wake the Hendersons but they were ghosts too, bleeding and lying and retreating from you and *this will only feel worse every second you don't listen* . . .

"Lucy! What's happening?"

That voice again.

It brought her back to her body, but that was a curse. She felt crushed, her neck in agony, strained and cracking, her skin loose, like it was slipping away, rotting away, but at least it was a sensation because the Oracle was coming into her mind again and draining her ability to be anything and she was so afraid of what waited in that blackness beyond herself because she could feel that it only held worse for her . . .

But that's not true. You can feel good again. We learned from the first of you, how to escape the absence. Jason showed us how to feed it, how to keep it at bay.

Lucy saw Jason's "wisdom," layers of it all at once: neighborhood dogs split, organs catalogued; girls in tears, bleeding; his younger brother screaming, hand forced to the stovetop; a man sleeping under a tarp by the railroad tracks, kicked in the head until he stopped moving . . .

She tried to blink it away, to focus on the natural light coming in from the desert sky, but the visions would not leave her, and she wanted them to sicken her, but whatever it was in the Oracle that Jason had taught how to feel was rewriting her code, teaching her this was good, that this was how to escape the loop, how to stay on, how to make herself feel anything at all, and *the absence is returning you don't have to feel low the boy is there he's calling for you he's nothing we don't need him he's only good for how he can make us feel* . . .

How he made *us feel,* Lucy thought, and she saw his arms wrapped around her as they sat on the desert floor and then she was shaking worse and she felt something stir, low in her body, and wondered if the salvage sequence had been initiated. Maybe the Oracle had no use for her anymore and the others had risen from the caves and they would soon be discovered and killed and something would grow from her womb and emerge from her and stand swaying in the desert, her body nourishment for the strange new plant.

Or is it feeding me that vision, because it doesn't want to think about Brewer? Because this thought is mine?

You weren't loved. Not once. Not now.

She tried to focus, to turn toward Brewer and her thoughts of him, and the clarity they seemed to bring.

Pain roiled in her guts. Her neck throbbed. Her sight filled again, and she could see herself, splattered with blood, her face hideous, angry beyond her own awareness, her arm swinging down, wrench in hand, striking one of the seer's eyes blind. The sight line shifted toward Brewer on the stairs, shocked.

He's terrified, watching you, this is what he thinks of you he doesn't love you he fears you he hates you he doesn't know what you are what you can be you have always been part of us we have always been inside of you.

No, she thought, *that was never you. It was* because *of you. Never for* you.

Another wave of pain wracked her body. Lucy wondered at how long Marisol had managed to go without killing Steve. The pressure was relentless, and she wanted so badly to feel good again, to have an end to the nothingness and destruction and the creeping voice inside her skull.

She shook terribly. One of her legs faltered beneath her, leaving her sitting on the desert floor.

A voice outside of her head. Hands on the front of her shoulders, setting loose spasms through her body. "It's not working, Lu. I can't watch it do this to you."

He had come to her, abandoned their plan.

She met his eyes.

"Oh, fuck. *That blue.* It got into you bad."

He *was* terrified, but *for her.*

He's already dead, like the rest. Only a matter of time. But you can feel good right now. You can get back on.

"Stay in front of me. Keep me in this place," she said. "Don't let them back in, not all the way."

Let us in.

Flames again. Luke Olsen's memory, stealing her sight, striking Brewer from her perception. She could smell the fire this time. Familiarity in the scent, beneath the smoke. It reminded her of Carol's favorite perfume. Luke took another step back, and she knew why the Oracle was showing her the blaze.

My house, she thought. *The Hendersons.*

"He's already dead, like the rest."

It was that *knowing,* the final erasure of hope that the Hendersons might have survived, that she felt in her chest. But the ache of losing them was real and present, and even as she watched the house burn she felt it moor her within herself, in the body she knew.

They wanted her broken and controlled by the rules of their world. But something was changing inside of her.

Lucy tucked her legs beneath her with trembling hands and reached out to Brewer.

"I'm here, but it keeps coming back. Forcing me to see. Help me stay. Sit here. Hold my hands."

He could have run, guessed it a trap, pictured himself being pulled down to her, her teeth on his neck, tearing away.

He could have pulled the trigger then, figured Lucy for mad or lost or both, and sent their last bullet through her brain, setting her free.

Instead she felt his hands on hers.

A vision struck her eyes, trying to erase any knowledge of what was happening. She saw two fires then: the people who made her and the people who loved her, all consumed, and she felt the familiar bright white tremors of her rage filling her up, threatening to negate her, to pull her toward the empty malice of the Oracle's hunger.

But she also felt immense sadness for what had been lost, and what may be lost still, and she allowed it because it was real and hers and even though it hurt it wasn't an absence.

She felt all of this at the same time, and she realized the Oracle's invasion had altered her mind, fracturing the layers of her perception far beyond what her own trauma and time as a child ghost had done, and as she had in the past she allowed her anger to ascend, pictured it as a beam running to the sky, and this time something new happened.

She closed her eyes, and her body remained on the desert floor, Brewer before her, but her mind, at long last, cleaved

right

in

two.

And then there were three of her.

The Lucy from her old life, terrified and abandoned and mocked, crushed by fear and grief.

Confused, opening her eyes to flickering light and finding herself in another room she'd built in her mind, blank screens on the wall, its earthen floor lush with dark green ferns.

Bucket was still there, smiling.

"I thought you'd never come back."

And the other Lucy, a series of animal instincts, a creature born of this new world, seeking continuation at any cost.

Finding the pleasure in seeing any living thing that wasn't her fall bleeding to the ground.

And she found herself deep in the caves, dozens of eyes looking to the surface of the stone dome, where something grew and waited and demanded to be fed.

And a body, not entirely hers,
trembling,
stolen,
steadied by the hands of a young man who held her and waited for her to return.

"It's coming, Lucy. It wants in."

A huge thud against the door to Bucket's room.

"You have to do something."

"It wants the stimulus. That's all that really matters to it."

The weight fell on her, pressure in the darkness, and she was all of them, and none of them were themselves anymore, all drones in service of whatever the Oracle had become, reduced to sensory organs feeding constant need.

They shivered and shook and watched layer upon layer of murders on loop and fell upon one another when their urges demanded it, And some of them had softened, their skin splitting, something slick emerging from their bloated limbs, allowing them to climb the walls of the ancient cave and bring the queens' harvest to the floor, where it would be set free, carried to the world on rushing waters.

"I don't want to feed it. It's already so strong."

Another thunderous crash against the door.

"You have to, Lucy. You have to give it what it wants. You have to match its signal, or overwhelm it, so it can't broadcast in here anymore."

"But I can't be that Lucy, anymore. I never wanted to be her. They made me."

"I'm sorry, Lu."

Bucket stepped closer to her, the smell of his cheap cologne sweet as spring to her senses. He put his arms around her and whispered in her ear.

"You have to end this."

She fed the hive, let them feel what she felt. The sick pleasure in the violence, in crushing and not being crushed.

She filled their eyes with what she'd done.
Ben's skin peeling away, folds of his face bunching under her nails,
fresh red rivers running down.
Ashley's nose and teeth crunching under stone, the feeling of her
body shaking under Lucy's.
Bradley's face crumbling with each swing of her wrench, the thrill
of blinding an animal that saw you as prey.
Toni's head opened and emptied and smoking next to the barrel
of Lucy's gun.
Ben again, resurrected by the Oracle only to have one eye staked
and the other gouged, his head and throat pulped flat under the
hammer in her hands.
And Lucy did not ignore the feeling that coursed through her and
them, the body rewarded with the thrill of not dying, the flesh never
so alive as when it asserted its need to continue atop a pile of dead
predators.
She could feel the hum of their pleasure as she fed them her fresh
sense memories, and she dove into the feeling and gave them more,
the warmth of Ashley's blood on her skin, the momentum of her body
weight swinging through a boy's head, his one remaining eye gone
wide knowing death was coming, the path of the bullet destroying the
symmetry of a once-perfect face, the seep of Ben's optic fluid around
a splinter of charred wood,
And they loved all of it, and the creatures in the cave were swaying
and moaning and
always,
always,
always
wanting more.

The sound at the door subsided; something sated had turned its
vision toward Lucy's

Symphony of death, loops of suffering harmonized
and speeding their pace.
Her anger the engine, untethered and rising and feeding the masses
everything they needed to feel good again.
And she let them have it all, opened her mind and showed them
Marisol, writhing on the floor, the hectocotylus cracking her
skull and coiling in her head, gray matter liquefying and running
from her nose.

"It's working, Lucy. Look."

The screens in Bucket's room grew brighter, the IMTECH logo
glowing from their centers.

Then text:

COM SYS RECOVERY, PLEASE WAIT.

She said, "I'm sorry, Bucket, but

I'm giving them everything,
And she showed them Bucket colliding with the windshield,
And the bodies falling from trucks, necks snapped, skin flayed,
spines twisted.
Faces peppered with glass.
She even gave them Bucket's face.
Swollen.
Split.
Flesh falling away.
His last breath.

"It's okay. There's no choice."

The screens in Bucket's room went blank for a moment, leaving him
and Lucy in blackness,

and then a single blinking symbol appeared, the waves of a signal
flashing

red

and

red

and then

Green.

She felt her eyes open, a third field of vision. Another layer beyond
the room
and the cave
and the knowledge of her body.
"Something's happening, Lucy.
One of your eyes.
It ain't blue anymore.
Can you tell me if you're in there?"

She felt something come rumbling back to life, the growl of a terrible wolf curling in her belly, trying to pull her away, so she

Added another layer to the loop,
Gave them Jake's face and neck being peeled away, exposing
tendon and vein, a scream dying in his throat,

But the growling grew louder,
and Bucket was fading,
the room itself beginning to darken and dissolve,
and the green signal started to blink out

And there was the screwdriver emerging through the skin in
Emmett's neck,
And Steve's flesh falling away, dripping flames to the ground,
But it wasn't enough, the hunger of the Oracle insatiable,

The absence never ending,
And even the accident, her parents' bodies burning, passengers
crushed under the bus after it had ejected them and rolled over their
bodies, wasn't going to be enough. But then she thought about the
Oracle, and wondered how much power it had at that moment,
divided and invading all

Three.

Of.

Her.

So she extended her mind into the cave and let the anger pour
from her and fill what minds it could and she imagined her hands on
the Oracle's precious eggs,
squeezing tight,
Waiting for the perfect moment when the surface would collapse
and the blue-black birth fluid inside would run down her arms.
And she believed the things would squeal when they were
crushed and the thought gave her such joy that the rush of the
impulse extended through the minds she'd entered and a few of the
twitching drones realized that they had found
Another way to feel good.

His hands were cold. Sweating. Quaking worse than her own.
But he didn't let go.
"Are you still . . ."

There.
She felt less of the thing outside the door. The growling subsided.
The signal light returned to steady green. The rest of the room, including Bucket, disappeared. She walked through silence across blackness, toward the glowing screen.

She reached out with one hand and touched the symbol.

The screen rippled, her finger disturbing the surface of a pond.

The signal light throbbed in time with the beating of her heart,

letting her know they were connected,

and then she felt something cold and simple and without thought
pulsing inside her body,

and all it wanted was information.

She gave it everything she knew,

a frenzied rush of death and destruction,

forms of infection and growth,

every shape the Oracle had assumed,

visions of the eggs lying in wait inside the East Bear Caves, stolen from

Another place, where the Oracle had reasserted its dominance,
And any slave who had dared to crush its progeny found themselves
being salvaged,
Each birthing a hectocotylus that sought to redeem whatever
was left of the meat
that had betrayed it.
And others were being sent, blind with rage, into the light of

The desert, where Lucy and Brewer sat,
facing each other.
Neither knowing yet
If any hope

Remained inside the signal and she realized then that the Oracle
had given her

the gift of revisiting all she'd seen,

which included

Steve's sign.

And she imagined a single screen inside a communications trailer, which had sprung to life,

and she wondered if the static swirled slowly until the black and white pixels separated enough to show them

the truth.

And after the whole of the message had been sent, she allowed herself to see only these words, flashing and repeating ad infinitum:

TACTICAL/TOTAL ERADICATION ONLY OPTION!

And she thought it the strangest prayer she'd ever seen.

"Lucy, they're coming this way. We gotta go!"
But she couldn't move, and she wasn't sure if it was

Her transmission

Or

The Oracle

that held her in place.
She only knew that she had to find some way to sever the connection.

And she reeled back through her memories,
experiencing them as quickly as she could,
though in this space, outside the Oracle's feedback loop,
they only hurt.

And she thought of poor, half-blind Jake and how the Oracle had rejected him from the hive,

and she thought of Emma's father saying, *"Can you tell them that the Devil needs their eyes to hold their souls?"*

And she thought of Ben Brumke, speaking again as a scared child after she plunged a shard of burnt wood into his skull.

And she knew there was a flaw in the interface design.

And she knew what she had to do.

"I'm not here, Brewer. Trapped inside. Even if you carry me, they'll see.
They'll follow."
"I can't leave you."
"Don't leave me."
"So what the fuck do I—"
"Blind me."
"Lucy, I don't know . . ."
"*Trust me.* It needs my eyes."
"Lucy."
"The knife in my pocket. Set me free. Help me run. *Please.*"

And she could see herself through the eyes of the hive. Distant
but growing closer.
Brewer standing on shaky legs, head hung low, moving behind her.

And she could feel something inside the transmission, a ticking, switching between two tones in rapid succession, some message being sent in return, though she couldn't tell what it might say.

And then she saw the edge of the razor jutting from the utility knife
handle in Brewer's hand,
the color of the world tainted blue on that side of her vision,
and she felt Brewer's other hand separate her eyelids,
and he said,
"I trust you. I'm so sorry, baby."
And there was pressure,

then pain like she'd never known,
and she screamed,
and the suffering was exquisite.
The kind to make you wish for death.

Lucy breathed deep, and screamed again,
and tried to find comfort in the fact that the other two versions of
Lucy had completely disappeared,
and the pain was finally
Hers
Alone.

One hand over her punctured eye, the other hand wrapped in Brewer's, and she felt herself pulled, nearly dragged, stumbling over rocks and brush. She wanted to open the other eye, but something about keeping both closed saved her from dizzying.

The pain wanted her to collapse unconscious, to be carried and treated and placed in a sterile environment. Flowers would be sent.

But she heard sounds behind them—shouting in the distance, voices cruel and cold, wanting her filled with fear before they fell on her, wanting her to understand that her trespass against the Oracle and its children would not be forgiven.

There was another noise, closer—squealing from the "exhaust vent" in her neck.

The Oracle, screaming through its beak, trying to escape a body whose mind it could not possess.

"Brewer, you have to pull it out of me."

"Not here. We can't. They're too close."

His voice echoed off an object in front of them. The pipeline?

The sound of both the infected and the thing in her neck grew louder.

"I need to know, Lucy. Did you get through? Do they know?" Brewer's voice sounded desperate.

"I reached something the Oracle had hidden. Something built into the device. Gave it Steve's message."

"Did they respond? Are they going to do what they need to do?"

Lucy thought of the simple alternating clicking pattern she'd heard through the transmission in Bucket's room, and she wondered if she'd imagined all of it, another trick of the Oracle. But then she heard the escalating, thrumming rage of the approaching swarm, the intensity of its desire to send her to oblivion, and she knew she had done *something* beyond its control. Hurt it in some way. And she also knew that she had found a way to fight against it from inside its own realm, and she'd found a way to escape its possession, and there was nothing magical or special about her that had allowed that to happen. So even if Brewer did what she thought he wanted to do, even if she was entirely wrong about her desperate plea and it was sent to some dead-end server, maybe there was a chance for others like her to stop the thing in the Oracle from controlling their kind.

Maybe.

That was the best you ever got, anyway. She had given up on certainties.

So she said, "They responded. They know." And as quickly as Brewer heard that he was yelling directions at her, that she had to duck, she had to get on her hands and knees, she had to crawl forward a few feet more, and he guided her by pushing forward on her hips, and she felt cool earth beneath her hands and heard something heavy rushing above her head, and she cried out as she felt the weight of her ruptured eye pulling toward the ground, the blood behind it an immense weight pressing down.

"Okay, you can stand now."

But she couldn't, and her legs were jellied again, and she wondered if the Oracle had found a way—despite her destroyed eye—to sink back into her mind. Its squealing had ceased, but she felt it moving beneath the thin skin of her neck.

She felt fresh sun on her arms and opened her remaining eye for a split second.

We're on the other side of the pipeline.

Pain insisted she close both eyes, showered her vision with fireworks and crystal castles in procession, all of it threatening to fade to black. She tried to stand again, and failed.

Then Brewer was grunting, finishing the crawl beneath the pipe. She felt him next to her, then she heard him moving quickly to another section of the pipeline.

A cacophony of screaming from feet away. The swarm had reached the pipeline. She heard their bodies pressed against it, the scrape and clatter of them climbing and crawling, and still she couldn't move, couldn't run, and she wondered if they'd find a way to feed her consciousness to the abyssal absence inside the Oracle, and there was a hand on her ankle, viciously tight.

A voice, ragged and torn from a parasite-swollen throat—"We will have the girl."

A single gunshot.

The sensation of her body, so heavy. Someone lifting her off the ground, moving as fast as they could.

Then a voice. Brewer. "We're not gonna make it far enough. Fuckin' fuse was too—"

Then pressure, and heat. A massive concussion that sent her flying blind through space.

For a moment she believed she'd died, and that the flying sensation would never end. Then gravity brought her tumbling to the ground. She spun, and something snapped in her leg. Static found her again, and blackness followed.

———

She woke to the feeling of the razor entering her skin.

"They have been at your wife with knives . . . and opened her up like a flower in bloom."

Her instincts told her to spin, to kill whatever was penetrating her, but the throbbing hell of her sliced eye and a new pain radiating from her right leg told her otherwise, and all she could do was moan.

Two more slices through her skin, fast, lighting up her nerves, and then she heard Brewer say, "Let . . . fucking . . . go, goddamnit," and she felt the Oracle pulled from inside her neck, the tissue around the intrusion swollen and sending her a sensory outline of the creature's squirming shape as it retracted.

"Fucking *nasty. God. Damn.*"

The Oracle's squealing reached a fever pitch.

Lucy felt the vibrations of a heavy object slamming into the ground near her, heard something squelching with each thud.

The squealing sputtered, then died off entirely.

"Holy hell, girl! How the *fuck* did you put that thing on your neck?"

She heard him settle to the ground near her, grunting then moaning in pain.

What if I'm only hallucinating him? How are either of us alive?

She opened her good eye.

He was really there, but at the sight of him she had her doubts he'd be alive much longer. His face and shoulders and neck were a map of scattered lacerations, all of them bleeding fresh. A jagged chunk of black PVC penetrated the meat of his left arm, which hung loose, the hand stark white.

Wait. Still alive. They'll know.

"They're coming for us. We have to keep going."

Brewer laughed.

"All right, *one*, we ain't exactly in 'going' condition. I mean, I probably look great, but the day's been pretty rough on you. I don't want to freak you out, but something's at a weird angle in your leg. And *two*, they're not coming. Not right now."

He must have read the confusion on her face.

"Here. You gotta see this, if you can. Look down this little hill a pinch. Can I move you?"

She wasn't sure there was any way she could move that wouldn't hurt like hell, but she said, "Yes."

"I'll try to be gentle, okay?"

And he was, and they both had to move in miniature, each shift triggering new jolts of pain and involuntary screams. But soon she was back where she'd been at the pipeline, sitting between his legs, leaning against his shrapnel-torn chest. She tried to ignore how little warmth moved between their bodies now, and the way that Brewer shook against her.

"You see *that*? Rodney built a hell of a bomb."

Lucy heard the pain in Brewer's voice, mixed with an odd sense of admiration.

She squinted, let her remaining eye focus. They were maybe thirty yards from the pipeline, on a slight rise. Below them was a charnel house, a mess of torn limbs and viscera that had once been the swarm that followed them.

And down the center of the territory they'd blown to high heaven, between two blood-soaked swaths of soil, ran the new river they'd created.

The eggs. They'll spread now.

"This was what they wanted," she said.

"That's probably what they're thinking right now, whatever's left of 'em. But it ain't what they're getting."

"What do you mean?"

"When I was dragging us up here, I heard a plane. *First* plane I've heard since all this shit went down. What are the odds of that? No— they came to *our coordinates*. Your message got through like you said."

Lucy wanted so deeply to believe him, to allow herself the joy that might bring. But she'd also noticed he was bleeding from both ears, so Brewer saying he'd "heard a plane" didn't mean he'd heard *their* plane, the one that would take the truth back to the bastards at the border and force them to end their experiment.

He might not have heard anything at all.

But what if he *had*?

Lucy decided to let it stand as the truth. She'd given others kind lies before they died. Didn't she deserve this?

They heard my message.

The joy fell to low tide, eclipsed by the pain in her eye and neck and leg and, well, everywhere. Still, she felt it, and was glad to have had it.

"So what do we do now?"

"'*Do*'? Come on, Lucy. *You're looking at it.* And who knows for how long? So will you sit here with me?"

She nodded.

Brewer leaned forward a bit and reached out his one good hand. Lucy curled her fingers into his, closed her eye, and thought of what Chris Carmichael had said on the last day of school.

"This makes it stop."

"This is real."

. . .

Poor Chris.

And she wanted to say so much to Brewer, to find a way to make his heart full, to thank him for saving her from the swarm, to thank him for pulling the Oracle from her neck, to tell him he'd been good like his grandma had taught him, to say, "Worst. Date. Ever," and know that he would laugh, to tell him he was kind and strong and that she truly loved him in a way she'd never loved another human being.

But there was something perfect in the quiet, and the way their bodies rested together, destroyed and finally free to stop fighting, so she let the silence stand and tried to block out the pain and feel only his breathing and the faint beating of his heart.

When Brewer's hand grew colder and his body fell back, she allowed herself to fall with him, and she kept her eye closed. She stayed in that darkness with him and listened to the wind and the sky, and it might have been minutes or hours after that when her ears captured a beautiful new sound—something with engines soaring far above them.

A plane.

Huge and powerful and directly over their stretch of ravaged desert.

She grabbed his hand tighter then and thought, *You were right. You heard it.*

Brewer.

Brewer.

We did it.

She squeezed his hand tighter still.

I love you.

Then came the flash, so bright it was daylight inside her mind, and Brewer's hand was warm again, and she felt their bodies lifting into the air before the sound of the explosion moved through her, and she knew that she and Brewer would soon be dust, swirling together, undone and freed from the world, and she thought, *We are all going to be okay,* and for the first time in forever it felt like the truth.

acknowledgments

I mmeasurable thanks, first and always, to my wife, Jessica, for holding down the fort while I disappeared into various hotels and camp trailers to write this novel (and further thanks to her parents for letting me crash in their trailer for days, only to emerge pale and sunblind, clutching my manuscript and hissing at anything moving). And thanks to my kid for being a cool customer while I was gone, and welcoming me back with hugs, pranks, and chocolate chip pumpkin bread.

This book wouldn't exist at all if not for the boundless faith and patience of Mollie Glick, who gave me wisdom and encouragement and kept me on her roster of authors for twelve years waiting for the right novel (and then stormed the gates with this book once it was a reality). Thank you!

Paul Tremblay gave me some excellent advice that led directly to the publication of this book. So not only is he very tall and very nice, he is owed a beer or two the next time we cross paths.

Thanks to the awesome Creepy Campfire Tales audience at Telluride Horror Show for letting me test drive this book with y'all. You helped me calibrate the kicks in this thing and I'm so happy you finally get to read it.

Stephen Graham Jones and Craig Davidson have been inordinately kind to me. I look at them as comrades, inspirations, and brothers-from-another-mother.

If there's humanity to the horror in this book you can thank Dallas Mayr (aka Jack Ketchum) who encouraged me in so many ways, but especially showed me how empathy sits at the core of work that makes you feel something. Like anybody who was lucky enough to know him, I miss that guy.

Huge thanks to Joe Monti and Madison Penico at Saga/S&S! Your hard work and enthusiasm have elevated this novel in a way that makes me very proud of and excited about what we've accomplished.

When you're a writer and the grind gets you down, there are certain people you can depend on to lift you back up. In addition to being talented professionals, John Skipp, Gabino Iglesias, and Sadie Hartmann are whirlwinds of positive energy, and their enthusiasm means the world to me.

Props to my hometown of Bend, Oregon, which might bear more than a few similarities to Turner Falls.

Shout-out to Freedom, the computer program that blocked my internet access and helped me escape my own dopamine compulsion loop so I could get some writing done.

And finally—whether this is your first time reading my work or you've been following my dark stuff for ages—thank YOU for picking up this book. Without you these books are just me working out my weird shit by the pale light of my monitor. With you this is fun and thrills and maybe even some catharsis or you and me feeling a little less alone. So . . . THANKS!

Jeremy Robert Johnson
November 2019